Praise for *Forbidden* and *Banished*

"Lush, lyrical, romantic. *Forbidden* transports readers into a vividly imagined place and time."
—Claudia Gray, *New York Times* bestselling author, on *Forbidden*

"The harsh beauty of the deserts of ancient Mesopotamia come to life. Your heart will break as you root for Jayden to triumph over the many struggles that threaten to tear her world apart, and the ending will leave you thirsting for more!"
—Sara B. Larson, author of *Defy*, on *Forbidden*

"A romance with all the push and pull that goes along with impossible love, and Little elevates the story by creating a perilous landscape, both outward and inward, as Jayden must deal with the hardship of desert life as well as her own desires."
—ALA *Booklist* (starred review), on *Forbidden*

"A fast-paced, entertaining choice."   —*SLJ,* on *Forbidden*

"Rich historical details are deftly woven into Jayden's narration. Jayden's story becomes as much about finding herself as it is about finding love."
—*BCCB,* on *Forbidden*

"Descriptions of the landscape are evocative. Just as good is her pacing. This will heighten anticipation for a no-doubt exciting conclusion."
—ALA *Booklist,* on *Banished*

"*Banished* will appeal to fans of Kristin Cashore and Morgan Rhodes."
—*VOYA,* on *Banished*

Also by Kimberley Griffiths Little
Forbidden
Returned

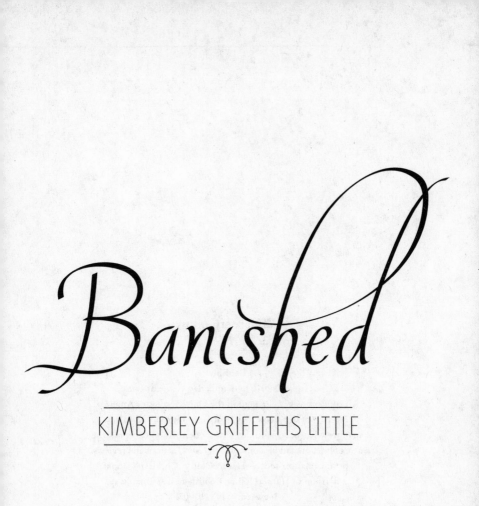

Banished

KIMBERLEY GRIFFITHS LITTLE

HARPER
An Imprint of HarperCollinsPublishers

Banished

Copyright © 2016 by Kimberley Griffiths Little
All rights reserved. Printed in the United States of America.
No part of this book may be used or reproduced in any
manner whatsoever without written permission except in the
case of brief quotations embodied in critical articles and reviews.
For information address HarperCollins Children's Books,
a division of HarperCollins Publishers, 195 Broadway,
New York, NY 10007.
www.epicreads.com

Library of Congress Control Number: 2015950813
ISBN 978-0-06-219502-9

Typography by Torborg Davern
16 17 18 19 20 PC/LSCH 10 9 8 7 6 5 4 3 2 1
❖
First paperback edition, 2017

For Kari,
my sister and best friend,
who blesses my life immeasurably

1

A dirty, callused hand slapped down over my mouth and the stale breath of a man hissed in my ear. "Don't move or I'll slit your pretty little neck."

I clawed at the stranger's cloak, trying to push him off, but he was too heavy. A moment later, I realized my ankles were tied together. I couldn't run, couldn't even move. Shrieks gurgled in my throat as if I was drowning, his hand cutting off my air.

Last evening's fire was nearly extinct and a cold, wretched moon shone a pillar of silver across the hollow I'd nestled myself into. This was my last night in the hills of Mari before I headed into the desert with my camel.

Only one day into my journey to find Kadesh and I was already dead.

The sharp tip of a blade pressed against my neck, and I whimpered.

I'd planned to be gone by dawn. Leave behind the city of Mari, and Sahmril, my baby sister who was lost to me when her adoptive parents refused to give her back. The promise I'd made to my mother to keep her safe was broken.

"Give me the frankincense of the stranger we killed." The man's foul breath dragged across my face. He was referring to Kadesh, the boy I loved, who'd been murdered by Horeb, the prince of my tribe. I'd watched Horeb plunge his sword into Kadesh and then order his soldiers to drag his body off.

Shock flooded me when I realized who my attacker was. I wrenched his fingers away from my mouth and with a raw voice said, "Gad? What are you doing lurking about the cliffs of Mari?"

This man was a childhood friend of Horeb's and one of my own tribesmen. His body pressed against mine, and I writhed in disgust.

There was only one reason Gad was in the foothills of Mari, far from the oasis of Tadmur where my tribe camped for the summer. He was a member of Horeb's army.

Horeb, my betrothed. The man who'd attacked and scarred me. Blackmailed me for the murder of his father to hide the fact that he'd killed Abimelech so he could steal the tribal crown. He thought the kingship gave him the right to murder Kadesh—because Kadesh had stolen me away. Horeb was the boy I knew as a child, ran foot races with, fought with stick swords, and tended baby camels with.

He was now the king of the Nephish tribe, and he'd been hunting me for weeks. If he found me he'd either kill me or lock me up in chains as his wife. Guarded by soldiers so I wouldn't slit my own wrists.

Nausea rose up my throat as Gad's beard grazed my cheek. He smelled vile and filthy. "Tell me where the frankincense is," he murmured, his hand hovering over my face. "If you refuse, I'll shove my dagger into your heart—then strip you naked to find the nuggets myself."

Flashes of that night when Horeb tried to rape me at the oasis pond crashed through my senses. I couldn't relive such an attack again.

Gad grinned and I knew he was thinking the same thing. "It's too bad Horeb's paying a ransom to get you back. If not, I'd be doing more than just stealing your frankincense."

I tried to swallow. "But I have nothing!"

"Liar! You were seen at the camel markets in Mari. You had frankincense and now I want the rest of it."

"I spent everything on the camel—I can't walk to Tadmur on foot!"

His fingers slinked along my waist and hips, fumbling in my dress pockets.

"Touch me and I'll kill you," I threatened, shifting as he searched, which freed my arm to reach the knife strapped to my thigh.

An amused smile spread across Gad's face. "There's a rumor that you're fairly adept with a knife."

I shuddered. So Horeb was bragging about the fact that he'd

branded my body with a knife to claim me as his so nobody else would want me.

"Where is Horeb?" I asked to distract him. "I thought he and I would travel together."

Gad's laugh was scornful. "You're a terrible liar."

"And when I see him next," I continued, "I'll tell him *you're* a deserter and a thief—and tried to attack his betrothed."

Surprise streaked his ugly face. He obviously didn't expect me to fight back.

"I know you're on the run. Give me the wealth."

"I don't have anything!" I said, spitting at his face. He slapped me, and my head slammed the ground. My eyes swam with tears. I could only insult him so far. For all I knew, Horeb was already here in the Mari hills, only a shout away.

My camel was on the far side of the boulders, looking skittish and uneasy. Her fur glowed white under the pink light of dawn.

Gad's grin cracked his face, showing stained brown teeth. He snatched up my cloak next, still sitting on top of me, and greedily searched the folds and inner pockets.

Of course, I was bluffing. The last nugget of frankincense, the one I'd saved for medicinal purposes or an emergency, was tied to my chest, but so small it wouldn't buy much.

With Gad's attention on my cloak, I slid my hand down to retrieve the dagger strapped under my skirt. My fist curled gratefully around the hilt.

The morning sun hit the horizon, and a blazing dawn streaked the sky.

"Nothing!" Gad muttered. After checking the rope around

my tied legs, he jumped up to tear apart the campsite.

While he searched my rations pack, I began to quietly saw at the rope around my ankles. I spoke out loud to hide my task. "See? I have no frankincense. You've climbed into the hills for nothing."

Ignoring me, Gad grabbed the halter of my camel and swung her head around. She bellowed and stomped her feet. Then he proceeded to hunt through her blanket and decorative tassels, even peering into her ears and mouth.

"Leave her alone!" I shouted.

"Damn!" he yelled when Shay bit him on the shoulder. Without hesitation he hit her head with his fist. Fury boiled in the pit of my belly at his treatment of my well-bred camel, but I tried to focus on freeing myself.

Just as the rope began to fall into pieces, Gad raced toward me with a roar. Before I could crawl away, he threw me flat on my back again, the dagger falling to the ground.

His touch made me sick. Instinctively, I shoved my knee into his soft belly, but he had more leverage and began to rip at the folds of my dress, breathing heavily. "The frankincense is strapped to you!"

"No!" I screamed, flailing my arms and legs, trying to maneuver my dagger to stop him. There was no other way out of this.

Suddenly, Gad stopped and swung his head around. "What's that noise?"

Low, hideous growls came from the cliffs above.

My camel screamed in fright, galloping across the campsite

to the head of the desert trail.

A striped gray hyena slinked along the cliff above us. Saliva dripped from its teeth. The animal's ribs showed; it was obviously starving and sick. The coarse fur on the back of its neck rose in attack mode, teeth grinning as it howled at us.

Fear soaked my body in rivulets of sweat. "I think he just found his dinner."

Gad fumbled for his sword. Before I could take another breath, he slashed at my dress and spotted the frankincense bound to my chest. "You sly girl." He grinned with pleasure just as the hyena launched itself from the edge of the cliff.

My breath came in terrified spurts. "No, no!" I moaned. "Get off me! The hyena's going to attack us both!"

But Gad was determined to steal the only thing of value I had left—and steal my virtue with it. Panting, he ripped at the cloth binding the frankincense to my chest, his face lighting up with greed and lust. Before I could form a coherent thought I gripped my dagger and thrust it straight into his soft stomach.

The sensation was sickening. Bright red blood dribbled down his cream-colored shirt into the waistband of his trousers, the hilt of the knife still tight in my fist.

My chest convulsed in horror at what I'd just done. "I—I never—"

Gad stared at me, terror in the whites of his eyes. He tried to speak, but only a trickle of red slipped through his lips.

Scrambling backward on my hands in the dirt, I screamed, "Shay, come!" My camel's ears pricked up, however she hesitated at the sight of the hyena slinking along the earth in stalk mode. But a moment later, she came hurtling toward me. Sweat trickled into my eyes as I swept up my blanket and satchel. I lurched to my feet, and then clawed my way up onto Shay's back, wrapping the halter around my wrist to keep from falling back down in the process.

When we raced out of the small clearing, I stole a glance behind me. Clutching at the wound in his belly, Gad fell to his back, groping for his sword. The hyena paused and sniffed at the scent of fresh blood pouring from the hole in his stomach.

"Oh, dear God in heaven," I moaned. I'd wielded my knife out of pure desperation. But even if Gad managed to fend off the wild hyena, I knew he didn't have long to live.

Burying my face in my camel's neck, I shuddered with sobs. Not a moment later, Gad let out a chilling, unnerving scream. I could hear the hyena's fierce teeth crunch down on bone, imagine the slobbering mouth and powerful body pinning the Nephish tribesman so he couldn't fight back.

"Go, go!" I urged the camel, closing my ears to the man's agony. I couldn't have fought both Gad and the hyena and stayed alive, but I was flooded with guilt.

After weeks of fear and loneliness in these hills while I crafted my plans to search for Kadesh, I'd just survived my first deadly encounter.

Tears of terror were cold on my face, wind smearing the salt across my cheeks. My camel tore headlong down the rocky hillside. I swore the ride jolted the bones from my skin. Every ounce of strength washed away, leaving me limp as a worn rag.

When we slowed at the bottom of the hill, the words of

Hannah, the desert woman I'd met many days ago, echoed through my mind. I latched on to them as though I was a child again, clutching my mother's nightgown when I had a bad dream. Hannah and her husband, Gedaliah, with their young children had traveled through the Edomite lands three moons ago.

They had told me the story of a man who wouldn't show his face, but who healed their son's arm with frankincense. Frankincense. Such an unusual possession. Not many people in these poor deserts owned the expensive nuggets.

The woman's voice came to me again: . . . *and he owned the most beautifully decorated sword.*

Instantly, I had pictured Kadesh's Damascus sword with its etchings and the imprinted symbol of his frankincense tribe. The man Hannah described had to be Kadesh. Somehow he'd survived Horeb's attack and ended up back with the Edomites. Not the wild men who'd tried to kidnap Leila and me and stolen our camels on our migration to the summer lands, but someone he trusted. A friend I had forgotten Kadesh mentioning long ago.

Once we were out of the Mari hills, I urged Shay forward to find the southern trail and start our journey for answers. If there was only a small chance Kadesh was actually alive in the Edomite city, I still had to know the truth—even if the perils of the desert tried to destroy me.

2

The sun was past its high point when I reached the foothills on the far side of Mari. I allowed my camel to find her own path down to the valley floor while my face crusted with dried tears.

I'd killed a man.

The knowledge horrified me, but Gad would have taken my frankincense, attacked me, and then dragged me to Horeb for his reward. I wanted more than a dagger now. I needed a sword, and I needed to learn how to fight with it. Because Horeb would find me. Just as Gad had.

After fleeing the death scene of my campsite, I'd scrubbed Gad's blood from my dagger and strapped the weapon to my leg again, then dug my heels into the camel's sides. The city of Mari was soon a distant mirage. Before I reached Tadmur to the west, I planned to follow the trail of wells to the land of the

Edomites, but the crossroads was still several days away.

It soon became obvious Shay hated traveling as a solitary camel. She didn't have the comfort of other camels, just as I didn't have the consolation of other humans. She roared and shot evil looks at me over her shoulder. At one point she tried to turn around and head back to Mari. The skin of my palms became battered, my arms drooping around the leather halter to keep her moving forward.

"Silly girl," I scolded. Banishing the unknown that lay ahead, I wondered if I'd lost my mind. After all, I'd watched Kadesh and Horeb fight in front of me, with a dozen witnesses. The blood-soaked cloak Horeb had tossed at me as proof of Kadesh's death now wrapped my shoulders in an irony of comfort and despair.

A scorching sun baked the earth. Sweat oozed in slow trickles down my back. Closing my eyes, I bowed my head, maintaining my balance by stretching my arms over Shay's sides and lying on my stomach.

I woke in the late afternoon with an ache in my back. My legs were sore from the chafing, red bruises forming like blisters on my inner thighs.

I kept on, desperate to put more space between me and Mari before stopping for the night. Orange and purple twilight shot across the western sky. Day turned into dusk and still we rode, silent and exhausted.

Loneliness I could handle, but knowing I was *alone* as far as I could see wreaked havoc on my mind. The insidious torture of your own thoughts was the reason people went crazy if they got lost in the desert. I shoved the stories out of my head, but they slithered back like snakes to torture me. Stories of corpses found off the trail. Skeletons half-eaten by wild animals. Travelers going mad when they panicked.

When darkness swallowed the world around me, a jiggle of fear crept along my spine. A small hollow near the edge of the plateau looked like it would make a secure place for sleeping. There were clouds to the west so I knew that sometime during this week I'd end up drenched. But rain also meant water.

I tapped Shay's neck with my stick and dismounted, tying her to a fat shrub. "Now for a fire," I said out loud, to comfort myself.

Using my flint and knife I managed to get smoke, then a tiny flame. I blew on it, feeding it dry leaves. I was glad to see clumps of dried camel dung, good for my fire, not far from my little camp—a strong sign I was still on the correct trail. Camel dung meant others had passed along this way.

The stars were in full bloom by the time I snatched a lump of hot doughy bread from the coals. I broke the bread into steaming pieces to eat.

I checked the constellations and was relieved to see I was on course. Day one was over. I finished the bread, ate a handful of dates, and drank a cup of water, making sure to pull the spout's strings tight so the skin wouldn't leak.

I unwrapped my last piece of frankincense and marveled at its comforting spicy smell, remembering Kadesh's warm strong hands when he'd poured the handful of nuggets into my palms so long ago.

After I mixed the frankincense shavings with two drops of water to make a paste, I rubbed it into the abrasions on my hands from the leather halter. Next, I sewed up the front of my dress where Gad had torn it, using my finest bone needle and thread.

A chill winter wind swept down from the north and I curled around Shay's body, holding Kadesh's cloak to my face to breathe in the last of his faint smell.

My first dance of womanhood had only been a year ago. The dance that had sprung a well of emotions and strength I'd never known before. Joy for womanhood and marriage. Grief for the death of my mother and baby brother, Isaac. Pain for Horeb's violence. Longing for Kadesh. And now fear for the most dangerous journey of my life.

Emotion seared the back of my eyes when I thought of my baby sister, Sahmril, who was now with the Mari nobleman Thomas, and his wife, Zarah. "My sweet sister," I whispered. "I promised to take care of you. I promised so many things to so many people and failed you and Leila. That's why I have to make this journey. So I don't fail Kadesh, too."

An eerie wind moaned across the hills and dunes. Reaching out from my bed, I added a stick to the fire. My hair whipped about my face like a loose veil. Under the shelter of my blanket, I slipped off the heirloom ankle bracelet Kadesh had given me, studying the symbols of the gnarled tree and halo of sun etched into the silver under the moonlight.

The tree and sun was a symbol of his tribe, and a promise of his love. Even though hunger squeezed my belly I'd rather starve than give up the precious gift.

As I tightened my fingers around the finely crafted chain, a swelling of devotion surged through me. My destiny lay in front of me on an unknown road. There was no going back, no matter what secrets Kadesh might be hiding in the caves of the Edomites.

I awoke before dawn and ate a piece of leftover bread, buried the fire under the sand, and was on the road before the sun hit the distant horizon. In the summer months we rarely traveled during the heat of the afternoon, but in the winter months it was possible. During daylight I could see the trail and the sun's course more clearly.

Over the next few days, I kept my path southwesterly, passing craggy hills and even a stretch of shale and black volcanic rock. On the fourth day, after a rain-filled night, I awoke to see outlines of figures coming out of the north behind me: camels with riders. My fingers fumbled with the harness and my gut curled into a tight knot. Even though I was weary riding late into the evening and then rising before dawn, I *had* to stay ahead of Horeb. The Edomites my family had encountered the previous year were unruly thieves, but there was shelter in their caves and a place to hide from Horeb's army.

Mounting Shay, I kicked her into a gallop. As a lone rider I wouldn't be as easily spotted, but I needed to get ahead of the next hill.

After an hour, I slowed and stared behind me. No sign of the riders any longer. Most likely, it was just a traveling family, but I didn't want to take any chances.

The sun finally broke through one of the dark clouds, making me blink back the easy tears of self-pity.

I turned directly south, skirting the road to Tadmur where my sister Leila lived at the Temple of Ashtoreth. The fertile springs of the summer oasis on the outskirts held harsh memories of Horeb's attack and sexual rites for the goddess.

I trudged on, but before I could stop for the night, a fierce wind began to blow. Gusts of sand whipped about the dunes like grainy white butter, creating a ghostly moaning in the hollows.

Sand lifted in loops and whirls from the earth as though performing an intricate dance, just before smacking me in the face.

After several hours riding against the battering wind, I finally halted and made camp. When I bent over the beginnings of a fire, trying to keep the flames lit, a blast of cold air instantly erased my work. The night went dead. More layers of sand kicked up, obscuring the stars overhead.

My camel pranced around the campsite like a skittish newborn. I jumped up to hold her halter, afraid she'd run off and get herself lost. But as she reared up, the stirring sand flew like stinging nettles into my eyes. Tiny grains pelted my arms and face, biting my skin as if a cloud of fleas had descended.

"Shay, stop!" I ordered her. "Calm down!"

Then I heard a roar growing in the distance. My heart crashed to the bottom of my gut. I knew that sound.

A sandstorm.

Holding tight to Shay's halter, I strained to see into the darkness. Dunes lay farther to the south. Now those hills of voluminous sand were being swept toward me. I only had seconds before I would be hit with the full force. With every passing moment, the noise grew more deafening, shutting out the world around me.

I threw my shawl over my face and drove my camel forward to find shelter. Shay spewed forth a series of obnoxious brays, gnashing her teeth, but she plodded forward and then suddenly stopped in her tracks.

"Keep going, girl," I urged her.

She whined and butted her head into my shoulder. I fell to my knees and patted the ground, crawling blind. The earth began to slope downward.

The slope appeared to run along an edge in the earth. There was just enough depth to take refuge. "Please no animals or scorpions," I prayed.

Wriggling on my belly, I crawled into the crevice.

After I was down as far as I could get, I covered my head with my arms. The continuous howling overhead was wearing at my nerves.

Shay folded herself next to me, for once staying quiet. The large animal made a shelter of her own and I buried my head into the curve of her neck, throwing my blanket over the both of us.

Hours passed as I hovered in the twilight of wake and sleep, dreaming of Kadesh as we swam together in the Sea of Many Waters. An indigo twilight sky danced on the warm blue waves along the coast of the southern lands. Rugged cliffs overhung the beach, so dazzlingly high they pierced the early pinprick of evening stars.

Groves of frankincense trees grew beyond those cliffs.

Secretive, haunting, and enigmatic as ever.

Kadesh's arms slipped around my waist as he bent to kiss my neck. His lips were warm, tickling my earlobe. Happiness bubbled up while we jumped wave after wave, splashing as if we were children.

The sea ran in rivulets down his beautiful neck. Drenched hair plastered his face in dark tendrils. I could see my own happiness mirrored in his eyes.

Walking backward, Kadesh pulled me to shore, tucking my hands firmly in his.

The last rays of sunset fell across the perfect white beach, sending sparkles across the sand. My soul ached at the beauty of this land, its languid, spicy air and calm shores.

All at once, my feet slipped and we fell back, laughing as the warm water splashed around us. I floated on my back, catching my breath, and then we pulled ourselves up through the final breaker.

My dress was a sodden tangle around my knees, but the waves receded and the world fell away when I walked toward Kadesh. His arms were around me, his lips tasting mine. "Come with me, Jayden," he murmured, giving a tug on my hand.

I lifted my head with a jolt, reality shattering the dream. The roaring had died to small gusts of whimpering wind. I didn't know what time of day it was.

Slowly, I crawled out of the hollow and stared in horror at a world that had drastically changed overnight. Sand dunes had sprung up where there used to be flat ground. Two enormous boulders were nearly buried. Cracks in the rocks dripped fine white sand in a slow trickle like an hourglass.

My camel towered over me, sand clinging to her eyelashes like dull jewels. The fine silt drenched me in white, clinging like lice to my skin, and making my teeth crunch. I was jangling with tension and exhaustion, but I was alive.

Moments later, panic clawed at my chest. If the desert had changed, I didn't know how I was supposed to find my way.

3

Three weeks had now gone by, with no sign of the Edomite land.

No sign of another living person since that first day.

I tried to calculate my distance, the number of hours I'd walked or galloped my camel to estimate if I'd gone too far, was drifting aimlessly, or still a hundred miles away. The changes brought about by the sandstorm delayed my journey, and I wondered if I was walking in circles.

If only I could conjure my father out of the sands and let him lead me to safety. Let me cry all the tears in the bottomless well of my soul.

Finally, one evening, I peered into the dusk of the endless desert surrounding me, unable to tamp down the screaming anxiety that was turning me mad.

Scanning the mountains up ahead, I felt a small measure

of hope. Wasn't this the same plateau my family had crossed after coming out of the canyon lands so many months ago? The setting sun splashed red against the rocks, deep as the stain of Gad's blood. "Please, let this be the land of the Edomites," I prayed.

The trail ended on the raw edge of a mountain that tumbled downward in sharply woven boulders and deflated caves and hollows. From the top of the ridge, the sight conjured up a magical, sunken world.

This *was* the same plateau, but I'd arrived at it from a different direction.

Slipping my hand along my leg, I caressed the dagger strapped to my thigh and hidden by my dress. This time the Edomites would know I was a woman, easily kidnapped for slavery. Not a young girl to be left alone by the death threat of a protective father.

I made camp on the ravine's far ridge. Relief stung my sunburned eyes when I added a few drops of water to the last of my flour and baked it. I ate a date in Kadesh's honor, and then saved the last handful to eat with him. It was my first meal in two days and it was all I could do not to devour it all. I tightened my sash against my hollow belly and tried not to think about food.

I'd been traveling for more than twenty days, not counting the days I'd spent in the hills of Mari. I'd given no thought to provisions for my return trip.

If Kadesh was truly dead, I couldn't make the trip to the southern lands to find his family and beg protection for myself.

My only choice would be to return to the Temple of Ashtoreth and my sister, Leila, to avoid marrying Horeb. But in reality, that was no choice at all.

Unable to sleep more than a few hours, I was back on Shay at first light.

The path dipped, lowering me into ravines as rugged as an old man's face.

The canyon walls tightened around me, growing tall as imposing giants, the colors an exquisite array of reds and pinks. I reached out to touch the soft sandstone to make sure I wasn't dreaming. What memories these canyon walls held—sweet memories of Kadesh touching my hand for the first time, gazing into my eyes with secret passion.

My camel strained forward, sensing the water up ahead. At midafternoon I spotted the wooden well rising from the ground. Not a mirage or hallucination any longer.

I slid off Shay's back and ran. Falling to my knees, I shoved the wooden covering off and thrust my hands into the dirt. With frantic fingers, I scooped out rocks and sand until I hit water.

Taking one of the empty water skins, I forced it down, my shoulder disappearing into the earth. A moment later, I pulled up the leather pouch, heavy with fresh water. I drank, giddy with the sweetness. There was a reason the Edomites guarded this precious water. I continued drinking until my stomach bloated, then I filled the leather bucket and Shay gulped it down within seconds. Watering the camel would take at least an hour so I sat back on my heels to rest and stare up at the red walls. Vivid and beautiful, they were like a painted mural on a phantom temple.

Nearly a year ago, Kadesh had uncovered this very well, filling bucket after bucket for me and Leila so we could drink and wash after the scare the Edomite bandits had given us.

All was silent this time. No Edomites galloping on their sleek steeds, demanding payment—or my virtue—for a chance to drink.

When Shay was finally satisfied and began to nibble sprouts of winter grass, I filled the buckets again to wash my hair, combing out the tangled strands with my fingers and rinsing until the dirt and sand was gone. Then I washed my face and clothes, sitting in the sun to dry. Blood from Gad was stained permanently into the fabric of my dress. My hems were ragged, my fingernails broken, my hands and feet callused. I hadn't used any lotion or creams since leaving the temple months ago, when we'd traveled to Mari to find Sahmril. I was sure I looked like a wild woman.

A shadow moved within the rock fissure up ahead and I was on my feet in an instant.

Tying off the leather water bags, I grabbed the halter and jerked Shay closer so I could mount. The camel complained so noisily I was sure she'd wake the dead. If the local tribesmen had not previously been aware I was here, they knew it now.

After climbing onto the camel, I wrapped Kadesh's cloak around my shoulders. Lifting the hood, I tucked my hair inside.

"Go on," I commanded, forcing my voice not to shake.

Spitting out protests, Shay jerked her legs forward. We swayed around the next bend in the narrow canyon in hopes of finding a hiding spot.

And walked straight into a mob of Edomite tribesmen.

4

A scream hovered in my throat, every nerve so taut I couldn't draw a decent breath. But the Edomites didn't gallop forward to encircle me. They weren't stopping me at all.

At least forty men, all with swords on their belts, had lined themselves along the narrow canyon path. Each horse stood by its owner, the halters held stiffly at their sides.

The Edomites' eyes bored into me, watchful, curious, but not hostile. If they wanted to, they could cut me into a hundred pieces before I managed a single cry. With small movements I pulled Kadesh's cloak closer around my shoulders.

Holding Shay's halter between my sweaty fingers, I made my way through the strange and silent gauntlet. My camel appeared completely unaffected, plodding her usual, slow gait.

The Edomite tribesmen were watchful, but not warlike.

Then one of the men came forward and I sucked in a gasp when I recognized him as the same man who had robbed my father of our camels to pay for water rights. A second man I didn't recognize quickly followed.

I tried not to shrink into my cloak, but my hand went instinctively to my leg. The man's black eyes flickered to the spot as well and I bit back a whimper. I despised him for humiliating my father when he'd threatened to slit his throat, shaming my father in front of his own family.

"If you're a woman, let your hair show," he commanded.

I didn't speak, afraid to admit who I was.

"Pull down your hair," the second man said, waving a hand to dismiss the first rogue, who slunk back to his horse with a growl. The older man faced me with piercing gray eyes. "You haven't fooled us, woman." Despite his orders, his voice was gentler, his eyes a shade kinder.

I sat taller on Shay, a weary indignation rising inside me. This man had no idea what I'd endured to get here. The brutality from Horeb; the humiliation of the temple bedrooms with Leila as victim; the loss of almost my entire family; the High Priestess Armana, the woman who wanted to chain me to the goddess statue of Ashtoreth; and finally, the death of Kadesh at the hand of my betrothed. The past year flooded my mind and strengthened my resolve.

I wasn't going to let the men of Edom harass me. They would not have me. Not alive, anyway. I'd already learned there were worse things than death.

I locked eyes with the older Edomite and slowly pulled

back the hood of my cloak, loosening my tangled, long hair. There could be no doubt as to my gender, but I was dirty, my face chapped red from the wind, my eyes bloodshot from sun and lack of sleep. I wavered on my camel, more exhausted than I'd ever been in my life. It took every ounce of strength to stay upright and not slide into a heap on the ground.

The man studied me, his face impassive. I waited for him to arrest me for trespassing and stealing their water. Instead an unexpected smile quivered at the corners of his mouth. "We are probably distant cousins through the tribes of Abraham's grandsons, are we not?"

I willed my voice to steady. "In Mari, where I've traveled from, I heard tales of a lone man—a stranger—living here in the caves of the canyon lands. Is this true?"

The Edomite leader put a hand on his sword belt. He scrutinized my face, my tattered clothing, and my beautiful white camel. "If this man you speak of wants to be known, he'll let you find him."

All at once my mind cleared, like early morning fog disappearing from the banks of the oasis pond. "Is—are you the man Kadesh called Chemish?"

I felt his surprise even as he tried to hide it. "Yes, I am Chemish. Which merely confirms my suspicions about who *you* are, woman of the Nephish."

I sucked in a breath. He'd known who I was the moment I'd stepped foot into their canyons. I should have realized the sentinels with their horses had been gathering while I watered my camel.

"A solitary woman is safe in the canyon lands," Chemish said, never taking his eyes off me. "Although she is a fool for traveling without her tribe. I advise you to stay on the main paths," he added with a slight bow. Regally, he waved to let me pass, but before I could order Shay to move, the Edomite leader gave a small clap of his hands.

A young man about my age ran to the elder man's side. "Asher, send a message through the ranks and to our sentries on the cliffs. The woman of Nephish is to remain safe while in our lands."

"Yes, my lord," the boy said, dark sympathetic eyes catching mine.

I flushed and loosened my grip on the reins, letting Shay take the lead. Passing the sentry of sober Edomites, I darted glances in every direction for signs of Kadesh. If he was here, why didn't he come to meet me?

Perhaps I needed to face reality. That the hidden man who had healed the young Benjamin with frankincense was *not* the man I loved. That Kadesh truly was dead. It was the only reasonable explanation. But I was grateful Kadesh had told me about his friend. The older man was the reason I was still alive. The reason the rogue Edomites hadn't swarmed and carried me off.

But the army of these fierce rose-walled canyons was lined up at the ready—as though they had been expecting me. The realization filled me with hope.

Soon I came upon the long narrow crevice I'd explored on my family's journey to the oasis the previous spring. This was the same closed-in gorge where Kadesh and I had stumbled upon each other and he'd told me a little about his frankincense lands. The place where he had kissed my palms and told me not to be afraid. The day he'd gazed into my eyes with such meaning and whispered my name with such emotion, I'd had to look away for fear I would throw myself at him.

Those memories had sustained me for months. But those same memories had also become a torture.

I shook my head to cast aside the tormenting thoughts and entered the opening to the narrow path. The air stilled, our steps muted. Blue sky peeked through the rock slits overhead while the sheer walls twisted and turned. The ache in my heart spilled over. This place brought back a rush of emotion.

If the unknown healer was actually Kadesh would he still find me desirable—or be disgusted by the slash of Horeb's scars across my chest? I'd hidden them from Kadesh when he'd found me at the Temple of Ashtoreth, but what about after we married? Could I hide my body in the dark of the marriage tent forever?

Shay plodded through the seemingly endless tunnel while shadows filled the passageway. My camel slowed when we finally entered the wide, open courtyard where I'd sat with Kadesh so long ago.

I was stunned once again by the flat limestone cliff carved like an enormous gate. So high I had to tilt my head back to see it properly. We paced the perimeter of the sandy courtyard, peering down other pathways branching off in the tumbling cliffs of the Edomite mountain kingdom.

I chose the path that lay more in shadow, following a gut instinct. A second area led to a myriad of dusky caves, stone steps cut into the rock side to reach them.

My camel grunted, impatient for me to dismount. "Not yet," I said, but Shay folded her legs and kneeled to the ground, giving me no choice but to jump off.

Walking on my own, I peered into numberless hollows along the walled avenue. The air turned motionless. Not a breath of a breeze. Prickles rose along my neck and arms. Each cave opening was like a single dark eye watching my every step. My camel ignored the surroundings and chewed her cud, sighing and grunting behind me.

"Silly girl," I told her over my shoulder, and my voice echoed in my ears.

Just then a shadow moved above me. My heart stuttered. Swallowing my anxiety, I spotted a second series of rough-cut steps. Using my hands, I climbed the staircase, breathless.

"Is someone there?" My voice was strangely loud in the utter stillness. Someone *was* watching. I could feel it, sense it. "Kadesh?"

The shadow didn't confirm or deny the question, but a man spoke from the darkness, the timbre of his voice low and rough. "What is a lone woman doing in the land of the Edomites? Don't you know the Edom men are savages? You might not be alive until sunset."

My pulse thudded in my head, but I wasn't going to leave until I knew for certain the man Hannah had told me about wasn't Kadesh. I moved to the opening, his heavy rich cloak swishing about my feet.

The past month of travel dragged like weighted chains tied to my ankles. It was all I could do to climb the steps of the cliff. How horrible I must look with my wild, tattered hair and bloodstains on my worn dress. "You can't frighten me," I said, my voice echoing off the dense walls. "Chemish gave me permission to search this land." I took three small steps upward. "I'm Jayden, daughter of Pharez and tribe of Nephish. I'm looking for someone and I thought you might know—"

I caught sight of a shadow crossing the blackness of the cave. Quickly, I climbed the last ten steps, my heart jammed in my throat.

"I know who you are," said the man, and his voice was suddenly right *there* next to me.

And that was the moment I knew. This was the voice I'd heard in my dreams all these long and terrible months. My voice broke despite my resolve. "And I'd know you anywhere, Kadesh. I'm wearing your cloak. Marked with your own blood." Under the sinking afternoon sun I laid the last nugget of frankincense on my outstretched palm. "Frankincense brought you to me the first time—and frankincense helped me find you again."

His laugh was strangely callous. "How could that be?"

"A family of the desert told me of a stranger who healed their son with the power of the frankincense." When he made no response my trepidation grew. "Kadesh, I've grieved for so many months over your death, too many to count. But you live. *You live!*"

"If you can call this living."

His aggrieved answer left me unbalanced. This was not the reunion I'd been longing for. "What does that mean? What are you saying?"

His next question was abrupt. "Who gave you my cloak?"

He was mere steps away from me, but locked in the cave's darkness. Purposely keeping me at bay. "Horeb gave me your bloodstained cloak as a wedding gift. Proof of your murder."

His voice held a strange despair. "My dreams have always been filled with you, Jayden, but any hope was stolen when your betrothed attacked me that last night in Mari."

"And I watched it all—locked inside Dinah's house! But if you live, Horeb can never take anything away from us again. I'm here. I found you." Tentatively, I stepped into the cave's opening, unsure of myself. Wanting to run to him. But something was clearly terribly wrong.

Kadesh's shadow paced the stone floor. "After Dinah and Nalla dragged you back into the house, Horeb's soldiers held me down while he plunged his sword into me and left me to die. For Horeb's plan to succeed—to rule the western deserts from Akabah to Damascus—he needs you as his wife. You give him the security of a tribal law fulfilled. The decency of family and stability on the throne."

"I know how ruthless and vile he is, but how did you escape? Both Horeb and Nalla told me you were dead."

"I have no more memories until I woke weeks later,

cared for by Chemish's wife."

"I should have run away with you the night of Hakak's wedding! If we had gone away together all those months ago . . . none of this would have happened."

"No. We'd both be dead if you had come with me that night."

"At least we'd have been together," I whispered.

His laugh was brusque. "Instead, you're Horeb's wife."

His statement shocked me. "No! I am not Horeb's wife!"

A dreadful silence swept through the canyon. A sinister foreboding. There was something Kadesh wasn't telling me. What had happened to him?

"I suppose I should believe you because you're here and not in Horeb's tent. But fate conspired against us. Horeb only had to take you back to the tribe with him to declare you his wife."

"I escaped Nalla's house before Horeb could kidnap me. I ran away to the Mari hills and nearly died of starvation until I met Gedaliah and his family." I took another step closer, all the love I couldn't contain rising up within me.

"Stay where you are! Don't move again."

His voice. So different, so changed. So terrible. "What did Horeb tell you? Why do you hate me so?"

I could see the details of his shadow now, his head buried in his hands. "Oh, Jayden, I could never hate you, but rumors and gossip spread like a sandstorm. I was told Horeb had taken you to his bed after he proclaimed my death. There was no way you couldn't marry him after that."

"Horeb has lied about everything," I said, tersely. I moved

again, frantic to touch him, real and solid, not a dream any longer.

"Come no closer, Jayden. Please."

An odd sense of clarity washed over me. "Gedaliah's wife, Hannah, told me the man in the Edomite cave kept his face covered. . . . You were scarred by Horeb's sword, weren't you?"

I sensed his eyes studying me. "I'm sorry you came so far for nothing. You're free to leave now that you know the truth."

"No, Kadesh. I'm not afraid of you or of Horeb any longer. Next time he and I meet I will kill him for everything he's taken from us. One of his soldiers even attacked me in the hills of Mari."

"Oh, Jayden."

The sound of my name on his lips turned my heart inside out. I sank to the parapet, shadows chilling my face. "Whatever Horeb did to you doesn't matter to me."

He gave a brief snort of laughter. "You shouldn't say that before you see the monster he created."

My senses crackled. "I've lost my mother and my sisters. I survived the grief of your death. I've crossed the desert and mountains, alone and hungry and exhausted. How could I be afraid of anything else?"

Before he could stop me, I plunged into the cave's entrance. Kadesh whirled, retreating, but my eyes had adjusted to the dim light. The cave was adorned with a simple fire hearth. Rugs and pillows, pots and candles. He lived here, not as a guest, but as one of them. "You made a deal with the Edomite band of robbers not to harm me, didn't you?"

"They spotted you when you crossed into Edomite borders. We didn't know who was hiding beneath my old cloak. You might have been Horeb here to finish me off, his army awaiting his signal to attack. It's only a matter of time before he returns."

"I should never have believed Horeb when he said he watched you die."

"A sword in the skull usually kills a man."

My breath carved a dagger across my tongue. "What do you mean?"

"It's taken two moons for me to ride a horse or camel with any sort of competence," he said. Now I could see that he held his arm in a sling against his chest. He wasn't completely healed. This was the reason he hadn't tried to find me.

"I was asleep on my death bed for the first few weeks while Chemish and his wife nursed me back to the living. When I woke again, I realized how much time had already passed, and I knew Horeb would have already declared my death." His head lifted. "I also knew you had no way to stop your family from forcing you into the marriage."

"I came close to killing Horeb once," I confessed, my dark thoughts spilling out. "Sometimes my own lust for revenge horrifies me—because that means I want to kill the *king of my own tribe*. It's treasonous no matter how much I despise him. But I don't want any deed to stop me from being with you—in this life or the next."

"If our fears convict us, then we are both condemned."

Holding myself at bay when he was so close was torture.

"Are you an Edomite? Is that why you've been staying here, because Chemish is a relative?"

"No, Jayden, I'm not an Edomite. That band of rogue men last year stole my gold, too. The men in these red lands are merely distant cousins, just as they're yours."

"Why do you keep it a secret, always speaking in riddles?"

"Because I do have secrets. More than you know. I wanted to take you with me to the southern lands, but now . . . it will be too hard for you. Our women are too different. There is great wealth, but also great danger."

"I survived the journey here alone. And it's still my dream to go with you." The setting sun shifted, slanting across the cave's entrance and submerging me in a pool of brilliant light. I lifted my eyes to this mysterious man I loved. "Kadesh—please let me in."

He held up his hands to stop me, and the gesture was a stone in my chest. "You don't want to look at me."

I tossed aside the worries I'd carried for so long. "I want to look at every part of you until the day I take my last breath. You *survived*. And healed your wounds with the magic frank-incense. I *can* see you, right here, right now. Hiding away. But you are no monster to me."

Before he could speak again, I closed the distance between us. "I'm going to take you for myself. At last. Forever." Lifting my hands to his face, I traced the mangled skin running the length of his left cheek.

The scar was jagged; Kadesh's face had been sliced sev-eral times by a knife, then sewn together with stitches that made me hurt to look at them. A black linen patch covered his left eye.

"You lost your eye. That's the truth you're trying to protect me from. But the only thing that matters is you survived."

I gazed unflinching at the fine angle of his jaw, the thick dark hair falling to his shoulders. Kindness, integrity, and honor were a part of him. Traits that made up the deepest fibers of his soul and linked my heart to his.

Before he could pull away, I grasped his hands. His skin was warm, his fingers strong and fine, just as I remembered. I lifted his palms and placed them against my face. Only a heartbeat of space separated us. To see him, to touch him, was everything I had dreamed.

"I won't ask you to live with a disfigured man," Kadesh told me. "I'll give you food and water, coins and guards to accompany you back to your father. But know I will always love you. Until the day I leave this world."

"How can you say these things? I want to spend the rest of my life with you."

"A scarred man would bring you shame."

"Then look at *me!*" I cried.

Before I could stop myself, I jerked his cloak from around my neck and allowed it to slip to the ground. Then I untied the belt around my waist. My dress drifted along my bare shoulders.

"Light a candle, Kadesh. I will show you the scars of *my* life, but I'm not going to be afraid any longer. I want you to know the truth."

"Jayden, you don't have to do this—"

Despite my determination, my fingers shook as I picked up one of the candles and bent to hold it in the fire's coals. Under the wavering yellow, the pale white lines of the cuts Horeb had given me using my own dagger showed clearly on my neck and shoulder. An eternal reminder of the night Horeb had tried to rape me at the pond. The same night he'd murdered his own father, our king.

Kadesh groaned. He touched my neck, and then gently traced his fingers down the white slash etched along my shoulder. I shivered at his touch, and then reached out to wipe away the tear that slipped down his face.

"Knife wounds don't go away. I know that, too."

"These aren't new scars," Kadesh said with a quiet fury. "Horeb attacked you. Long before we ever went to Mari. Long before he tried to kill me. Why didn't you tell me when I saw you at the temple of Ashtoreth?"

"I was afraid just like you. Ashamed of my own actions. I scarred Horeb that night, too. So there would be proof. I've already made a vow to kill him the next time I see him. But as long as I have you with me, I won't ever be afraid again."

"You are an amazing girl, Jayden, daughter of Pharez." Kadesh's voice was so tender my body ached. "You are as lovely as the day I first saw you from the cliff top, dancing in prayer at your mother's grave, pouring out your love and sorrow."

I stepped into the circle of his arms and leaned forward to softly press my lips along the ragged scar on his cheek. Then I kissed the emptiness where Horeb had stolen his sight. He was blind, and I ached with a grief that ran deep and terrible. The disfigurement could affect his role as Prince of Sariba. His ability to be a warrior and king.

Kadesh pulled me tighter and his tears of agony ran down my neck. I wanted to take away his pain. I didn't care what he looked like. I only knew that I loved him and would do anything for him, just as he'd done for my family.

"I should have gone to your father that very night," Kadesh said softly. "I should have protected you."

"If you had stayed at the oasis, Horeb would have killed you in your sleep. The night of Hakak's wedding, the night we fell in love, Horeb saw us—we were already as good as dead. No more regrets," I added, my fingers in his hair as he kissed me. "On the night of our marriage, I will dance for you with jewels and perfume and silks."

He wrapped his cloak around me as the sun began to sink. "Jayden, are you truly ready to be tied to the mystery of the southern lands?"

I stared into his beautiful face and nodded. "Your home will be my home. Your secrets will be my secrets." Kadesh lifted me up into the strength of his arms and my toes left the cave floor. His long hair brushed against my bare shoulders and I closed my eyes as he kissed my face and neck again.

The power of the ancient Mother Goddess was deep within me, intense as ever, but also familiar and sweet. She'd brought me here. Watched over me. I didn't know why I had ever been afraid.

Taking my hand, Kadesh led me out of the cave. Slivers of

lingering sunlight dripped down the narrow canyon walls. "I have something else to show you."

My white camel kneeled at the bottom of the cave's steps, and he clucked his tongue to beckon her to us. Kadesh lifted me onto Shay, pulling himself up to sit in front of me so I could lean against him. My arms went around his waist, my chin in the crook of his neck while we navigated the maze of alleys and crevices. A moment later, the city of Edom spread below us. A spectacular fortress of blood-red cliff walls and towering sandstone.

A brigade of Edomite men sat astride their black and chestnut mares. The horses' hooves danced, eager to charge into battle. And then a hundred men poured across the floor of the valley, surging from the cracks and fissures of the canyon.

A thrill ran through me. "What's happening?"

"I'm gathering an army to travel back to my homeland. Chemish is enlisting his brothers and cousins. Yesterday one of our scouts returned. The story of a wounded southern man has leaked out. Just as you heard rumors from Gedaliah's family, so has Horeb."

His words turned me colder than a river in winter, but then his warm, beautiful eyes sought mine.

"But first, I was getting ready to send the Edomite army to see if there was any chance I could still rescue a certain girl of the Tribe of Nephish from the clutches of my enemy." He touched my cheek and gave me a half smile. "Only she found her way here first."

Kadesh *had been* coming for me, just as he'd promised. But

I wasn't the same person Kadesh had left at the Tadmur oasis so many months ago. So much had happened. So much had changed.

The warriors on their fierce steeds gave me great satisfaction. In the far reaches of the desert, Horeb and his men were unaware we would be ready for him if they found us on the trail to the secret southern lands.

"I wasn't planning to be defeated a second time," Kadesh said. "If we want to stay ahead of Horeb's army we need to leave without delay. Flee these lands and head south."

Every bone in my body was exhausted, but there wasn't a moment of spare time. I noticed the way he protected his left arm. Being blind in one eye would hinder his vision, too.

A hot wind lifted my tangled hair, spinning it about my face. I tried to calm my thudding heart. I had to be ready for whatever lay ahead, whether it was victory or death.

There were no more secrets between us, but there was still a war to fight if we wanted any kind of peace. Survival was going to take all my focus. Every ounce of precious life. To win a future that would finally belong to us.

5

hemish's wife, Isra, arrived to take me to her family home.

My fingers lingered in Kadesh's hand, reluctant to let him go. "Isra will care for you. Sleep well, Jayden. Tomorrow we ride out."

"You'll take care of Shay?"

"Asher has already tended to her with food and water."

When I glanced over my shoulder, I could see Asher's dark silhouette watching us from the mouth of the cave. He nodded an assurance for my camel's well-being and gave a small bow.

Isra slipped her arm through mine. "Welcome to the land of Edom," she said, leading me to a set of stone stairs a short distance from Kadesh's cave. Her eyes sparked a rich dark brown, a startling green color circling the irises.

This home was much larger, befitting an Edomite ruler.

Luxurious rugs and tapestries decorated the floors and walls. A girl of about ten grasped my hand and motioned for me to sit while she washed my feet in a basin of water.

"I'm quite filthy after weeks on the trail," I said with a self-conscious laugh.

The girl lowered her lashes shyly. "This is a custom reserved for honored guests."

Isra hovered, providing soap and hot water from the fire. "This is my youngest child, Zilyah. She's such a blessing to me, as is my son, Asher. We've heard so much about you, Jayden. The stories are spreading across the city. Stories of a girl traveling such a great distance with only one camel. It's a miracle you're here—alive. I'm sure your mother would be so proud of you. Worried, but proud, as any mother would be for their daughter."

"You know about my—" Emotion rose up my belly hard and fast.

Tenderly, Isra cupped my face, knowledge in her eyes. "She might have left this world, but she hasn't left you. I sense her in you, Jayden."

"That's my greatest wish, to someday be like her. I've tried so hard to keep my promises . . . and feel like I've only failed . . ." My voice trailed away, the words inadequate.

"Eat a few morsels, child. I promise you'll sleep soundly tonight. No lonely fears to guard against on the desert."

There was a hot lentil soup, fresh bread, dates, and fruit. My stomach was so tight and hollow I could only eat a little even though it was delicious.

After we ate, I spotted a bath in the far reaches of the cave. Light from a dozen candles sitting in niches revealed the cave was divided into several rooms. "Where's your husband?" I asked, embarrassed.

"Chemish will sleep in Kadesh's cave tonight so we can have some privacy."

"I'd love a bath and a clean dress," I confessed, guilty for craving comforts from total strangers.

"I prepared it just for you, my dear." Isra left me behind a curtain for privacy, and I undressed and climbed into the tub, scrubbing every inch of my body and in between each toe. Zilyah helped me wash my hair twice, and then poured bowls of warm water over my head.

I was tempted to throw my tattered dress into the fire, but instead I washed the fabric with the last of the soapy water, scrubbing at the embedded dirt. After wringing it out, I hung the dress along one of the stone walls to dry for packing in the morning.

Shivering, with damp hair, I stood by the fire to put on the dress Chemish's wife had left for me. It was a deep green color with threads of gold running through the fitted bodice and flared skirt. Embroidered sleeves fell below my wrists. It was one of the loveliest dresses I'd ever worn, and I was grateful for her generosity.

"It fits perfectly, Jayden," Isra said with approval, a candle in her hand.

"The dress is too lovely to travel in. I'm afraid it's going to be in shreds by the time we arrive in the southern lands."

She waved away my words, the gesture reminding me of her husband, Chemish. "After birthing five sons and a daughter I can't fit in it any longer. It's been sitting in my chest for years. But Jayden," she broke off, darting a quick glance behind her. "Please stay here with me. The trip to the lands of frankincense is horribly difficult. Some don't survive. And traveling with all those dirty Edomites—pah! You couldn't bribe me enough!" Her eyes widened in a joking manner, but there was an underlying seriousness.

"Aren't you related to a few of them?" My lips quirked upward.

The woman laughed softly. "Chemish is even taking Asher on the journey. He needs more caravan experience before he leads one of his own someday."

I remembered the young man studying me with curious eyes.

"You'll be safer here," Isra pressed. "And I'd love someone new to gossip with. Our little village up on the plateau where we farm and raise our sheep is becoming quite dull."

"But I wouldn't be safe. Horeb is on the desert tracking me. And—and I must be with Kadesh."

She kissed me on each cheek. "Young love cannot be apart. It was wishful thinking on my part, but I wish you safe travels." Isra paused. "I can see why Kadesh is taken with you. You have a spirit about you, a way of holding yourself tranquil and composed. But underneath your serenity lies a fiery will for survival and devotion to those you love. So different from—from the other girls who have tried to enchant the prince of the Sariba kingdom."

"Other girls?" I fought for composure. Of course there would be women who would desire Kadesh for a husband. "A prince is a coveted position indeed."

Isra led me to a hanging tapestry. Behind the wall lay a bed piled with pillows and blankets against the winter chill. "Sleep well, Jayden."

Homesickness washed over me with a swift fierceness. My hands curled into fists of weariness and anxiety. I wished Shay was here so I could curl around her warm belly. I hadn't slept without her for nearly two months, since I'd purchased her in the camel market at Mari.

I lifted my eyes to the roof of the cave. "Oh, mother," I whispered. "Are you watching from the world of spirits? Do you see me here in this world of fear and death?"

A moment later I heard the rustling of blankets on the other side of the tapestry, and then Isra softly singing to her daughter. The melody wound around my heart, reminding me of all the lullabies my mother had sung to me and Leila whenever we were tired or frightened or ill. My throat filled with a lump of grief. I was nearly seventeen, but I still needed my mother's love and guidance. Desperately I tried to capture her face and voice in my mind and hold on to it, despite the tenuous grasp.

Sleep became impossible. Finally I rose and tiptoed to the entrance of the cave. Stars and moonlight traced Isra's melody, silver light dripping along the stone walls like mystical water.

My arms and hips began to sway to her voice, marking the beats, my bare toes silent on the cold red sandstone. A sacred night enlarged before my eyes. Isra's song swathed my thoughts, and my body sang its dance. Just as I'd danced at my mother's grave, I danced the love for my family in an eternal bond that wouldn't diminish no matter how far apart we were.

Turning in small circles, I reached my arms to the heavens, yearning to grasp my mother's spirit. The faces of my family flashed across my mind, and I knew with certainty I had to return to the oasis at Tadmur. I had to get Leila from the temple. I had to convince my father and grandmother to come with us. I couldn't leave them behind.

Once I was safely living in the southern lands, it was certain I'd never see them again. I'd never know their fate. Kadesh's Sariba kingdom was a land of bounty and peace. If they came with us, my family would be well taken care of.

The idea was insane, but I had to go north—*opposite* the direction Kadesh and the Edomite army planned to go—and get the family I'd promised my mother I'd care for.

Shivers rushed along my arms. Horeb had been in Mari, but where was he now? Aligning himself with the Assyrians in the north—or rounding up an army in Damascus? If his spy in the hills had managed to kidnap me I'd already be in his captivity and tied forever to a marriage bed I loathed.

Horeb would use threats and blackmail against my father and sister to lure me back to his prison. Without Abimelech, my father didn't have an ally in the tribe any longer.

Horeb's sinister connection to the High Priestess Armana

could also prove to be Leila's downfall. She could be mistreated. Sold as a sex slave. Forced to have children to be sacrificed to the goddess of Ashtoreth.

Misery awaited my family if I left them in Tadmur. I couldn't wait for that to happen. I had to go to Tadmur now—before Horeb got there.

All at once, something glittered below the stone staircase where I danced. Halting, I held myself as still as the stone. Moonlight glinted off the hilt of a sword.

My eyes widened when the sound of cautious footsteps paused. A male figure glanced up at me and his eyes gleamed, like a wild cat.

It was Asher. Wordlessly, we stared at each other. Had he been watching me dance? The scene reminded me of the night long ago when I'd danced on the desert after burying my mother. The night Kadesh couldn't sleep after the burning of his wound, and caught me unawares.

What was Asher doing out this late? He must be coming to see his mother, to fetch something. After all, this large, sumptuous cave was his family home. Tentatively, I smiled as though our encounter was nothing, but he didn't return the gesture. Instead, his face was impassive. It soon became clear I wasn't supposed to be outside on the terrace of the cave.

He didn't move, didn't speak. Then a second figure slipped out of the darkness. Quickly, I stepped back and shuddered. It was the same scar-faced Edomite horseman who had stolen our camels last year to pay for usage of the well—blatant thievery when we were dying with need of water—and lewdly suggested taking me and Leila for payment as well.

I'd hoped I'd never see him again.

What did Asher have to do with that awful man?

My bare feet made no sound as I darted back inside the cave and made my way past the fire. For another hour I tossed and turned, reliving the long day with all its emotions, unable to shake the sight of the two Edomite warriors meeting in the dead of night.

When I finally fell asleep, I swore I felt the soft press of Isra's lips against my forehead. A voice whispered, "Sleep, child," but I didn't know if the voice belonged to Isra or my mother.

6

In the early light of dawn, Isra embraced me good-bye, while her daughter stared with shy curiosity. "I'll pray for your safety every day, dear girl," the woman murmured as I thanked her for her many kindnesses.

Quickly, I headed to Kadesh's cave. When I spotted him, he was crouched at the entrance cooking breakfast. Seeing him engrossed in his task made my breath catch. For so many months I'd thought he would only live in my memories.

A laugh bubbled up my throat as I raced up the staircase, my hair billowing. He was the same, but different, too, and I was suddenly shy around him.

"Dawn's creeping fingers are here, my love. As soon as we eat, we're gone. Here's a brush for your hair—although I confess I love the tangled look on you." Kadesh ran his fingers through my curls and I trembled at his touch.

"Maybe I can start looking like a real person again instead of a wild girl."

"You look completely real to me," Kadesh said, encircling me with his arms.

I loved the feel of his body, his warmth, his strength, his heartbeat thudding against my ear. "You feel completely real—" I started to say in agreement, but before I could finish he pressed his lips against mine, so gently, so sweetly, I wanted to weep. My legs turned weak and my soul rose with an inexplicable happiness.

The kiss deepened, but Kadesh abruptly broke away, his chest heaving as if he couldn't bear the power of our physical contact. "Jayden, daughter of Pharez, I'll honor and cherish you until I die."

I traced the terrible scar around his blind eye and Kadesh clung to me, burying his face in my neck. I held him tight while the morning sun streaked the rocks a brilliant pink. I drank in the miracle of him, grateful Horeb's blade hadn't marred the rest of him.

"You are more lovely than any of my dreams, Jayden." Smoothing his thick dark hair with my hands, I marveled at the reality of this moment, at the reality of him, solid in my arms.

I shook away his compliments. "I'm sunburned and travel weary—and need ten more baths."

"You saved me from rotting alone in this cave for the rest of my life." His tone turned serious as he gazed down into my face. "You saved me from a wicked despair growing in my soul. There were nights I thought I'd die in this cave. Never see you again. Never go home to my uncle and family."

I recognized the hurt in his eyes. "I don't believe that for one moment. You are too strong and compassionate to sit in a cave for the rest of your life. Even while you recovered from near death, you've been healing people and spreading your gift. Gedaliah's son is proof of that."

"I'm astounded you traveled such a great distance, alone."

A smile crept across my lips. "I was highly motivated. And I bought a marvelous camel."

He chuckled at my words. "She *is* a worthy camel. You chose wisely, my desert girl. I admire your spirit, your determination. I am *your* servant for the rest of my life. And one day . . ."

I leaned into him, drinking in his warm and spicy scent. "And one day?"

"One day I won't sleep in a cold cave, alone. I'll take you to the marriage tent, and we'll never be apart again."

"To be safe in the southern lands and never spend a single moment apart will be our very own creation of heaven."

We stared at each other for a moment, wishing the future was already here, and then Kadesh gently tugged on my hand. "Our army and journey awaits."

The unsettling scene from the previous night returned. I had to tell Kadesh what I'd witnessed. "Something strange happened. Late last night, I saw Chemish's son, Asher, speaking with someone."

"I thought you were tucked safely away with Isra."

"I couldn't sleep. I was missing home . . . missing my mother. I went out on the terrace of Isra's cave."

"But Asher was with his father."

I twisted my hands together. "He was down below the staircase. I know he saw me, too. Our eyes met."

"He was watching you?" Incredulity lined Kadesh's words.

"No, Asher was meeting the Edomite who robbed us last year. The thief who stole your gold, nearly killed my father, and threatened to defile me and Leila. There was one reason I was afraid to come to these canyon lands to look for you: that man. What is he doing so close to the Edomite leader's home? In the dead of night?"

The muscles in Kadesh's face tensed. "His name is Laban. Yes, he's a true Edomite, and no, he's not a man of God or honor. But," he paused, his gaze dropping away.

Something twisted inside me. "No, Kadesh," I started. "No."

He gripped my hand in reassurance. "Laban is coming with us to the southern lands. Last year, Chemish banished him from the city, and he's been out on the desert, but we've called him back to travel with the army. For penitence—and because he's the best fighter we have. He swore allegiance to Chemish."

"My skin crawls to look at him."

"You won't have to ever look at him again. He'll be in the front guard. I'm putting you in the middle for protection with Asher as your bodyguard."

"But won't I be with you?"

"Of course, but I'm the caravan leader and tracker. I'll

have many duties while we journey. I don't want you to be left alone. And I trust Asher completely."

Kadesh called for my camel while I retrieved my satchel and water pouch from the ledge of the cave's entrance.

Morning sunshine filled the hollows of rock. Kadesh sat on Shay so regally, his back straight, cloak flapping against Shay's flanks in the soft breeze. It wasn't the same cloak he'd worn when I'd seen him for the first time perched on the cliff watching me dance over my mother's grave a year ago. I now wore the rich brown cloak with its foreign detailing. The cloak he currently fastened about his shoulders was simpler, the same forest green material as my dress. I suspected Isra had crafted it for him—and purposely given me her old dress.

We'd come so far, but the most arduous journey still lay ahead. We were both scarred, but together we were healed and whole.

"I love you," I whispered. The wind caught my words and carried them down the red stone cliff. The expression on Kadesh's face washed me in courage and serenity. When I reached Shay, the camel groaned, spit, and shook herself as I stroked her soft fur. "There's something else I must do before I go with you to your secret homeland."

"Jayden, it's risky to delay—"

"We don't know where Horeb is, or how close he is to finding us, but I can't leave my family in Tadmur. I can't bear the thought of never seeing them again."

"We'll send for them once we get settled."

"They'll never come on their own. And another six months from now might be too late. *We* might not survive, and if we do, Horeb will use my father and sister as hostages. To black-mail me into coming back. He could torture them, keep them captive—to lure me back in the hope of rescuing them."

Kadesh's face was thoughtful, his hands gripping my arms while I spoke. All I wanted to do was bury my face in his chest and forget Horeb existed, but I gritted my teeth and continued.

"To hide out in the hills of Mari and make this journey alone to find you—only to return to Horeb's clutches when he uses my family against me. We both know he will do exactly that. He needs me to legitimize his throne and himself in the eyes of the foreign tribes he's aligning himself with."

"Surely you understand the great risks if we go north to the oasis?"

I placed my hand on his face. "I took a great risk coming here alone. My life has already taken an enormous turn. I can never go back to the girl I was."

Kadesh winced and I could tell it hurt his honor that he hadn't thought of rescuing my family first. His first instinct was to save me. We both had an aching need to flee hard and fast and leave these lands forever. "When I think of Horeb hurting my grandmother. Imprisoning my father. Forcing himself on Leila and then taunting me to return to save her life—if he lets my family live at all. I can't trust him."

"You're absolutely right, Jayden. We need to take them with us now. I'll let Chemish know of the change in plans, and to use the safest route we can back to Tadmur."

"What do your scouts say about Horeb's army? Have you heard anything?"

He didn't answer at first. "Horeb was in Damascus searching for you—and signing treaties with the Assyrians in those northern lands. But the Edomites have vowed to protect you with their lives."

"I will owe them a huge debt of gratitude, and I hate to put them in danger. Perhaps I should travel alone, in disguise, and then catch up to you with a—another caravan."

Kadesh stared at me as if I'd gone crazy. "I would never let you go alone—never again."

"But I know you need to return to your uncle. And I'm asking you to put your own family aside for me—once again."

"You are my family, Jayden. Forever. Once we're in the frankincense lands you'll see how hidden away and safe we are. Nothing can touch us there."

I nodded wordlessly, uncertain, but I'd cling to the promise of hope.

A hundred men on horseback came into view, their sleek horses jangling with decorations. Dancing on their hooves, ready to ride into the empty desert. Behind them, a string of camels was packed with supplies and bedrolls.

Chemish rode up, accompanied by his son, Asher. The two of them dismounted and bowed to me. Chemish said, "You're looking well this morning, daughter of Pharez."

"Sleep and a bath suit me. I'm grateful for your family's kindness and hospitality."

Kadesh formally presented me to the young man. "Jayden, this is Asher, Chemish's son, and an Edomite prince. I've asked him to take a special role as we travel. Especially since Chemish has asked me to be his captain over any skirmishes we might encounter."

I glanced up at Kadesh curiously. "You have soldiering experience?"

"Military training comes with the responsibility of overseeing my uncle's caravans the past two years." Kadesh paused, slipping a hand reassuringly along my arm. "I've assigned Asher as your personal bodyguard—with Chemish's permission, of course."

"What about the Edomite prince's permission?"

The young man stepped forward, back erect, his expression solemn. "I volunteered to do anything Kadesh needed from me. This journey is more dangerous than a normal caravan trip. Kadesh is like my elder blood brother. I'd follow him to the ends of the earth if he needed me."

Kadesh put a hand on the boy's shoulder. "If you recall, Asher, you *have* followed me to the ends of the earth before. A place called Sariba, my homeland."

"I was thinking it was all just a bad dream," Asher quipped in return.

I stared between the two of them. "The trip is that bad?"

"One day at a time keeps the madness of the empty desert at bay," Kadesh said lightly. "For now, look forward to seeing your family in Tadmur. And pray we're faster than Horeb."

Chemish began calling out orders to the Edomite army.

Asher helped him arrange the pack camels within the ranks of soldiers, organized into companies of twenty for traveling.

Asher's humility piqued my curiosity. He didn't walk or speak as an heir of a kingdom. No arrogance or pridefulness in his demeanor. So unlike Horeb and the Maachathite tribe men. But what did that late-night rendezvous with Laban mean? What would a young man like Asher have to do with a hardened thief? Despite Kadesh's assurances, I dreaded spending the next few months so close to that man.

I needed to learn how to protect myself. To fight Horeb when—and not if—the time came. For it would come. I knew it. I wished I'd taken the chance to grab Gad's sword, after the hyena finished eating him and slunk off into the hills.

"How do your horses endure the desert between wells?" I asked. "Horses need more water than camels. Or are they magical camels in disguise?"

Chemish's face crinkled into a smile at my question. "We only take our horses away from our lands during the winter months when food is more plentiful and there are occasional ravines with rivers flowing."

"Our horses have another secret, my lady," Asher added almost shyly. "One evening around the hearth, I will tell you the story."

"But it's not the custom for women to sit at the fire with the men. . . ." I blushed. I would be the only woman of the company.

The Edomite army split in two, half going before me and

the other half behind me as I joined the caravan. It was comforting to be cushioned from any strangers we might encounter.

Sand swished under the horses' hooves. Winter sun warmed the top of my head. The pack camels carried our food and water, and for the first time in weeks I could doze while my camel followed the other animals. I didn't have to be afraid I'd wake up to Horeb and an army surrounding me, a knife at my throat.

We pushed through the day, past dusk and the moon's rising. We had to make it north to Tadmur as fast as possible, and then leave again just as swiftly.

When we made camp the men brushed down their horses, corralled them together, and then fell into their beds. Kadesh created a sleeping spot for me, tying blankets between scrub bushes for privacy. The same customs I'd experienced on the trail since I was born. As second nature as breathing.

I spotted sentries posted around the camp. Others would take their place during the watches of the night. Kadesh and Chemish squatted together under the partial moon. The scouts had arrived from the north, four bedraggled men with lathered horses. The male voices were low, but carried in the stillness, despite the rustlings of sleeping men, the neighing of the horses, and grumblings of our camels.

"What is the news?" Chemish asked.

"We found them," the first man said. "The Nephish army traveled west from Mari to Tadmur—"

I slipped out of my bed, unable to lie still. "I can't let you do this," I said, kneeling behind Kadesh. "You and your army get nothing but the possibility of death. I can't in good conscience—"

Chemish held up his hand. "We all hope to avoid a confrontation, daughter of Pharez. Nobody is hungry for war. We know these deserts well. It's the reason Sariba and the Edomite kingdom made an alliance a generation ago. We plan to slip past Horeb, and we'll succeed."

Kadesh brought me closer, his presence calming me as the fire's flames flickered against the men's faces. "It's the middle of winter," he said thoughtfully. "Horeb's men should be on the open desert with their camel herds following the rains, not at the oasis."

"They waited several weeks at Tadmur," the second scout said, "thinking Horeb's betrothed would return to her family after escaping them at Mari."

I cringed at words I never wanted to hear again: Horeb's betrothed. But the scouts dared not call me by my given name.

"We heard a strange tale," the first man added. "One of the Nephish prince's scouts must have discovered her camp. Pieces of his body were found in the Mari hills."

Chemish jerked his head in surprise, and his son, Asher, glanced over at me. "How do you know the body belonged to a Nephish soldier?"

"His sword and bedroll lay near the remains of an old fire," the scout continued. "Horeb's army must have assumed she turned northwest to Damascus to try to lose herself in the big city. Upon his arrival in Damascus, Horeb got into a skirmish with the Adummatus, long-time enemies of the Maachathite tribe. In fact, the Nephish and Maachathites have declared an alliance and fought together to strengthen that treaty."

The second scout shook his head. "The Maachathites are old enemies, but the alliance appears strong."

"Fighting the Adummatus in Damascus is good news," Kadesh said. "They'll be licking their wounds and resupplying. But there's something you aren't telling me?"

The scout leader nodded soberly. "The Nephish princess was spotted by merchants when she traveled to the Edomite lands. They sold the information to Horeb, who is now making plans to reverse his army's directions—and intercept us as we head north."

Those figures I'd seen in the distant desert. Wearing the male cloak hadn't fooled them. Horeb knew where I was. I'd been afraid of this, but to have my fears confirmed made it somehow so much worse.

Sensing my distress, Kadesh squeezed my fingers in his. "How far away are they?"

"A few weeks by the regular northern trails—less if they cut through the mountains. Knowing they're highly motivated to retrieve Horeb's bride—"

"Jayden is not his bride!" Kadesh said sharply.

The scout bowed his head. "I apologize, my lord. I meant—his betrothed."

Those words didn't help either. Kadesh jumped up from the hearth, his expression a mix of impatience, anger, and sadness. Turning back to the scout, Kadesh added, "We are also highly motivated to retrieve my betrothed's family from Tadmur."

"Who is to say which motivation is the strongest?" the man said with a helpless shrug.

His words were a clear reference to the fact that the outcome of our journey was completely uncertain and fraught with intolerable danger. To be traveling toward Horeb was insane.

Kadesh rubbed at his face, wincing when he got too close to the jagged scar surrounding his blinded eye. "The Edomite army and this prince of Sariba will show you who is stronger—and who will win."

The second scout spoke up. "We should turn now before it's too late, and go south along the Red Sea, which will take us home to Sariba. We have Dedan forts that will protect us if the Nephish and Maachathites catch up."

Kadesh had once told me the Dedan forts had been built by his family. The forts protected the frankincense caravans along the dozens of journeys they made every year to deliver the costly spice to the cities and towns along the Red Sea, the Canaanite lands, and the great rivers of Babylon.

"I won't run from Horeb or be outmaneuvered by him," Kadesh said. "If we come upon his army, we will kill them and be done with it. We don't have a choice. You know that, Chemish," he added, turning to his friend. There was a tone of respect in Kadesh's words, and a willingness to listen to the older man's experienced suggestions.

"We have a good chance of reaching Tadmur before the King of Nephish," Chemish said. "As soon as we have the princess's family we flee south—and never confront him at all."

"The timing is risky, my lord," the scout interrupted. "We have no friends in that country. We might become the slaughtered army."

Kadesh eyed the men sitting about the campfire. "If we ride hard, sleep little, we can cut our time nearly in half. Are you with me, Chemish? Asher?"

The father and son stared at each other briefly. "We came to help you," Chemish said. "We won't leave you to die a second time at Horeb's hands. If that man is allowed to continue, he will spread death and destruction over all the desert lands— bribing and killing to force the smaller tribes to join him."

Kadesh's chin lifted. "Join him or face extinction."

A bitter taste was in my throat. "When we get to Tadmur," I said, "we'll need to get my family and leave again within hours."

"Exactly, my dear," Chemish said, touching my arm with his fatherly warmth. "And once we're beyond the borders of the Red Sea and reach the far southern regions, we'll lose the Nephish army along the borders of the Empty Sands. They won't know how to survive that country."

I pictured Horeb's army losing their way in the Empty Sands, dying of thirst. The Empty Sands was a realm where there were no wells or shrubs—a place where no one who ventured in was ever seen again.

If Horeb got lost, his army would be forced to kill their camels one by one to stay alive. And when the camels were gone, his men dead, Horeb would curse God and die. The scene in my imagination brought an awful satisfaction, but also horror. I knew what it was like to be so hungry and thirsty I wanted to claw my throat out. To weep without tears because I was so dehydrated. To be coaxed by desert demons to lie down in the soft, warm sand and never wake up.

The circle around the fire quieted. There was nothing left to do but retire to our beds. I gathered Kadesh's cloak around me as I moved away from the fire. The night was filled with the usual noises. Rustling rodents. A stirring of wings from soundless owls and bats overhead.

Even with an army surrounding me, I was troubled. So much could happen between here and Sariba. So much *would* happen. On the way to my sleeping area, I saw Laban slip away from the fire. His shadow disappeared into the darkness. The man sent shivers down my neck and I avoided his presence, pretending he didn't exist.

I spotted Asher's figure walking in the opposite direction to his bedroll and wondered whether the two of them had just held a private meeting. Or was it a coincidence to see the pair only moments apart? I was too tired, too weary, to ponder it.

Sometime in the middle of the night I was awakened by a light touch on my shoulder.

"Kadesh!" I jerked upright. Blackness surrounded me as though I'd gone blind. But the stars were gone now along with the fire.

"It's me," a male voice whispered. "Asher."

Instinctively, I pulled up my blanket.

"Kadesh sent me to wake you. We leave within moments."

I stumbled to my feet, sleep clinging like cobwebs. "That was a—a short night."

"Nights are always brief while traveling."

"Where's Kadesh?" I asked, wishing he were here to wake me.

"Your camel managed to loosen her ropes and strayed off—"

"Shay? I hope she's not lost! Although she never got me permanently off the trail on the way from Mari to Edom."

"Then she's a good camel. You're fortunate to own her."

"I bought her in Mari because of Kadesh. I mean, his generosity paid for her." A flush burned my cheeks. What did he think of me—a girl from a different tribe chasing after a man to whom she wasn't officially betrothed, let alone married?

"With frankincense, right?" Asher asked.

I glanced up from rolling my bedding. Dawn brushed a pale hue across the sky and his features were becoming more distinct in the morning light.

"Don't be afraid of his secrets. We all know him well. We work for him, actually . . ." His voice trailed off as if he were uncertain about how much he should confide.

"What do you do for Kadesh?"

"We run his caravans through our mountain canyons. One day we hope to build a beautiful city in the cliffs of Edom's red land. The crossroads for all caravans."

"You are a prophet to see into the future?"

He glanced away as though I'd embarrassed him. Having

a personal guard was disconcerting. I don't know why Kadesh should be so worried since I was protected by a hundred Edomite soldiers. But once again I found myself wishing I had a sword of my own and not just a small dagger.

Every time I looked at the weapon it reminded me of Gad. The sight of his blood dripping from the bronze blade. The thought of needing to use my blade again in the future brought little comfort. Thrusting a dagger into someone meant face-to-face combat. So close you could smell your enemy's breath.

Asher stared at me curiously. "Are you all right?"

I started, realizing I'd been lost in thought. "Edom has the potential for great wealth, then," I stammered, trying to pick up the thread of our conversation.

Asher paused on the path, holding out an arm in case I needed to steady myself, but careful not to touch me.

"I suppose the frankincense trade could grow enormous," I said, bypassing his chivalrous hand. "As cities and towns multiply from Damascus to Salem. Nineveh to Babylon."

"We don't just manage Kadesh's caravans and maintain the tribal forts and wells for greedy wealth." A lock of hair fell over his serious brown eyes, and my eyes dropped to take note of the well-crafted slingshot tied at his hip. "We're his partners in all things. Alliances, trade, protection, war."

"Why would you risk so much for a girl and a tribe you have no formal treaty with?"

"The Sariba Prince is one of the finest men I've ever known. We are blood brothers in many ways. We—I love him. I would do anything for him."

His underlying meaning dawned on me. "This army is for Kadesh and his tribe's safety, not me personally."

Asher's eyebrows shot up. "I didn't mean to imply that—"

I tried not to laugh at his expression. "You don't have to justify your devotion to him. I know of Kadesh's generosity personally. I can imagine he elicits the same from his friends."

"No, you don't fully understand. We're here to help you—because you are the woman he now loves."

"Your loyalty is noble and kind. *More* than kind because one day I will owe you my life. I pray to the God of Abraham our lives are spared. That war with Horeb will come to naught."

A calm steadiness stared at me through those solemn brown eyes of his. "With that I agree wholeheartedly." He directed my attention up ahead. "We're gathering at the trailhead around this cliff outcropping."

I walked behind him, bewildered. One moment Asher was timid and unassuming, the next he was speaking passionately about his loyalty to Kadesh. The next he was holding clandestine meetings with the ugly Laban.

The first horses galloped ahead and a cloud of fine dust sprayed the air. Kadesh rode up on Shay, my wandering, frisky camel. Bending to kiss my hand, his whisper of love brushed my skin as he helped me onto the white camel.

When I kicked Shay's sides to take my spot in the caravan, Asher's words came back to haunt me. What did he mean when he said, "The woman Kadesh *now* loves?"

Those were not careless words, but had the power of a

subtle insinuation. The power to turn my world completely upside down.

Had there been another girl in Kadesh's past? Had he loved someone before we'd met? And if so, why had he chosen to keep her a secret?

7

We pushed hard, rarely dismounting, eating and drinking as we rode. At night, when we stopped, Asher began showing me various moves I could do with my dagger—thrusts and slices and parries, making me practice with both my right and left hands so I'd be able to continue if my arm or hand was struck in a fight.

Those first few evenings, Asher watched with amusement. Finally, he allowed me to try the moves with his own sword. It didn't take long before even I could see my improvement.

I had a long way to go to defend myself against Horeb or his men, but I felt a glimmer of hope. By the time I faced him I'd be even stronger. As long as I didn't face him until we reached the southern lands.

"Kadesh observes our lessons for a bit each night," Asher said after a few days, "but doesn't say anything. What does he think about me teaching you?"

"He suggested it himself when I told him I *must* learn sword-fighting. I need to be able to defend myself. I don't want to be a helpless girl."

"You're anything but helpless," Asher said, admiration clearly in his words.

"I just need to figure out how to get a sword of my own."

"Ask for one when you get to Sariba—as a wedding gift."

I looked at him from the corner of my eye and smiled.

A group of Edomite horses swept past, their powerful leg muscles rippling as they galloped. Coats of black and amber gleamed richly.

I stuck my dagger back into its sheath. "How can your steeds ride so hard and so swiftly for so many hours?"

"We breed them to survive with less water during the cooler months. I promise they eat well each evening," Asher added.

"You also promised to tell me their story."

"We found the secret for teaching endurance in the harsh desert. We put the young horses we're breaking into a pen, and then leave them there without food and water for three days."

"Three days?" I was shocked. "Surely, they would die of thirst."

"It's worse than that. The pen is built within sight of a spring or a river. The horses can see the water. They can smell the water. So close, and yet so far."

"It must be pure torture."

"When I was a boy I ran away the first time I watched the

horses ramming their sides against the paddock, screaming for water. By the end, the horses are frothing at the mouth, the whites of their eyes rolling. When my father finally opened the gate the young horses rushed down the hill, galloping like fiends toward the water—that's when my father whistled and called them back to him."

My own throat burned at the thought of their terrible thirst after the brutal sun of three days. "Why would he do such a cruel thing?"

"To see if they would obey his voice above all else. To put their love and devotion for my father above their own needs, even death."

A strange awe rushed over me. The desert was a cruel master, but forged a devoted reverence of its stark power to the nomadic tribes.

"If my father takes the time to train well, the horse will turn away from the water and run back to him before they drink." Asher wrapped a fist around his leather halter, eyes flickering to my face and away again. "If they can overcome their own desires no matter how desperate, they can be trusted. They've proven their worth. A horse more prized than gold or jewels."

"Or frankincense," Kadesh added, suddenly at my side.

"After enduring the test of obedience, our horses can travel all day during the winter before needing water."

A smile played around Kadesh's mouth. "But you can't eat them like a camel."

"You're a tease," I told him. "I'm curious. How did your

two families become so close?"

"My uncle Ephrem and Chemish met in the lands of Dedan during their early caravan days."

"Kadesh is like an older brother to me," Asher said. "My father once told me the story of a time when he and Kadesh ventured through the Empty Sands. Rescuing one of my cousins who had lost his way on the final trail to the Sariba kingdom."

"I've never heard of anyone surviving the Empty Sands." I stared at Kadesh sitting on his horse. There was so much more to him than I knew. The awareness left me slightly breathless. I was learning that the man I loved was heir to a powerful throne I was ignorant about—and a past of which I knew almost nothing.

When we stopped for the night, my legs trembled after straddling Shay for so long. All the hot, claustrophobic hours I'd spent trapped inside a camel litter during my early childhood when I couldn't walk fast enough to keep up made me appreciate the luxury of napping on a pillow once in a while.

I hobbled Shay next to a stand of shrubbery. A lone Edomite horse was eating a patch of grass near an outcropping of rocks. Its leather halter trailed on the ground, and I reached down to grasp it. The animal gave a low whinny.

Intelligent black eyes studied me, and the rich dark brown coat was silk under the starlight. I lifted my hand to its nose. "You are well taken care of."

I expected a skittish bolt from the animal, but instead she

thrust her face toward me, as though craving my touch. Her neck was warm against my cold hands, and her back arched beautifully, unlike any horse I'd ever seen before.

"You're gorgeous," I said when the mare nuzzled my palm.

Asher spoke from the shadows. "Her name is Hara. She's my horse."

I took a step backward so our fingers wouldn't touch when he took the halter from my hands. "She's splendid. I can see why the Edomites love and protect their animals so fiercely."

"I'm surprised you still think so after my story of torture, my lady."

"Please don't call me that," I told him lightly. "It feels very strange."

"Our customs demand I not call you by your name."

This was true. In different circumstances we wouldn't speak to each other at all.

"I *could* call you Princess," Asher went on.

"Oh, no! I'm hardly that."

"But you were to be princess—queen—of your Nephish tribe," he said soberly.

I squirmed. "You know quite a bit about me."

"I need to for Kadesh's sake."

My eyes cut through the shadows. "What do you mean?"

"One day you will officially be crowned Kadesh's wife and princess of the Sariba lands—and then his queen to rule at his side. Since I'm his loyal friend and your personal bodyguard, there's nothing I wouldn't do to protect you both."

"I—thank you." If he were younger, I could call him by his

given name, but I was fairly certain we were close to the same age, which made the situation more complicated.

I turned toward the hot fire crackling in the makeshift hearth and saw Kadesh had already set up my private sleeping area. There was food and small talk, but most of the men were already settling in for another early start.

Every day brought us closer to my family, but we were headed straight toward Horeb, too. The idea made me wild with anxiety.

Kadesh folded his hand over mine, pulling me close. "It's my turn for the first watch. But you have only to call out if you need me."

I wanted to curl up in his arms and sleep soundly all night. I wanted to forget the threat of Horeb, forget that Kadesh had an unknown past, and that Asher and Laban were conspiring about something. The worries hovered, keeping me on edge, and I wished I could forget the world around us and start all over again. How utterly lovely to begin a fresh history with Kadesh. Erase our pasts as though they never existed.

Perhaps when the trek to Sariba got underway at last, we could finally expunge the old and officially declare our new life.

8

After a week of hard riding, we came within sight of the city of Tadmur. Next to Tadmur lay the oasis, a shadow of darkness on the desert and a shadow on my heart. Horeb's attack on me, the murder of Abimelech, the loss of my sister to the temple—these memories stole the blissful summers I'd had here as a child.

My mind swept backward, like brushing cobwebs from the corners of the tent. I saw myself giggling as I chased after the new baby camels. My mother's voice singing while she cooked and washed, my grandmother Seraiah guiding my fingers as she taught me how to weave at the loom. In the background of my memories, my sister Leila joked and gossiped with Falail as they pretended not to watch the boys polishing their daggers and stringing their bows.

Lazy summer days. Pomegranate juice dripping down my

chin. Competitions with Leila to see who could pick the most fruit from the date orchards and grape vineyards.

Now my sister resided in the luxurious temple apartments, living the life of a priestess of Ashtoreth. The thought of her worshiping the bewitching idols of Ashtoreth and sleeping with strange men distressed me.

The sky bulged with stars when we approached the outskirts of the oasis. My eyes burned from lack of sleep. My body jangled with nerves at the immediacy of the city lights of Tadmur. Our arrival was a relief, but also mixed with dread. What would we find here? And could we survive the encounter with my tribe?

Kadesh pulled up next to me, reining in his horse. "We cut our travel in half. It's astounding you made this same journey on your own," he added softly. "I'm more in love with you every day." He brought my face toward his, so close his long hair brushed my cheek. "I believe we have spectators."

I sensed Asher behind me and ran a finger down his face. "We'll just have to wait until later."

"Chemish's scouts have brought word that we have three days before Horeb's arrival from Damascus."

"Three days—that's good, isn't it?"

"It is if there are no complications. If anything slows us on the travel south—" Kadesh stopped.

I shivered with foreboding. "By the time we get Leila from the temple, Horeb could be only one day's ride behind us."

Kadesh was sober. "If we have trouble of *any* kind, we're doomed. Meeting Horeb in the open desert is not how I want to fight him. We need to at least reach the mountains bordering the Red Sea. We'll have cliffs and caves to conceal us and from which to fight."

I searched his dark, beautiful eyes. "Why do you fear he could slaughter us? Our army is twice as large. What else is troubling you?"

He pressed his lips together, not meeting my eyes. "We've learned Horeb has gathered more men to his cause. Not only the Maachathite tribe but the Adummatus as well. Just like the Maachathites, the Adummatus have been eager to grow in strength and wealth."

A coldness spread through me, and every particle of my being wanted to flee. "My father once said the Adummatus were born without mercy in their veins. Reveling in war to gain power. Why won't Horeb just let me go?" I whispered.

"I took his wife," Kadesh said with a quiet shrug. "He can't let me remain alive. Your knowledge of his guilt as his father's murderer won't allow you to live, either."

I breathed in, trying to focus on rescuing my family. We were here now. So very close to success. "What's the plan you and Chemish have made?"

Kadesh clasped my freezing hands in his warm ones. "We intend to surround the perimeter of the oasis, keeping two scouts in each direction while you sneak into the oasis to your grandmother's tent. I'll go into Tadmur to speak with the High Priestess and beg for Leila—or buy her if I have to. We'll help your father pack and leave by nightfall. Tomorrow we go south permanently. We'll make another hard push to widen the distance to give us more lead time. Remember, in Sariba I have an army bigger than Horeb's."

Sariba was our only hope to come out of this alive. But the mysterious frankincense lands were three moons away from here. "The very air seeps with deception and betrayal. As though this day might be my last."

"Jayden, I can't ride in with you and risk being seen. The Nephish militia has been ordered to slit my throat on sight."

I wavered on my camel. "Horeb left a militia at the oasis?"

"We're sending Asher with you. Because he's young, we're hoping he'll be mistaken as a cousin. Just get to your father's tent as quickly as possible."

Without speaking, I climbed onto the back of Asher's horse, clutching the folds of his shirt to secure my seat. It was odd to be so close to the boy, to smell his scent, to feel my body against his. But his horse, Hara, could run faster than our camels, and it was safer to ride together.

Kadesh kissed my palm, his eyes grave. "Stay together at all costs."

A shout came from behind and an Edomite scout rode hard, Chemish on his heels. They pulled up their horses, dust flying.

"My lord," he addressed Kadesh, lowering his scarf from his mouth and bowing his head to me. "We've just learned about a death decree for the princess of the Nephish."

I thought I'd be sick. "A death decree?" Asher reached behind him to grip my arm so I wouldn't fall off.

"Who ordered it?" Kadesh asked.

"Either King Horeb or the tribal council—for crimes against the king and her tribe."

I pressed my forehead into Asher's back. "For breaking my betrothal," I whispered. "For running away with a man I wasn't married to. For the death of Abimelech. All of it."

"You're walking into a trap," the scout added.

Defiance rose in my belly. "I won't be frightened away. We've come all this way. I won't leave without my family." My eyes met Kadesh's and Chemish's. "You know Horeb will hurt them."

Kadesh's expression was determined, yet solemn. "All I know is, I don't want to lose you. Not now. Not after everything."

"The Edomites will surround the oasis, correct? And there's no sign of Horeb's army?"

"Not yet," Chemish answered. He pursed his lips. "It's up to you, Jayden and Kadesh, whether we go in or leave."

A heartbeat of silence passed.

"We go now," I said. "Quickly."

If I learned my family was slaughtered, I'd never have a moment's peace for the rest of my life.

Kadesh nodded once, a steely look on his face. I gave him a wavering smile, memorizing his eyes above the pattern of the rich head scarf wrapped around his face. He held out his hand and we locked fingers.

For one brief moment, only he and I existed in all the world. And then Kadesh broke off and galloped away, Asher and I following.

The morning sun fell onto the eastern hills when Kadesh turned east at the crossroad between the oasis and Tadmur, leading twenty-five horses and men with him. Another twenty-five galloped west toward the Damascus road. A contingent of Edomites had already gone north, and the twenty-five behind me and Asher would bring up the rear, guarding the southern entrance to the oasis.

As we approached, my breath caught. Groves of date palms spread their thick leaves, encircling the pond. The shining water was like fine quartz glass.

No one spoke. No sentries shouted.

My pulse thudded in my throat. I could hardly breathe.

Asher slowed when we entered the palm tree groves. Leaves rustled, cool and mysterious. I'd run through these same trees fleeing Horeb after he'd murdered his father. That moonless night caused me to lose my way, and I fell into the pond just before Horeb attacked me.

When we skirted the water's edge I tried to shake off the memory. The moment I recognized my father's tent it seemed as though my mother reached out to grasp my heart in her hands. Waves of emotions deluged me. I felt her loss more keenly than ever.

Cautiously, Asher passed another tent. The hearth fire was cold. The faint smell of smoke lingered in the air. A moment later we rode up to the back door of my father's tent. I slid off Asher's horse and tried to steady my legs.

The sun teased the tops of the hills as though holding its breath, too. A nervous sweat broke over me. When I pulled my scarf away to cool my face Asher bowed his head in deference, but I tore my eyes from his, focusing on the task at hand.

Creeping into the oasis on the edge between night and dawn was surreal. A place so familiar and yet so far removed from my heart now. An image of my mother's hands rolling out bread dough appeared before my eyes. Distinctly, I could see the rings on her fingers. Her hair tucked up in a quick knot while she told stories of her childhood and recited our family history.

I glanced about the rest of the camp, but the only visible sight was the shadows of sleeping camels. The smell of last night's cardamom spice from the men's hearth-fire teased my nose.

"Go with God," Asher whispered. My head whipped around, but his scarf was back over his face. With a quick nod, I lifted the rear tent flap and slipped inside.

I drew a breath. My mother's beautifully carved linen chest sat neatly in the corner. I stood in place to compose myself, and then rushed to the chest, lifting the lid with both hands. My mother's dresses and blankets and shawls still lay in neat folded piles. Her slippers and sashes in bright, embroidered colors. The veils she'd worn over her black hair. I buried my face in them to capture her smell, to hang on to her forever.

The empty room felt strange, like time was poised in suspension.

A sense of foreboding came over me and my hand went to my dagger. If my father was sleeping in the main room, my grandmother Seraiah should have been here in the women's quarters. Had she gone away for the winter with Judith—or was she *gone*? I'd counted on my grandmother's persuasive words to convince my father to come with us.

Walking to the partition wall, I peered around the tapestry to the main room.

Someone was asleep on the floor, the small form nearly like a child's under the blanket. Before I could take another breath, the figure lifted its head. "Who's there? Speak, or be gone! We don't welcome strangers to the Nephish tribe. Certainly not in the middle of the night."

"Grandmother?" I rushed toward her and fell into her arms.

Seraiah reached a hand to my face, her long, gray hair tumbling about her shoulders. Her knotted fingers traced my cheek as she wiped away my tears. "Is it really you, or am I living a peculiar dream? Perhaps I *am* awake and I've merely left this mortal world?"

"You're awake and I'm here. It's really me!"

My grandmother clasped me to her chest while tears ran down her beautiful, wrinkled face. "Jayden, oh my darling girl. I feared I would never see you again!"

A swell of love and sweet relief overwhelmed me. "You look more beautiful than a perfect oasis rose, grandmother."

"Pah!" she spluttered. "Older, wobbly, and so wrinkled I'm sure I've turned into a basket of prunes. Come, the morning is chilly." She lifted her blanket and I slid in beside her, holding my hand tightly in hers as we lay side by side, our faces close, tears running down our noses.

"I thought you were dead, Jayden. Oh, the terrible tales

Horeb told on his way to Damascus to enlist the Maachathites—and now the Adummatus—to join him. We're no longer the same peace-loving tribe we once were when your mother was alive. My old heart is broken."

"What stories did Horeb tell everyone?"

"He bragged that he had killed the stranger, Kadesh, and that his men carried his body away to be eaten by vultures. He said you'd lost your mind and were wandering the desert, so he was gathering an army to rescue you and bring you safely home."

"Oh, Grandmother, it's all lies. You know that."

"I also heard terrible reports from Nalla and Dinah's relatives. They watched Horeb murder Kadesh. They said he was surrounded and had no chance." She paused. "We all feared you had died on the desert as Horeb claimed—while he shed the tears of a grieving widower—which I didn't believe for a moment. Or—Horeb hinted that perhaps you had killed yourself when Kadesh died."

I shook my head. "Never, despite a deep despair for so long I wasn't sure I'd survive."

My grandmother brushed her hands through the strands of my hair. "Where have you been, my child?"

"I spent weeks hiding in the hills of Mari. Then I purchased a camel with Kadesh's frankincense and journeyed south to the Edomite kingdom to find him. I heard stories, too. That perhaps he was still alive. I carried that hope with me."

Seraiah's expression was thoughtful. "And you found him, didn't you?"

"Yes, he survived Horeb's brutality."

"Then Kadesh *is* a man of miracles."

"In many ways, Grandmother. In so many ways."

"I'll never forget the way you two looked at each other the night of Hakak's wedding. So secretly. So furtively right under Horeb's nose."

"But Horeb did hurt Kadesh. He lost one eye, and he's terribly scarred."

Something rustled outside, and my grandmother pushed back the blankets and sat up, nervous. "My darling Jayden," she whispered, "you can't stay any longer. It's much too dangerous. You shouldn't have come back."

"But I came to get you and take you with me to the southern lands."

"Oh, no, my dear." She shook her head. "I'll finish out my life here at the oasis and be buried in this spot like so many of our family over the years."

"I can't think of never seeing you again."

My grandmother wrapped her thin arms around my shoulders. "You don't need me any longer. You are a woman of enormous compassion and courage. You have the love of a fine man in Kadesh. I will dream of you and your children. Happy and prosperous. Just like I once was with your grandfather."

I sat up on my knees to cling to her.

"Help me up, Jayden. I want to tell you a proper good-bye."

"No good-byes," I cried softly. "I sneaked into camp to take you and Father with me—and Leila. Horeb will make your lives miserable. He'll use you against me. We must flee."

"Pah!" she spat again. "I'm not afraid of him. Besides, Judith and I have made a pact of peace, despite her rage toward us. We don't speak unless we have to, but we'll live here at the oasis until our deaths. Two widows with no husbands and nowhere to go."

"But—where *is* my father?"

Seraiah's fingers tightened in mine. "Jayden, I don't know. Pharez disappeared three days ago."

The words shocked me as if she'd thrown a bucket of cold water at me.

"He left for Tadmur to get Leila from the grasp of the High Priestess of Ashtoreth. The knowledge of your sister living there turned him into a madman."

"Who told him she was there?"

"Judith delighted in confirming that bit of information," she answered with an abundant dose of scorn. "When Pharez returned from Mari without you, we were all sure you had died somewhere on the desert, or had escaped to Damascus, which is why Horeb went there to search for you. As days turned into weeks, the thought of Leila living at the temple was more than he could accept. I advised him to go to the temple and demand his daughter back."

"Oh, no." I could hardly take in what she was saying.

"I've sent my only living son to his doom. No one has seen or heard from him since, and I'm too old to walk there myself. I've been praying, asking God to let him walk through those tent doors. Instead, God brought you."

"I'll find him myself," I vowed.

"If you're lucky enough to find him alive in Tadmur, you should flee immediately. It's the only way you and Kadesh can slip through Horeb's grasp. There's no time to lose." My grandmother wobbled to the tent doors and snapped them open. Daylight surged through. Frantic, she pulled me past the tapestry to the back door. "Ride into Tadmur as fast as you can. The tribal council has a death decree on your head. You've been charged with the murder of King Abimelech."

"But *Horeb* killed his father!"

"Horeb framed you for the murder with the help of Judith. And there's a rumor you killed one of Horeb's men in the Mari hills. Not two months ago."

I spluttered. "I—I didn't. I mean, I didn't mean to. There was a hyena . . ."

"Horeb brought the man's body here for burial before leaving for Damascus. They said his own sword was stuck through his belly—"

I tried to think clearly, nausea closing up my throat. "But I used my dagger. Not his sword." When the hyena attacked, Gad must have used his own sword on himself to avoid being slowly eaten to death.

"You were officially declared a murderess, dear child. And I can convince no one to stay the death decree. You're the scapegoat for Horeb."

I flew to the door, anxious to summon Asher. Once again, the idea of my imminent death took my breath away. "I've stayed too long. We're sitting in a viper's nest!"

My grandmother wavered on her frail, old legs and I clung to her, and then kissed her hard on both cheeks.

Her whisper was harsh. "Go, go!"

I reached for the door panel, but before I could grasp the edge, the doors thrust open. Two Nephish elders grabbed my arms and flung me to the floor. Then between them, they hauled an unconscious Asher into the tent, a knife pressed firmly to his throat.

9

I leaped back, protecting my grandmother from the swords in the small space of the tent. "Leave Seraiah alone. She knew nothing of this."

The two elders dropped Asher to the floor with a thud so hard I winced. They'd torture Asher and then kill him. We should have come in the dead of night. I should have grabbed my grandmother immediately and left everything else behind.

Chemish and the rest of the Edomites had known this trip to Tadmur was dangerous but they'd volunteered for my family's sake. Now I would be responsible for all of their deaths.

"If we're lucky, the old woman will die soon," one of the elders said without pity. "Once we finish with you, girl, we can finally be done with the clan of Pharez."

"Are you insinuating my father is dead?"

"He disappeared, leaving his elderly mother alone," the

man replied. "He's most likely dead. If not, he should be."

"How dare you speak of my father that way? He was a general for this tribe with King Abimelech while you two were still infants."

The council member sneered. "Which confirms that Pharez and his family were always plotting to overthrow Abimelech and his son, Horeb."

"Both of you do Horeb's bidding with blinders on. You're both fools!"

The second elder grabbed my long hair and bent my neck backward. "And you have become a threat to the existence of this tribe." His breath was foul as he traced the blade of his knife along my neck.

"Get off me!"

"We have a death warrant for the daughter of Pharez." He twisted my hair harder and I bit back a sob as he brought me to my knees to bow before him.

"I came here for my father and grandmother, and I will gladly leave this minute."

"If you're as innocent as you claim, why did you bring a guard with you?"

I tried to think of a way to save Asher. "He's not my guard. He's a boy and his mind is—is touched, like that of a child."

"You're a bad liar. We found him pacing before the tent like an Edomite soldier. With a horse of finest Arabian quality. Which now belongs to us."

"You can't take his horse! It's his most precious—" I stopped, cursing myself for saying anything.

The taller of the two men pressed a foot on Asher's back when he began to stir on the carpet. "That's why the animal now belongs to us."

Despair engulfed me. Where were Kadesh and Chemish? Where was the rest of the Edomite army? The silence outside the walls of the tent was deafening. Had Horeb's army arrived early? Was a battle now raging out on the desert?

Asher stirred again, letting out a moan.

"The boy can be discarded later," the first councilman said. "He's nothing to us—only the means that brought you back here, daughter of Pharez. Who is the fool now?"

Despite the knife poised along my neck, I drew myself up defiantly. Before I could speak, my grandmother stepped forward. "Leave my home, Enoch and Balzer. I've known you both since you were babies, and you have no right to enter this tent without permission, especially with women present and Pharez missing. Your wives will be ashamed."

"We have no quarrel with you, Seraiah, so stay out of this."

"But you invaded *my* home! I will take this up with the court of the tribal council."

"*We* are the tribal council while King Horeb is gone," Enoch said. "And we have an order to arrest your granddaughter for the murder of King Abimelech, including sedition against King Horeb."

"I'm not a traitor!" I pleaded. "Or a murderer."

"You broke the tribe's code of honor by leaving with a foreigner who was not your husband. Adulterers are sentenced to death. And so are assassins."

"I didn't kill King Abimelech. Allow me to speak before the council. You should permit me that at least." I jerked against their fists and the blade nicked my skin. Blood trickled down my neck.

"Women don't speak before the council."

"Let me find my father first. Please!"

"Stop this charade!" Seraiah growled. "Get out of my home, or I'll see you both tried for your crimes against women."

"It was Judith who set the punishment for Abimelech's murderer," the man called Enoch said with a smile.

"If you could open your eyes to the truth, you'd know Abimelech's killer is Horeb himself. He's framing me. What did I have to gain by his death?"

"Your words are treachery," the man called Balzer said. "You do yourself no favors."

Asher's head lolled upward, his eyes glazed over. He had a knot on his temple the size of an ostrich egg.

Balzer took a length of rope from his belt and tied Asher's hands together, then dragged him upright. Asher's face was bruised and swelling. His lips moved. "I'm sorry."

Guilt washed over me for bringing him to such an end.

Enoch retrieved a scroll tucked inside his shirt, and unfolded it. "This is the decree of your crimes signed by the tribal council."

"Is it signed by Horeb's own hand?"

The tall man's eyes were void of any benevolence. "It doesn't need to be. He left us in charge."

"Horeb didn't sign it because he wants me alive," I told

him tersely. "To make his kingship legitimate."

"Daughter of Pharez, your punishment for the murder of the king is death by stoning."

My grandmother sank like a wisp of silk to the floor. "Stoning," she moaned.

"No!" Asher roared. Balzer kicked him into silence and the Edomite prince slumped against the carpet again.

My words scraped out. "You're breaking the law. I'm not ignorant even though you treat me with contempt."

"You're a whore with the Sariba prince and an assassin."

"The Council of Nephish has another law," I said icily. "No one is stoned for murder without the king signing the order—and without the king's presence at the delivery of punishment. When Horeb returns, you'll both lose your heads. He wants me alive so we can be married."

"Why would he want a tainted girl any longer?"

"Because," I said slowly. "It was decreed long before you ever sat on the council that the son of Abimelech and the daughter of Pharez would take their seats as Nephish king and queen."

"Perhaps Horeb has found someone else."

"What are you talking about? He'd have to change the law."

Except I was supposed to die today, with or without Horeb's presence.

A chilling smile crossed Balzer's lips. "Perhaps Horeb has decided he will mingle his royal blood with the Goddess of Ashtoreth so that a divine ruler can lead the Nephish at Horeb's side."

"Horeb and the High Priestess?" I was returned to the night of my cousin Hakak's wedding, seething while Horeb flirted with Esther, one of the initiates of the Temple of Ashtoreth. I'd thought he might be in love with her, but it appeared to be only a ruse to ingratiate himself with Armana. The pieces of Horeb's plan came together in my mind. "That's how Horeb's army is being funded. He's bribing the other tribes for treaties—through the coffers of the temple and the High Priestess Armana."

"Armana will be our queen," Enoch said, smiling at how he'd managed to enlarge the threat against me. "Your sister could become Horeb's mistress. She will give him the clan of Pharez *and* the temple divinity and wealth."

The suggestion of Leila and Horeb together made me sick to my stomach. "You aren't fit to wash Leila's feet."

Balzer wrenched me upright. "The sun has risen. Death by stoning to take place upon sight of the assassin."

I was sure their warrant for arrest said none of those things, but I was at their mercy. I could only stall to give Kadesh and Chemish time to get here. Stumbling over the limp body of Asher, I was dragged from my father's tent.

Enoch and Balzer yanked me down the oasis path and my grandmother's wail followed me. The morning was fragile, filled with a surreal, hazy light. I could barely grasp the fact I only had minutes left to live.

Somehow, word had spread that I'd been captured. Already, tribal families were emerging from their tents to watch me taken to the stoning cliff on the desert perimeter of the oasis, away from the city.

My eyes searched for signs of Kadesh and the Edomites. *Where were they?*

Nasib, another council member, walked up to us and spat at my feet. "So you've found the murderess."

I flinched, but held myself upright, despite how fast they were dragging me through the rocky sand. "Let me tell my grandmother good-bye," I said. "It's my final right."

"If it were up to me," huffed Enoch, "you would get nothing except a mouthful of vinegar wine."

"My blood will cry against you from the dust," I told him. "My soul will follow you until you drop dead from your own sins."

Balzar hit me across the jaw and my head flung back with the impact. "Silence, prisoner!"

The paths were filling. Older men and women, boys too young for raiding, young children skipping along the path carrying early spring wildflowers in their fists. As though we were all going to a party.

Two men came to speak to Enoch and Balzar, their eyes flickering to my face. "Fighting in the west," one of them said in a low voice.

My body tensed. "Who's fighting?"

Balzar gave me a withering look. "Your stranger brought an Edomite army with him. Our militia is taking care of them."

"The Edomites will destroy you."

"You underestimate the number of militia King Horeb left behind." Enoch smiled wickedly. "The slaughter of the Edomites will be finished soon."

The sickening fear in my belly increased tenfold. "Never," I whispered under my breath.

Within moments, we were at the stoning cliff's edge, the place marked for the death of enemy prisoners and convicts of Tadmur. The spot was on the outskirts of the city and not very high. Most of the time the hollow below the stoning cliff was a place to bury rubbish and the carcasses of dead animals.

Behind me, my grandmother and Asher were jostled through the crowd, held in check by tribal council guards. Asher's hair fell in blood-streaked clumps over his bruised eyes. They'd taken his sandals and stripped him of his cloak.

Guilt gnawed at me to think what I'd brought upon Chemish's son. "This boy has done nothing," I tried again. "He doesn't deserve such harsh treatment. Give him his horse and send him back to his people."

"Soon he won't have any people left," Enoch said.

"That's enough!" snapped Seraiah. "Prisoners aren't treated this badly, not even when captured from a raiding tribe."

"As a person of rank I deserve a trial." I pressed a hand against my stomach. My arguments were fading along with the last moments of my life.

"Final good-bye," one of the guards announced.

The crowd pressed forward. Curious and hate-filled eyes surrounded me. I heard a baby crying among the women and the sound reminded me of my sister, Sahmril, in her first hours of life a year ago.

My grandmother was shoved forward. "Say good-bye, old woman," Balzar ordered.

Her hands stroked my hair as I clung to her, the horror of what was about to happen turning me feeble and weak. Vomit rose up in my stomach.

"Oh, my child, Jayden," she murmured.

"Is there any hope?" I whispered into her gray hair, trying not to cry in front of my tribe.

"There is always hope." She brought me closer, her black marble eyes latched on to mine. "Whether you die this day or one day far into the future in the southern lands, I will see you in the spirit world. Go in peace, my daughter. Know that you are beloved, and will never be forgotten."

My grandmother kissed me on each cheek and then placed her palms on my head as though blessing me.

Two soldiers wrenched me from her arms. Seraiah was hauled to the edge of the cliff and placed in position to watch my death.

Rough hands yanked at my arms, pulling so hard I let out a shriek. I barely had time to take a breath before I was pushed over the craggy overhang. When my feet tripped at the edge of loose rocks, I caught a glimpse of Asher. He stared into my face, his eyes filled with a strange light.

And then I was falling through emptiness.

10

The crowd quieted and silence reigned above me.

A moment later, I crashed to the ground. The impact knocked the air from my lungs. My bones shuddered, and a cloud of dirt rose up around me. Crawling to my knees, I gasped for breath, the sound raw and hoarse. My shins ached. I was sure I had bruises as dark as the ones on Asher's face.

How did I get to this place, this moment, to be stoned by my own people? All I had wanted was to be a part of them, to belong to the circle of women. To be loved by my aunts and cousins. A year ago, we'd danced and laughed, eating sweets, swaying to the drums of Nalla. I'd waited nervously in Aunt Judith's tent, dressing for my special night to celebrate my betrothal to her son. What would my mother say to see her tribe treat her daughter like this? I'd lost the one person who could have fought for me.

That betrothal night had begun a chain of events leading to this. My death.

Under the hot sun the full force of what I'd done drove at my heart like a dagger. I'd turned my back on all of them when I loved Kadesh and not Horeb.

But my execution was Horeb's doing, murder done by *his* hand.

I brushed at the sweaty strands of my hair and watched Asher slammed to his knees on the cliff's edge, hands tied behind his back. He stared down at me, agony crumpling his face.

My grandmother wept, her back bowed with age and grief, her tiny figure so slight it hurt to see her. A few women hid their eyes, but Aunt Judith pushed forward from the crowd. Hatred and revenge twisted her features into ugly lines.

I returned her stare without guilt. She had a part in my death, but I knew I shouldn't die with hatred inside. I tried to feel pity for her, remorse for not loving her son. But can one love a monster, even a broken one? Perhaps that had been my task. Horeb's soul had been twisted by envy and greed, but also by fear. Fear of not being loved. Fear of not being important. Fear of being second place in his family. I could be sorry for that. He'd made gruesome choices, but I was paying the price.

I didn't want to cry, but the tears were coming anyway. I would rot here, stoned to a bloody pulp. After stoning, no one would mourn me. No one would speak my name again.

I bowed my head, praying for strength to endure the looming horror—just as the first stone hit my arm. Even though I knew it was coming, I was shocked. My chin snapped upward, and a look of grim satisfaction crossed Aunt Judith's features.

The people on the cliff remained quiet, expressions hardened by the awfulness of my guilt, and their own guilt to stone the girl who would be their queen. How pathetic and tragic it all was.

"Where *are* you, Kadesh?" I screamed into the empty blue sky.

As though they had become one singular mind, the people of Nephish picked up a stone from the piles at their feet. Their fists curled tight. With ghastly cries, one by one, my people heaved the rocks at me, and I watched as they sailed through the air.

The stones found their mark. My body was pummeled. My skin rose with instant welts. Dark red bruises formed on my arms. Two fingers on my left hand bent strangely at an odd angle when a large rock struck with a velocity and fierceness that dazed me. My shins were bleeding under my skirts.

I put up my arms to shield myself, but my skin was soon streaked with ribbons of blood. I ducked and darted through the debris, trying to avoid a direct hit to my skull.

I sought refuge but there was nothing except barren emptiness. Nowhere to run but a second drop into a deeper ravine. I'd be killed for certain if I attempted the jump. I wanted to live a little bit longer, even if it was only for a few more minutes.

Scrabbling through the field of rocks and animal skeleton bones, I tried to cover my body with the debris of dead things.

Above the jeering cries, I heard my grandmother's feeble voice cry out. Covering myself with bones was useless. I needed to bury myself underneath a layer of it, like a second skin. A hole was what I needed. I found a low spot and dug my fingers into the dirt but my energy was waning from the injuries and hot sun.

I was now in agony. Every moment death came nearer. A direct blow to my temple would kill me instantly. The pain was so intense I began to pray for my demise.

I looked up to whisper a final good-bye to Seraiah. My lips parted and I saw my grandmother fumbling with something behind Asher. What was she doing? Nobody was paying attention. They were jeering and shouting and picking up more rocks.

Seconds later, Asher staggered to his feet, his rope bonds broken. Astonished, I watched him throw them to the ground and jump down the cliff, darting around boulders, racing toward me.

"Are you a fool?" I cried when he reached me. His right eye had swollen shut. His clothes were shredded, his wrists bleeding from the rough ropes. "Now they'll kill you, too."

"I'm going to make sure *you* do not die," Asher said softly. "That is the promise I made to Kadesh." A fresh barrage of rocks rained down, and when I crouched, the young Edomite proceeded to coil himself around me like a snake, using his body as a shield.

Asher grunted as the stones thumped his arms and shoulders, but I was safely cocooned in his arms, his head bent over mine, eyes closed tight as he withstood the blows.

I'd never been this close to another man in my life except

for my father and Kadesh—and not even Kadesh had ever sheltered me so completely with his body. I forced my mind to remember Kadesh holding me enveloped in his cloak, covering me with kisses. I dreamed of all the good things while my spirit left my body.

"You're not going to die," Asher repeated in my ear. "I promised Kadesh. And now I promise you."

My eyelids flickered upward. We seemed to float in a mirage of pain. My lips moved, but nothing came out.

"Stay with me, Jayden," Asher said, holding me to the thread of life spooling away from me. "You're in shock, you're bruised, but you are not going to die."

"It's not the end?" I sensed Asher's heartbeat under the fabric of his tunic, saw the pulse in his throat, and heard each ragged breath he made.

"Will you be all right if I rise to my knees for a moment?"

"Don't stand! They'll kill you with one single blow."

Another rock skittered past in a cloud of dust. I cringed, grabbing onto the folds of his tunic, but he gently released my fingers. I watched his hands flicker at his waistline. With one single motion, he'd untied the slingshot hidden in his waistband. Swiftly he placed one of the large stones into the pocket of the sling. The next instant, the sling was whizzing in a circle through the air above us, creating a peculiar buzzing sound. Not more than three breaths later, Asher released the stone.

I jerked my gaze toward the cliff, following the stone's trajectory. All at once, Balzar dropped over the edge headfirst to the ground. Screams came from the women.

"Got him," Asher muttered. Before I could speak, he had a second stone whizzing in his sling. He was so swift I could hardly see his hands move. Another tribal council member slumped to the ground.

The stones stopped raining down on us. The screams from the cliff grew. I watched my tribe scatter, dashing in all directions to escape Asher's deadly slingshot.

"What's happening now?" The cloud over my eyes lifted. The noise of panic was split asunder by the sound of galloping horses.

Asher let out a yell of relief and helped me rise to my feet. "Edomites on the cliff tops!"

Dozens of Edom's soldiers bent over their horses in full gallop, swords flashing in the sunlight. Nephish women raced back to the oasis, shrieking, although the Edomite army wasn't attacking them. Just driving them away from the stoning cliff.

"My father and Kadesh are pushing them back." The emotion in Asher's voice was palpable.

Holding me upright, Asher staggered across the field of bones. "I can walk," I protested, but I kept slipping and falling.

Before I knew what he was doing, Asher lifted me into his arms to wade through the pit of death. "You're cold. You're shaking."

The morning sun was a blessing of warmth on my face. "We're alive," I whispered into the hot skin of his neck while he picked his way through the death field of debris and bones.

A horse approached, galloping fast. I flinched, afraid a

member of the tribal council was about to mow us down with a sword or club.

"Let me down! We need to run!"

"Ssh," Asher murmured. His hands brushed my bloodied hair from my eyes so I could see more clearly. "Everything will be all right. Trust me."

I touched the boy's swollen skin. "How did you manage to get the ropes off your wrists?"

"Your grandmother loosened them. I just wish I could have gotten to you faster."

The advancing horse wheeled up in a cloud of dust. I cowered against Asher, but it was Kadesh leaping off the animal, his cloak swirling, arms reaching for me.

Raw fear laced Kadesh's words. "Is Jayden alive?"

"She's alive," Asher said. A wave of emotions crossed Asher's face. Determination, pride, and relief. He truly loved Kadesh.

Kadesh lifted me from Asher's arms and placed his cloak around me. Fear of my death etched the features of his face. "I almost lost you again."

"I don't think she'll have any lasting effects from the injuries," Asher told him. "She was able to bury herself and prevent the worst. No broken bones or gashes too deep to be healed."

Kadesh brought the young man to his chest in a brotherly embrace. I heard his choked tears of relief. "You have wounds to be tended as well. I'm surprised either one of you is still coherent."

"What happened out in the desert?" Asher asked.

While Kadesh placed me on his horse, their words slipped around me in low, urgent tones. "We encountered a secret militia. We should never have sent you both in. I'm so sorry."

"Where's the militia now?"

"They're dead," Kadesh said flatly. "And so are the two men who sent you over the cliff to be stoned. Their declaration of capital punishment was unlawful. It meant nothing that you are Pharez's daughter and were Horeb's betrothed. Nobody in the tribe seems to care that your father has disappeared, either. Which is extremely baffling."

"So you heard he's not here," I said flatly. The sky overhead was too bright. "Seraiah said he went to the temple and never came home. He would never have left her by herself. Not on purpose."

"Especially with a rogue tribal council," Kadesh agreed. "We'll go to Tadmur ourselves and trace him."

"Hurry," I whispered. When Kadesh reached down to take my hand, I flinched. I was horrified to see my torn nails, dirty and bloody. I cradled my hand in my lap, trying to hide the broken fingers.

"You're hurt, Jayden. You need to be tended before we go to Tadmur. I'd rather leave you at your father's tent to rest."

"No, I'm going to the city with you. What if another tribal council member shows up to finish me off? I don't trust anybody here."

"We'll need to find a camel litter for the journey south, too. You'll be recuperating and healing for several weeks. Nothing has gone as planned. We *must* leave no later than dawn. We're not safe here."

Asher pressed a hand to Kadesh's shoulder. "Don't frighten Jayden."

Kadesh softened his voice. "Believe me, she's my utmost concern."

Asher bowed his head. "I apologize for my familiarity, my lord."

Kadesh let out a small laugh. "Please don't call me those high-minded titles. We've been friends since you were an infant and I held you in my arms, Asher. Without you, Jayden would be dead. We owe you her life." He paused for a moment. "While Jayden is tended by her grandmother, we need to find a doctor for you, too, Asher. The city would be best."

"I don't need a physician. You know my father knows how to use frankincense and herbs. I'm only grateful Jayden isn't hurt worse."

Kadesh glanced at Asher when the younger boy spoke my name for the second time that day. We weren't kinsmen and it wasn't proper. Realizing his error, Asher glanced away, tightening the slingshot at his belt.

When we arrived back at my father's tent, Seraiah had hot water, towels, and medicine ready. Despite her frailty, her strength came alive when she was helping me. "What a strange day this has been," she said, clucking her tongue.

I lowered myself into the tub, wincing with each sting. My pulse raced with the need to find my father and Leila and get away.

My grandmother poured hot water over my shoulders.

"You're freezing cold, dear girl. You're in shock."

Images of my tribe's hateful faces throwing stones in the hopes of killing me wouldn't leave my mind. I sank deeper into the water, wincing at my broken finger. Every single part of me hurt so badly it was all I could do not to weep.

"Sitting in this tub while you tend my wounds reminds me too much of the night when Horeb attacked me." My voice was woeful, my spirit struggling to remain optimistic.

The look on my grandmother's face was scathing. "Both times at the hands of Horeb. So there is nothing else to say."

"Please come with us to the southern lands," I pleaded.

Her lips quivered. "I'm ready to leave this sad world, Jayden. Even though I'm disgusted with my tribe, I will peacefully return to my God."

"I hate the thought of you not in this world."

My grandmother smiled wanly and left me to soak. When the water grew cold, I dried off with one of my mother's towels. My grandmother applied ointment to each wound and then wrapped me in a blanket to sit in a warm spot where the winter sun shone. Sitting knee to knee with me, Seraiah bound my bruised fingers together with a clean bandage and snugly tied the ends.

"Asher saved my life, didn't he?"

"I knew he would," Seraiah said calmly, not looking at me.

My eyes flickered to her face and then away, not wanting to bring attention to her observation.

Carefully, my grandmother folded the dress Chemish's wife, Isra, had given me. The beautiful green gown was torn and filthy. "There's no way to mend this," she said, slipping a clean, soft dress over my head.

"Isn't this—?"

"I retrieved it from your mother's chest. Her dresses . . . well, your mother would want you to have them."

"Oh, grandmother," I murmured. "I can still smell her perfume."

She placed a hand against my cheek and then fastened me up. The cut and style accentuated my curves when I tied the wide, red-trimmed belt at my waist.

When Seraiah held up a mirror, a younger version of my mother stared back. I'd kept my head down during the stoning so my face held no bruises. "You are your mother from twenty years ago."

I lifted an aching arm to my necklace, touching the silver strands my mother had fastened around my neck on my betrothal night a year ago. There had been love and pride in her eyes. I couldn't begin to imagine what she thought of me now, looking down from the spirit world.

Grief burst from my mouth and my grandmother pulled me close. "There, there, sweet child. I know you miss her terribly. You faced death this morning with grace and a prayer in your heart. Your mother is near; I can always feel her here in the tent where she loved and served her family."

I nodded shakily.

"She would have helped you with the betrothal. With your feelings for a man from a foreign land. Because, Jayden . . . your love of Kadesh is still dangerous and forbidden. Besides Horeb, there are those who will try to stop your union."

"What do you mean?"

She tried to ignore my question, but I pressed her. "Who else would want to stop Kadesh and me from marrying?"

"Kadesh is not the only one relieved you're still alive."

I almost laughed. "Why would Asher stop us? He adores Kadesh and told me he'd do anything to help us forge a strong union for the throne of Sariba."

"That boy carries a secret torch for someone," Seraiah said sagely.

Her words startled me. Was she implying Asher secretly loved me?

I glanced across the room and the boy's shadow hovered at the tent door. "Is all well?" I called.

He parted the doorway. Despite the bruises on his face, the young Edomite appeared in immensely better shape now. The grime was gone and he'd changed into a fresh tunic. "We need to leave for Tadmur. The guards of the city will help protect us from rogue Nephish tribal members."

It was time to say good-bye forever to the grandmother who had repeatedly saved me.

Asher's glance shifted between us. "I will do all I can to keep your granddaughter safe," he vowed.

Seraiah studied him as though she knew his thoughts. She understood people so well I often suspected God whispered directly into her ears. "Be careful of the swelling around your eyes," she told him. "Put a salve on them and cover them as much as you can while they heal. Your horse can follow the caravan on its own."

Asher nodded, bowing awkwardly as he backed out of the doorway.

My grandmother kissed my cheeks. "Horeb will be defeated, of that I'm certain, but be careful not to let anyone in Sariba defeat your spirit. Nobody can triumph over you unless you allow them to, Jayden."

"You're speaking in a secret code," I accused. "Who in Sariba wants to defeat me? I don't know anybody there."

"In Tadmur we stand in awe and fear of the High Priestess of Ashtoreth. There are cunning idol worshippers in the frank-incense lands and Kadesh grew up among them. Their beliefs could hold great sway among the citizens, and we don't know Kadesh's internal alliances."

"But his motives are worthy!"

"I don't doubt Kadesh. It's the politics of his kingdom that's uncertain. Nobody creates such a wealthy and powerful secret land like Sariba without making enemies along the way."

Her words were sobering. I hoped when we began the journey to the southern lands Kadesh and I would have the chance to talk about his kingdom and his hopes and dreams.

"Forewarned is forearmed," I said lightly, but I was certain I would shatter to leave her here in Tadmur alone. The silence between us swelled with affection and sorrow. "I love you with all my heart," I finally whispered.

My grandmother kissed me again, and I slipped from her grasp and fled the tent, tears blinding me.

11

When I came out of the tent door, I almost knocked Asher over. "I'm sorry," I mumbled, turning away to hide my shaking shoulders.

"Jayden, wait!"

I turned back, conscious of my mother's lovely gown and the fresh kohl with which Seraiah had dressed my eyes. My once dirty, bloodied hair, now washed and brushed, flowed down the length of my back. "You really shouldn't use my given name."

His face flushed, eyes traveling up my new appearance. "I apologize. Perhaps, after nearly dying together, I feel as though we are tied together in blood and death."

My mouth went dry at his intimate words. Self-conscious about how he'd wrapped his body around mine, I brushed it off. "You must think I'm a silly girl chasing after Kadesh across the desert. I wouldn't blame you for being angry at having to save me in this strange place. Nearly dying for your efforts. You've left your homeland to fight a war not of your making."

"You crossed the desert alone with only a single camel and food for a fortnight. You faced starvation and death. You fended off the Nephish scout's attack. I would never consider you silly."

When he stepped closer, my stomach twisted. "My admiration is immense. You left your family to follow Kadesh and create a new home with a royal family you know nothing about. You'll certainly be a stranger in a very strange land."

I gave a nervous laugh. "You make his homeland sound daunting."

"Doing what you've done takes courage and a tremendous amount of selfless love. Kadesh is blessed. Someday—" His voice cracked. "Someday, I hope to be just as loved."

I squirmed at the personal words.

"You are so unlike the Sariba women of the frankincense lands," Asher added.

"I'm sure they're more sophisticated than a poor camel herder's daughter."

"No, you are so much more—"

I cut him off. "Please don't say anything you might regret."

He stepped back and swallowed hard. "Come," he finally said, "we must be on our way."

It was a short ride to Tadmur, but the gatekeepers weren't pleased to spot a band of Edomites riding toward them.

When we reached the city pylons, Chemish and Kadesh dismounted to speak with the guards. It was decided Chemish, Kadesh, and I would go to the temple to find Leila, while two platoons of Edomites kept guard along the city plaza. The remainder of the army would stay at the city gates, awaiting any news of Horeb the scouts brought from the desert.

Tadmur was peaceful, so different from Mari under siege a few months ago. Still, a current of foreboding skulked around the edges. As we walked through the marketplace, whispers came from citizens speculating that the sign of Edomite soldiers might be a precursor to King Hammurabi of Babylon preparing an invasion of the western lands.

The Temple of Ashtoreth loomed on its hill above the city plaza, glittering under the sun with white pristine walls and blue paved tiles.

Kadesh and I followed the series of staircases to the golden double doors on the east side of the public entrance. Gardeners, messengers, slaves, and officials hurried about their daily tasks.

I reached out to cling to Kadesh's hand as we neared the public doors, despite the open arena with all of its watching eyes. His fingers clasped mine reassuringly.

Before he could speak, we were at the temple door to Armana's private offices. Unease crept up my neck.

Leila was within these gilded, luxurious walls.

The doors opened at the hands of a butler. A moment later, a woman appeared wearing a flowing blue dress, her hair adorned with curls and gold dust.

I clenched my fists within the folds of my cloak while

Kadesh gave a bow of greeting. "We're here to visit Leila, a novice of the High Priestess Armana."

The woman's eyes settled on me with a hint of recognition, but she didn't acknowledge it. "Please come to our waiting room. Visitors are not allowed to go farther without an explicit invitation."

Down a short hallway was a small room where luxurious chairs and couches sat tastefully arranged. A table held a profusion of gloriously scented yellow roses, pale pink orchids, and lavender irises. A wide window overlooked an inner courtyard where a fountain sprayed the air with a heady mist.

Statuesque figures of the goddess had been placed about the courtyard. Beyond the elaborate columns I glimpsed the inner temple halls. The entire compound evoked lushness, but an underlying sexual tension filled this place, too.

My palms sweated. Beads of perspiration broke out on my forehead. A tinge of desperation filled me.

Chemish paced the floor, agitated. "I hate to leave my men outside the city. I fear an ambush."

He'd barely finished speaking when the door opened and the most beautiful woman I'd ever seen glided into the room. "I'm Armana, High Priestess to our Goddess Ashtoreth," she said in a low voice. Her full lips were red with pomegranate stain. Lavish jewelry adorned her throat, ears, and wrists, her hair a flowing mane of ringlets and gold filigree ornaments. She swept the silk train of her rose-colored dress about her sensuous hips, and when she raised her eyes, expertly lined with black kohl, they fastened on Kadesh.

"To what do I owe this fascinating visit from the Sariba Prince?"

"We're looking for Pharez, the father of Leila," Kadesh told her. "From the tribe of Nephish. We understand he came here looking for his daughter a few days ago, and never returned home."

The High Priestess purred, "That's because he's a silly man."

"Don't speak of my father that way!" I burst out.

Armana's head whipped around and she looked at me with narrowed eyes. "A man named Pharez arrived looking for his daughter. Instead of waiting for an appointment and going to the taverns like any other reasonable man, he demanded I produce her immediately. When we did not—because she was busy with her *duties* to the goddess—he went into a tirade, shouting, throwing vases, and breaking one of our precious statues of Ashtoreth herself."

"Then you're holding him against his will?" Chemish asked point-blank.

"Of course we're not holding him! We aren't a prison. The men who stay here arrive of their own free will and then remain for the beauty, music, and culture."

Chemish gave a derisive laugh. Armana looked down her nose at him and turned back to Kadesh. "Will you take refreshment with me, Prince of Sariba?"

Kadesh frowned, clearly perplexed by the High Priestess's insistence on using his title. Something else about her words bothered me, although I couldn't seem to identify it. "What is the protocol for visitors who want to see their daughters?"

Armana lifted one pretty, bare shoulder in a shrug. "An appointment, of course. But if someone shows up unannounced they are treated the same as any disruptive parent. We call the Tadmur royal guard. Pharez was seized for unruly behavior."

I moaned inwardly. "Where is he now?"

"He was charged with destruction of temple property and trying to kidnap a priestess." She gave a faint smile. "As far as I know, he's still in the dungeons of Tadmur."

"You are the most evil woman I know," I spat, lunging toward the High Priestess.

"Guards!" Armana screeched.

The mahogany doors flung open. Three temple guards marched inside with swords drawn.

Armana's eyes narrowed and one eyebrow arched like a cat's. "Take them to the Tadmur prison to visit the prisoner named Pharez of Nephish. But I warn you," she added. "He has a high price on his head. If not paid by the next moon, he'll be put to death."

The room swam before my eyes. When the temple guards led us away I stole a glance behind me. Armana's expression was oddly triumphant, as if she had planned this.

I should have bit my tongue and kept my head. All my outburst had done was to get us escorted out. And I hadn't even had a chance to ask to see Leila.

Outside the temple again, we were transferred to a pair of dungeon guards. Chemish was released and ordered to leave the city. He slipped away with one of his scouts, giving us a quick backward glance. I watched the two Edomites fall into step, their heads bent together. Anxiety tugged at my belly. This day was lasting much too long. We should already be on the road to the southern Red Sea highway.

Kadesh gave me a smile I returned apprehensively. I had to remember he was alive. I was alive. My father and sister were still alive, despite the terrible circumstances.

We made our way down to Tadmur's dungeons, following the jail keepers into the bowels of Tadmur. A network of stone corridors and chambers underneath the city ran parallel to the city's sewer system. The stench was overpowering and the filth appalling.

These rock walls had absorbed years of sweat and rancid food, as though the smell had painted the stone.

A dank hallway stretched before us, disappearing into darkness. No windows graced this dismal place. No light penetrated.

If we ran into trouble, I hoped Chemish and the Edomites could find us.

"The girl should stay behind," the guard said, eyeing me. He carried a bowl of something brown and lumpy. A small lantern in his other fist gave the only light. "She won't want to see this."

"I refuse to be left alone." I bit my tongue and tasted blood. "I can only imagine the insanity my father is living under. I had no idea it would be so appalling."

"I agree," Kadesh said, keeping me close in the claustrophobic darkness.

A solitary candle flickered. The darkness and heat were

stifling. I could only imagine prisoners died here during the hot summer months without fresh air or decent food. The filthy air and slimy walls reached out to caress my face. My stomach heaved. "I take no responsibility if she gets sick."

"Down there!" the guard shouted next, halting on the disgusting floor.

All I could see was a black hole in the rock, like a well. Kadesh took a candle and held it over the pitch blackness. "Dear God in heaven," he whispered.

Before he could stop me, I peered far down into the dank hole. Three men stood in a pit of water and sewage, tied with rope to walls blackened by years of vulgar filth.

One of the figures was unmistakably my father. He wore only a loincloth, his gray hair matted and greasy, ribs showing under his skin, wrists shackled by bronze chain fastened to the wall over his head.

I dropped to my knees. "Father, up here! It's me, Jayden!"

Kadesh's arms went around my waist, holding me back from falling in.

"Bring him up!" I cried. "Please! He'll die down there."

The guard's sinister smile flickered in the shadows. "They usually do."

I swayed on my knees, my hands reaching down into the hole, but falling far short.

"Jayden, come away. You can't see this," Kadesh said.

"Father," I called out again. His head hung to one side; whether he was asleep or dead I couldn't tell. I was glad my mother wasn't here to see him like this.

"The desert man called Pharez," Kadesh demanded, pointing down the hole. "We're here to get him released."

"He destroyed temple property and tried to kidnap one of the girls."

"The girl was his own daughter."

The man grinned in the candlelight. "Maybe she didn't want to leave the temple."

Kadesh wouldn't rise to the bait. "Has he been seen by a judge?"

"No money for that."

"Is that the problem?" Kadesh asked. "He needs bribe money?"

"Don't insult me. Payment for damaged idols, drapes, chairs. That's how it works."

Kadesh's eyes fixed on the jailer's face. "If payment is made he will be released." It was a statement, not a question.

"What's in it for me?"

Kadesh looked as though he might wring the man's neck. "I assure you by the time we leave you will be more than happy." He withdrew a silver coin and tossed it on the ground at the man's feet.

The jailer snatched it up. "Pay the rest on the way out. But be warned," he added with a snarl. "I have my own men who will haul you back here and shove you in a hole if you cheat us."

"I promise you'll never see us again."

An eternity passed while we waited for the guard to drag my father up on the rope. His legs and arms dangled as though he were already dead.

My eyes watered when my father's thin body slumped to the cold floor at my feet. Despair and illness were written into every crevice and wrinkle of his face. "Oh, Father, what have they done to you?"

His limbs quivered when he tried to sit up. "Jayden?" His voice was so hoarse, I was sure he hadn't spoken in days.

I embraced his hands. "It's me," I whispered. Skin sagged along his stomach, and his beard had gone completely gray. I clung to him, weeping, so grateful to see him after all these months. Wrapping my arms around his emaciated body, my shoulders shook with sobs of sadness and guilt. It was obvious he hadn't been eating properly for a long time. He didn't look well at all.

Trembling, my father's fingers plucked at my hair. His eyes were rheumy and watering. Kadesh helped him sit, holding him up so he wouldn't fall over. "I went looking for my daughters in Mari, following the camel markets."

Shame burned my cheeks. "I was in Mari," I confessed. "Kadesh helped me find Sahmril. She's been sold to a nobleman at the palace."

He nodded, and began to shake again. Kadesh took off his thick cloak to wrap around him.

"Did you get to see her?" I asked.

Weakly, my father thumped his chest in a gesture of mourning, his mouth going slack. "The palace had already burned. They died in the blaze during the chaos."

"No, Father. I saw her for myself. Sahmril was well with the adoptive family. She was just beginning to toddle on her little legs. She looked—" My voice broke as the memory of her sweet face sprang to my mind. "She's beautiful. She looks just like Mother."

My father held his face in his hands, his shoulders shaking with emotion.

"They treated her well," I assured him. "They call her Ramah."

His hands slipped from mine as he sank back to the floor. "I've lost my wife and all my daughters." His tone was detached and odd, and it frightened me. "Leila to the temple. You to a foreign boy without marriage. Sahmril to a strange family."

"Kadesh, please let's get him out of here." I placed a hand against my father's sallow cheek and bent low to his face. "Someday we *will* get Sahmril back."

He wept soundlessly, tears running like rain down his withered cheeks.

"Sir," Kadesh said with fresh urgency. "We must leave as soon as possible."

"Leave?" he echoed.

"Pharez, I love and care for your daughter more than life itself. Please come with us to my kingdom. We'll give you a new home, a new life. You'll have the best doctors and regain your health. I will give you anything you ask if you'll grant me the betrothal of your daughter."

"After Horeb's brother, Zenos, died, I dreamed of Horeb and Jayden together on the Nephish throne."

"Ssh," I whispered. "Don't think of things so long ago."

"You can live on your own terms," Kadesh told him. "You'll be a free man."

I brushed my lips against my father's fingers. "I love you, Father. You must come with us to the southern lands so Kadesh and I can marry. We need a proper chaperone," I added, attempting to smile.

Without waiting for a response, Kadesh placed his hands underneath my father's frail body, lifting him up into his arms. I tucked the cloak around him and then we made our way back through the clammy, rat-infested corridor. "Pharez, I'll have my men retrieve your tent and camels."

My father nodded, but I wasn't sure he understood we were leaving the oasis, never to return.

"Get him out of here," the guard said, waving his lantern in our faces.

"I'm returning to the temple for Leila," I said in a low voice to Kadesh. "I know the priestesses. If I go myself they can't accuse you of being there to kidnap her—and drag you off to this horrible prison."

"I understand, but it's too risky to go alone. I don't trust Armana."

"I don't either. Maybe Asher—or the Edomite army—could accompany me for protection, although they'll have to wait outside. I can show them the rear entrances where I'll bring Leila out."

"I don't like being separated, but time is running out. Help Leila pack as quickly as possible. We'll meet at the crossroads between the southern gates of Tadmur and the oasis. Be there no later than sundown."

"Agreed," I said, trying to hide my anxiety with a small smile.

A small leather sack bulging with silver and frankincense was laid on the jailer's table as we exited the dungeons of Tadmur and burst out into fresh air again.

Kadesh pressed a second pouch of valuables into my hand. "You know what to use it for," he said.

I nodded, and once again, I was racing toward the Temple of Ashtoreth.

12

A sher met me at the temple, leading a group of Edomites. My heart thrummed and my legs wobbled with fatigue. His band of brothers surrounded the plaza as I slid off the back of Asher's horse. One of them was the rogue thief, Laban, and I jerked my head away when he leered at me.

Asher put out a hand and then quickly dropped it. "I mean no disrespect, my lady. Are you sure you're up to this after the horror on the stoning field?"

An awkward silence passed between us. "I'll be fine."

"Please be careful. I distrust everyone at the temple."

"I do too, but I don't fear for my life."

Asher's eyes were on me as I climbed the green tiled stairs. Once through the courtyard and inside the doors, I requested an audience with the High Priestess for the second time that day.

The girl at the desk blinked her eyes.

"I'm Leila's sister."

"It's a pity you didn't remain here at the temple," she said. "We received an endowment from the Assyrian governor who comes to the temple when he visits Tadmur. You had potential. You missed the Court of Goddesses when the initiates graduated to priestesses. Leila now wears a crown of jewels. You would have been at her side."

"I chose a different life," I said, trying not to let her rattle me.

The young woman leaned across the desk, jangling her gold bracelets. "You could have been even more valuable than Leila. You have a presence, and yet a beguiling purity. From the moment you danced, Armana wanted you for herself. To train personally."

I was astonished. "But I'm not—"

"You haven't looked into a mirror lately, have you?"

"I'm sure I'm quite hideous. Especially after this morning."

"That's true," the girl said, wrinkling her nose at my wounds. "But Armana called you unruly. *Wild.* With jewels and silks, no man could resist you."

I choked on the sweet, cloying incense filling the halls, not wanting to hear her snake-like words. "Just call for Armana."

"She's already here."

I whipped around to see the High Priestess standing in the doorway. She was serene. Perfect in her eloquent beauty. But shrewdness spilled over her eyes. "You've returned."

"Only to get my sister. Please," I added, wishing I didn't have to grovel. "My father is heartbroken, my grandmother dying. She needs to come home."

"What do I get in return for one of Ashtoreth's anointed priestesses?"

"I have a cache of gold and frankincense in payment for her life," I said, holding out the pouch Kadesh had given me.

Armana transferred Kadesh's pouch of coins and frankincense to the palace guards, waving a hand through the air as though it was nothing. "We already have storehouses full of frankincense and myrrh for our temple ceremonies." She gave a smug smile, the gold shavings sprinkled in her hair glittering balefully at me. "What else do you have?"

"Isn't my sister's soul and virtue enough for you?"

Her eyes latched on to mine. My heart slammed against my ribs. We stood only inches apart. Her breath was sweet, her skin lovely. She was a dream in her gown and jewels but she also frightened me. I had no other bribery or enticements to offer for Leila's freedom.

I slipped my hand down to my dagger, not daring to break the gaze between us.

"Are you afraid, Jayden?" she said softly.

Sweat trickled down my neck. "Of course not."

"Then you won't mind uniting with one of the priests of Ba'al as payment for your sister. It's early spring and the Sacred Marriage Rites are upon us."

"Don't insult me."

"You're insulting *me*," she said, grabbing my arm. Driving

her fingernails into my flesh, she added in a low, terrible voice, "I thought you said you'd do anything for your sister."

"You know I would never agree to that."

Her brown eyes studied me. Laughed at me. "Then perhaps you'll agree to my final offer. I will give you Leila," she said, breathing the power of the Goddess across my face. "And *you* will give me a night with Kadesh, the prince of the frankincense lands."

Outraged, I grabbed my dagger and swung the blade at her—inches from slashing her perfect beauty. Instantly, the guards pounced, their swords at my neck. "You want me to give you a night with Kadesh—just like you spent nights with my betrothed, Horeb, the prince of Nephish?"

She didn't disclose any surprise, but there was no mistaking the hard glint of guilt in her eyes. Accusing her of consorting with Horeb had been a gamble, but Horeb drunkenly admitted he'd been visiting the Temple of Ashtoreth the night he tried to rape me at the pond.

Armana laughed. "Why shouldn't I have both your men? You're obviously having a difficult time keeping them close and well satisfied."

"I will kill you before I let you touch Kadesh."

She waved away my blade and swept the train of her gown across the room. "I have guards waiting for my orders to carry you out of here. Maybe still alive—maybe with your tongue cut out."

"What kind of game are you playing?"

"This is no game, stupid girl," she said, reversing her path to swing back around to me, venom on her face. "As the High Priestess of Ashtoreth, I want the most valuable man in all of Mesopotamia, the wealthiest, the most coveted. It's the season for fertility and new life. Abundant blessings from the goddess. And Ashtoreth wants a love child to raise up to do her will. A child who will adore the Goddess with perfect love and obedience—willing to be sacrificed for Ashtoreth if necessary."

"Have you lost all shame? You'd give your soul to the Goddess and sacrifice an innocent baby?"

Armana snaked out her arm to grab a lock of my hair, pulling me intimately close. "The Goddess of Ashtoreth and the Prince of Sariba would create the most perfect goddess child together."

The image of this woman and Kadesh together—lying naked on a bed of silks in a candlelit room—made me nauseous.

"I know what you're thinking, Jayden. The picture of Kadesh and me in your mind. But denying me the man you love means never seeing Leila again. Now go get him for me. He and I will become one with the Goddess and create the world over again in her image."

"Bring me Leila first. I want to see my sister."

Armana snapped her fingers, her red mouth a slash of poison. "You don't get to make bargains with the Goddess, heathen girl!"

"Let me see her!" I demanded. My voice echoed off the stone walls, and before I could stop myself, I shoved past Armana and flung open the doors to the inner hallway.

Two guards glanced at me, startled, but I was already running down the corridor. The High Priestess had forgotten one thing. I'd lived here for weeks, and I knew exactly where to find Leila.

The dimly lit halls were filled with voluptuous goddess statues. Wall sconces flickered heat and melting wax. Doors and courtyards branched off, sculpted columns rising overhead. I was running deeper into the enemy's lair. Asher and I had never planned any sort of signal in case I was in trouble. I would just have to find my own way out—somehow.

I came to a polished staircase and leaped the steps as the sound of chasing guards drifted into the distance. The stairs disappeared up into shadows. I quickly took the corner landing to a new hallway, and then a smaller staircase before the guards could figure out where I'd gone.

Here were the bedrooms where I'd recovered from Horeb's brutal attack. The baths and saunas I'd enjoyed with their luxurious water, scented soaps, and rich towels.

After glancing in both directions, I burst through the bedroom I'd shared with my sister. My chest heaved from running up so many stairs, the bruises and cuts from the stoning flaming with fresh pain.

The bedroom was empty. No lamps were lit. Afternoon sun drenched the floor from the long windows. I stared at my reflection in the mirror. Big dark eyes set in a drawn face, a tangled mess of hair falling past my waist. The hem of my mother's dress was filthy where I'd kneeled at my father's dungeon hole.

No wonder Armana taunted me. She was confident she could sway Kadesh with a flick of her little finger. I pushed the High Priestess from my mind. Night was coming much too fast. With every passing hour, Horeb was moving closer.

"Leila!" I hissed into the stillness. "Where are you?"

She should have been here dressing for the evening meal.

No other girls were in sight. The suite was emptier than it should have been, but my eyes focused on the strange details. The bedclothes were thrown back and wrinkled. Crumbs of cake lay on the table. A half-empty flask of wine stood next to it. No hairbrushes or jumble of jewels were on the dressing tables, but a forlorn ribbon trailed off the edge next to a broken comb.

The closet doors hung open, swinging on their hinges. Except for a forgotten dress, a torn shawl, and a pair of old sandals stuffed into the corner, it had been emptied.

My mother's prized alabaster box was gone, too. I'd left it at the temple with Leila because there was no room on my camel for anything but food and water. My mother's wedding gift didn't belong at the temple; it belonged with me. Putting a hand on the wall to steady myself, I turned the corner to where the bureau stood. One by one I pulled open the drawers with shaking hands. They were vacant, too, except for a few forgotten silks. It was as though someone had recently packed and left in a hurry.

Lurching out of the closet, I ran to the adjoining suite and pushed through the double doors into a huge upper hall.

Golden light, laughter, and music surrounded me.

Abundant food weighted down the tables, more than I'd seen in months. Girls in silk dresses and intricate hairstyles stretched across divans. A few were singing, others sipped red wine; giggles, whispers, and jokes filled the air.

My eyes blurred with the sight of so many people and so much sumptuous richness. "Leila?"

My presence didn't appear to be noted. The musicians in the far corner played loudly while drums pounded a familiar sensuous rhythm under the soles of my feet. In the center of the large room girls were dancing, their legs drifting in and out of exotic linen dresses, their breasts bared like the women of Egypt, accents of gold collars about their necks.

I hid behind a curtain when I spotted several foreign men watching the girls dance. My heart pounded until it hurt. I stared at the girls, trying to identify Leila.

There was laughing and clapping while two girls wound bloodred silks around a statue of Ashtoreth in the far corner. The girls appeared drunk. The room was hazy with incense and the heat of the wall sconce torches.

One by one, the Egyptian men chose a temple priestess and disappeared through open doors into rooms lit with candles. Rooms adorned in heavy drapes and plush beds.

My stomach churned. I felt ill.

And then I saw her. My sister, wearing a see-through lavender gown, swaying as though she'd been drugged, her eyes half closed.

"Leila!" I screamed, darting forward, but my voice was

small, blanketed by the music and party. I pushed past girls hovering over the food tables, the circles of dancers and men who were touching them as they moved to the music, their eyes on fire with desire. Pushing through the crowd was like swimming upstream through a torrent of water during a storm.

"Leila!" I shouted again. Not a moment later, I watched, stunned, as the foreign men surrounding her grabbed my sister and two other girls. Picking them up, they put the girls over their shoulders and moved swiftly through a set of double doors on the far side of the room.

Leila's head flopped. Her black hair drifted down the man's back, her arms limp. She was clearly not coherent.

Jostling through the crowd, I stumbled over goblets left carelessly on the tiled floor, forgotten silk shawls sliding under my feet. When I reached the same double doors, the room beyond was empty. I kept going, my legs heavy as tree stumps.

Another staircase went down and I took the steps two at a time. One of the kidnappers glanced up and saw me. He shouted to the others, and they picked up their pace. Then, as if taunting me, he grabbed a wall sconce and dripped hot wax along the steps above him.

When I slowed to avoid burning my feet, the men and the captive girls disappeared. Halls branched off in several directions. They were gone. As if a magical door had swallowed them up.

A servant girl rounded a corner, carrying a tray. "Who are you?" she asked, reaching out a hand to touch my arm.

"Those girls—the men—who came through here just now. Where did they go?"

Her eyes darted about the empty corridor. "I'm sure I don't know who you mean."

I took her arm and shook it. "You had to have seen them. They have my sister."

"Who's your sister?"

"Leila. She's—she's one of the newly ordained temple priestesses."

The girl nodded, as if unsure how to answer me. "Yes, I know who you mean."

"I was upstairs. There was a party, dancing. And foreign men. They took Leila and two other girls . . . and disappeared."

The servant girl bit her lips and backed away from me. I could tell she wanted to turn around and pretend I didn't exist. "The High Priestess Armana has been entertaining dignitaries from Egypt. A few girls volunteered to go with them to Egypt. A caravan leaves tonight."

"Egypt?" I echoed. "Where do the caravans leave from? Tell me."

A vision of Leila's empty suite of rooms—clothes torn from hangers, drawers emptied in a hurry—pieces of her left behind. She'd packed haphazardly. Or someone had packed for her.

"Tell me!" I urged.

"Those doors over there. Down that staircase to the bottom of the temple. The delivery area."

I pushed through the door, my breath heaving, and found myself stumbling down a circular set of stone steps. When I reached the bottom, I pushed through the final door and out into a wide hallway. Servants were moving crates, organizing food baskets. Nobody paid any attention to me.

A young girl sorted linens by color and size. "Did a group of Egyptians come through here?" I asked her.

She stared at me as though she couldn't speak. Finally, she nodded and pointed to one of the doors leading to the outside. "Through there."

I ran down the hall and pushed open the door. Cool evening air rushed across my face. Fresh camel and horse tracks were visible. Footprints and mud and chariot wheels.

The foreign caravan was gone with hardly a trace. If they had even come this direction. Or had I been duped as to which route they'd taken? I'd heard of underground tunnels connecting the Temple of Ba'al and the Temple of Ashtoreth. Those foreigners could have easily slipped through those secret passageways.

My sister had been kidnapped. The High Priestess Armana had arranged it all.

I fell to the ground, pounding the stone, wishing I'd run faster, wishing I'd screamed louder.

I stared down at the empty sand with its hollow imprints of camels and wagons. I'd failed my sister, and there was a good chance I'd lost her forever.

The night was silent, the hills of Tadmur hovering shadows of doom.

What would I tell my father?

In a daze, I slipped around the wall of the temple to the

closest gate and followed the path back to the plaza. Every part of my body screamed in pain, but my heart hurt worst of all.

"Jayden!" a quiet voice called out from a shadowed alley behind me. It was Asher.

I whirled. "You startled me. How did you know it was me?"

"I have a tendency to recognize the people I save from death." He was trying to coax a smile from me, but I was too exhausted to respond.

Asher helped me onto his horse and then slapped the reins, joining the Edomites who came out of the evening like specters and enclosed us in their ranks. Moments later we rode out the southern gates of Tadmur. Away from the oasis, away from the camp of Nephish. Away from the western roads to Damascus—and away from Leila.

I spotted Kadesh and my father at the crossroads waiting for us, and ran into my father's arms so hard I almost knocked him over.

"Jayden," he said, his voice trembling. "Where's Leila?"

"Don't tell me she's still packing." Concern lay in Kadesh's eyes, despite the smile of optimism he forced onto his lips.

I shook my head and Kadesh held me carefully, so as not to hurt my wounds. "Where's Leila?" he asked gently. "Did you see the High Priestess?"

Armana's request to use the body of the man I loved was seared into my mind. I wanted to banish her ugly words, but it was almost impossible. "She was her usual lying, manipulative self."

My father began to tremble, and I knew he feared the worst. I reached for his hands. "Leila *is* alive. I can tell you that much. But she's gone. I watched her carried away on an Egyptian caravan. Her bedroom had been cleaned out. There was a party, the girls were drunk and more wanton than I've ever seen before . . . somehow I know it was planned. Purposeful."

Kadesh shook his head. "Why would Armana send priestesses to Egypt? She wouldn't let such valuable girls go without being paid handsomely."

My father tore at his gray hair. "Leila barely survived the journey to Tadmur a year ago. How can she travel to Egypt? It will kill her." He slumped to the ground, groaning, and Kadesh knelt beside him, holding him while he trembled with grief. I watched the two men I loved comfort each other. My chest filled with such a hard knot of emotion I couldn't even speak.

Finally, Kadesh lifted my father from the dirt, speaking in low tones while Chemish brought his camel. Then he took my hands. "I almost lost you today, and now I have to ask you to bear even more as we begin this long journey while you're hurt and not well."

"You gave me a gift placing Asher as my personal guard. I'm still alive because of him."

A huge bull camel lumbered up, led by one of the Edomites, a large litter already perched on its back. "I don't need a litter for traveling, Kadesh. I don't need to be spoiled," I said.

My father spoke up. "Your grandmother decided she'd rather die with her family in the Empty Sands than live with a tribe that would stone you and leave her son to rot in prison."

A rush of joy surged through me. "Seraiah is here?"

My father nodded and Chemish said, "We must leave immediately. We've procured rations and will travel until midnight. We'll push hard this first week to keep ahead of Horeb."

My father winced at the mention of Horeb's name and turned away to mount his camel, one slow step at a time, as though he'd aged twenty years.

I climbed into the litter with my grandmother and embraced her fiercely.

"I decided it was better to face death on the desert than be left behind with Judith," she said dryly. "Besides, my son looks terrible."

I peered through the window at my father. He tucked his legs around his camel's broad back, but he was gaunt as a skeleton and completely gray now, his hair, his beard, and his face.

My grandmother leaned in to inspect me. "You should have washed your face at the temple."

"Is that all you can say to me after such a day?" I teased her, but the horror of all that had happened was beginning to wear. Dread gnawed at me. "I could always run back to Tadmur and jump into the well at the plaza for a proper bath."

"And give Kadesh a heart attack the moment you left his sight."

"If my appearance is so bad, how can he stand to look at me?"

"Underneath the bruises and dirt is a most beautiful woman.

You've caught the imagination of every single Edomite here. To them, you're already their princess. And well deserved, I might add. Loyalty to your family. Unwavering courage despite grave threats."

I pressed my face into her neck, so grateful to be together, but every part of my body screamed with pain. "Then why do I feel as though I failed? I was ready to give up in the stoning pit, and then Leila was kidnapped right in front of my eyes."

"Pah! A true princess behaves just as you did today. The tribe of Nephish abandoned our family," Seraiah went on severely. "They left your father to die in jail. They stoned you—and made me watch—while you prepared to die with dignity and honor. The people of Sariba will love you just as we all do."

Our hands clenched together while the bull camel lurched forward. The time had finally come to leave the lands I'd known my whole life, and Leila and Sahmril were not with me. A great wail rose up inside me, but if I gave in to all my sorrows I'd never survive this journey.

"What do my cousins Hakak and Falail and Timnath think of me? I'm sure Aunt Judith poisoned them with ugly lies."

My grandmother used humor to break my desolate mood. "I rather fancy wearing jewels of jade and sapphire—and smelling like frankincense."

"You sound like you're sixteen again."

"No matter how old you get, a girl feels young in her heart. It's the body that gets to be a problem."

I pushed the curtains aside. The sun was setting, its gold rays splashing the world with a luxuriant hue. Despite all I'd been through, the sky's color created a good omen as we headed to a land with caches of golden frankincense nuggets.

13

I quickly learned Chemish possessed skills similar to a physician. When we stopped late that night, he soaked herbs and ground roots to make poultices for my cuts and bruises, showing Seraiah how to apply the herbs to my skin and make a plaster. He warned me the next day would prove to be worse, and he was right. I ached so badly I could hardly move as we raced from the borders of the Assyrian Empire and headed south.

"I'm sure I look ridiculous," I said while my grandmother doctored me.

Beads of sweat dribbled down her face. "You're fortunate you have no broken bones."

"Lie down and rest," I urged her. "I can finish tending my legs. We have two thousand miles to go."

My grandmother lay back on the pillows and closed her

eyes. "Darling girl, I can promise you I won't make it that far."

"Please don't say that."

"None of us live forever, my dear, but I decided I wanted to be with you and your father in my last days."

"Were the women—Judith—treating you badly?"

"I was ignored and yet overheard their gossip. Would any of them have done differently if their betrothed treated them as badly as Horeb did you? Other girls have taken their own lives rather than marry a man they despised."

I winced. "I—can imagine."

"I had a dear friend when I was young who did just that. It was terrible. Nobody was allowed to speak her name again. But I've never forgotten her. Sometimes when I was out by myself at the well or tending the camels I'd whisper her name and tell her I still remembered." She paused. "Our life is in God's hands. I gave my heart to Him when I was young, trusting all would be well in the end. And it usually is. But many times I've learned that the hard way."

"I'm not sure I can endure anymore."

My grandmother gazed at me. "You've had more than your share of tragedy at the hands of others. Unfortunately, we can't take another person's free will away, or force them to make different choices, no matter how much we wish we could. Because of your role as betrothed to the heir you were caught up in circumstances beyond your control. All you can do is endure it well and carry yourself with pride."

I dipped a strip of linen into the herbal paste and massaged it into the bruises on my shins. "Unfortunately," I repeated.

"Don't let your heart turn to resentment, my sweet Jayden. You must forgive. It's the only way to find peace."

"Forgiveness? I almost lost Kadesh. I'm scarred for life. I lost Sahmril, my mother's jewelry, my camel to Dinah. Horeb hunts me like a wild animal. I refuse to be tamed and live under his rule."

"And that is *your* choice, my girl. You have every right to freedom and love. But Horeb won't accept it." Her eyes turned to the window, as if she could see what was beyond the night's darkness. "If I know him, he is gathering stronger forces. Making promises he can't keep to convince other armies to join him."

"What do you mean?"

Seraiah posed a question back to me. "Why would Horeb's army follow us all the way to the southern lands?"

"Because his pride has made him crazy."

"Perhaps . . . but what else?"

"He wants to make sure Kadesh is dead—kill him again. Then lock me up and force me into his marriage bed."

"What do the Maachathites and the Adummatus have to gain by joining forces with him?" My grandmother's hooded eyes were thoughtful. "He may be gathering Assyrian tribes, too. Moabites, Midianites. Horeb has other motivations, Jayden. Remember, he learned of his father's desire to join the Nephish tribe with Kadesh's Sariba kingdom. He knows Abimelech wanted to put you and Kadesh on the throne to join our tribes in fealty. I would swear on your grandfather's grave Horeb promised the Maachathites and Adummatus wealth and power—the promise of ruling the eastern deserts and waterways. Which means being in charge of all the riches of the desert worlds."

I wrapped a blanket around myself, tendrils of darkness wafting through the window to chill me. "This is so much bigger than I imagined."

"Horeb has seized a glorious opportunity. A chance at ruling the lands of Mesopotamia. Just as King Hammurabi is conquering and ruling the Babylonian cities of the great rivers to the east. All Horeb needs is the wealth of the frankincense lands, and you as his rightful queen to claim—and maintain— his legitimacy. And then produce lawful heirs. After all, he has the contract papers from Abimelech and your father."

The betrothal contract. Signed by my father and Horeb's father when we were children.

Seraiah reached out her withered fingers to touch my hand. "Despite hardships, pain, poverty, and death, you must believe in yourself and never give up."

"I just want peace with Kadesh."

"Our afflictions often make the good things that much sweeter. Opposition in all things."

I gazed through the curtains at the shadows of passing hills. With every alliance and every stroke of his sword, Horeb fought to prove himself worthy to his murdered father, his dead brother's memory, and to his tribe. Uniting the desert tribes with the lure of unimaginable wealth, Horeb would grow stronger, more resilient, and more zealous.

He would stop at nothing.

14

Over the next few weeks, while we journeyed toward the Red Sea, my bruises blossomed and then faded, the cuts stung less, my fever disappeared, and I could move about more easily without succumbing to whimpers of pain. Kadesh was solicitous, bringing meals and keeping us surrounded by his best warriors as we raced across the desert.

My father's silence lasted for days at a time. I often saw him staring down at his hands while he rode and I wondered what he was thinking about. On the first day I felt well enough to ride my camel again, I rode beside him, not speaking at first. I followed his gaze down to his hands. He was carrying one of my mother's necklaces in his fist.

When my father noticed, he slipped the necklace into his tunic pocket.

"One day," I told him softly, "I will find Sahmril and bring her to the frankincense lands. Leila, too. I'll unite us as a family again."

His face crumpled, the edges of his features caving into grief. "Everything has gone wrong since your mother left this world. That's when you ran away from home, our tribe. You broke your promises."

I tensed, not wanting to argue. "Those promises weren't my promises, father. They were forced upon me."

"You left with a stranger, a man we know little about."

"But *I* know him. He's good and kind and generous. He brought a hundred camels for you—with more to come for my bride price."

He winced when I mentioned the camels. Those same camels had been left at the oasis, along with our empty tent and other belongings. Horeb would destroy our personal possessions and steal the camels for his own. "Jayden, you traveled with a man you're not related to. Your reputation is tarnished."

"Kadesh helped me search for Sahmril in Mari—and we found her."

His face was drawn tight. "You deserted your sister at the temple of Ashtoreth."

"I begged Leila to come with me, but she's determined to be a priestess." *And is as stubborn as you,* I wanted to add.

"Horeb told me you'd gone to Mari with the stranger. He sent me to find you and bring you back home so the marriage could take place."

"Did Horeb also tell you *he* was in Mari? He found me at Nalla's house—and then he killed Kadesh in front of me."

"No, it was Kadesh who kidnapped you and then *he* tried to kill Horeb."

"Horeb lies, Father. He attacked me, he killed Abimelech—"

"Silence!" Pharez held up his trembling hands. "I won't listen to this."

"You see Kadesh's blind eye and mangled scar? Horeb did that. And then he gave me Kadesh's bloody cloak as proof. I want you to trust me. I want you to believe me, because I'm your daughter. I've never lied to you. I've always told you the truth, Father."

"Until the stranger came into our lives. When he showed up, everything changed. *You* changed."

"Horeb and I were never right. He's the one who changed as he grew up. And, after Zenos' death he changed even more."

My father tried to wave my words way. They were too difficult for him to hear.

"I never meant to love someone else, but why do I have to choose between Kadesh and my family?" I grasped my father's hand, and his fingers were icy cold. "Mother would not have asked me to make that choice. She'd want me to be happy. Father," I whispered. "I'm so sorry. For everything."

He leaned close to brush a finger against my cheek. "You're bruised, and your fingers are broken," he observed, staring at my linen-bound hand. "Stoned by our own tribe." His voice broke and he went silent for several long minutes while our camels' padded feet pounded the earth. Then he said, "Maybe I've been the blind man."

Tenderness surged through me. "Father, you loved Horeb like a son. That shows the goodness of your heart."

"Perhaps, but also the blindness of my mind."

We rode along in silence. Chemish led us to the trail that brought us in line for the wells that paralleled the Red Sea mountain range. These trails and wells would take us all the way to the land of Sa'ba. Cleverly, Chemish skirted his city of Edom to avoid anyone he knew who might pass information to Horeb. I was sorry he had to miss seeing Isra and his daughter.

Later, scouts arrived with news of the Nephish and Maachathite armies. It hadn't taken long for Horeb to learn of my stoning and the deaths of his tribal council. He'd be angry they hadn't captured me. Furious that I had an army with me and had slipped through his grasp again.

If Horeb resupplied with fresh camels in Tadmur, there was a real possibility he could catch up. At the pace we'd been traveling for so many weeks, from the Edomite lands north to Tadmur, and now crossing back over to go south, our animals were becoming tired. They needed a real rest. More than just a few hours at a time.

I spoke to Kadesh about my concerns of Horeb catching up to us. "He doesn't know the terrain where we're going," Kadesh assured me. "He's never experienced the Empty Sands firsthand. He could lose half his men trying to follow us."

"Don't underestimate Horeb. He'll do everything he can to make it to Sariba, even if it kills his men and he crawls on his belly into the palace to slit my throat at midnight."

We stopped in the late afternoon, earlier than usual, to

partake of a day of extra rest. We'd arrived three days ahead of the usual pace, and Chemish ordered extra food and rest for all the animals.

The sea sparkled under the lowering sun. Boats and fishing vessels bobbed on the waters off the shore. The port of Akabah was at the northern tip of the Red Sea. Busy and bustling, larger than Tadmur, with vast neighborhoods, shops, a city plaza, thronging citizens—and the tang of sea salt spicing the air.

At the marketplace we purchased fresh melons, grapes, dates, and bags of wheat and barley, and then set up camp along the seashore. The beach stretched wide and flat as my hand. A haze of mountains hung in the distance, so faint they didn't seem real. Those were the mountains we would follow south to the land of Sheba and then nearly straight east to Kadesh's kingdom of Sariba.

Thunderous waves crashed along the shoreline. Tossing off my sandals, I ran into the warm water, recalling rare childhood trips. Remembering the dream I'd had of me and Kadesh swimming in the southern sea. His eyes holding mine while he held me on top of the surging water. Spectacular kisses as breakers rushed around us on the beach.

Digging my bare toes into the wet sand along the shoreline, I sat down and hugged my knees, enjoying the glorious fresh air. Fingers of orange and mauve clung to the horizon, as though the setting sun was scrabbling to stay on top of the earth, just like I clung to the images in my dream. Behind me, campfires snapped. When I glanced to my left I caught Asher watching me.

I rose to my feet, brushed the sand from my clothes, and strolled down the beach where waves broke in frothy bubbles. He didn't follow me, but I could feel his eyes on my back.

We slept soundly that night, grateful for the extra hours of rest. In the morning, the Edomites fished along the shore. Kadesh grasped my hand and we waded in the warm waters, salt clinging to the hem of my dress.

"I wish we could stay longer," I told him. "What other place could be more beautiful, more perfect and sweet?"

Kadesh glanced down the coastline. "Wait until you see my homeland. Vistas and waterfalls you could hardly dream up in your imagination."

"I have a good imagination," I said with a smile.

Holding hands, we watched the Edomites playing in the ocean with their camels, laughing, eating great chunks of fresh-baked bread from the marketplace.

Farther down, Asher was conversing with Laban, who was gesturing toward the city of Akabah. "What are they talking about?" I asked Kadesh. "Why, out of all the Edomites Asher grew up with, does he spend so much time with a man twenty years older than he is?"

"I haven't noticed any particular attention between them," Kadesh answered. "On long journeys we make friends with all our companions. If we didn't we'd be horribly bored and fights would break out."

"Still . . ." I said, letting the word linger. "I've seen them talking together before. It bothers me that Asher is my bodyguard and yet spends time with the one Edomite I despise completely."

"Perhaps he's merely conveying a message from Chemish. He put Laban in charge of the front lines."

My instincts said otherwise, but I changed the subject. "Are we getting close to Sariba now?"

"I'm sorry to dash your hopes, but we've barely begun. There are a hundred wells between Edom and my homeland. One well a day—at least for most of the trail. We'll follow the delta for a few days. The spot where it enters the sea is called the Fountain of the Red Sea. And then there is a range of colossal mountains we must climb when we turn east for the land of Sa'ba."

"I never knew I lived in such a magical land."

"You won't think it's so magical when you grow weary and sore sleeping under the stars."

"How could I grow tired of any of this when I know you're nearby?" I reached up to smooth his hair back from his patch and he winced—whether from physical or mental pain I didn't know, and he never said. Having only one eye affected his ability to hunt and fight, too. I'd noticed he had assigned more Edomites to hunting duty. I wondered if he worried the people of Sariba would not accept a scarred prince. It must have weighed on his mind.

Feeling a surge of affection, I rose on my toes and pressed my lips against his. His breath caught, and then Kadesh kissed me back with such melancholy, tears pricked at my eyelids.

"This journey just makes me love you all the more," Kadesh murmured. "Before I become completely distracted by you, let's see how well you fare using a sword in soft sand. I know you've been practicing with Asher, but I'm going to show you another technique."

"I only wish I had a sword that fit my size," I said.

"When we get to Sariba you'll have the best sword my bronze workers can fashion."

"I'm holding you to it."

"The thought of you fighting Horeb's soldiers sickens me," he added. "One wrong move and they'll take off your head."

"I don't want to be caught unawares. I have to be able to fight for my life."

"I suppose with many weeks of travel ahead of us you have time to learn quite a bit."

I could guess what Kadesh was doing—playing out an imaginary death scene, just as I'd done when I'd watched Horeb's soldiers carry him off to be killed.

I smiled. "I think that means yes."

"I want Asher to continue teaching you, too. More experience with different styles of fighting. And, as your guard, he'll be the one close by if we're ever attacked on the desert."

"When we reach Sariba, your duties to the throne are going to demand much of your time, won't they? I'll have to learn how to function on my own, maneuver palace life."

Kadesh appeared relieved that I understood his role as prince and general of the Sariba army.

I leaned in close, my lips against his cheek. "But I claim

your nights, Prince of Sariba."

His arms went around my shoulders, and he brought me close, his fingers brushing through the strands of my hair. "I want Asher to teach you the slingshot and how to shoot a bow as well."

"All of that, too?" I teased. "And just a moment ago you were reluctant to let me learn just one weapon."

"Asher is the best with the sling."

"His skill saved my life."

"I'll be eternally grateful." Kadesh took on a more serious tone. "You're not afraid, Jayden. I've seen it in your eyes, your face when you pull out your dagger to practice."

His compliment was high praise, but he had no idea how frightened I'd been the day Gad attacked me. Sheer terror had caused me to shove my dagger into the man's chest. Perhaps this is what happened during battle—an immense sense of self-preservation.

"My father had no sons," I mused. "I used to listen to him and the other men relive their battle stories and raids. I tended the camels with him out on the desert—until my mother made me become a girl."

"I was the one to help my mother when my father was away on business. She used to confide in me, rely on me. . . ." Kadesh's voice trailed away.

"But no more?"

Tension formed around his mouth and I placed my hands in his cold ones, bringing them to my lips to warm them. "You sound very close to her."

"We *were* very close." His words seemed to travel up from a dark place deep inside.

"Your mother—what is her name? She grew up in the Dedanite nation, right? We're getting close to the Dedan forts, aren't we?"

He started, as though a fog had sprung up around the campfire. "Her name?"

When he didn't answer a long pause strung out between us. "Kadesh, tell me what happened to her."

He shook his head, his thoughts far away. "Not now, not on this journey. I can't think of her and remain focused on getting us to Sariba safely."

His words left an empty spot inside me. What secret was he carrying that he couldn't share with me? Surely he trusted me, but I could tell the subject was off limits. When he pushed me away I was more rattled than I wanted to admit. Was this how it would be when we arrived in Sariba?

In three days we arrived at the Fountain of the Red Sea. Kadesh led the caravan through a narrow ravine, bringing us down to banks of sand along a slow-moving river. Previous torrential storms had left high watermarks on the canyon walls. Breathtaking sandstone cliffs towered about us.

We slept under a grove of date palms. The trickle of water singing through the rushes under the tamarisk trees was soothing. I slept heavily, but awoke before dawn. The camp remained silent, but in a few hours the world would rush to life with the sunrise.

I took the opportunity to gather my clean dress and soap to bathe in an actual river. A half-filled bucket from a well was never sufficient.

With bare toes, I stepped along the spongy bank, making my way to a covert spot. The grasses were soft, a luxury to my callused feet.

I placed the clean dress on the bank and furtively glanced about. Silent as a grave. Quickly, I dropped the dress I'd been wearing since leaving the Temple of Ashtoreth. My stomach clenched as I entered the river. The water was cooler than I expected, but after a few moments, the temperature was perfect and refreshing.

To immerse myself was true bliss, and it was glorious to swim, the water dream-like against my bare skin. Farther out, the water grew deeper. I ducked completely under and washed my hair twice, swishing my neck to rinse the soap.

Floating on my back, my eyes closed, I could conjure my mother and Leila's chatter and laughter when we'd find a river to bathe in. I saw myself slipping on the wet banks. Chasing soap bubbles across the water. Pictures floated across the night sky—my mother scrubbing my hair. Me as a little girl shrieking when she combed out the wet knots.

Laughter bubbled up my throat, along with the sting of loss pricking my eyes. I wasn't sure I'd ever remember my mother without a combination of both happiness and sorrow.

I clung to the hope I'd find Leila in Egypt one day. I couldn't imagine what the goddess temples of Isis in that foreign land wanted with her.

Thinking of the women of my family made me want to dance. Moving through the water, I spun in slow circles, the water rippling about my swaying hips. My arms arched overhead, flinging drops of water from my fingertips under the last of the crescent moon.

Holding myself still, I practiced hip circles, the drops and lifts my mother had taught me. Placing a hand against my abdomen, I swirled on my toes in the soft mud. When I touched my naked skin, I thought of dancing for Kadesh on our wedding night. I needed to practice if I was to be ready to dance with the seven veils for him—as well as in the marriage tent when we were alone at last.

The tamarisk trees rustled and I was startled out of my reverie. Rising from the water, I glanced about. A flash glittered beyond the trees. I scrambled up the bank and grabbed my dagger from its sheath, my breath raspy.

No growls or snuffling came through the brush.

"Is someone there?" I called in a harsh whisper. Hurriedly I dried myself with the towel I'd packed. My thighs were taut with nerves as I threw the dress back over my head.

Just as I shifted the dress around my hips and reached for my sash, Asher stepped out of the shadows.

My stomach dropped sickeningly. "Have you been watching me?"

"No, my lady, no!" The young man strode forward to reassure me and then stopped. "I was on watch and heard noises. I had no idea it was you. I apologize for intruding."

Heat rose like wildfire from my toes to my damp chest. My hair was heavy and wet against my neck, my stomach queasy at the sight of him. The stars were quickly fading now, the river a hazy gray in the early morning. "Do you speak the truth?"

The young man pressed a hand against his heart, reminding me of Kadesh. "I do not lie. I had no idea you were out here."

Seeing him here at the river was too reminiscent of the night I'd fallen into the pond and Horeb had attacked me. My heart was racing, my lips dry, but I had to trust Asher would do no such thing.

A terrible thought reared its ugly head. I used to think that about Horeb, too.

"You saw nothing?"

Impulsively, Asher took a step forward. "When you walked up the bank you were the loveliest thing I've ever seen in my life."

My mouth opened and I spluttered, "How am I supposed to respond to that?"

"That was stupid. Unforgivable. I didn't mean anything, my lady. Please don't speak of this to Kadesh. I mean—it's true I think you are one of the finest girls I've ever known. The most brave, and the most beautiful. But I would never hurt you. I'd never do anything to make you hate me."

Confusion tumbled inside my mind. "Of course I don't hate you."

He looked so relieved I almost laughed. "My father—all

the men—think the same. We've heard the stories of what you did to save your sister. The attack from the man in the Mari hills. I've never known any girl like you before."

"I've also made a hundred mistakes. Often in the same day."

Dawn created pink streaks behind his head, lighting his youthful face. He was actually quite handsome.

I shook the thought away and attempted to walk up the slope of the bank, but he was standing in the middle of the path I needed to return to my sleeping quarters.

Asher toyed with the leather strap of his slingshot, and I could tell he wanted to say more. "You have my complete allegiance and devotion, my lady."

"You've demonstrated that most faithfully," I said, my voice louder than I wanted, keenly aware of the listening trees. "I'm grateful, but it can never be more. You understand that?"

Asher's expression dropped as though a small flicker of hope had drained away. "Jayden, if you ever have need of my heart, it's yours."

I was speechless. The hope he harbored was foolish and unreasonable, but anything I said would belittle his tender, boyish emotions.

Asher's fingers brushed against mine and I quickly sidestepped him. "Get some sleep, Asher," I said, making my voice brisk. "Before the camp rises."

I couldn't get to my bed fast enough. When I lay down, I couldn't stop my heart from pounding.

Asher had denied it, but I knew he'd seen me rising naked

out of the river. He'd seen me squeezing the water out of my hair, reaching for my clothes. I didn't want to hurt him, because he was a boy in love, but I hoped no one else had seen our encounter.

Every hour my mind conjured the memory of Asher's eyes when I walked out of the river. I could still feel his breath when he wrapped his body around me to save me from the stoning. Why had he chosen me for his affections, the girl of the prince he clearly loved so greatly?

The questions perplexed me during the day. Made sleep elusive at night.

I couldn't even ignore him due to our sword-fighting practices.

I was finding it difficult to ignore him at all. When we packed up the animals the next morning, once again I noticed Asher and Laban conferring with each other, heads bent, their movements quick and deft, surreptitious.

Asher passed something to Laban, a leather packet of some kind. No, it was a thin tablet for writing. Laban stuffed it in the folds of his cloak and glanced up to see if anyone was watching. Quickly, I averted my face, tying my water pouch to Shay's halter, but still wondering what their conversations were about. Further, what had been etched on the writing tablet?

I bided my time and bit my tongue. A few days later, we entered the borders of Dedan—the tribe of Kadesh's mother. Dedan and Sheba were brothers, sons of Abraham and his second wife, Keturah. The current Queen of Sheba was their descendant, which made Kadesh a great-grandson of Dedan, and cousin to the queen.

The oasis near the capital of Dedan was just as exquisite as the Fountain of the Red Sea. Nestled in the midst of the magnificent Hijaz mountain range, there were miles of towering red cliffs. Caves and tombs lay nearby, reminding me of the Edomite canyons.

At the oasis lake, jasmine perfumed the air. Knee-high grasses and lush wildflowers of red and purple surrounded the perimeter. Groves of date palms grew as far as I could see. Orchards of orange trees and grape vineyards. Pistachios and almonds.

Kadesh's mother surfaced at last, even though the memories were not his own. "My father met her on one of his caravan trips when he was first learning the frankincense trade." He glanced at me meaningfully, recalling our first encounter, when he'd crouched on top of the cliff while I danced over my mother's grave.

"I hope your father wasn't bleeding to death when your mother met him," I said, hiding a smile with my scarf.

He laughed, reaching for my camel's halter to bring me closer. "And if he had he would probably have endured the stitching and burning of his wounds much better than I did."

It was good to see him in better spirits. His parents' courtship and marriage obviously pleased him, but what could the dark secret be? Why wouldn't he share their current status with me?

"My father entered the city with hundreds of camels laden with frankincense and myrrh. His wealth impressed her family. My mother was intelligent and educated by a private tutor. She knew art and history and appreciated the finer things in life. My father negotiated a treaty with the Dedanites, and the construction of forts began. Resting places for travelers. A safe spot, with Dedan soldiers for protection, as well as water and food. We now have forts under construction from here north to the Edomite lands. That's how I became allies with Chemish. We have plans to build forts all the way south to the kingdom of Sheba, at the bottom of the Red Sea. One day the caravan trail will be faster. Easier to reach the cities of Salem and Damascus to the west and north. Including the eastern Babylonian cities along the Euphrates."

"What an ambitious undertaking." We rode past one of the half-constructed forts on the outskirts of the walled capital of Dedan and I was impressed.

"Next time I'll take you into the city and let you meet my crazy Dedan cousins. For now, we'll stop one night here, resupply, and try to make the kingdom of Sheba by the next full moon."

"The *next* full moon?" The vast distance ahead of us was astonishing. "You have a complicated family tree—as well as complex friendships with people in every city and land."

"Comes with driving caravans since I was young enough to maneuver a camel. Chemish is a longtime ally of Uncle Ephrem and my mother's family. A skilled horseman, general, and doctor. His friendship and alliance has saved my life more than once. Fortunately, we have enough camels to carry thirty sacks of food. We'll need to fatten up as we continue south. The last few weeks of the journey are the worst. How is Seraiah faring?"

"Becoming more frail, but stubborn and feisty as always."

Kadesh winked at me, a gesture that tugged at my belly. He looked unexpectedly sensuous with his swarthy black eye patch. "The soldiers are all secretly in love with her."

I couldn't help grinning. "They all wish they had a grandmother like her."

The gates of Dedan glinted in the setting sun, monstrous pylons cunningly crafted of hewn stones embedded with carnelian, onyx, and red polished jasper.

I climbed back into the litter with Seraiah, our bull camel placed in the middle of the caravan for safety. The wooden frame rattled, and a male voice called through the curtains. I pulled the drapes back and found Asher wearing ragged, filthy clothes. He'd smeared dirt on his face and knotted a cloth about his forehead in a style I'd never seen the Edomites wear before.

"Kadesh is sending a group into the Dedan city to get

supplies. We don't want to be identified."

"You look more like a beggar."

"Precautions so your Nephish leader doesn't know we've come through here. We don't want to leave any trace behind in case his scouts are in the city."

"Seraiah hasn't been well," I told him. "I'd hoped we'd spend a night here."

"My father and Kadesh have decided to move the camp to the southern boundaries of Dedan while we purchase supplies."

"What if someone recognizes the camels?" I asked.

"We're taking our oldest animals and removing their finery so we'll appear as poor desert gypsies. We'll meet outside the city later." Asher went on. "One of the scouts believes he sighted a Maachathite lodging at one of the Dedan inns."

"It doesn't necessarily mean he's with Horeb, does it—I mean, the Nephish."

"If there's a Maachathite soldier in Dedan lands, he's with the Nephish, no doubt on that score."

My hands began to sweat. "But if you've spotted a Maachathite spy, that means the army could only be a day or two behind us. I thought we'd left them at least two weeks behind."

"Scouts are usually several days ahead. In fact, we already have scouts in Nahom and Sheba. They rotate, some staying in the cities, others riding back with fresh horses to bring us news."

I gazed past him to the camels and horses being organized to go south of the fortified city. A few other men were dressed similarly to Asher. "I—" I lowered my voice so as not to disturb Seraiah, who was sleeping. "How often have you visited the southern lands?"

"Only once about a year ago. My father took my mother and me to visit Kadesh and his family. When his—" The young man stopped, and I wondered what he'd been about to say. "Why do you ask this?"

"I'm sure it's silly. I once heard a rumor about magical serpents that guard the frankincense trees. Did you ever see one? Are they dangerous?"

He smiled. "Don't worry, my lady. The kingdom of Sariba is a dream on earth. A piece of heaven itself, fashioned by God's hands."

An odd premonition spiraled up my belly. Asher was keeping something from me—from us—too.

"You'll fit in perfectly, my lady. You and Kadesh on the throne will mark days of glory that lie ahead."

I waved away his flattery. "Asher, please. Stop that."

His face held a look of pleasure. "You just said my name out loud. For the first time."

Embarrassment flooded me, and my face grew warm.

"I don't say these things to flatter you, my lady. I speak only truth."

"I could never accuse you of lying." I lifted my eyebrows, referring to the reassurance he'd given me that morning on the bank of the river when I'd emerged from my bath.

How did I know he hadn't been spying on me from the

moment I walked to the water's edge? What if he'd watched me undress and bathe and dance? I'd done nothing to be ashamed of, but a strange guilt spread through my belly. I worried I'd done something that would hurt Kadesh if he knew about the incident at the pond. So many things about Asher made me uneasy.

A flush rose up the boy's face. Had I struck at the truth?

"Have you always lived at home with Chemish and Isra?" I asked, feeling bold.

"Mostly. From the ages of ten to fourteen, my parents sent me to Salem to live with my uncle, who provided schooling for me."

"So you know how to read and write?"

"Yes, I'm my father's scribe when needed."

"You have many talents, then," I murmured.

Another Edomite rode up, wheeling his horse before Asher could say anything more.

"We leave now!" the man shouted.

Asher mounted in one fluid movement, grasping the reins of his horse in his fist. He shot a quick glance back at me and gave a nod of farewell.

Closing the door of the camel litter, I sank into the cushions, placing an arm across my eyes. So Asher was educated. The writing tablet he gave Laban was most likely his with a message written by Asher's own hand. But I didn't believe for a moment Laban knew how to read.

I glanced over at Seraiah to see how she fared. I would have sworn my grandmother's eyes blinked closed as she pretended to be asleep.

Two hours later we set up camp on the south side of Dedan. Kadesh helped my father erect a shelter for Seraiah. She was barely situated when she began to develop a cough.

Chemish fixed a hot brew while my father paced in front of the makeshift tent.

I tended the fire, trying not to fret. Worry tugged at my father's face, as though the weight literally pulled at his skin. He finally pulled me aside. "Chemish says her heart is failing her."

Seraiah made a whimpering sound and I dropped to the rug next to her. "My heart is not failing *me*," she said in a raspy voice. "My heart is failing my body. This pathetic, diseased vessel wants to return to dust while my soul climbs toward God."

"You promised to see me married," I reminded her. I didn't want her to give up and leave me. I wanted her to see the frankincense lands, to see my wedding. "And wash my first baby at his birth."

Her breathing was shallow. "I shall do everything I can to fulfill my promises, my dear Jayden, but life doesn't guarantee us anything."

"She needs to rest," Chemish said. His eyes held sympathy when he took my father by the elbow to his own hearth so they could talk. The aroma of cardamom seeped into the air, the comforting smell reminding me of home.

Seraiah grasped my fingers. "I think that Edomite doctor dropped a sleeping potion into my tea."

I smothered a smile. She was correct. "You must get your rest," I said, tucking the blankets around her frail bones and lifting my voice in pleas to God to spare her. A brisk wind roared down the Hijaz mountains, snatching away my feeble prayers.

Later that night, the sound of shouts woke me. I sat up with a start, but my grandmother blessedly slept on.

Jumping up, I stared into the midnight blackness. The fires were out; not even glowing coals remained, which was odd. Had the fires been purposely stamped out?

The skin along my neck prickled. There was no moon. Even the stars were hidden by high clouds.

Before I could take a step forward, horses shot past my shelter, so fast I felt the wind they created. Crouching, I dared not call out. There was a flurry of activity up ahead, and the sight of men without faces, scarves hiding everything but their eyes. More shouting and yelling—and then silence again.

I snatched up my dagger, accidentally slipping a finger along the blade and drawing blood. *What is going on?*

I dared not leave my grandmother alone, but seconds later both Kadesh and Asher materialized out of the blackness.

"Jayden!" Kadesh said with relief.

I jerked at his shirt, trying to breathe normally. "You're alive."

Asher held up a candle stub, pointing to the blood on my finger. "Are you all right?"

"It's nothing, just careless with my knife." I tucked the blade back into its sheath and wrapped a piece of linen to stop the bleeding. "I heard shouts. Who was on those horses that just flew past?"

"A few of my scouts on their way to Dedan," Kadesh answered, but he wouldn't look me in the eye.

"What happened tonight?"

"Two of Horeb's scouts infiltrated our camp."

"*No,* that can't be. Horeb will know where we are by morning."

Asher shook his head. "It's worse. Horeb is only a day north of Dedan."

"H-How did they know where we were camped?"

"They followed us back after an encounter we had with them in the city."

"We have to leave. Now." I heard the panic in my own voice.

Kadesh rubbed my cold hands. His dark eyes glittered under the starlight. "Horeb's scouts can't confirm our location. They're dead."

My legs weakened. I sank to the sand, shivering.

"As soon as we knew someone was following us," Asher added, "we raced back here, destroyed the campfires, and then confronted them in the desert. They tried to escape back to Dedan, but we caught up to them."

Something about this didn't make sense. Horeb's army wasn't supposed to have caught up to us so quickly. I looked at

Asher curiously, remembering his last encounter with Laban. He'd given Laban a message—could it have been meant for this night?

"It's almost dawn," Kadesh told me. "We're packing up now."

I gave a nod, standing as he departed to organize the companies with Chemish.

Asher turned to follow, but I stopped him. "Prince of Edom," I said, my voice stronger than I expected.

"Yes, my lady. Do you need help taking down your shelter?"

"No, I can manage. But I want you to answer a question. May I have your sworn word that your answer is the truth?"

He frowned. "Of course. I've pledged my allegiance to you."

"I've seen you with Laban. A man I don't trust to do anything that does not benefit himself."

"You're a good judge of character, then."

"I'm sure you know the story of how he treated my family last year—and Kadesh, a sworn brother of the King of Edom. Why do you confer with him? Why did you give him a letter? I saw Laban hide it in his cloak."

Asher's eyes fastened onto mine. "You did?"

"I know you're a trained scribe. Which comes in cleverly useful for writing correspondence."

"Yes, I gave him a letter. A letter to take into Dedan for a caravan going north. The letter is for my mother to give her news of the journey and assure her all is well."

"Why couldn't you find a caravan yourself?"

"As your assigned bodyguard I wasn't sure Kadesh would send me into the city."

I gazed at the flurry of camp breakdown. "The raid tonight seems ill-timed. Horeb's army wasn't supposed to be so close."

"He has good scouts."

"No better than ours who know this land so well."

Asher bowed to me. "I'm sorry, but we must hurry from here."

"Yes, we must," I replied.

When he walked away from me, I swore Asher was trying hard to hold himself in control. To not look back at me with guilt. Had he just lied to me—or only told half the truth?

I pictured the stops we'd made at Akabah, the Fountain of the Red Sea, the Midianite town, and now Dedan. All places I'd seen Asher with Laban. Every one of them a convenient location to leave directions for Horeb's army to follow us.

Shaking off my irrational thoughts, I bent to wake my grandmother then gather our personal items. I jumped when Seraiah's hand clenched my arm.

"Grandmother, you startled me. We must leave. Horeb is upon us." To my horror, my voice shook.

"I heard your conversation with Asher," Seraiah said.

I pressed my lips together. "I must be imagining things. None of it makes any sense."

"You must tell Kadesh," Seraiah said soberly.

"How can I cast doubt on a boy he's known since a babe? Chemish's own son?"

"We live and die by God's will, not because of a secret Nephish spy."

I merely nodded, fearful of what was to come if we didn't leave immediately. But I couldn't stop thinking about Asher and Laban as potential spies for Horeb.

16

It was still dark when our caravan raced away from the Dedanite city and its rich, fruitful oasis.

The weather turned hotter—and worse, humid. My clothes stuck to my skin, and there was no relief at night either. We weren't as close to the beach any longer, but traveling a wide coastal plain of mudflats and barren soil, mountains a hazy dream far to the east.

The first two days south of Dedan we didn't even stop at night to camp but pushed on with only brief breaks and water stops. There was almost no vegetation for our camels to eat and the wells were more brackish. Dragging buckets from the small, hand-dug wells took hours to water the animals, slowing us down even more.

When I napped in the heat of the afternoon I woke sluggish and ill, as though I'd been poisoned. I couldn't imagine making this trek during summer. The heat, humidity, sand, and salt were almost more than I could bear.

Seraiah slept fitfully, waking at dawn soaked in perspiration. I cooled her face and neck as best I could with a wet cloth, but her strength was diminishing. I spent afternoons fanning her with palm fronds.

Occasionally, I glimpsed tents far off the main trail, flocks of goats or sheep picking the desert clean of greenery. A lone tamarisk tree here and there made a solitary landmark.

Beds of black lava rock stretched from eastern volcanic peaks until the flat plain dropped into the sea. Our camels complained bitterly, but there was no avoiding the sharp rock without going far out of our way.

"The mountains we have to climb will come soon enough," Asher told me when I asked about the hard rock.

Shay swiveled her head with a grunt, as if she understood the trail would become progressively more difficult.

"How far?" I asked, using clipped words. I found myself impatient with him. I really needed to talk to Kadesh, but there was never the right moment, or a private place.

"A few weeks. The mountains are grand and majestic, but full of animals to hunt. My slingshot and I will provide for you, my lady."

"I'm not yours to worry about," I reminded him.

He gave me a sober glance. Asher was my guard and stayed close at my side, but often a flash of Horeb stalking me crossed my mind. Did Asher remind me of Horeb? This harmless boy was nothing like him, but Horeb was never far from my thoughts. By now, he would have discovered his dead scouts at our Dedanite camp.

"We'll make it to Sariba first," Asher assured me. "They don't know the trail like Kadesh does. They'll have to stop more often and longer for supplies. As his army grows, so does his need for camels and water bags and food."

"As his army *grows* . . ." I echoed. Fingers of alarm snaked down my throat. I was exhausted. "I'm going to check on my grandmother."

"Have I said something to offend you?"

"Of course not," I said irritably. "It's Horeb. Everything *always* comes back to Horeb. We're exposed here in the open desert. I'm being hunted every day."

Asher unhooked the slingshot from his waist. The sling was woven of black and white goat hair just like our tents. Two straps came together in the middle with a pouch to center the stone. The sling had been used so often it had become soft as fine, supple leather. "You'll feel better if I can capture some game tonight."

I gazed at the flat land with its poor, brackish water. "All I've seen for days are scorpions and spiders."

"We're getting close to the Shazer oasis. There are birds and locusts."

I stared at his sling, picturing it dyed black. "That looks just like—" I began, pairing the sling with another image. Kadesh's eye patch. I glanced up, but Asher didn't say anything, although I was certain he'd deduced what I was thinking.

"I think I need another sword lesson," I told him. The hour

practicing on my own each night wasn't enough. "Chemish, your Edomite brothers, my family—their deaths will be on my head. All because I ran away with Kadesh."

"We made choices, too. Loyalty and friendship to save those we care about."

"If I'd married Horeb, my family would be safe. King Abimelech would still be alive. Horeb killed his father because Abimelech formed an alliance with Kadesh—grounded on my union with Kadesh, and not Horeb at all. Don't you see?"

Asher shook his head. "I see it completely differently. You saved Kadesh's life. He would have died in the desert if you and your father hadn't taken him in and healed him. Sariba would have lost its prince. That country might already be in the process of being destroyed. At least you have freedom and peace."

"That's ominous. What do you mean?"

"There are forces at play that want to rid Sariba of its royal family."

"What sort of forces?" I asked. Kadesh had never mentioned any of this.

"Kadesh knows if he doesn't agree to certain stipulations, he will never be king—"

"You're speaking in riddles."

"I can't be much clearer. These are things Kadesh needs to tell you himself. But know this, if he doesn't marry you—the girl he loves—Sariba will not be the land everyone has loved for so long. A darkness will come over it, one that can never be erased."

I glanced up and found Kadesh staring at us. Startled, I

asked, "How long have you been listening, Kadesh?"

Asher shifted uncomfortably on his mount, as though he'd been caught spreading gossip.

Kadesh guided his camel closer. "When I met you, Jayden, I knew that I loved you. I also knew my homeland had a chance again. Before I found you at your mother's grave, I was dying from thirst and the wound in my belly. I started hoping I would die. Because death would save me from having to make terrible decisions—even though those very decisions might save my country."

"Kadesh, what do you speak of?" I began. "I thought we were running toward light and peace. But now . . . we have death behind us in Horeb's army—and death waiting for us in Sariba?"

Kadesh pressed his face against my palm. "Jayden, we have enough to worry about to stay ahead of Horeb's army. He's the imminent threat right now. But Asher is correct because when I formed an alliance with Abimelech, I knew Sariba had been given a second chance."

My mind trembled with a thousand questions. This was the most Kadesh had ever said to me about his homeland and the problems he was facing upon his arrival. "I've doubted the choices I've made. Fearing I'd brought death to you all."

"You made the best choice, Jayden," Kadesh said quietly. "For my family, for my kingdom—and most of all for me. While I was recuperating in the caves of Edom, I was devastated to think Horeb had you in his possession. That I'd lost you forever. You are our hope for a brighter future."

"But can I be when I don't even know what you're talking about?"

"I promise all will be clear when we get to Sariba. I'll tell you everything." But Kadesh's voice dropped. He was still reluctant. Almost as though he were afraid to tell me.

"I believe you," I finally said. "But Horeb is still after us. War *is* coming."

"Yes," Kadesh agreed. "War is coming from many fronts."

"I won't stand back and see those I love slaughtered."

"We're not going to be slaughtered—"

I held up my hand to stop his words of appeasement. Shifting in my seat, I stared behind me at the empty desert. It was almost as if I could feel Horeb reaching out to me with an unerring vengeance for blood.

17

Before dawn while Seraiah slept, I practiced with my sword. The various thrusts and swings Asher and Kadesh had taught me. After Asher had drunk his morning tea we parried together. He showed me how to improve my stance and use various strategic steps during a fight.

"You once watched a fight between Kadesh and Horeb," Asher said. "Try to remember the moves and strategy he used to get the better of Kadesh."

"Horeb tried to cheat."

"Then learn how to be a better cheater," Asher said with a quirk of his eyebrow.

"Easier said than done," I snorted. "He tried to cut down Kadesh when he was turning and recovering. Going for his shoulders, even his back."

"Being quicker and smaller will give you an advantage."

"It's true Horeb is larger, heavier. He does move slower."

"Remember," Asher said soberly. "During a fight for your life you must use every skill and maneuver—and cheating—to stay alive. Horeb and his men won't give you a second chance."

Fighting Horeb would not be a regular game of parry. It would be life-and-death.

"Next lesson I'll teach you how to disarm your opponent."

I liked the sound of that. While the men loaded Seraiah into the litter and strapped the bull camel and our possessions into place, I spent a bit of time learning how to use the sling-shot of soft, brown deerskin Asher had created for me. The straps were the perfect length for my arm.

A stream of birds flew over the waters of the Shazer oasis. Grouse and swallows twittered in the trees. I spied a population of pink and white flamingos standing in the far reaches of the spring waters.

Holding the laces between my fingers, I spun a small stone in the pouch to launch it. I was oddly proud to wear my sling on my sash belt and my dagger in its sheath. No longer did I strap it to my thigh hidden under my dress. I needed fast and easy access.

Rocks crunched behind me just as my stone hit a small hare. As I felt his arms slip around my waist, I leaned back against Kadesh. "An excellent shot. Jayden, princess of the northern deserts, I do believe you should be a queen someday."

My lips twitched with laughter. "Is that a marriage proposal, Prince of Sariba?"

"A proposal a thousand times over," he said in his distinctive accent. The familiar longing coursed through me. "I wish you weren't so keen on swords and slings."

"This war with Horeb is about me—you—us. Not Sariba. I refuse to be cornered in a sewer hole with only a dagger to defend myself."

"You always have an answer to all my arguments. I'll make you queen and lawyer both."

Turning, I lifted my face to his. "Trust me, Kadesh. Please trust me."

His hands slipped down my arms and we stared at each other in a new way. Our relationship had become tentative, cautious, filled with new, emotional dangers the past few weeks as he continued to stay silent about his parents and homeland.

Kadesh gathered me up with the intent to kiss me, but I placed my palms against his chest. "If you truly love me, you will believe I can help you. I will guard your secrets with my life. Do you believe that?"

"I do, but I—I can't break down with a hundred men who need me to be their leader. To keep up their morale through the worst part of the journey. This is not the place to discuss my family or the political business of my country."

I knew he was right. My arms went around him and we held each other, not speaking. Kadesh buried his face into my neck and I ran my fingers through his soft, thick hair, wanting him desperately, but feeling cautious. "Kadesh," I finally said in a low voice. "I fear there might be a spy among us."

He reared back, shock on his face. "What are you talking about?"

"Laban and Asher—"

"Asher is not a spy!"

"Asher may be an unwitting accomplice."

"But I trust Asher with my life. He's a boy, only eighteen. His conversations with Laban are nothing more than camp tasks. I'm sure of it."

I shook my head. "I've seen them pass messages between them."

"That makes no sense. Like what?"

"Thin tablets for writing correspondence. Asher admitted he'd written letters home. But I saw an exchange three times. Why would he use Laban and not ask you or Chemish—or personally give them to a caravan headed north to deliver?"

"Because he already has the important task of protecting you."

"Why the furtiveness between them? Horeb caught up to us faster than we ever expected. He was *upon* us at Dedan. We barely escaped."

"That's true," he said slowly. "But I don't understand their motive. If Horeb overcomes us on the desert, we'll be slaughtered—including Laban and Asher."

"Not if Laban is paid first and slips away."

"He swore allegiance to me and this trip to Sariba. Because he knew I needed the best fighters."

"Or perhaps because he saw an opportunity."

Kadesh began to pace, casting glances over his shoulder at the men engaged in their morning tasks about the camp. "I don't want to suspect them of treason. . . ."

"I hope I'm wrong, Kadesh, but something is going on. Please, just be extra cautious."

When we returned to camp, the animals and men were ready to leave. Kadesh scooped Seraiah up from her makeshift camp bed as though she weighed nothing more than a feather. After placing her into the litter, he yanked on the camel's ropes to pull the animal to its feet.

Heat steamed from the dew-frosted rocks as the sun hit the ground.

I tended to my grandmother, coaxing her to drink a soothing herbal tea and nibble a date. She wasn't well and her strength was leaving. I sang and told stories just as she had done for me all the times I was ill as a child, but my spirits felt depressed with the weight of Horeb so close. Constantly, I checked behind us, dreading the sight of his arm bearing down.

Leila's whereabouts in Egypt never left my mind either. Why had Egyptians taken her, and where had they gone? Egypt was enormous. A person could be hidden away there for the rest of their life. And what would be the High Priestess's motive for selling the girls? Except sex slaves, especially beautiful ones, brought a high price of gold.

A warm wind parched my throat. Spring was flinging itself at us and my worries over Horeb, and Leila and Sahmril, who were now both missing, were flinging me into a state of madness.

"All of Leila's belongings and dresses were gone," I told Seraiah, going over the events at the Temple of Ashtoreth. "Even Mother's alabaster box."

My grandmother's black eyes were shrewd. "I suspect something but have no real guesses. I don't trust that Armana *hasn't* sold her into slavery in Egypt."

I shuddered to hear her own fears mirroring mine. As I helped my grandmother lie down again, her long gray hair lay matted in coarse threads across the pillows.

"Perhaps Leila merely gave in to temptation," Seraiah said quietly. "But I suspect the girls were lured away from Tadmur on some sort of pretense."

"What could be worse than prostituting themselves in the name of creating a divine conduit to the goddess?"

"Many things could be worse, my darling girl. Sacrificing women to the gods who rule over Ba'al and Ashtoreth. Gods such as Moloch and Elkenah."

"You mean girls—like Leila—volunteer to die for the Goddess?"

"That, and worse. Sacrificing children, babies. In the belief it will keep the Goddess happy and the land and women fertile."

The images she conjured made me sick. "If Leila knew these things she would never have joined with the priestesses at the temple."

"Unless she . . . was influenced by something else. Lied to by someone who wants to use her in some way." My grandmother's fragile fingers fumbled for mine. "Jayden, listen to me. There are rumors the Sariba goddesses use magic. That they have magicians to help them. I don't know how much of the gossip is exaggerated. And . . ." She paused while I stared at her in horror. "I don't know if Kadesh's royal family is part of it."

I was horrified. "Kadesh would never condone such horrible acts."

"But the royal family must know and doesn't stop it. City governments work hand in hand with the temples for many civic functions and taxation."

"You don't think Kadesh, that he—goes to the temple to appease the Goddess?"

Seraiah's breathing grew labored. "You need only look into Kadesh's eyes to know he has a good and honest soul, but I worry after hearing of Leila's disappearance. She was safer in Tadmur." She shifted on the thin mattress, trying to get more comfortable, her eyes closed now. "I must rest now."

"Are you warm enough, Grandmother? Have you had enough to eat?"

She was already asleep, her fingers cool in my hot ones, the skin thinner than the fragile wings of a butterfly, her veins a mass of blue streaks. She curled on her mat like a small child, her back hunched with age.

I pulled a blanket over her shoulders, stricken anew over my sister.

Magic. The word hurled terror down my spine. What was Leila caught up in? Kadesh had never even hinted at something so powerful, so sinister in the southern lands. Magicians. People who used spells and magic as their livelihood. Would I be able to identify them? Would I recognize their curses and enchantments, the tools of power and persuasion?

A chain of events had begun months ago that I didn't understand and had no way to stop. Did the threat of powerful magicians explain Kadesh's agitation, his melancholy?

When we camped that night, I refused the erecting of a shelter. "We'll stay in the litter," I told Kadesh. "Seraiah is too fragile to move."

At one moment my grandmother became restless, eyelids fluttering. But then she quieted, hardly moving. Refusing food and water. Her mind seemed to float between this world and a world only she could see, her lips often moving as though speaking with someone who wasn't there. I held her small hand in mine, not daring to press it for fear I'd crush her delicate bones.

That night I sat beside her, hardly moving myself.

At midnight her eyes opened. "My last wish," Seraiah whispered, "was to see the well of Hagar, our Egyptian mother. The desert of Ishmael's exile. The spot where God's miracle of water kept them alive."

"We'll take you there," I promised as we both drifted off into an edgy sleep at last.

We were to leave at daybreak, but dawn hovered at the edge of the world, tentative and delicate. Lingering, it seemed, just for us. Knowing we needed extra time this day.

When I woke, my hand was still clasped in Seraiah's. Her fingers were cold. I pulled the blanket up close to warm her, but then I saw her still, wax-like face, the features marbled like a fine statue, her chest not moving, I knew she would never be warm again. At least not in this life.

My grandmother had passed through the veil of death sometime during the night. Her purple-veined hand was folded around mine, already stiffening with the signs of death, but a smile remained on her face. The youthful, mischievous smile I'd known my entire life.

I dropped to my knees, bowing my head over her lifeless form. *"No,"* I whispered, grief rising up from the bottom of my soul to choke me. "No, sweet Grandmother. You can't leave me, I need you too much. I have no other woman of my tribe left to help me, to teach me. You promised to stay, at least for a few months longer."

I'd known in my heart she wouldn't make it to the southern lands, but I'd hoped and I'd prayed. Now I held her cold, tiny body in my arms, weeping for all I had lost. My grandmother had protected me, helped me survive, had fought for me before Horeb, Judith, and the tribal council. She didn't blame me or chastise me. She'd supported my choices to chase after my dreams—to live the life I wanted to live.

Cradling her face with my hands, I whispered, "You've blessed me so much, my sweet, funny, and wise grandmother. I'll never forget the night of my betrothal celebration, when you transformed into a young girl, shaking out your hair, laughing as though it were your own betrothal all over again. Dancing with hips of wisdom and beauty. Teaching me the ways of our ancient mothers who live in the world beyond this one."

My tears fell harder, staining my face, but I tried to smile despite the loss of my last ally in womanhood. "Perhaps you're luckier than me. You're with Grandfather, my mother, baby

Isaac, your sisters, and our heavenly mothers." I swallowed past the thickness in my voice. "One day you and I will dance again together. We'll laugh and sing and cradle babies together."

Movement at the door made me lift my head. Kadesh's figure filled the opening of the cramped door of the litter. His face crumpled at the sight of Seraiah's gray, unmoving form. "Oh, Jayden, I feared this. I'd hoped my physicians could tend her when we arrived in Sariba."

I pressed my fingers against my temples, a throbbing headache forming. "Even when we left Tadmur I don't think she had much time left. In the end, I think that's why she wanted to come with us. But *I* needed more time with her. I wanted her to see the beauty and wonders of Sariba."

Kadesh brought me close and brushed away the tears running down my face. "I did, too. She would have loved every piece of it."

When my father came to the door, I left him alone to say good-bye. Outside the litter, I sank to the earth and buried my face in my knees. Slow moments ticked by. The sun was shining, and a light breeze bowed the grasses out on the desert. Just like every other day. No wavering mountain on the horizon had shifted its position to mark this day of grief.

The sky arched overhead like a brilliantly blue glazed bowl, and yet, my heart was a hollow of hurt that couldn't be filled. My grandmother's death was the fifth loss in our family in little more than a year.

When my father stepped out of the litter he looked worn down. He'd lost his home, his tribe, his camels, and his position.

He moved like a broken man without hope, but all he said was, "I'll bring water for you to wash her."

"Father," I called. Jumping up, I ran straight at him and wrapped my arms tight around his middle. He patted my back with his big hands, murmuring words I didn't understand. But I knew he was weeping into my hair.

Finally he released me, touching my shoulder as if he didn't know what to do next. "We'll find Leila," I promised him. "And Sahmril."

He didn't speak. I wondered if he'd lost hope. It would be so easy to lie down and never move again. Let the desert swallow us up, dry out our bones, and then tumble those bleached bones across the sands.

"Your grandmother loved you with all her heart," my father said suddenly. "As did your mother." We gazed at each other and then he walked across camp on shaky legs without looking back.

Soon Kadesh brought heated water, clean white sponges, as well as a small pot of frankincense oil and myrrh to perfume Seraiah's body.

I worked alone, clenching my teeth, willing myself not to cave in to the fresh grief. I cleansed my grandmother's body with warm, salted water, and then dressed her in her finest red dress.

When I tied the sashes around her waist, I sang her favorite song of the desert. Sweet, haunting words of sleep and dreams, of fresh rain washing away the worries and strife of life. Outside the litter, I heard the men tamping down the campfires, hiding evidence we'd been here.

When I placed the final pieces of jewelry on Seraiah's neck and wrists, the hot sun was heating up the interior of the litter. I melted to the floor, stroking her bony arm. "Please tell my mother I'm doing my best to keep my promises." I paused, trying not to fall apart. "I sometimes wonder if she sent Kadesh to us when I danced at her grave. I wonder if she led him to the cliff to find us so we could save each other. I'm so lost and afraid. I need you *here* to help me figure out the mystifying secrets of my new homeland." But my words fell on silence.

I'd combed out my grandmother's silvery hair and now it was long and loose, free as though she were a child again. "Oh, Grandmother, I love you," I said, lifting my head to see if I could spy her spirit fleeing upward into the skies.

When I finally opened the door of the litter, Kadesh and my father were waiting for me. Asher stood off to the side with Chemish, their clothing smudged with dirt. Grave-digging tools clenched in their fists. Sympathy lining their features.

We buried my grandmother in the midmorning light, and I was grateful the harshness of noonday hadn't yet sapped our strength. This time I stood to the side and watched. I didn't need to pile the rocks as I'd done with my mother's grave. This time my father and I were not alone in our grief.

When my father tried to replace the mounds of dirt by himself, Chemish lifted my father's hands away and completed the task. "This is a fitting spot for Seraiah. She's close to the spirits of her ancient grandmothers."

I spent a few moments at my grandmother's grave after my

father and the others left to ready for our departure. I danced briefly, reaching my hands to the sky to show her how much I loved her. Finally, I made my way back, too, knowing we had to keep moving.

"Jayden, you should ride in the litter," Kadesh said when I approached. "Mourn in private this day."

Soon our caravan was moving down the flat straits again. The camels looked particularly magnificent. They swept forward in pounding strides, galloping nearly as fast as the Edomite horses. When we climbed up rises and down into hollows, their necks stretched forward as though drinking in air.

A flock of gray falcons skimmed along the distant Red Sea shoreline. Two eagles floated on an invisible pocket of air, gliding as elegantly as Hakak had danced on her wedding day. The same day I'd secretly danced for Kadesh while he watched me from the folds of his cloak. My grandmother's hooded eyes had seen it all. And suspected everything.

The trail ended in a swell of sand dunes and rugged mountains. Those same mountains mocked us with their height, even as they shaded the trail.

Kadesh pointed to a vertical path cut into the side of the jagged peaks. Several thousand feet of stone and precarious ledges stabbed the sky. "We need to climb that escarpment straight up those cliffs until we reach a plateau. When we reach that new plain we'll continue south to Nahom and then straight east to Sariba. We're getting closer," he added.

"You have a strange sense of time," I told him, trying not to droop as we entered the third month of travel.

"Before we head to Sariba, we'll visit the Queen of Sheba in her city of Ma'rib."

"You *know* the Queen of Sheba?"

"She's my distant cousin, remember?"

"You said your great-great-great-grandfathers were brothers about a hundred and fifty years ago. I didn't think you had family gatherings."

Kadesh lifted his eyebrows to grin at me. "The queen is our ally in the frankincense trade. Normally I oversee the caravans only as far as the land of Sheba. Her kingdom facilitates the routes north along the Red Sea, which we just traveled, all the way to Damascus, or west to Egypt."

The ascent up the mountain was slow while our animals picked their way along the steep and twisting path. Every moment I worried we'd tumble backward in an avalanche of loose shale.

At one point, I looked down to see the blues and greens of the ocean below us in a sheer, vertical drop. I wobbled in my seat, feeling light-headed at the dizzying height.

"A dazzling view," Asher said behind me. "But alarming. Just keep Shay focused on the camel in front of her so she doesn't lose her footing."

Conversation ceased as we concentrated on the climb. I imagined Seraiah in the litter, the camel struggling under the burden of the swaying carriage, and cringed. It was better she lay in the peaceful desert where God had communed with our ancestors, but I missed her good humor and wit terribly.

We reached the top of the escarpment at sunset. The

mountain range shuddered off along the eastern shores of the Red Sea. Sweeping furrows of rock slashed straight down to the sandy beaches. Buzzards and hawks wheeled overhead in the blustery winds.

We approached the city of Ma'rib within the land of Sa'ba, making camp at a spring on the outskirts. The golden, arched gates of the city of the queen sparkled under a red ball of setting sun.

Being here seemed to have cast a spell over the Edomites. They talked of nothing except the Queen of Sheba's beauty and mystery. What would Horeb do when he came through? Would the queen allow his new army to pass without cross-examination—to travel onward in determination to kill us?

I ate my dinner in silence. It was the best one we'd had in days—wild asparagus and scallions with lentils and chunks of roasted rabbit.

After eating, Kadesh rose to leave for the city. "I haven't seen the queen since my caravan passed through here last year. I hope she recognizes me," he added dryly, touching the scar on his face and adjusting his eye patch.

I glanced at the filthy hem of my cloak and the dirt under my fingernails, grateful I didn't have to meet her. I hadn't had a true bath since the river at the Fountain of the Red Sea.

"Jayden," Kadesh said. "I hope to introduce you tomorrow before we leave again."

"I'd be mortified to appear at all. I have nothing but ragged dresses."

"When we marry, she'll be at the top of the guest list. For

now, stay here and rest, my princess of Sariba."

"I'm not a princess yet." I lowered my voice. "Is it pessimism to fear there are forces that are still going to try and stop our union?"

"I promise there's no one who can stop us from uniting in marriage."

Asher stepped around the campfire, an odd look crossing his face. The two young men gazed at each other, unspoken words passing between them.

Why did I keep getting the feeling there was an unknown threat still ahead of me in the land of Sariba? Something or someone who would stop us from marrying?

And it wasn't necessarily Horeb.

My grandmother had also alluded to it with her warning of the powerful Goddess cult.

I'd hoped we'd be leaving the Goddess temples behind with Tadmur, Mari, the cities of Babylon, and the land of Canaan, but it was a foolish hope. Idolatry had spread to every people and every city; there was nowhere to hide from the influence of Ba'al and Ashtoreth.

Now I had to worry about a goddess in Sariba that lured its citizens to partake of the illicit activities. My grandmother only knew gossip and rumors, but there had been real fear in her eyes when she spoke of the Goddess in the mysterious southern lands.

Forces would try to pull me away from the life I loved. Or from Kadesh, to whom I'd vowed to devote myself.

I'd already stood up to the High Priestess Armana, fought

her, and challenged her. I could do it again.

But there was something bigger than the Sariba goddess lying in wait for me. Another woman who would fight me for Kadesh. A girl who had a royal claim to the boy I desperately loved. A girl who would destroy me to win Kadesh back.

18

Stars pricked the sky like silver pins when Kadesh set out for the palace. My father followed me about camp. He watched me cook, sharpened his knife, lost in his own private thoughts. Chemish urged him to sit at his campfire, but my father pleaded fatigue and retired early. Exhaustion from the journey was winning out over other distractions.

Kadesh's family relationship with the powerful Queen of Sheba was a soothing balm. We were safer here with the Sheba army than out on the desert, alone. Tonight I didn't have to fear an attack when I fell asleep.

Soon after the evening meal a servant arrived from the city with a handwritten letter. Asher read the message and came toward me. "Kadesh says the queen has summoned you to the palace."

I glanced at my shabby clothes and soot-smudged hands. "I

couldn't possibly meet the queen like this. Tell them I can't—"

"Kadesh sent his assurances. I'm to take you straight there."

I plucked at my appearance while we walked. I was ashamed to go to the palace so bedraggled and fought the urge to turn around and run back to the campsite.

Inside the golden gates, hundreds of citizens crowded the wide avenues. Shops and restaurants rose up on both sides of every road. Families and couples mingled, others walked home from work or tried to strike last-minute bargains as shopkeepers closed for the day.

We passed an outdoor theater ablaze with lights. I could hear actors on a stage, the audience laughing. Such a strange sight.

The city of Ma'rib was completely unlike Mari under siege last summer with its wary citizens and Babylonian soldiers on every corner. The palace sat on an expansive grassy knoll, lamps burning in every window. The architecture reminded me of a crumbling old castle we'd passed on the road into Sa'ba.

I'd day-dreamed about what it would be like to live there, its dark empty windows filled with warm yellow lamps. Kadesh and I would be perfectly content away from the insanity of the world around us. Safe to raise our family and dote on our children.

Now I stared up at the palatial bastion of the Queen of Sheba, sick to my stomach.

Lanterns were strung along manicured pathways. Perfectly tended gardens exploded in a profusion of blossoming color in late spring. Giant palm trees spread their wings of green in carefully planned rows. Cushioned chairs had been arranged under small canopies for citizens or dignitaries to engage in conversation along the walks that paralleled shimmering ponds. A fountain shot sparkles of water into the night air, turning various colors of the rainbow under the lanterns.

"Do you like it?" Asher asked, close at my elbow.

"I'm speechless at such loveliness."

A moment later, Kadesh strode toward us on the paved walk. His cloak swirled about his legs and my stomach jumped at the magnificent sight of his bearing. "Are you finished with your meeting?" I asked when he greeted me.

"I received a message when I checked in with the secretary of state. My appointment time is between the first and second watch of the night. But," Kadesh glanced up from the note. "The queen requested the presence of the girl of Nephish."

"How does she know about me?"

"I mentioned you to her myself. When I notified her we had left Tadmur and were on our way back home."

Kadesh corresponding with queens who ruled powerful kingdoms was a life I knew nothing about. "Have we—have I—done something wrong?"

He shook his head and smiled. "She just wants to meet the girl I love. She's sending one of her maids to fetch you at the east doors. Asher, will you escort Jayden there while I go back to the receiving room foyer to wait? And then you can return to camp. We should have scouts arriving tonight. If they get to camp before I do, please send them to Chemish."

At the mention of scouts, my palms turned clammy. I

both yearned for and feared the days when the Edomite scouts returned with news of Horeb's location.

Kadesh bent down to kiss my palms, and then lifted his head to look into my eyes. "The palace maid will turn you from a dusty traveler into the princess you already are."

Asher held out a hand to direct me to the eastern doors. "This way, my lady."

We'd barely passed the fountain when Laban appeared at the corner where two paths met. He nodded at Asher, and his mouth cracked into a smile filled with bad teeth. I sucked in my breath, my skin crawling. It still bothered me he was on this long journey—even if he was a ruthless soldier known for his skill in a battle. I suppose if the man ever managed to kill Horeb he'd rise in my estimation.

"What's he doing in the city?" I said to Asher. "How did he know I was here?"

"He didn't know; it's a coincidence, I'm sure. He has an assignment to purchase supplies for the animals," Asher said, moving ahead on the path while I slowed. Realizing I wasn't at his side any longer, the boy turned. "I have a list to give him that Chemish prepared."

Servants and palace guards brushed past me while I watched Asher speaking with Laban. But hadn't the young man told me Laban couldn't read?

A few moments later, he ended his conversation and returned to my side. My voice was edged in sharpness. "Don't give me silly excuses about letters and food supply lists. What are you really writing for Laban?"

Asher cast a glance downward. "If you must know, we have an envoy of spies following Horeb's armies. We report on our location and plans going forward. They're helping to protect us, my lady. Protect you. Which I do gladly. And"—he gave me a sheepish smile—"Laban can slip in and out of places like a shadow. He knows these towns and cities well. We're in good hands."

I chewed on my lip, staring at him. "If you say so, I'll trust Laban then."

At that moment a young girl appeared. With a curtsy, she murmured a greeting in an accent reminiscent of Kadesh's. "My name is Zara. I've been instructed to take you to see the queen. Please follow me."

I didn't obey, but glued my feet to the ground. "I'm sorry, but I can't."

"My lady?" Confusion flitted across Zara's face.

"What's wrong, Jayden?" Asher asked, moving closer while Laban slinked away into the evening's shadows.

"Have you looked at me lately?"

"I look at you every single day."

I rolled my eyes and Zara blushed, immersing her attention to the study of her sandals.

I lowered my voice. "I refuse to meet the Queen of Sheba in a dirty cloak and with grimy feet."

"Lady Jayden," Zara interrupted. "My task is to *prepare* you for the queen's receiving room."

Before I could speak again, the girl took my arm and whisked me down the path. Zara gave three distinct raps on a door under an awning and we were ushered inside.

The castle was an explosion of hallways and receiving rooms larger than either of the goddess temples in Tadmur and Mari. Ceilings so high I had to crane my neck to see the intricately carved upper windows.

Fluted ashlars and pillars crafted to resemble actual granite from Egypt ornamented every corridor. Arched windows decorated with carved grapes and filigree overlooked gardens and shimmering pools. Everything was gold and carnelian, topaz, and amethyst.

"Come, my lady," Zara said. "The queen doesn't normally see people on the last day of the week. She made an exception because the prince is her cousin and you're only in Ma'rib for one night."

She hurried me along floors painted in hues of rose and magenta. The texture was smooth as glass under my rough feet, as if I were walking on pillows of air.

All at once, Zara pulled me inside a bathing room. The girl's fingers were deft as she stripped off my dress before I could utter a word of protest. Next, she dunked me into a large square tub of warm water. With expert skill, she scrubbed my skin until it was raw.

"Your elbows and knees are a disaster," she murmured under her breath.

"I'm sorry," I said, embarrassed at the condition of my body after more than two months on the trail.

Zara lifted her chin and blinked significantly.

"I've said something wrong."

"A lady never apologizes for her state of disarray when she's been traveling. All of our women and servants—even the queen herself—need much care and grooming after a trip north, or when they travel to Egypt or Nubia. That's why I'm here."

"I've never had a personal servant before."

I thought Zara was going to faint from shock. "That's dreadful. They say *you* are a princess, too."

She was appalled, when actually I was only a poor nomadic girl whose father couldn't even afford a dowry of camels.

Her eyes lowered. "They say you will be princess of Sariba—and that your betrothed is hunting you in the desert."

I let out a choked laugh. "Who are these people who tell you these things?"

Zara pressed her lips together, focusing on exfoliating the skin along my ankles, where brown dust was embedded in every pore. Next, she washed my hair, lathering and rinsing quickly. The coarse, brittle texture disappeared as she combed out the tangles from weeks of wind and sun. Running a light mixture of rose oil through the strands, she turned my hair into soft, silky strands.

A knock sounded at the door. "We're almost ready!" she called as another girl poked her head inside. The girl disappeared and Zara doubled her swiftness, if that was possible.

Over my head went a gown of flowing brocade. She tightened a silk sash around my middle. "You have a tiny waist," she observed. "Especially for someone so tall. You're thin as a flower stalk."

"It happens during long treks."

"I can only imagine! Never would I want to make that trip."

"There are wonderful vistas and mountains and oceans to be seen," I said, wistful for my deserts.

Zara led me to a dressing table next. Brushes, jeweled clips, and a smattering of face creams and makeup lay in a wide array. She proceeded to apply a delicate cream to my chapped skin and sunburned nose. "Take some with you. You'll need to apply this to your face for the rest of your life to preserve your stunning looks."

"The word *stunning* is much too strong," I contradicted.

Zara lifted an eyebrow. "Just wait until you look in the mirror. Now hold still." She applied fresh kohl and a lavender color that actually glittered to my eyelids, then a touch of rouge to my cheeks. Last, she brushed out my hair in strokes to speed its drying, fluffing out the ends. Expertly, she created a twisted pile of curls, fastening it all in place with amethyst clips. Tendrils of hair floated along my neck.

Sitting there brought back a wave of memories when Leila helped me with my hair and makeup on the night of my betrothal celebration. That was one of the last times we'd giggled and talked about the future, just the two of us, in the back room of Aunt Judith's tent. I'd called her an Egyptian goddess when she wore a skimpy skirt and jewels in her navel. It was the first night I'd danced before the women of my tribe. The night I'd felt the power of myself, and the glory our Mother Goddess had given us at creation.

I missed Leila's sauciness, her daring, and the sisterhood

that tied us together, even if we were a continent apart. When we saw each other again I hoped our hearts would still be knitted together. That we could begin a new future.

"Come, it's past time!" Zara commanded, snapping me out of my nostalgic reverie. "But first, look at yourself."

She led me to a bank of mirrors under the high, arched windows. I didn't recognize the girl looking back at me. The transformation was incredible. My face had a lustrous glow, my eyes were larger and darker than ever, and the gown was exquisite. Zara had done my hair in true elegance. The amethyst stones made a stunning replacement for my usual clips of bone.

"Now hurry!" Zara grabbed my hand as I slipped my feet into gold sandals.

The royal receiving rooms weren't far from the dressing rooms. Strategically located for travelers fresh from the desert.

To approach the throne room, Zara escorted me through a courtyard. Painted tile floors lay beneath my feet, warm from the day's heat. Massive columns rose in archways overhead.

A guard opened a set of double doors overlaid with ivory panels.

Zara whispered, "Good luck, Lady Jayden!"

She ran lightly down the hall. I reached for her, but my fingers only found empty air. "Where are you going?"

She halted. "You do this part alone."

"But—I—"

She came back to squeeze my hand, and then impetuously leaned in as if to tell me a secret. "I've heard the Sariba lands are the most beautiful in all the world. But be careful. Ma'rib gossip says the women are cobras that will eat you alive."

I was so astonished I couldn't even form a reply. In an instant Zara was gone in a flutter of waving fingers and flying dark hair.

With a deep breath of trepidation, I walked through the door.

19

The throne room had paintings along the walls depicting battles from long ago; queens and kings with flanks of soldiers riding home in victory. The carvings in the floor glowed with white irises and drifting rose petals. Rows of columns held up a massive ceiling sculpted in stars and suns and moons.

Plush velvet chairs and couches lined the walls, but they were empty tonight.

When I advanced up the center of the room, Kadesh was already standing before the dais. He wore a gold-threaded tunic and his hair hung loosely about his shoulders. His cloak was missing, which struck me oddly since I'd rarely seen him without it. He looked almost like a stranger, except for his smile.

His eyes traveled over the dress I was wearing and my hair decorated with jewels. The look in his eyes made me blush.

How I wished I could run to him, but I reminded myself to proceed with decorum, holding my head straight so the jewels didn't fall off.

I took another step to grasp the hand he held out to me, but a woman's voice rang out. "Stop where you are. Come no closer."

My eyes jerked from Kadesh to an elegant woman sitting above us on the gold throne. Lamps situated on tables about the perimeters of the hall cast shadows of light and dark. The Queen of Sheba wore a gown ten times the worth of mine, the cut impeccable. A gold crown studded with diamonds, emeralds, and rubies perched on top of her head. Strands of pearls looped along the sides of her ebony hair.

She pointed her chin at me, but directed her words toward Kadesh as though I wasn't standing right there. "Is this the girl you've been telling me about?"

The abruptness of her manner surprised me. I'd expected to be introduced, not merely referred to like an object.

"Your Majesty," Kadesh said with a bow. "May I present the princess of Nephish, Jayden, daughter of Pharez, great-grandson of Ishmael from the family of Abraham."

"A fine lineage," the queen acknowledged stoically. "My great-grandfather once met Abraham and the prophet Melchizedek when they visited the holy city of Salem."

There was a brief moment of silence. I didn't have a clue what I was supposed to do. Except curtsy to her. Which I did, slowly, my head down, legs shaking, ordering myself not to fall on my face.

The queen and Kadesh were cousins, but she was older by at least ten years. I knew nothing about her family or politics or character.

"How old are you, daughter of Nephish?" The queen spoke with a serene but detached tone.

My shaking voice betrayed my nerves. "I'm in my eighteenth year."

Pointedly, the queen turned to Kadesh. "What have you *done*, my cousin?"

Kadesh raised his eyebrows. "What are you referring to? I've done nothing."

"You're going to bring the wrath of your own kingdom down on your head."

I sucked in a breath. She disapproved of me. I'd done nothing to deserve it, except come from poverty.

"You've gone against every law of propriety and decorum to travel with her, unmarried, with a rabble of Edomites, no less."

"I can give you a dozen reasons, my queen," Kadesh said, with the faintest trace of impatience. "Very good life-and-death reasons—which you probably already know. Jayden's father travels with us as well. We are never unchaperoned. And, just for the record, my rabble of Edomites is quite the opposite." He bowed again and lifted his head to smile at her. I could see the boyishness in his face, and his efforts to get her to relax.

The queen's expression never changed. Surreptitiously, I glanced about the throne room, wondering if she had to keep up a distant decorum in front of the guards and advisors who stood as shadows about the dais.

The queen leaned forward, putting a finger to her lips while she stared. "Is she . . .with child?"

Kadesh was immediately irritated. He glared at the queen and came toward me, but my own outrage spilled out before I could stop it. "Your Majesty. Queen of Ma'rib and the great land of Sheba. You invite me into your throne room and then insult me? You deride my virtue? Question Kadesh's honor as well as the honor of my good parents? My mother who is dead from childbirth and to whom I made promises that I have faithfully kept?" My voice continued to rise. I couldn't seem to stop myself. "My honorable mother who taught me exactness in decorum—"

"Jayden," Kadesh whispered, pressing my fingers in his. "This is the queen. . . ."

I swallowed my emotion, keeping my voice low. "Yes, she's the most beautiful and powerful woman on earth. But she knows nothing of me or my family, and yet assumes the very worst about us."

I didn't realize my whispers carried through the hall, snaking around the columns and sculptures. The queen's intuitive lavender eyes held mine. The ridges of her face grew softer, filled with a morsel of respect.

Yet my voice still shook. "I've never known such an honorable man as Kadesh, except for my own father. He has never—we have never—how dare you accuse us of such great impropriety." I stopped, conscious of the fact that the queen was not talking over me. Or trying to stop my words from tumbling out of my mouth. Perhaps I'd sealed my fate and would now be thrown out.

She gave me an even smile. "I'm glad we've been able to get to know each other, Jayden. I can see why my cousin likes you. You are very beautiful as well as spirited. I admire those who defend and love their parents, too."

I inclined my head, acknowledging her words.

"But from the view of my throne, you have a serious problem. You have broken a covenant with your tribe. With your betrothed."

Her words startled me, and I had to refrain from gasping.

"Do not underestimate my knowledge," she continued, "even though we live in the far southern reaches of the uttermost parts of the earth."

The queen conveyed a calmness I didn't feel. But she received people here in this room every day of her life. She'd been trained to meet with politicians, ambassadors, and other royalty of the desert kingdoms.

"I use scouts and spies liberally," she said matter-of-factly. "I'm already aware an army made up of Nephish, Maachathites, and Adummatus is en route. My kingdom is in its path. I have no quarrel with these tribes. I've been in a peace-keeping treaty with the latter tribe for far too many years. I won't fight them for you, Kadesh—although I could, perhaps, make things a bit 'difficult' as they travel through my lands."

Kadesh entreated her. "You know I would be grateful—"

"Then again," she interrupted, "they may try to skirt Ma'rib—and me—completely. Avoid any confrontation.

Bypass my border taxes. It might be foolish to seek them out, and I won't destroy them for you. Your war is not my war, and I won't bring the peaceful people of Sa'ba into it."

"I understand," Kadesh said, but I could tell he wasn't happy. We'd both secretly hoped she could stop the advancement of Horeb.

The queen rose from her throne and descended the stairs, closing the gap between us. The draperies of her gown flowed like water over the inlaid ivory and parquet floors.

Movement caught the corners of my eyes. Advisors and castle guards in crisp uniforms with ferocious sabers at their belts stood in the shadows under flickering wall sconces. Listening to every word we spoke.

I was foolish not to realize our conversation would be public—even if they were trusted advisors to the queen.

Suddenly, the monarch of Sheba stood right in front of me. Barely a hand's width of space between us.

"Dear cousin Kadesh," she said in a gentle tone I hadn't heard before. Her eyes glanced imperceptibly into the corners of the room. Two soldiers moved forward as if to restrain us from accidentally touching the queen, but she waved them back with a flick of her wrist. "Once you arrive in your kingdom, I trust you will know when you need to call upon me. Send scouts with word. We'll be ready. Right now go home and organize your Sariba army. Prepare for war."

My jaw dropped. *Prepare for war?* The words were so chilling. So matter-of-fact.

Kadesh inclined his head toward hers, but his eyes were on

the guards. "I'm already making plans. I'm eager to get home and meet with my generals and captains."

I was surprised at this news, and yet not surprised.

Softly, the queen added, "Use our code word so we won't be deceived by imposters."

Kadesh nodded, as if he knew what she was referring to. There was so much past history between them I felt off balance. The lands of Sa'ba and Sariba had political maneuvers, correspondence, and the strategy of a hundred desert tribes.

The queen's eyes locked onto mine. "And you, young lady. I wish you luck as well as God's blessings."

"Thank you, my queen," I acknowledged. "But as for luck? I don't understand."

"I could wish you happiness in your future life, but you're going to need more luck than anything else. Fate can be quite fickle, and luck a rare commodity. You're going to need providence as well as courage. Most of all, you're going to need your wits. Trusted guards and maids. And a foolproof plan." With these last words of advice, the Queen of Sheba gazed significantly between me and Kadesh. "A difficult task lies before you. Horeb's motivations are as great as yours. He's amassing larger and more dangerous armies than just a few small tribes. A treacherous combination. Horeb is a man who wants to rule the world."

With that ominous prediction, the ruler of Sheba swept her gown about her feet and returned to the dais. Before the gilded throne, she indicated our audience was over. I bowed deeply, holding out the heavy brocade skirt of my own gown, puzzling over her words and the double meanings.

When I lifted my head again, Kadesh was kneeling at the dais. The queen put a slender finger, heavy with jeweled rings, under his chin. He lifted his eyes to hers and they gazed at each other for several moments. Then Kadesh took her hand and pressed his lips into her palm.

I couldn't tell if they spoke. If they did, it was so quiet I wasn't able to discern any words.

A strange envy rose in my chest. Was there more to their relationship than Kadesh had told me? Even if I had ten maids bathing and dressing me I would never be as beautiful as she was. In my heart, I was just a simple camel herder, a girl of absolutely no consequence in the queen's sphere.

Before I arrived this evening, had Kadesh and the queen discussed his choice for a wife? Had she chided him, berated his wisdom?

My throat burned with unanswered questions when Kadesh retrieved his cloak and we left the receiving hall. His hand was on my arm, but I walked the corridor in a daze. I was no match for the women of these foreign lands. I didn't doubt my feelings for Kadesh, but I wondered if I was a thoughtless girl chasing a foolish dream.

Not a moment later, Kadesh whispered, "In here, Jayden."

"What—" My words were cut short as he opened a door and tugged me into total darkness. The door shut behind us. Darkness surrounded me. My heart was in my mouth. "I can't see. Where are we?"

"Give your eyes a moment to adjust."

It didn't take long before a torch lit up the narrow hallway we were standing in. "What's happening?"

Before Kadesh could answer, the Queen of Sheba appeared—seemingly out of nowhere—beckoning us into an antechamber, a small furnished room, barely big enough for the three of us.

"Sit down, Jayden," the queen said. "I'm sure you're feeling light-headed."

She was right. I sank into a soft couch. "What's going on?" I asked.

"My cousin and I need to speak freely," she said gently, pressing her hand into mine for a moment to reassure me. It was as if she had become someone entirely different from the impersonal woman I'd met in the throne room.

Kadesh glanced about the simple paneled room. "It's been a long time since we met here."

"And that's a blessing," the queen said wryly. "Unfortunately, our peaceful days are over. You need help, my cousin-brother," she added, sinking to a chair.

"But I thought you said—" I started.

"Decorum can be a disadvantage in the public receiving halls, dear Jayden," the queen told me.

I blinked at the change in her personality, confused.

"Kadesh, you've been gone a long time and you need to know what's happening in Sariba. Running away last year only exacerbated the turmoil."

"I didn't run away," Kadesh objected.

"It's understandable after—after all that happened—to

want to roam the deserts, get lost in the cities, and forget the pain . . ."

"But my flight led me to an answer to my prayers," Kadesh said, gazing at me as if I was everything to him. Only moments ago I'd been jealous of his relationship with the queen. I had to come to terms with the fact Kadesh probably knew many women and had friendships and alliances with a multitude of people I would never know.

The queen's next words astonished me. "I wanted a more private audience with both of you, to tell you I approve of your Nephish princess, Kadesh. My words in the throne room were for the benefit of my advisors."

Still standing, Kadesh towered over us both. "You put on a good performance, my queen."

"I've had a lot of practice," she said, lifting an eyebrow. "But there are two more things I must tell you before you leave Ma'rib." Her brows knit together, creating lines along her previously smooth face. She was older than I'd first thought.

"You're worrying me now," Kadesh said.

"You *should* be worried. First piece of advice: marry Jayden as soon as you get to Sariba. If you two are going to marry, then don't wait. Announce it soon. Make the preparations for the wedding of a king. For you will soon be king, I predict."

Kadesh's face went white. "My uncle?"

"Ephrem is alive, but unwell, I'm sorry to say. You know his health has been failing. He may survive a year—and he may not. But a true king must have a lavish wedding nobody will forget or question. A wedding so sumptuous and extravagant

Jayden will immediately become legitimate in the eyes of the people of Sariba. And will erase her betrothal to the Nephish king. She must be your unwavering choice as the wife of your heart. Not just as an alliance—there can be none now since the Nephish leader is on your heels. My spies tell me he's closer than you think. *And*—this is the worst news I have to tell you—the Nephish king has allied himself with the Assyrians from Damascus."

"The Assyrians!" Kadesh spun about the room, aghast. "The Assyrians dominate the northern deserts. I would never have dreamed Horeb was powerful or savvy enough to pull it off."

"The Assyrians have long wanted to wage war with Babylon and King Hammurabi. They'd love to overthrow him. And to find the secret frankincense lands. Because we—you—hold the wealth they need to conquer Babylonia."

"Horeb is no fool, then," Kadesh said, shaking his head from side to side. "By following Jayden to Sariba he gets her, has a chance to kill me again, and takes my throne."

The queen nodded sagely. "Horeb wants to rule the world and is cunningly aligning the two greatest kingdoms on his side against us. And . . . he has other alliances you should be warned about—and should fear with all your heart."

"What are you talking about?" Kadesh scrutinized the queen's face.

Even though he asked the question, I had a feeling he knew exactly what she meant.

"You need to take care of it," the queen added, so softly I strained to hear her. "The sooner the better."

"I'll handle them."

"This evil can't be *handled* any longer. It grows powerful and insidious, spreading not only from Sariba but to my own city of Ma'rib. When Horeb arrives, there will be all-out war and many innocent people will die."

"But Horeb only wants revenge. And Jayden."

"Kadesh, I fear you're being naïve. It may have started with revenge, but his hunger for power grows. That's why he made this Assyrian alliance. They hope to rule the world just as King Hammurabi rules now. Taking control of the wealth of the south is intelligent and strategic. To own the frankincense and spice trade, the seas and ports, the caravan trails and wells. When he has it all, the king of the Nephish can squash Hammurabi and the Babylonian kingdoms in a matter of months."

Kadesh rubbed at his face, horror in his eyes. "The life we know will be decimated."

"And so will peace be forever decimated. The Assyrians and King Horeb will rule with tyranny and cruelty. That's why we *must* succeed. At all costs. Even if the cost is repulsive to us."

"Why the secrecy from your advisors?"

"They say I'm overestimating the threat." The queen sighed. "I'm afraid once we're under attack it may be too late. Your army is better trained and equipped, and with more loyal and willing soldiers."

"But we are small—"

I darted a glance at him, the unexpected admission turning my stomach upside down. I thought Sariba had a hundred thousand soldiers.

The queen said, "I remain hopeful. That's why you need to get home as fast as you can."

"I wish I'd known this sooner. . . ."

"It's difficult to write these warnings in letters that are sure to be opened and read by others over the space of many months."

Gravely, Kadesh paced the small room. "I can rally my country and my army, but I don't want to carry out . . . your request. How *can you even consider it?*"

"Believe me; it makes me ill to contemplate. I've hardly slept waiting for your arrival. But there is no other way. We need to stop them before we're the ones lying dead in cities of ashes."

I went absolutely cold. "What are you referring to? What could possibly be worse than Horeb and war?"

Kadesh's eyes remained on the queen's face. "Are you positive?"

"Prepare your special forces. But we need to move slowly so as not to alert the wrong people."

"You're frightening me," I said. "Please, what's going on?"

The queen took my hand in her cool one, her fingers laden with jade and rubies from the Nubian coast. "Jayden, your only worry is Horeb. And even *he* is a pawn in a much bigger plan, though he does not know it."

Both of them spoke in riddles. I was more afraid now than ever.

"Horeb is bringing the largest army we've ever had to face. Keep Asher with Jayden at all times, Kadesh. They'll try to kidnap her and use her as leverage."

"Who will? Horeb only wants me to legitimize his throne. And make sure I never speak the truth about him."

"Dear girl, the Maachathites, the Assyrians, everyone will try to use you in a battle for power against one another. They are all enemies who would grab the chance to stick a sword in one another's backs."

"Trust me," I said. "Nobody will get the chance to get close to me."

The queen laughed sadly. "It's not a matter of trust, my dear girl. The Goddess of Sariba is watching, waiting for us to make a wrong move. A black widow ready to pounce and eat us alive."

20

I was shaking on the return trip to camp. I couldn't stop thinking about the queen, her unparalleled beauty, the warnings, and the need for a clandestine meeting.

My growing suspicions about Sariba and Kadesh's riddles about his past life were coming true. Something bigger than me or Horeb was happening here. But what did the Goddess of Sariba have to do with anything—except my sister Leila was a follower of Ashtoreth. And Ashtoreth was a sister Goddess to Sariba. That was the only connection, right?

Perhaps the queen was subtly referencing my sister in all this talk of war. Did she think I'd abandon Kadesh and turn to the religion of idol worshipers? Leave him to be overthrown in a revolution?

I stopped on the dark trail. "What is the Queen of Sheba to you?"

Kadesh looked puzzled. "She's my cousin, my strongest ally. Two tribes linked by generations of blood and family."

A sick sensation churned at my stomach. "Cousins marry all the time. We both know that. What better way to unite two kingdoms than through you and her? I'm surprised you haven't already joined together." I hated the words, but I had to speak them out loud. "If things are as bad as you both say, wouldn't that be the best solution?"

Kadesh grasped my hand, whirling me close. "What are you saying, Jayden? You want me to marry the Queen of Sheba?"

"No! Of course I don't *want* you to. But she—you—" Tears bit the corners of my eyes. "The way she looked at you. The way you kissed her hand."

His eyes searched mine under the starlight. "I've known her all my life; of course we love each other. We're family, but she's also more than ten years older than I am."

"Age never stopped marriages between royal families before."

Kadesh put his hands to my face, leaning into me, his lips a breath from mine. "The Queen of Sheba has her king, a prince of Ethiopia. They have children. The wealthiest royal couple in the known world. Long ago, King Hammurabi tried to woo her, but she refused, although he would never admit it."

"I see." My voice sounded small and foolish. "I'm sorry. The queen has just given us disconcerting news, and I'm acting like a jealous child."

He wrapped me in his cloak and pressed his lips into my hair. "There was never a question of her and me. She married while I was a young boy. *You* are my love, and will remain so for the rest of my life. I only wish we were already married. I'm sorry you misinterpreted tonight's meeting. If we were already married so many things would be easier. I just want to get home and show you my world. But . . . the queen gave us sound advice. My aunt Naomi will help us prepare a royal wedding fit for a king and his bride and leaving no doubt as to my loyalties and alliances."

Just when I thought I understood what was going on, more rose up to confuse and confound me. Foreign alliances, Assyrians, magical goddesses. I'd been flung off a cliff with no way to keep myself from dashing against the treacherous rocks below.

"I have a gift for you, my future wife," Kadesh added, brushing his lips against my forehead.

"A gift?"

"Call it an early wedding present." Kadesh slipped his hand into the folds of his cloak. A heartbeat later, he produced a resplendent sword in a casing of finely tooled leather with brass trim.

I could hardly speak. *My own sword.* "It's—it's simply gorgeous."

"Unsheathe it," he said, just like an excited child on the best morning of spring.

I pulled out the weapon from its leather sheath. The bronze-colored alloy gleamed under the starlight. Most remarkably, the handle was engraved with the same etchings of the Sariba homeland as Kadesh's sword.

"It's just like yours," I whispered. "Oh, Kadesh!"

I stared in wonder at the beauty lying between my open palms. A year ago I could barely lift Kadesh's sword, but this was shorter, lighter, just my size. And I was stronger now, practicing every evening until I dropped into bed.

"I had it specially crafted for you—and ordered a silversmith to engrave the Land of Sariba's stamp for you."

"You must have planned this long ago. To order it specially."

"The sword was tooled right here in Sheba. It's been waiting for us the last few months."

"But up until recently you were arguing against me having a sword."

"I don't want Horeb to ever see your face again, but I know it's foolish not to have you prepared in every way possible."

I ran a finger along the gleaming bronze, testing the sharpness of the edge with my thumb. "This sword will forever bring your face and strength to my mind." I moved closer, giving him a teasing smile. "Shall we spar right now, Prince of Sariba?"

He gave a low chuckle. "We'll work on foot moves tomorrow—maybe more than that—my beautiful Jayden."

His fingers lingered on my cheek, but a weight remained on my chest.

"I'm bringing danger to your people. I want your family to love me, but how can they look upon me with any degree of welcome when we're about to be ravaged by Horeb's army?"

"Try not to think of things that may never come to pass."

We stood under the stars and I savored his hands on my

waist, the touch that set my nerves on fire. I slipped my hands inside his cloak and wrapped myself tight against him. A wind howled across the edge of the Empty Sands that bordered the land of Sa'ba. This refined country boasted running water and every comfort, but it still lay under the watchful eye of a deadly desert.

"I'll try to banish my fears to those Empty Sands and imagine Horeb's army carried away by the deadly winds. Never to be seen again."

"Jayden," Kadesh whispered, pulling me closer as his lips touched mine. I'd forgotten how miraculous his mouth was. My hands gripped the back of his head and his warm lips softened as they tasted mine. An ache of yearning filled me.

I knew this would be the last moment of comfort before we left Ma'rib and embarked on the final leg of the journey. I tried to forget all the danger waiting for us and bask in this moment. A moment that would have to last until our wedding night.

At night I practiced using my new beautifully etched sword. Tying rock weights to it, Asher forced me to swing the sword a hundred times over, again and again. The muscles in my arms burned so fiercely I could barely lift my satchel the next day.

But miraculously, even after just a week, the sword felt so much lighter my moves instantly became quicker. When I sparred with Kadesh or Asher we used wooden practice swords to prevent injuries, although one evening I caught Asher when he wasn't paying close attention, snatching at the hem of his cloak.

"Ha!" I cried. The Edomites who were watching applauded my success and I grinned with the praise.

The men finally broke apart and went off to bed. I sighed with contentment, feeling stronger, closer to being able to hold my ground in a real fight.

I'd barely headed to my own sleeping spot when unexpected shouts broke the quiet night.

Two Edomite scouts rode hard into camp, kicking up dust, their horses white with lather under the light of the fire. The men circled, yelling for Chemish and Kadesh.

I stood stock-still, staring at them. The cries of alarm portended bad news. My heart lodged like a stone in my chest while sweat trickled along the inside of my dress.

Edomite soldiers, half-dressed and ready for bed, surged toward the scouts. Chemish and Kadesh rose from the fire, their dinner half-eaten.

"My lord!" the first scout cried to Kadesh.

"Let's speak around the fire," he told them. "Get some food."

"There's no time." A wild look was in the man's eyes. "Horeb's army left Ma'rib a week ago. They've caught up. They're right behind us."

Chemish instinctively pulled his sword from its sheath.

I bit down so hard on my bottom lip I tasted blood.

"How close?" Kadesh asked quickly. "How soon?"

"They're fast on our heels," the first scout replied. "A day at most. We rode as fast as we could. Our horses are nearly dead."

"How many?"

"An army bigger than our eyes could fathom stretched clear across the desert."

My legs couldn't hold me. I sank to the ground, my sword falling next to me. "Dear God in heaven. We're dead."

"Take care of your horses," Kadesh ordered. "Let them breathe while we pack. Stay at the rear of the company so they have a little more time to recover. If you're our rearguard you can alert us if we need to stop and organize ourselves for a fight." Turning to the Edomites, he shouted, "We pack and leave immediately!"

Voices raised in questions and alarm. Underneath it all fear laced the words. We thought we'd had time to get to Sariba safely.

Laban stepped forward. "How can we fight if we travel all night and all day tomorrow?"

"That's the point," Kadesh said, his face filled with distress. "I don't plan to fight at all. I won't sit here waiting to be ambushed by three organized armies. With our small numbers and no reinforcements, we'll be slaughtered in an hour."

Chemish spoke up, agreeing with Kadesh. "Our best chance is to stay ahead of them. I'd rather die in Sariba than out here."

"Organize your animals and companies," Kadesh shouted again. "We leave within the hour. Seth and Jabal, your job is to destroy the well. Leave no water for Horeb."

"That's cruel to his animals," Laban muttered under his breath.

I watched Kadesh try to hold his anger in check. "Your

words are madness. We're talking about one of Horeb's camels—or our lives."

Laban waved his sword in the air, pacing before the fire. "I won't be a coward. I'll take my chances here. All we have to do is talk to them. Sign a truce of peace."

Chemish stared at the man as if he'd gone insane. "You swore allegiance to Prince Kadesh. You're an Edomite, which means you're my citizen, a member of my army."

I found myself walking forward, my sword heavy in my hand. The words of the Queen of Sheba pounded in my head. "None of you know Horeb like Kadesh and I do. He hasn't come all this way to sign a truce for peace. He'll take me and then kill you all in the most brutal fashion."

Kadesh moved closer to Laban. "Why would you want to face thousands of Assyrians and Maachathites in the desert? There won't be time for talks. They'll march right over us before we have a chance to utter a single word."

Chemish gave a grunt, brushing off Laban's words. "You're a crazy thief, Laban, but you're not suicidal. You know what we're up against. The whole purpose for our expedition is to get Kadesh and Jayden to safety in Sariba."

"We've been traveling at breakneck speed for months," Asher said from behind his father. "That's why we have our own small spy convoy so we know where Horeb is and how to avoid him."

"Shut up, you fool!" Laban hissed.

Dead silence followed his outburst. Kadesh and Chemish stared between Laban and Asher, a terrible disquiet spreading like a disease among the Edomite soldiers. The men began to murmur again, gathering about, their faces darkened by sun and hardened after weeks of desert trekking.

Nothing made sense. Asher had assured me the letters he was writing for Laban were left in strategic locations for our scouts and spies. Correspondence home. Receipts for supplies.

But neither Kadesh nor Chemish had ever mentioned them.

My eyes bore into Laban's face as the memory of furtive meetings came together in my mind. I looked at Asher, who appeared completely unsettled. "There's something more going on here," I said, stepping forward.

"Stay away from him, Jayden," Asher said, cutting in front of me. "Laban is a madman. Don't anger him."

"Don't patronize me!" I screamed. With both fists, I swept up my sword and swung it toward Asher, catching him under the chin.

Asher's eyes widened. He held out his hands to show he was unarmed, but at the moment I didn't care. When he tried to move backward, a trickle of red dribbled down the length of his throat.

"I could take you right now," I told him evenly. "I could kill you."

"Jayden!" Kadesh stepped between us. "Drop your sword! How could you threaten the prince of Edom? These are strong accusations."

I flicked my eyes across Asher's face, not lowering my sword one bit. "Haven't you noticed how much faster Horeb has been traveling the last few weeks? In a land and on a trail he's never seen before? Despite the fact *we've* been traveling hard and fast most of the way. It's impossible to move three armies at our speed. To water hundreds of animals at each well."

"Perhaps he hired guides," Asher suggested.

"*Perhaps* he hired a mercenary thief and a traitor." My words were soft, but in the horrible quiet everyone heard them. "Kadesh," I ordered. "Search Laban's pack, all of his belongings. He's been leaving secret missives at each town and city. He's been telling Horeb where we are, how to travel, where the wells are. That's the only thing that makes sense."

"No, Jayden, you're mistaken. Laban has been sending information to our own spy envoy." But Asher's voice shook with apprehension.

"If Laban has nothing to hide, then Kadesh won't find anything, will he?"

"Laban can't read or write," Asher said. "How could he have placed letters or notes to Horeb or anyone?"

"Because you've been helping him," I said. "You're a pawn in Laban's treason, Asher."

The eyes of the entire Edomite army were on me. The murmurs, the arguments, the talk all around me was making me dizzy. I was crazy to accuse the son of Chemish of being a traitor. But Asher and Laban had secrets that needed to be exposed. Especially with the news of Horeb so close. We could all be dead by morning.

"Not many people in camp can read or write," I added. "Except a trained scribe."

Chemish surged forward. "Are you accusing my son of

conspiring with Laban to lead Horeb's army to us?"

"Conspiring? I don't know. Only Asher and Laban can explain themselves."

Finally I lowered my sword, glancing toward Kadesh. I wanted his help; I wanted him to believe me. I'd just put myself on the outside of every man who had crossed the harsh desert to help me and my family. I'd just questioned every single one of their loyalty.

"The girl is dreaming up a tale of complete insanity!" Laban shouted. He plunged the tip of his sword into the sand with defiance. "Search her belongings! Horeb is *her* betrothed. Perhaps *she's* leading them to us!"

His accusation took my breath away. I was accusing Asher of hurting his own father, his own people. Of exposing me, a girl he secretly loved. None of it made sense. Perhaps I was merely exhausted, my mind conjuring a mirage? I couldn't think straight any longer. But I was in too deep with my accusations to back down now.

But as for Chemish and Kadesh, perhaps they'd been too trusting, too blind to see the strange relationship between Asher and Laban. Laban a man of forty with a history of rogue fights and thievery. And Asher, a young man barely past youth, the son of the Edomite leader, who should have very little to do with a man who was normally on the fringe of society.

"Oh, Jayden, what are you doing?" my father said. He took a step toward me, shaking his head, telling me to stop. He thought I was putting us all in peril. But that was Horeb. Horeb who was within hours of us. Death was coming quickly. I could envision it. Taste my own bitter fear on my tongue.

Without another word, I dug the tip of my sword into the sand, leaving the handle upright at my waist. I turned to Kadesh, and our eyes met. Perhaps the imminent battle made me overly confident, but my gesture said I wasn't backing down. Something wasn't right, and it hadn't been for many, many weeks.

All eyes were on us, but in the shadows of midnight I couldn't fathom what Kadesh was thinking. I'd just challenged him in a very public setting, the Prince of Sariba, the man I loved, the man who was soon going to be my king and ruler.

I said, "If I'm wrong I will pay the consequences, my lord. But I won't die at the hands of Horeb without knowing the truth."

Kadesh unsheathed his own sword and punched it into the sand. "Unload your packs. Chemish and I will search their belongings."

Asher turned pale. Laban spat on the ground. "This is an unjust search. I won't be subject to the whims of a woman!"

Chemish advanced toward the man. Despair filled his countenance. "I am your king and you will obey my orders—or suffer the consequences."

Asher was so pale in the firelight I thought he'd be sick. He wouldn't look at me, turning his back while he spread his belongings on the ground for his father to inspect. Among his personal bedding and clothing were his scribe tools: several thin tablets, a cake of ink, and writing stencils. "Father, I never meant this to happen," he said in a strained voice. "I never thought . . . I wanted to be useful. Laban promised the letters were for *our* scouts, *our* spies keeping check on Horeb's army in each city."

Chemish's face twitched as he stared at his son. "Asher, are you a fool?"

"I wanted to help save Jayden—the girl I—I was helping us all get to Sariba more safely."

His words punched me in the belly. "The letters you wrote weren't for a phantom envoy of Edomite spies. Laban was delivering them to Horeb's operatives. Horeb has known where we are every step of the way. That's the only way he could have navigated foreign lands and roads to gain more than a week of time."

"You were right all along, Jayden," Kadesh said. "It's the only thing that makes sense."

Out of the corner of my eye I watched Laban back away from the fire, trying to slip through the companies of Edomites.

"Laban!" I cried, but the other men had already seen him and grabbed the man.

Kadesh shouted, "Bring Laban to me."

Chemish's face held a strange mix of rage and sorrow. He kicked Asher's scribe tools and sand flew through the air. "Have you lost your mind?"

"I—I wanted to be useful. To prove I could help."

"Did Laban promise you anything in return for sending us all to our deaths?" Chemish asked.

"He said he had a cache of gold and silver. That after the trip I would be well paid for my work to help our expedition."

"He lied to you. He used you. And you were a fool to believe him. Never would I put a rogue Edomite to such an important task. Laban was only here as a fighter. And for that he was going to be paid well upon our return home." He paced the campfire in agitation. "Away with all of you! You have your orders. Pack immediately. We travel all night!"

The night became surreal. My chest pounded with fear of unfathomable proportions.

The Edomites groaned, returning to their orders with tired bodies and unsettled hearts. The din surrounded me, the stir of dust and sand while the men packed bedrolls and prepared their animals. Grabbed their dinner. Smothered the fires.

It was as though I were watching the entire scene from a great distance. My chin jerked when a flicker of movement out of the corner of my eye caught my attention.

Two men dragged Laban over and dropped him to the ground with his pack for inspection. For a moment I lost sight of him in the dark beyond the fire's dying light. A whoosh of sparks blinded me as someone kicked sand into the flames.

Far across the clearing, Laban rose from the task of emptying his pack, moving so quickly in the shadows nobody noticed. At that same moment Kadesh turned toward Chemish who was about to snap the writing tablets in half. Kadesh bent to stop him, murmuring, "Don't destroy the evidence."

I swore I was swimming through sand, wading through a black tunnel when Laban sidestepped, grabbed his sword from the earth, and lunged at Kadesh. Silent as a specter of death. Purposely striking at Kadesh's blinded left side.

Before I could think, I wrenched my own sword up from the earth with both fists. My eyes blurred when Laban's face appeared before me. I swung hard and our blades crashed together, the deafening sound of metal clanging wildly.

Laban gave a scream of agony. The glitter of his sword arced under the starlight. My bones reverberated from the impact, and the grip on my blade weakened from the force of the collision. I nearly dropped it, but his sword went flying.

Something wet spattered my face and Laban lurched toward me. Wheeling backward, I saw his hand was bleeding, blood flowing down to his elbow. Three fingers had been sliced off.

The night came back into focus. "Kadesh!" I shrieked.

I hefted my sword, ready to attack again, but Chemish and Asher tackled Laban to the ground. The Edomite kicked and fought, and Seth came to their aid. Soon Laban was pinned to the dirt.

Kadesh whirled toward me, his eyes wild when he comprehended what had just happened. "Jayden," he said, panting as though he'd been running. "You took down his sword. You stopped him."

My legs gave out and I dropped to my knees. "I saw him come at you. On your blind side. He was going to kill you."

He staggered toward me. "Jayden, you saved my life."

Laban continued to fight and struggle against the three men holding him down. Finally, Chemish punched him in the face, knocking him out. The Edomite king rose again and jerked his son close. "You're fortunate I don't knock you out cold, Asher. Now finish unloading Laban's pack."

Asher obeyed, shaking out the rest of the contents. A piece of correspondence written in Asher's own hand was wrapped up in Laban's extra shirt. Chemish scanned its contents and his face looked terrible. "How could you betray us? What did the man offer you besides money?"

"I never thought the letters were a betrayal!" Asher cried. "I'm sorry, father. Please forgive me."

Laban clawed his way up to a sitting position, holding his bleeding hand against his chest. "We're outnumbered ten to one," he snarled. "Horeb was going to offer us wealth *and* safety if we surrendered."

"You think you can sign a truce for the Edomite army?" Chemish's laugh was harsh. "For the Prince of Sariba? As though Horeb wants peace, you idiot. He didn't gather three armies, follow us for thousands of leagues across the empty sands just to sign a truce and give you bags of gold." He turned to Asher. "I've raised an idiot!"

Shouting to Seth and Jabal, Chemish ordered rope to tie Laban and Asher up. "I can't stand the sight of you," he told Asher. "How can I call you son?"

"We could have ended this before any bloodshed—and walked away rich," Laban yelled.

Chemish gave him a derisive glare. "Riches for you maybe—but death for us. You were a pawn in Horeb's game."

"Perhaps Laban isn't an idiot or insane," Kadesh said in a terrible voice. "If Horeb caught up to us out here in the Empty Sands, we'd be forced into signing whatever papers Horeb wanted us to—to prevent an outright slaughter. And then Horeb would take Jayden. And *then*," he added, "he'd ride into Sariba with his army—with *us* as his prisoners, and declare himself king. End of the so-called war. But he wouldn't stop there. The Assyrians, Maachathites, and Adummatus would plunder Sariba, forcing us into servitude while they controlled the frankincense and every trade route of the deserts."

"I didn't know what Laban was planning," Asher said. "The correspondence was cryptic. He lied to me."

"Your astuteness comes far too late," I murmured, and Asher winced.

"Where were the letters placed?" Kadesh demanded, standing over the young man. "Which cities?"

"The Akabah port, the Fountain of the Red Sea, the city of Dedan . . ." Asher's voice trailed off.

Kadesh looked incredulous. "Where was the first?"

"At the well south of the Edomite land."

Kadesh ran his fingers through his hair with a groan. "He's been able to follow us from the start. When the scouts came in tonight with news of Horeb's army, I thought it was bizarre so much luck was on his side. It all makes sense now."

"Jayden," Asher said quietly from where he sat tied in ropes. "You must believe I never meant any harm to come to you. Laban said we would kill Horeb and I could take Horeb's gold and make sure you were safe."

I closed my eyes. He was soundly unprepared for a conspiring thief like Laban. "Once Horeb captured Sariba he would have cast you both off. Or had you killed."

"All I wanted to do was to earn my own wealth, a place in

the world. I wanted to take Edom out of our poverty. Finish building our city." He glanced up at me. "I just wanted to save you, Jayden. I didn't want Horeb to hurt you. I could have protected you."

"You're no match for him, Asher," I said softly.

Kadesh's voice shook with rage. "You thought you could protect Jayden by bringing Horeb closer—a man you know nothing about? The Nephish King vowed to take Jayden and keep her as a slave wife. Jayden is not yours to protect. You were her bodyguard—nothing else! An assignment meant to teach you to grow up to be a man and a leader."

The words were harsh. Asher was shamed before me. Love had blinded him in incomprehensible ways. A foolish, naïve boy who had so much to learn. A boy who might never rule the land of Edom after this.

While Laban squirmed on the sand, Chemish spat into the fire pit now buried by sand. "A kingdom is hard-won through blood and sweat and protecting those you love at all costs. You've grown up sheltered in Edom. I brought you on this journey to learn how kingdoms, politics—war *and* peace— truly work. How we fight for the things we love: our families and country and faith."

Jabal and Seth hefted Laban between them. "What shall we do with him?"

There was a pause of silence.

"He's a traitor," Kadesh said. "He'll be executed before we leave. I won't take any chance of him leaving his last missive of information. Destroy the rest of the tablets and papyrus, Seth.

And destroy Asher's scribe tools."

Asher made a strangled sound. He dropped to his knees before his father and Kadesh. "My lords, please, have pity on me. I am your son, your brother. I'm not a traitor. I love my kingdom. I love Sariba. I didn't know Laban's plan. I would never have allowed Horeb to destroy us—or to take Jayden as his slave."

Kadesh whirled about, snapping his cloak. "Horeb's motives and actions are nothing you can stop or change, Asher." To Jabal and Seth he said, "I'll announce my judgment shortly. Punishment to be meted out before we leave."

Without looking back, Kadesh left the perimeter of camp. He shoved past the salt brush growing up through the sand. Strode down a hollow into the emptiness of midnight. My heart ached for him. I wondered where he was going.

The two Edomites checked that Laban's and Asher's wrists and ankles were secure. "Guard them," Chemish added, and he stalked off to see how the caravan was coming together.

It appeared as though we were ready to flee into the Empty Sands—the worst portion of the trip. Hotter weather. Fewer wells. And Horeb literally nipping at our heels like a mangy wolf.

I sheathed my sword, my hands still shaking. My stomach was ill; I wanted to throw up. I'd never felt this kind of sickening pain before.

Asher's eyes pleaded at me. "Please, Jayden, you believe me? You'll speak to Kadesh for me?"

"Don't, Asher. Don't beg me to do anything for you."

Then I turned on my heel and followed Kadesh into the darkness.

I found him kneeling on the dirt, his back bowed over, his head in his hands. What terrible decisions he had to make. How horrific our trip had become.

I yearned for my grandmother. Seraiah would have wise words for me, for Kadesh.

With quiet steps, I approached and knelt in the warm sand. Kadesh's shoulders tensed and I placed my hands on them. "Let me share your anguish," I whispered.

He raised his face to the heavens. Shafts of silver moonlight glazed the scarred side of his face. "I'm Prince of Sariba. Soon to be its king. And I don't know what to do. How can I execute men I've known my entire life? Men who volunteered to fight with me? To die with me?"

"But they thought they could defy death. And defy you. They thought they had a better plan. A plan that would mean all of our deaths—or slavery."

Rising to his knees, Kadesh pulled me against him. His face sank into my belly and his arms wrapped around my legs. I didn't hear his sobs, but I felt them. "To order an execution so far from home. Years before I ever thought I'd have to make such a decision."

I stroked his hair with my hands. "Laban is a traitor to you and his country and Chemish."

"But *Asher*! Chemish's own son! I saw him in Isra's arms

when he was three months old." He glanced up at me and there was a moment of silence between us. "Asher is in love with you, isn't he?"

I swallowed, scraping at the dryness in my mouth. "I believe so."

"Has he divulged his feelings to you?"

"Not—not in words. But in deeds."

"You should have told me."

"You have so much more to worry about than a boy with an infatuation."

"It's not an infatuation for Asher. I saw the way he looked at you tonight."

"Can he be forgiven? Can he atone for his stupidity and grave mistakes?"

"What he's done to our army, to you, is not easily brushed aside. Atonement is another question altogether." Kadesh's arms loosened when he sat back on his heels. I knelt down to kiss his eyes, his forehead, and the scar running along his cheek. "Never have I had to make a more excruciating decision."

"In one night, everything has changed," I said quietly. "You are being called to the kingship right here, right now. Without your Uncle Ephrem to advise you."

"I'm not sure I'm ready to be a king. Can I make these difficult decisions? Punish my best friend's child? Isra will never forgive me."

"A mother can never believe the worst about her own child," I said, thinking of Judith. Holding Kadesh tight, I wept with him. "But Chemish knows. He is a king, too. He will forgive whatever you decide."

"It has to be me, you know."

"What do you mean?"

"*I* must deliver the punishment to Laban and Asher. I can't ask their brothers, or anyone else. There *is* no one else. This was a crime against me and my country and my mission. If I stand as witness and judge both, I must be executioner as well."

We rose to our feet and embraced so tightly I could barely breathe. I clung to him, willing any strength I had left to seep into his soul. "I trust you to do the right thing for your conscience, for the good of your kingdom, and in the eyes of God."

"You know I have to punish, Asher. Despite his ignorance and naïveté. The other men have to know we won't tolerate any form of sedition or stupidity."

"I know," I whispered.

"You have more faith than I do, my love," Kadesh said bitterly.

"For tonight I'll have enough for both of us."

It didn't take long to organize the four companies of soldiers. They stood at attention for the verdict and penalty. Chemish's face was haggard, his expression broken. I couldn't begin to imagine his suffering.

Kadesh arranged to use Seth's bow and arrow while Laban was brought before the tribe.

The rogue thief stood alone before his Edomite brothers. There were bruises on his face and a split lip from Chemish's fist. His legs were tied with rope so he couldn't run. Two Edomite men stood on either side and blindfolded him. I hid my face, not wanting to watch his shame. Laban begged for mercy, and when that didn't come he screamed insults and rage.

Kadesh raised his voice so everyone could hear. "As Prince of Sariba and head of this expedition, and with full agreement from Chemish, King of the Edomites, I sentence Laban to death for crimes of treason and sedition, including regicide and the attempted assassination of his leaders."

No one spoke a word. A grave solemnity hung heavy.

Chemish stood soberly, not speaking. My father was somewhere within the ranks of the soldiers and I couldn't see him. When no one begged for Laban's life or put forth evidence to the contrary, Kadesh walked across the campsite. For a moment he stood directly opposite the convict.

I hardly dared to breathe when Kadesh lifted the bow, notched the arrow, and took aim. When he pulled the string taut, I saw a faint shaking of emotion. A heartbeat passed, and then Kadesh fired straight into Laban's chest.

The thief's raging words abruptly stopped when the arrow punctured his heart. He staggered, but still stood. Kadesh quickly notched a second arrow and fired it again. Laban gave a soft grunt and then fell face-first into the sand.

He hit the ground with a thud. The shafts of the two arrows snapped with a crack in the silence.

21

The screams of Asher were lengthy and horrible. Kadesh ordered him down a hill and out of sight of the camp to administer the punishment of twenty lashes. The camp was deadly silent as we listened.

I cringed with each stroke of the whip that echoed through the air.

There was a breath of relief when the screams finally stopped. We all waited, and then Chemish appeared, carrying his son. Asher was unconscious, his clothing bloodied and shredded. Chemish placed him onto his horse, tied him to the animal, and then rode beside him.

When Kadesh returned, his chest was heaving, his eyes bleak. Not a word was spoken while we mounted our camels and horses. The company, taking formation by groups, galloped into the darkness as the moon sank below the horizon.

Kadesh rode on my left and my father rode on my right, but not a word was spoken by anyone until dawn. I felt protected, loved, but the deep sadness would take time to absorb. The events of tonight would stay with me forever.

All I could do was ride beside Kadesh, pushing my camel in a never-ending race into a barrenness far worse than any we'd experienced up until now. A desert fraught with misery, glaring sun, and death. A desert without shade and little water. And Horeb's army breathing down our necks.

I wondered what Horeb would think when he came across our cold camp and found Laban shot through by two Edomite arrows.

The lands of the Empty Sands rolled in undulating waves on all sides of us—flatter and more desolate than anything I'd seen so far. So austere not a single tree stood in the endlessly unchanging terrain while dry riverbeds scarred the emptiness.

We dragged our camels through hillocks of deep sand. At times, my camel shied away or stopped altogether. She sensed death lay beyond those slippery dunes of gold.

The glare of the sun made my eyes hurt. For the first time in my life I beheld the sands that swallowed camels and men whole. A place as desolate as the moon.

"It's easy to lose heart out here. A stark land tries men's spirits," Kadesh told me. "Men often lose their nerve before they lose their water skins."

I tried to smile past my chapped lips. Even my eyelids were

sunburned, and I often rode with my scarf wrapped completely around my face.

We ate raw meat since we had no wood for a fire. Kadesh prepared a special concoction of garlic and spices to sweeten the meat so it was edible, rubbing it on like a paste.

No scrub brush, no hidden wildflowers for our camels and horses. At night they bawled, hungry. We didn't even have extra water to help fill their bellies.

Our water bags turned dry long before we reached each new well, even though we pushed the animals to travel late into the nights which were cooler and didn't sap our energy as much. I only hoped Horeb and his army was having a worse time of it. That he was losing men to starvation and thirst. Getting lost in the sands.

Asher avoided me, and everyone else. From the corner of my eye I'd watch him tend the men's horses, search for food for the camels, kneel for hours at each well, drawing water, volunteering for every extra task. The sight of him made my chest ache, despite the fact he'd brought Horeb within reach of us.

After three weeks I was stuck in a never-ending dream of sand fleas and scorpions. Tightening my belt every day against hunger pangs. My bones so weary I was sure I'd turned the age of Seraiah. Even so, I tried to spend a few moments with my new sword before going to bed, practicing the moves Asher had taught me. I often caught him watching me, nodding his head. Then, when he knew I'd seen him, he'd slink away into the darkness.

We were so hungry and thirsty by the time we reached the end of the trail of desolation, even the Edomites didn't show their usual joy at the sight of the well. There was only silence and exhaustion.

Wrapped in his dusty cloak, Kadesh studied the terrain surrounding the well. "The next well is home. We're almost there."

The next morning we learned Horeb's army had been spotted. They were still behind us despite the terrible final stretch, but had dropped back several days, even close to a week. He was still there, still coming, with no other roads or trails to distract him if he maintained a due east direction. But at least Kadesh would have a chance to organize the army of Sariba.

Three long days later, a range of mountains came into view. The Edomites let out a wild series of echoing shouts. I was so relieved I cried over my camel's neck but my eyes were dry from dehydration.

"The Qara Mountains," Kadesh shouted. Joy lit his face as he beheld the range of his homeland for the first time in more than a year. A burst of excited energy engulfed the horses and they danced and wheeled on the sand.

"The hills appear so far away still," I said, wishing we were there already, and safe behind the gates of Sariba.

"We'll be there in half a day," Kadesh replied, squeezing my hand in his.

My emotions were strangely mixed. At last we could stop. I would sleep in a real bed. There would be food and water. But melancholy washed over me as I realized I had a new home, strange people to meet, expectations I could barely imagine. And both my sisters missing.

Sorrow thudded inside my chest. I would never know my old life and home again. My palms ached to touch the coarse goat-hair walls of my mother's tent, feel her hands guiding mine with a needle, sense the kiss of her lips on my forehead, hear her voice raised in laughter and song. I'd never chatter with gossip alongside my cousins, Hakak and Falail. Or hold their babies. Or teach our daughters the dances of the women's world. Never again would I gather wisdom and unconditional love from my grandmother and aunts.

I brushed a fist against my eyes, trying to hide the pangs of loss.

Up ahead, Chemish slapped the reins on his horse's back while Asher followed him in silence. I'd barely heard the boy speak ten words the past three weeks.

The Edomites rushed forward, kicking up sand. I sat quietly on Shay's back, feeling my pain and sorrow—and yet a peculiar joy, too.

Kadesh seemed to sense my homesickness. "You're not alone, Jayden. You and I will face everything together; my family, our future—as well as Horeb's armies. I promise he can't hurt us here."

I wanted to believe him, but I'd heard the words from the Queen of Sheba's own lips. I'd listened to her fears of elusive enemies and growing armies. A force stronger than King Hammurabi who had conquered the entire eastern lands and rivers.

Was Horeb our true enemy, or only one of many in the strange city of Sariba?

The mountains grew taller when we turned southeast, heading for the coastline away from the desert trail. The camels began to gallop alongside the horses. I smiled at their enthusiasm, their intuition that we were close.

At last we came to a sheer drop of rugged cliffs. Below lay an ocean of spectacular blue. White-capped waves rushed gently onto shore. The faint roar of the water lured me like a siren. I smelled the spray of salt as waves crashed against the rocks. One of the most glorious sights I'd ever seen.

We are here. The city of Sariba had remained a mirage of my dreams for so long I almost couldn't take it in. We were now more than a month's travel east of the Red Sea, and two months south of the northern deserts where I'd been born.

The sweat on my brow cooled for the first time in weeks, and the hot wind of the barren desert disappeared like an ill gift tossed into the refuse pile. The ocean's humid breeze flapped my dress against my ankles, and streamed along my dry cheeks.

"The ocean is called Irreantum," Kadesh said. "The Sea of Many Waters." He reached for my hand and held it tight to his lips.

"It's just as you described." Affection rushed up my belly. We smiled without speaking, eyes locked, a thousand words unspoken and unneeded.

The pristine beach shaped like a half-moon called to us down below the gorgeous red cliffs. It was almost as though I recognized the waters of the dream I'd had those lonely nights searching for Kadesh in the Edomite land when I didn't know if he was dead or alive.

Sun-bleached sand spread soft as warm butter, reaching the walled city of Sariba nestled against a bank of low-lying hills. Even from here I could see homes and gardens built in steps along the lower plateaus.

Kadesh pointed straight north from the ocean on our right. "The Qara Mountains border the Empty Sands. I think heaven built this place of bounty for those who survive the desert crossing."

My eyes soaked up the luscious forests beyond the beach. "Such emerald-green hills. The Garden of Eden created all over again just for us."

"The frankincense groves grow in the foothills of the mountains," Kadesh added. "We have farms growing grains and cotton and maize. Orchards of fruit trees."

My father and Chemish came up behind us, overhearing our conversation. My father looked weary but overwhelmingly relieved, too.

"There's a freshwater lake in those mountains," Chemish said. "Streams and gorges and waterfalls."

"It will take months to explore," I said softly.

"You have a lifetime to enjoy it," Kadesh told me.

The camels and horses clambered down the rock path to the beach, not waiting to be led. When it leveled out, Shay galloped with the other camels, her legs long and awkward in the fine sand. Palm trees lined the perimeter of the crescent-shaped coastline. The swath of beach went as far as I could see, enclosed by rock cliffs.

The Edomites whooped and hollered. A few jumped off their horses to splash in the breaking surf. Others crashed straight into the water with their horses, water rising to their bellies.

"Come on, Jayden!" Kadesh said with a wild grin. We broke into a full run, racing each other as we left behind the older Edomites who were dismounting and then falling straight onto the sand to rest, arms wide, eyes closed in bliss.

My heart pulsed with delight. Kadesh turned his camel toward the water and the animal's head swiveled about as if flabbergasted to be standing knee-deep in the middle of the ocean.

"Go, Shay!" I cried. My camel had seen the beaches along the Red Sea, but we had never gone racing headlong into the waves. Shay lifted her feet carefully, as though the water was distasteful. Finally, she gave me a baleful stare, stepping tentatively like a prissy girl.

The Edomites were swimming and laughing. Their fine Arabian horses ran back and forth along the breakwaters, but I noticed Asher still sitting in his saddle, water splashing up onto his legs while the others frolicked.

After dismounting, my father stared toward the hazy horizon. I caught his eye and waved. He lifted a hand in return, not smiling, but not frowning either. I hoped he could find some peace and rest here.

Kadesh tugged at me. "Come on, let's swim and cool off."

I slid off Shay and tumbled into the clear water. "I've never swum before."

"I'll help you." He grasped my fingers and walked backward into the waves. My toes skimmed over smooth, tiny pebbles. "If you kick your feet you'll stay afloat."

It wasn't long before the water was up to our waists. Kadesh held his arms under me to keep my buoyant. Releasing my toes, which gripped the sand, I leaned back, gazing up into the blue sky. Strands of clouds hovered like tendrils of white wool.

Kadesh's shadow blocked the sun from my face. "Now pull your arms down," he said. "Up and down. Soon you'll be swimming on your own."

My fingers rushed through the water as Kadesh moved my body slowly along the rippling water. "It works! But my dress is getting heavy. It's pulling me under."

"All you have to do it put your feet down and stand up."

"But I'll sink."

Amusement crossed his lips. "No, you won't. It's not that deep."

My long hair floated all around me on top of the ocean, undulating like seaweed. Finally, I put my feet down and my bare toes sank into the bottom. The water barely came past my thighs. I was perfectly fine. When I laughed at my own silliness, Kadesh pulled me close. His hair was wet and unruly, and the faint scent of salt and frankincense drifted along his skin. He scooped water into his cupped hands and used it to scrub my dirty chin.

"There," he said. "Now you look presentable to meet King Ephrem."

I swayed on my feet, each wave pulling and tugging as if trying to swallow me up. "I only need a few lengths of seaweed to decorate my hair."

"Just the way I like you." He bent down to kiss me, and I tasted the crisp, clean sea on his mouth.

I murmured against his soft, wet lips, "If you present me to your uncle like this he'll be convinced you've gone mad."

Our lips parted and we stood quietly, hair dripping, smiling at each other. Kadesh pulled my fingers into his, locking us together. "Want to swim back to shore?"

When I saw the distance my eyes widened. "It's farther back to the beach than I thought." My toes dug into the sand to keep my balance, but Kadesh pulled me down into the water so we were crouching underneath the blueness. Setting me on his lap, he turned slowly in a circle. My dress swirled, the water heavy and light at the same time. The sensation was magical and exquisite.

The sinking sun lowered even more, the orange hue gilding the horseshoe mountains like they'd been painted with real gold.

"I love you, Jayden, daughter of Pharez," Kadesh said. His voice was quiet and husky while his fingers trailed the curves of my face.

"I love you, too," I whispered. My heart seemed to grow so large I thought my chest would burst. Our noses touched as we stared into each other's eyes.

"We've been through so much," Kadesh whispered.

I brushed his wet hair away from the black eye patch that would forever be a part of him, then kissed his scars one by one. "Separation, heartache, scars, and death," I said softly. "Wonderful and horrible moments both."

"I'll never forget how nervous you were when we stood alone in the narrow passage of the Edomite lands a year ago. The day you told me not to speak your name."

"You were overwhelming, Kadesh, Prince of Sariba."

"I could feel your heart even then, and I didn't know why you kept running away from me."

"I was betrothed—and yet drawn to you. I tried to deny it, but on the night of Hakak's wedding I couldn't any longer."

"Jayden, you are now *my* betrothed." I could feel him shaking, vulnerable. This year had been just as hard on him as it had on me. He faced even more difficult things now. King and general. A war to fight, his people to protect.

"Those are the sweetest words of the entire journey," I told him.

We stayed locked together for several long moments, not wanting to break apart. Not wanting to think about the monumental tasks that still lay ahead.

Kadesh held my hand as we swam back. The breakers grew more shallow and then we crawled up through the final wave, falling onto our backs to stare at a sky twisting with colors of crimson and purple.

Turning on his side to face me, Kadesh traced his finger up the curve of my waist. Then he placed a hand on my hip and brought his face toward mine, tugging away the wet strands of my hair where they'd become plastered to my face. "Jayden," he murmured, tasting my lips, my tongue.

My arms swept around his neck to hold him, our bodies woven together, legs tangled. I sensed his heart beating in rhythm to mine as though we were already one.

"We're making a spectacle of ourselves," Kadesh murmured after a few moments. "A crowd is gathering."

My eyes flew open.

Horses, camels, and Edomites were walking toward us. I touched Kadesh's mouth with my damp, salty fingers, wanting to kiss him all night long.

"Get to the city before the gates close!" Chemish shouted, waving an arm.

Kadesh smiled, his long, wet hair falling over my cheeks when we rose to our feet.

My father was on his camel and getting closer. Tufts of sand drifted with each step of the camel's large, padded feet. Quickly, I made sure my dress was still in place.

My heart squeezed when I spotted an Edomite off by himself—closer to us than the others—but alone. I looked away, trying to pretend I hadn't seen Asher, his sword and slingshot stuck in his belt. Stoically staring up at the city.

But I knew he'd been watching us.

Kadesh tilted my chin up, sensing my discomfort. "It's all right, Jayden. They can see we've been swimming out in the open. I was only kissing the girl I intend to marry."

Unfortunately he misunderstood the deeper meaning of

my distress. And Asher's personal torment.

At last we mounted our beasts while Chemish organized the company to enter the city. I might have been cleaner from my swim, but sand now caked my dress and the locks of my hair were clumped together. My appearance was demolished. I tried to run my fingers through the knotted strands and shake the sand from my gown.

A hundred of us were certainly going to make an entrance.

Asher stood quietly to the side. My bodyguard. My sword-fighting teacher. The last few weeks had been awkward between us. I'd felt his shame every time we had to pass along the trail or while in camp.

He cleared his throat to speak. "Remember, my lady, we've been on the desert for three months. Nobody expects us to be in our best dress. The servants at the palace will take care of you."

"Thank you," I mumbled. Those were the first words he'd spoken directly to me since the night of Laban's execution.

We were in a new place, and I hoped, a new beginning along with a better understanding between us. Earlier that morning, Kadesh had said he wanted our practice sessions to start up again in earnest so I'd be prepared for Horeb.

Word had spread of the prince of Sariba's arrival. The gates of the walled city opened with ceremony. Royal guards stood at attention in uniformed lines and official dress. When we passed through the imposing pylons, trumpets blared splendidly. The haunting, lyrical melody was so unlike any I'd heard before, and I knew at once I was a foreigner in a strange land.

A series of deep, guttural drums pounded next. The sound thrummed the soles of my feet, making me homesick for those childhood nights I'd danced with my mother and sister in our tent.

It had been too long since I'd danced; only a few times in the last several months, at Isra's cave and while camping along the river of the Fountain of the Red Sea. The dance connected me to my mother and sister, and the ancient Mother Goddess who'd given me spirit and life. The music and movements kept me grounded to the earth, to who I was, and to the women of my family who'd come before me—all of whom were now gone. I had no one to show me the way. No one to teach me how to be a wife and mother and woman of faith.

I'd missed those private, prayerful dances during this arduous trek.

The city's lights shimmered behind my watery eyes. It was as though part of me had died with my mother and my grandmother. Every generation gone but me and Leila.

Kadesh had alluded to the Sariba women who danced, and I was eager to learn more. Perhaps I could once more have a tribe of women in this land. Women I could be a part of and call my family.

A crowd of townspeople had gathered in the twilight: families of all sizes, merchants, tradesmen, innkeepers, and farmers. The Edomite soldiers flanked me on their Arabian steeds. Shay's bells were tarnished from dirt and sun, her colorful tassels soiled, but she held her head high as we padded past the guards and golden gates. I was proud of her unique and beautiful white fur, a rarity even in the western world where white camels were bred.

Dozens of colorful flags ringed the center square, but the flag of Sariba was the most dramatic. The image of a tree sprouting a myriad of gnarled, twisted branches set against a deep magenta color. The frankincense tree was silhouetted by the halo of the sun on the horizon of the Irreantum Sea.

We entered the plaza accompanied by the blast of trumpets and drums, a packed crowd of citizens following behind.

In the city square, beautiful wells had been built on raised beds of sparkling tile and flowers. Boasting of a never-ending supply of fresh water. Hand-painted tiles ornamented the well lids, including an overhanging shelter to give shade. I'd never seen anything like it, not even in the wealthy city of Mari.

Hanging lamps filled with olive oil were being lit by men with long torches. A wide avenue led directly to the palace and the small orange flames glowed up and down the thorough-fare. Similar lights lined the square. Streets branched off in all directions and the radiating lamps gave the entire city a warm cheerfulness.

"It's absolutely breathtaking," I said. "Enchanting."

"It *is* magical," Kadesh agreed as we jostled through the squeeze of people. "I never tire of seeing Sariba at night. Just wait until we enter the palace grounds."

22

The gates to the royal palace swung wide. Hundreds of the same shimmering lamps on the city streets surrounded the residence. I sucked in my breath at the columned portico entrance—as grand as the city.

Large doors carved in the lush pattern of frankincense trees and lustrous suns gleamed with a warm richness. Ten Edomites created a formal horse guard while Kadesh dismounted. His cloak swept behind him when he walked to the top of the glittering stairs. Underneath the porch roof, Kadesh turned to face the city.

The citizens of Sariba went wild. Their lost son had returned. By their cheers and shouts, I knew they loved King Ephrem and his nephew.

But I also heard an undercurrent of voices rising. Whispers of shock at Kadesh's scarred face, his missing eye. And whispers of me. A girl from a strange land. Someone rescued on the desert? Or a wife of one of the Edomites?

Prickles ran along my neck. I had the distinct feeling someone was watching me.

I glanced about, assuming it was merely the townspeople gossiping behind their hands but suddenly, to my left, a pair of black eyes met mine. The only man standing still in the waving crowd. He wasn't particularly tall, but cut an imposing figure as though he were larger than anyone else around him. Confidence and a keen, arrogant intelligence exuded from him.

A second man stood just behind his right shoulder. Also staring at me. Both of them wore impressive pleated white linen. Gold belts slung about their waists. Robes of black on their shoulders. Their heads were shaved bald, and small gold hoops pierced their ears.

My heart stopped beating for a moment. Who were these men and why did they stare at me as though they knew me?

When our line of horses and camels began to move down the avenue, the first man gave me a slow smile, inclining his head. He raised an enameled staff to me. The staff bore gold filigree and the head of a falcon with jade for eyes. His bow wasn't a form of deference; it was instead, rather mocking. A challenge of some kind.

My palms began to sweat.

"Jayden, you're pale," Asher said, pulling up aside me.

"I am?" A catch in my throat made it hard to breathe. With Kadesh at the top of the palace entrance and waving to his people, I was glad Asher had noticed my distress and not left me alone to fend for myself.

"Ignore the gossip. They mean no harm. Sariba doesn't get travelers from faraway lands very often."

I gripped Shay's reins tighter, trying to shake off what had just happened. Those men. Their black ominous eyes. "I understand their curiosity. Me, a lone woman with an army of a hundred Edomite men. I'm also aware the people of Sariba could easily deem me not worthy of Kadesh."

"They'll accept you. And they will love you. How could they not?"

"Please don't say these things," I whispered, grateful when my father rode up on my left and reached for my hand.

He gave me a sideways smile when I gripped his palm. "The Nephish tribe must stick together. Even in a land of beauty and peace."

Once the Edomites and camels had lined up along the outer staircase, my father helped me dismount. We stood with the rest of the crowd while Sariba guards, in distinctive uniforms of black and magenta, held in formation along the palace doors and gates.

"My beloved friends and fellow citizens," Kadesh called out in a loud voice. "How glad I am to be home!"

The roar in response to his words was deafening, quickly followed by laughter, cheers, and thunderous clapping. A single, explosive blast from one of the trumpets pierced the night, capturing the emotions of the Sariba citizens. Lights consumed the darkness. The Qara Mountains disappeared with the sunset. Giant shadows behind us. Pockets of deep gloom where the jungle grew. Where tranquil lakes lay motionless under the stars.

"King Ephrem and I will reunite after more than a year," Kadesh went on. "You will hear stories of dangerous journeys. Life-threatening, but our Edomite brothers saved my life. Our Dedan forts are strong. And . . ." He paused. "There is glad news to come."

His eyes sought out my face, and I gave a sharp intake of breath. Kadesh was referring to me.

Nerves hummed along my arms. Murmurs and speculation filled the air. Kadesh made no mention of an approaching army. He clearly didn't want to alarm them. It was the moment to celebrate the heir's return, but Horeb's presence loomed. Just beyond my sight. As if he'd be grinning wickedly at me if I glanced over my shoulder. How much time did we have before his army showed up on the western horizon?

"For now, my companions and I must rest, but during this week, we'll celebrate and rejoice in the blessings of our land." Kadesh turned and the palace stable boys began to lead the horses away for grooming and feeding. My camel was taken in another direction and it felt odd not to have her halter in my hand after so many months.

I ascended the palace stairs gripping my father's arm. When we stepped through the doors a brilliant foyer opened up, on fire with another hundred hanging lamps and wall sconces.

A lightheaded sensation swept over me. This was a palace not of stone and imported marble, but of magnificent tents. A hundred times bigger than anything I could have imagined.

Panels of finely finished goat hair hung on stout wooden frames set into the earth and lashed together in resplendent canopies.

Ceilings twenty feet high. Carpets created from intricate designs and colors. The foyer was an enormous square, halls and corridors breaking off at intervals. Ivory-inlaid mahogany and cedar tables from Lebanon sat next to artfully arranged sofas. Golden lamps adorned the tables, and chandeliers lit by innumerable candles hung over our heads.

Male servants and maids were everywhere, leading us to our various rooms. I said good night to my father. "Will there be food?" I asked, trying to pry a smile from his tired face.

He lifted an eyebrow, his old humor returning for a brief moment. "I think they'll feed us."

Two young girls scurried around me, eager to lead me to my room, but I stood still, gazing into my father's face. We were in a place and time I could never have imagined when my mother died.

"It's a new world, Jayden," my father said. "Your mother and grandmother would be in awe to see such magnificence."

I wished I could erase the melancholy in his eyes. "A new life," I whispered. "And a new beginning for all of us."

My father gazed over my shoulder in the direction of the western desert where the sun had fallen through the skies. Fatigue dug grooves into his face. He would never say it, but he couldn't live here permanently. He was a man of the desert. It was in his blood, his soul, so deep it could never be separated from the person he was.

I wondered the same about myself. Could I live in a palace

my entire life—even a palace created in the structure of a magnificent tent? Already the throngs of citizens, servants, and guards were giving me claustrophobia. I could only imagine how much worse it was for my father, a man who cherished his freedom and the open land above all else.

He kissed my forehead. "Sleep well, my girl."

I was thoroughly lost by the time the servant girls maneuvered several turns. Finally, we entered a short alcove-like hallway and the older girl pushed open a door leading into a suite of rooms. My knees buckled at the sight of so much comfort and charm.

"You must be tired," the girl said, holding me up by the elbow.

I was too busy staring. Painted, billowing panels swooped upward into an arch, forming a square in the center of the ceiling. A chandelier hanging at the top of the arch was crafted of burnished bronze with decorative holes and pinpricks formed into flowers and tamarisk trees. The lit candles inside superimposed a bright yellow pattern on the bedroom's walls.

Wide windows banked the wall on my left. Gardens glowed under lamplight on the outside pathway. When I walked over to peek through the window, a crescent moon shone among the stars in the night sky.

Farther down the garden paths stood palace guards, garbed in the same rich brown patterned cloak Kadesh had been wearing when I first saw him on the cliff at my mother's grave. Ferocious swords hung from their belts.

Luxurious carpets pillowed under my feet. I noted fine

glass ornaments, an inlaid writing table, and a cushioned chair just my size. I was tempted to drop myself into the chair and sleep for a week, but one of the girls gently guided me away.

"Not yet," she said. "We will bathe and dress you for sleeping."

We passed a wide bed sitting high off the floor. I reached out to touch the velvety mattress. Beautiful gold and russet linens were sewn in the same manner as Kadesh's rich cloak. Pillows and bolsters lay in an inviting arrangement on the bed. No more hard-packed earth with ants, spiders, and scorpions to keep at bay.

"I'm Tijah," the girl told me, grasping my hand in a gesture of welcome. I pictured my mother doing the same to a foreign visitor.

The second girl, a bit younger than Tijah, had gone ahead of us into the adjoining room. I could hear the splash of water. A set of small steps was decorated with a pattern of white-and-magenta tiles. A fireplace was set into the wall and the back of the hearth arched with more tiles. Orange coals burned in the grate. I was surprised to see a fire inside a home when summer's burning temperatures were upon us. But I was comfortable, not overly warm.

"The mountains and ocean cool Sariba at night," Tijah explained. "You'll want your blankets to sleep."

I stifled a yawn and wondered where Kadesh was. He'd been swept away after his speech. No doubt to greet his family. Uncle Ephrem hadn't attended the welcome party, but I was too sleepy to wonder what Sariba royal protocol rules were.

Tijah led me to the adjoining bathroom where a tub filled with water from a gold faucet came straight through the floor and tent walls.

"What strange miracle is this?" I asked.

"The Kingdom of Sariba—like that of Sheba and Egypt— is sophisticated and complex," Tijah answered. "We have running water in the palace compound."

She helped me undress while the other girl tested the water with her wrist. She added a handful of pink granules and frothy white bubbles began to form.

"Water is brought through clay pipes directly here to all the main rooms," Tijah went on. "We have cisterns and aqueducts that fill from the streams in the mountains. Our brother does pipe works. He's currently studying to be an engineer at the king's university."

"Then you two are sisters," I said, noting the resemblance. They both had the same wavy bangs cut across their foreheads. The same small chins and slight frames. I was taller than both of them. "What's your name" I asked Tijah's sister.

The girl didn't look up when I spoke, focusing on laying out beautiful sponges and choosing from a stack of thick towels.

Tijah leaned close. "Her name is Jasmine. She was born without hearing or speech. My brother, Timothy and I, care for her. Prince Kadesh allows many people of Sariba with physical or mental impairments to work in the palace or on the grounds."

A longing for Kadesh's gentle love rose up, searing my belly with fire. Already I missed him terribly. "But I'm here at last," I whispered. Kadesh and I would marry soon. Just as the Queen of Sheba had instructed. And Horeb's army would be conquered.

I imagined endless days exploring the mystical mountains. Swimming and fishing in their streams and lakes. Walking the splendor of a magical, new world. Raising children together, just as I'd dreamed. After all the heartache, God had finally granted us a measure of peace. All would be perfect when I found Leila. I'd bring her here to the palace and enlist Kadesh's help in finding her a good man to wed. Perhaps even a nobleman's son.

A soberness fell over me knowing the roads to Egypt were also filled with dangers. She was in a foreign land, and completely alone. Would she survive the harsh journey? Or was her corpse somewhere on the Egyptian deserts? What sort of men had kidnapped her? Her life might now be worse than one as a temple priestess.

I tried to throw off a thousand fears, but they lurked in the corners of my mind, like rats.

"Will you please dim the lights?" I asked, fully aware of my body's scars in the eyes of the two young girls. I was self-conscious and didn't want to engender questions.

Tijah looked perplexed, but she motioned to her sister to douse a few of the candles.

"I'm sorry," I stammered.

"My lady, you don't need to explain or apologize. I'm here to serve you."

Tijah helped me into the tub and kneeled to scrub my back and neck. The warm water was like silk, soft as a rose petal.

"I'm just an ordinary girl like you," I told her.

Tijah vehemently shook her head. "They say you are a great lady. A princess of your tribe. And a warrior, too."

I was disconcerted. "I've only been here a few hours and already I have a reputation?"

"The people of Sariba know everyone's business," Tijah confessed without shame.

Her statement reminded me of the women's world of my own tribe. The familiar relationships we had. Our intimate ties bound us together. They made us feel safe in a world of trials and hardships. But not any longer. Never again with the Tribe of Nephish. And how many true friendships could I cultivate as the queen of Sariba?

I kept the upper half of my body submerged under the soapy bubbles while Tijah sponged my legs and toes. "Are you well, Lady Jayden?" she asked.

It was my turn to frown. "Yes, of course, I'm fine."

"You've been hurt," the girl observed, lightly touching the long white scar along my neck.

I gripped the edge of the bathtub. I didn't want my mutilated body to become society talk.

"Your secret is safe with me. I'm sure a warrior girl who travels the deserts would have scars."

"Yes," I agreed carefully.

"I'll make you a salve of my mother's herbs, including myrrh and frankincense. Freshly harvested frankincense will fade those scars."

I glanced up to see Jasmine hanging up my cloak. "Please be careful!" I called out. "I have—I have a weapon inside. I don't want her to get hurt."

Tijah flicked her eyes toward her sister. Unspoken words passed between them. The dagger was brought forth and placed in a locked case Jasmine produced from one of the wardrobes. My sword and sheath had been laid on top of one of the bureaus, high out of reach.

"Your dress will need to be burned," Tijah told me.

"It used to be my mother's. . . ." I pressed my palms against my eyes, not wanting to give it up. I had no other keepsakes of hers. No clothing or jewelry or alabaster box.

"It's filthy and beyond repair." Tijah bit her lips, noting my expression. Softly she added, "We have a closet full of gowns for you."

I nodded without speaking as she set to work washing my hair, then rinsed it using urns of fresh, warm water Jasmine handed her. After toweling dry, I was dressed in a nightgown created from layers of magenta-and-gold satin. Tijah combed out my hair while Jasmine cleaned the bathtub.

The dressing table had a beautiful array of brushes and powders and a large burnished mirror. I caught Tijah's eyes as she rubbed ointment into my hair to rid the mess of its dry, broken tangles.

"My lady, tell us about your family. Have you no one other than your father?"

"I have two sisters I'm searching for. My younger sister was sold to a couple without children. I found her in the city of Mari, but they wouldn't give her to me—even though the prince of Sariba offered them wealth untold."

A crease formed above Tijah's eyes. "I'm so sorry."

"And I have an older sister named Leila. All I know is she was taken to Egypt. From the Temple of Ashtoreth in Tadmur."

"I've never heard of these cities you name."

The pit of my stomach ached. "How often do you get visitors here?"

"Almost never. We're so isolated. The return of Prince Kadesh with his company—and you—are the first in a year."

I tasted a bitter bite at the back of my throat.

"Tell me more about your sister, my lady."

"She's slim with long black hair. She's lovely and funny and temperamental. An Egyptian goddess when she dances. But her constitution is delicate. She becomes ill on long journeys."

"No wonder you're worried."

"I tried to bring her with us, but I was too late."

"Why did your sister go to the Temple of Ashtoreth? Girls in good families stay away." She stopped, holding a hand to her mouth. "I'm sorry, my lady, I didn't mean to imply—"

"You're right, Tijah. My sister was lured there after my mother died." There were several moments of silence and then I said, "Today, as we walked into the city, I saw two strange men in the crowd. It almost seemed as though they were watching me particularly."

"What did they look like?"

"White tunics, black robes. Bald heads and staffs. Dressed so differently from the other men here."

She frowned. "We do get a few foreigners now and then. Those men you describe sound like the magicians who arrived here a few months ago. Guests of the goddess temple of Sariba."

"Magicians!" I exclaimed. "For the temple?" The words of my grandmother Seraiah came back with force.

"They create potions for healing or charms. And they speak incantations to make their magic work. A girl in my neighborhood bought a potion for a man she's in love with. I thought it was silly, but they can make things happen . . ." Her voice trailed away as she focused on getting me ready for bed.

"How do they do that?" I asked. "How do they get their power?"

"Egypt, of course. That's where all magic comes from. And in Egypt when you speak a spell or a prayer, it becomes so. Just saying the words, or speaking someone's name as part of the incantation, is powerful. The words fly straight up to the gods. When a magician or a sorcerer creates a magic chant for you, or tends to you when you're sick, then your hope or wish or healing comes true."

I desperately wanted to lie down. "What are they doing here so far from home?"

I remembered how the men had stared at me, had raised their staff and bowed to me. I almost confided in the girl, but stopped myself. This young maid wouldn't know.

Tijah glanced at her sister, who was wiping water from the floor in the bathing area.

"Is there a Temple of Ashtoreth here?" I asked. Seraiah had spoken of Egyptian sorcerers and healers, and now I knew they existed right here in the frankincense lands. Egyptians had taken Leila across the western route to that strange and magical country where the people worshipped an entire pantheon of gods. Perhaps those Egyptian men could help me find her. If I had the nerve to approach them.

"No, the magicians are with the Temple of Sariba. They give the girls of the temple some sort of special drink, which makes them forget their names and their families. Any girl who joins the Temple of Sariba becomes a servant of the powerful Goddess for the rest of her life. She dedicates her life to worshiping her, sustaining her, and demonstrating complete obedience."

"And what does perfect obedience entail?"

"Please don't ask me anything else—I don't know!"

I reached out to grasp her hand. Her fingers were small, the nails worn from servitude. "Tijah," I said. "Are you afraid of the temple? Do you know someone there?"

The girl made a choking sound. "I can't, no, I don't know anyone. I've never gone there. I don't want to. Please don't make me!"

I was stunned by the force of her emotion.

"The Goddess is powerful," Tijah whispered. "She can hypnotize you into doing things."

"Nonsense," I said, but my words didn't seem to comfort her. "I promise you don't have to go there, or live there, or even visit."

"Promises can be broken," she said with desolation.

23

I studied the two sisters while Tijah brought me a plate of dinner. Jasmine set a pitcher of cold water and a goblet of wine on the table beside the bed. Tijah appeared to be her happy self again, but her outburst bothered me. She was afraid of something, but didn't want to tell me.

I drank the entire pitcher of water, but I could only nibble at the bread. My stomach was too empty and I was afraid I'd be ill if I ate any of the rich food.

The two girls helped me into the softest bed I'd ever spent a night in. Fine cotton sheets were smooth as satin against my arms and feet. Three months of knots in my neck and shoulders had eased after the hot bath.

My stomach had stopped rumbling with hunger, but my mind was in turmoil. Now that I was here I needed to use the connections of the royal family to learn where Leila was and bring her here.

Tijah brought me a hot herbal drink. "Sleep, Lady Jayden. You're exhausted from the journey. Distraught over your sister." Pulling a chair close, the girl smoothed my hair with her gentle fingers, reminding me of the times Leila and I soothed each other to sleep in the camel litter. "Don't torture yourself. We'll figure something out with the help of the palace government. Perhaps Aliyah can help us."

"Who's Aliyah?" I murmured.

"The grand princess. She's the most beautiful woman in all of Sariba. And as a royal princess she has connections to the Temple of Sariba, which means she may be able to find out where she was taken in Egypt."

The room grew fuzzy. My head slid down my pillow when the herbal drink took effect. I didn't want to talk to anyone at any temple. I didn't trust the High Priestesses, not in Tadmur, and not here. "Kadesh, I want Kadesh, I need to talk to him. I need *him*."

Tijah glanced at her sister. An odd look passed between them. I wondered if Jasmine could read my lips. If she understood more of our conversations than she let on.

"I suppose," Tijah said, choosing her words carefully, "after three months on the trail you became on more personal terms with the prince of Sariba. He is Prince Kadesh. As an outsider, we advise you to use his title."

My heart dropped to the perfect, hand-painted tiled floor. The servant girls didn't realize who I was. "Nobody has told you who I am?" A queer sense of betrayal came over me.

"Of course we know. You are Princess Jayden, of the Nephish. There was a bounty on your head, and our prince saved you from death."

"But—but—" My words slurred. "Will you please send Kadesh a message?"

The sisters glanced at each other again. "That isn't proper, my lady, while a guest of the palace. You need to wait until he summons you himself." Tijah motioned to Jasmine and the two girls scurried away.

"Kadesh and I . . . we're . . ." I tried one last time, but the splendor of the suite of rooms faded away, and I went into a dreamless sleep.

When I awoke, I had no idea what time it was. The bedroom had acquired a strange grayness, as if storm clouds hovered across the sloped ceiling.

My tongue felt thick, my mouth dry as a bone. Instinctively, I knew I'd been asleep for a very long time.

Untouched meals sat on the table next to the bed. Cold soup, drinks with settled dregs on the bottom, and stale, herbed bread on a ceramic platter painted with the emblem of the palace.

I pushed myself up on one elbow. Bit by bit pieces of the previous night returned. The fanfare of our welcome to Sariba, and the servant girls who had taken care of me.

I swung my legs over the bed. When I tried to rise I wobbled like a newborn camel. Rubbing at a crick in my neck,

I took slow steps through the splendid room, staring at the wondrous draperies and furniture. Not a speck of dust lay on the handsome tables with their intricately carved wood and armrests.

A hint of perfume lingered in the air. Perhaps it was the frankincense salve Tijah had rubbed on my scars. My head ached like I'd been ill. More likely exhaustion.

Had Kadesh come to see me? I wondered if Tijah would have allowed him entrance. It was odd the girls didn't know about our relationship. Perhaps Kadesh was waiting to make a formal announcement. First, he had to make arrangements with his uncle to sign the papers of our marriage covenant. Then he could sound the trumpets and proclaim our love to the world.

Becoming more awake by the minute, I realized I was ravenous. The magenta-and-gold nightgown swished around my ankles as I strode to the window. Flinging back the curtains, I saw a gray mist shrouding the world. Leaning on the open ledge, I peered down the paths in both directions, unable to see past the edge of the palace. It was as though the world had disappeared. No mountains to the north. No sky above me. Billowing clouds lowered upon the city, enveloping everything.

The mist glazed my arms with moisture. I shut the drapes again, impatient.

"You're awake!" Tijah exclaimed, bustling in the door.

"I feel like I'm still dreaming. I can't see a thing through the windows."

"That's the fog. We get much more fog and drizzle here in

the Qara Mountains than the deserts."

"I can't tell whether it's morning or—"

"Late afternoon. You've slept almost round the clock for two days. We need to get you dressed for dinner."

I sank into one of the cushioned chairs, trying to take in that I'd been asleep for nearly two days. "I don't own any finery or jewels for a palace dinner."

Tijah motioned Jasmine toward the wardrobe. The younger girl opened the doors and began to riffle through stacks of hanging dresses. "Tonight is the royal celebration dinner to welcome Prince Kadesh home. You are his guest and must look your best."

Her words slowly registered. "Who will be there?"

"The royal family, of course," Tijah began. "All the kingdom's dignitaries, heads of state, the general of the army. There will be music and dancing, too."

Trepidation crawled up my throat. I wanted to jump on my camel and run away to the desert for a few hours. "I need some fresh air."

"You'll get wet if you step outside," Tijah told me, escorting me to the dressing table. "We need your hair to stay dry so we can arrange it into curls."

"Curls?" I echoed. "It's already wavy."

Tijah smiled mysteriously. "You'll see what talents I have, my lady. And I hope if you like my service you'll consider retaining me for a long time to come."

Retaining her services was my decision? It was odd to have such power.

I still felt clean from the long soak two nights earlier. Jasmine had scrubbed me harder than my mother ever had. But she gave me a sponge bath now with clean linen and hot, fragrant water. Then I sat at the dressing table while the two sisters worked on my hair and face.

Tijah had a strange ceramic cylinder contraption she heated in the fire and wrapped about the long strands of my hair, creating a series of ringlet-type curls. Next she pulled my hair up into a loose knot, allowing the lovely curls to glide down my neck.

With gentle fingers, Jasmine applied a lavender eye color to the lids, expertly adding thick lines of black kohl above and below my eyelashes to create an exotic appearance.

Using a series of cream and lotions, the girls softened the rough skin of my arms and legs, dotting my wrists and ears and chest with a woodsy, sensual perfume. A bit of rose color applied to my face brought out my cheekbones. Pomegranate juice stained my lips.

While the girls chose a gown from the wardrobe, I caught a glimpse of Jasmine mouthing words to Tijah in the mirror. Her older sister whispered in return. The two girls saw me watching and hurriedly averted their faces.

My servant girls were talking about me. And it wasn't about the evening's dressing. "What is it?" I demanded.

"My lady, we were only discussing the perfect gown. And slippers to match."

"Tijah," I said, feeling bolder. "Please come here."

The girl advanced toward me with slow steps.

I forced her eyes to meet mine. "If we are to trust each other I must know what it is you're whispering about with your sister. She understands more than she admits."

"There are many things, Lady Jayden, that are just . . . puzzling to us."

I clenched my hands together. "Who is spreading gossip about me?"

"Some of the servants are saying—" she swallowed. "They're saying you killed a man."

"How in the world . . . ?" I lifted my face to the girl who stared back at me in the dressing mirror. I regretted killing Gad, but he'd given me no choice. Would the people of Sariba only see me as a girl who'd killed one of my own kinsmen?

"I must speak with Kad—Prince Kadesh," I stammered. "It's very important."

Tijah's eyes widened. "You need to request an audience first. It can take a few days to receive an appointment."

"But he's my—oh, dear God in heaven!" I cried out in frustration. Gossip about killing Gad had reached the palace ears, but *not* my relationship with the Prince of Sariba. "Please get me some water, and then let's finish dressing. If I sit here any longer I'll scream."

"I'm so sorry, my lady," Tijah said, obviously troubled by my distress.

Jasmine fetched a drink for me and then the two girls held up the dresses in the wardrobe for my examination. One was a slim piece in a deep forest green, the second a striking red with shots of gold. Lace trimmed the skirt bottom and sleeves.

"Perhaps the green is more soothing, more elegant," Tijah suggested.

I nodded my assent, and Jasmine knelt to help me step into the dress. Before she pulled it up over my legs she jerked her chin up, blinking in bewilderment. She pointed to my feet and then cast a pleading look at her sister.

Tijah stepped forward. "She says you have something odd on your foot."

I glanced down and realized Jasmine was staring at the ankle bracelet Kadesh had given me. The two sisters kneeled on the floor to peer at the frankincense tree made of silver, the halo of sun on the horizon of ocean waves. So perfectly the symbols of this land.

Tijah brushed the silver chain with her fingers. "Who gave you this?"

I unclasped the anklet and held it in my palm. "Prince Kadesh. Of course."

"How strange he would give you such a gift. Because he's—" Tijah glanced once more at her sister.

My patience disappeared, my voice raw at the edges. *"What?"*

Tijah wrung her fingers around the sash of her dress, twisting the cloth into cords. "It's just that . . . Prince Kadesh is betrothed to someone else."

24

Kadesh betrothed to another girl? That was impossible. He'd been gone for over a year. He'd told me he loved me a hundred times over, had given me gifts. We'd made so many plans for our future, a future I yearned for with every fiber of my being.

In a single moment my entire life had precariously tilted. I stood on a sharp precipice with no stone or floor beneath me, where falling meant certain destruction. Dazed, I glanced up. Jasmine blinked her eyes as though she were about to burst into tears.

"Jasmine says we're all heartbroken our beloved prince almost died," Tijah translated. "That he's now blind. Everyone is upset."

A cold numbness spread through my limbs. Servants talked, right? I'd certainly listened to the girls at the temple gossiping all day long. Perhaps this betrothal was just hateful rumors. After all, I was a stranger from a small, inconsequential tribe. My feelings didn't matter. Maybe someone was, this very moment, laughing at the joke because they hated my tribe—or didn't like a stranger coming in to marry their beloved prince.

Beads of perspiration broke out on Tijah's face. "Some are saying it's your fault our prince has come home scarred and wounded."

"My fault?" I gripped the silver bracelet so hard the edges cut into my palm. The same palm Kadesh had kissed so many times. "First I've killed a man and now it's my fault the prince of Sariba is blind? Who is saying these things?"

"The servants' quarters are buzzing with stories."

I strode the length of the bedroom, angry, confused, and fighting to stay in control. Whirling around, I said, "I won't be attending the dinner party. Tell them I'm ill. Actually, I don't care what you tell them." Without warning, tears began to form behind my eyes. I stifled them down. "Do you know where my camel is quartered?"

"The stables and camel corrals are located on the northern side of the palace grounds," Tijah answered. "A short walk from here. But you can't walk there by yourself."

I tried to breathe, to think calmly. The citizens of Sariba didn't want me here. Maybe I should leave, begin my journey back to the desert and find a new life somewhere else.

"You would have looked so beautiful in the green gown," Tijah added wistfully.

The girls watched to see what I would do. I realized I could sulk here in the bedroom—or I could find out the truth. Pivoting on my heel, I said, "Actually, dress me please. I *will* attend dinner."

"Yes, my lady!" Tijah waved her hands at Jasmine and the girl's brown eyes widened. She smiled so sweetly, so eagerly, I couldn't help giving her a tremulous smile in return, brushing away the stupid tears on my face.

Shakily, I stepped into the green gown for the second time. Jasmine helped me push my arms through the embroidered sleeves. She fastened the back and then tied sashes of various shades of green, the color of leaves and jungle and ocean, around my waist.

Tijah fixed my makeup and then finished arranging my hair, adding a fine mist of gold lacquer to keep the cascading curls in place.

"You look beautiful," Jasmine mouthed, fixing a stray curl.

The sisters led me out of the suite to the main hallway where endless, elaborate tent walls had been joined together to form the lavish palace.

"We're not allowed to leave this part of the palace. Go down this hallway, past several doors," Tijah instructed. "The royal dining hall will be on the right. You'll hear music. High-ranking ladies' maids will direct you where to sit."

I was sure I'd throw up when I left the relative safety of my room to venture down the grand hallway. Peaked ceilings as high as cypress trees floated overhead. Gilded chairs and luxurious carpets.

My mind kept returning to Tijah's words: Kadesh is

betrothed to someone else. Why wouldn't he tell me something so important, so life-altering? The information seemed to fill the corridors with appalling implications.

I wished my father, or even Asher, had come to fetch me. Instead, I was facing a crowd of strangers by myself. At the end of the hallway, a woman wearing sprays of jade and garnet earrings beckoned to me. "Please enter, Lady Jayden. You and your father will be seated at our guest table." I stood at the door, hesitating, and the woman sent me forward with a surreptitious push of her ringed hand.

The dining hall boasted elegant soaring columns. Velvet cushions in every color of the rainbow were set beneath long, low tables. A thousand lamps and candles. People lounged, chatting, talking, and laughing. So much color, so much light, so many people. Unsure where to go, I wavered, trying desperately to find Kadesh in the crowd.

In one corner, a musician thumped two different-sized drums while a flutist and a harpist played a high melody over the deep sound.

Various wines were presented on shiny platters. Servants in white linen and bare feet expertly moved through the hall.

"This way, my lady." Another woman was at my elbow, leading me to a table on my far left. Heads turned as I approached. Murmurs began. My name was spoken on both sides of me. Behind me, a female voice carried across the din. "That's the camel girl from the north." Her friend added grudgingly, "I expected worse. But why are they here? And why did they bring the Edomite army?"

I stared rigidly ahead, forcing myself not to clench the folds of my dress in my fists. Large urns bursting with flowers sat in the corners. Sweet perfume emanated from garlands of jasmine strung along the low walls of the perimeter.

"Your place is here next to your father."

I didn't know who had spoken, but my eyes finally focused. Chemish and Asher were already seated at the same table. My father's familiar, dear face locked onto mine. He gave me a wan smile, looking completely out of place. I think we both wished, at that moment, we were racing our camels out on the desert. But those memories almost seemed to belong to someone else.

After I was seated, I leaned in, unable to contain the desperation in my voice. "Where's Kadesh?"

"The royal family table," Chemish answered.

A servant set a plate of lettuces and herbs sprinkled with dried pomegranate, raisins, and almonds before me. I murmured my thanks, and then lifted my eyes, clutching at my napkin.

Kadesh sat directly across the expanse of the hall from me. He wore a white tunic, a royal purple robe thrown over his shoulders, and a crown of gold on his thick, dark hair, which suddenly looked longer, curling at the ends, as though I hadn't seen him in weeks instead of two days. Our swim in the ocean, the fevered kissing on the beach while waves rushed along our bodies, almost seemed like a dream now.

Was I an imposter?

Kadesh's eyes met mine and softened. My face felt tight. I studied the man I loved while he lifted a goblet of red wine, desperately wanting to touch him, to make sure he was real.

Was he really mine or did he belong to someone else? A thousand questions tortured me.

Trying not to stare at the royal table on the raised dais, I forced myself to eat tiny bites of the syrupy apricots that had appeared on the table. Grapes mixed with sugared almonds. My nerves were strung so tightly I was sure I'd be sick later.

The roar of talk and laughter covered up my unease. My eyes raked over the guests. Was the woman Kadesh had been betrothed to here in this very room? I studied every girl. Imagined Kadesh sharing secrets with her, sharing kisses, and tried not to gag on my salad leaves.

In the center of the royal family table was a gentleman older than my father. He wore his hair long like Kadesh, but it was pure white. His accompanying beard was also a silvery white color, long but neatly trimmed. His aged eyes drooped, hooded like my grandmother's, as though he possessed wisdom and knowledge over everyone else in the room.

Formerly a tall, broad-shouldered man, the man was now stooped with age. His hand shook when he raised his goblet of wine. "Is that the king?" I asked under my breath.

"Yes, that's King Ephrem," my father replied.

"Who is the older woman between him and Kadesh? His wife?"

"No, his sister-in-law, Kadesh's aunt. The sister of his deceased mother."

"And the men and women at the other end of the table?"

"King Ephrem's sisters and their spouses. A few of their adult children and grandchildren."

The familial relationships made sense. The siblings and their spouses weren't quite as elderly as Ephrem, but held themselves regally. The children were darling, ranging between the ages of three and twelve. Dressed in finery, a little wiggly, eating with their fingers and pretending to push each other off their pillows.

And then there was a young woman sitting at the royal family table. Perhaps a year or two older than me. Overwhelmingly beautiful and serene. Her hair was a shade lighter than mine, shimmering with gold strands. Her makeup and complexion were flawless while she delicately ate her meal and chatted with Kadesh. I stared between them, back and forth, not daring to ask who she was, although I was going to be sick if I didn't find out soon.

My father leaned in. "Jayden, attend to your dinner. You're shooting daggers at that princess."

"She's a princess?" I asked faintly. I finished swallowing a wedge of melon and the juice dribbled unceremoniously down my chin. Quickly, I dabbed a napkin at it, gulping water to help the piece of fruit down so I didn't choke on it.

I knew there were princesses here—I'd met the Queen of Sheba—but I hadn't expected a girl of such intimidating beauty to be sitting so close to Kadesh.

"Chemish told me her name is Aliyah. She and Kadesh have known each since they were children. Much like you and Horeb."

Briefly, I closed my eyes. "Please don't mention Horeb to me."

A pained expression crossed my father's face. I knew the subject of Horeb and our escape from the oasis upset him. And my father didn't know half of what Horeb had done to me.

I couldn't tear my eyes from the girl. *Aliyah.* She had to be the Princess Aliyah Tijah had mentioned. I watched her flirting with Kadesh. Leaning into him, touching his arm. While I sat far across the room as a guest without a name.

I pushed my plate away. "I can't eat. I'm sorry."

"You're not used to these rich foods," my father said, leaving portions of his own food untouched.

"I'm so tired I think I could sleep for a week." I tried to smile pleasantly, but I was faking every lift of my mouth.

I hadn't talked to Kadesh since our arrival and his attentions were being subverted by Princess Aliyah. Clenching my fists together, I suppressed the urge to take the dishes of sauces and yogurt and throw them.

Insight flamed within me, like a match taken to an overfilled oil lamp. If Aliyah was the same princess who was liaison for the royal family to the Sariba High Priestess, that meant *she* might also be a priestess in training. I didn't understand how a woman from the temple earned a spot at the royal family table.

Or was I jumping to conclusions? A political liaison didn't mean she was part of the temple. Only sat on boards and committees.

"Your first courses are almost untouched," Asher observed. "Are you ill, my lady?" He was still hesitant in his speech and manner after what had happened on the desert. As the son of the Edomite leader, his shame would haunt him for years to come. I wondered how he felt about returning home when this was all over. Seeing his mother and sister. His people who might never hold him in regard again. His life had changed irrevocably, and I couldn't help feeling sympathy toward him. He was still young, but was supposed to be a man.

I shoved down my fury at the flirting princess on the royal dais. "I think my stomach is now the size of a pea."

"You look absolutely lovely, Jayden," he added with a shy smile.

Chemish nodded his agreement. "Palace life suits you."

I tried not to blush. "I've been assigned excellent personal maids. They used their magical skills on a plain desert girl."

The compliments were words I wanted to hear from Kadesh. The room around me loomed wide and enormous, the distance between me and the man I loved as vast as the desert.

While we ate roasted lamb and crisp steamed vegetables, a group of drummers thumped their instruments. The sound echoed through the high-ceilinged room and the pulse pounded my seat cushions, reverberating through my bones. My whole being responded to the sensuous sound, and the desire to dance lit a fire in my belly.

But fatigue was taking its toll on me and the heat of the room made my neck perspire. Finally, the waitstaff served luscious cakes and berries artfully arranged on dessert plates, and then receded into the dusky background while the lamps around the perimeter were extinguished.

All eyes were drawn to the main floor where the lights glowed more ardently.

An ache of homesickness began in my feet and spread through my body. I wanted to move, to whirl, to feel the power and awe of the dance shoot through my hair and fingers and toes. My hips began to sway, my arms desperate to float overhead just as they had on the night of my betrothal dance. I wanted to relive the exhilaration, the intoxicating thrill of my shimmying hips.

A set of draperies opened on either side of the room and eight female dancers entered, spinning in dresses of magenta, white, and gold decorated in beads and coins. The girls' hair had been magnificently draped in jewels, their eyes large and exotic.

I clutched the edge of the table to keep myself anchored.

It had been too long since I'd danced. Months seemed like years. Watching the girls on stage transported me back to the night of my betrothal dance. The long-ago sound of trills and laughter rang in my ears, the sweet aroma of sugared dumplings filling the tent.

One dancer caught my attention with her languid moves and swirling dress. I leaned forward, my eyes sliding along the girl's hips and torso. Her body was strong and tall as a jeweled column, just like an Egyptian goddess. My gaze narrowed and I gasped into my linen napkin. Behind the exotic costume and makeup, I recognized the distinctive dancer.

It was Leila.

25

My father recognized Leila a fraction of a moment later and he rose from his seat, jaw sagging, dazed by shock. "Leila!" he cried, his voice hoarse.

"Father!" I hissed, clutching at his hand to keep him next to me. "Please."

Asher glanced at us, confusion in his face.

I shook my head at him. The room hushed, all eyes mesmerized by the dancers.

"She's alive, father," I whispered.

"But she was in Egypt," he said, slowly sinking back to the cushions. "How did she get to the land of Sariba?"

"I'm just as astonished as you are. But just think! She's here. We can bring her to the palace." I rubbed my bare arms, a chill turning me cold when I recalled those two men with their pleated linen, bald heads, and falcon-headed staves, who had watched me enter the city in the procession. They were Egyptian. They must be some of the magicians Tijah had mentioned. Were they the men who had kidnapped Leila and the other girls from the Temple of Ashtoreth? Instead of taking them to Egypt, they had brought them to the southern lands.

None of it made any sense, but instinctively I recognized the reason those foreign men had watched me so particularly and performed their mocking bow. Because they knew I was Leila's sister. I shivered, feeling those ominous eyes on me all over again.

The music changed, the flutes and harp taking the melody, slowing the pace as the dancers widened their circle.

Before I was even aware she had risen from her chair, Princess Aliyah drifted down the steps of the dais. The fabric of her long, red gown slipped along the brilliant tiles as she joined the dancers in the center.

Making eye contact with each guest, the girl danced slowly about the room. Her hands moved in sculpted poses. Fluttering, wrists rolling luxuriously, fingers arching delicately. She told a story while her hips circled, and I was envious. I wanted to dance, too. In the privacy of my mother's tent, laughing with Leila.

But right now I just wanted to grab my sister and escape this place.

As though she'd read my mind, Aliyah glanced up and her eyes locked with mine. Before I knew what was happening, she crossed the floor and pulled me to my feet.

Kadesh jumped up from his chair, brows pulled together,

and panic on his face. He didn't sit down, but continued to stand, arms folded over his chest.

"No," I protested. "I can't—" I wanted to slink back to my table, but my hand was stuck to hers as though stitched together with invisible thread. She pulled me onto the dance floor, and the music took over. We whirled and dipped in the circle of girls. I flung my arm toward Leila, but she was always just out of reach.

The audience's faces blurred. So many eyes on my body and hips. My face flamed, but I couldn't get away from Aliyah and her hypnotic smile.

Drums throbbed at the soles of my feet. I wanted to grab my sister and steal her away. Find out what had happened to her when I saw her disappear down the stairs at the Temple of Ashtoreth with her kidnappers. Mostly, I wanted to flee from the watching audience. It was humiliating to dance before Kadesh and the king and my father, but I also felt a compulsion to dance. To move my hips until I dropped into a dreamless sleep from which I'd never awaken. The dichotomy made my head ache.

Aliyah's touch mesmerized me. I couldn't seem to catch a proper breath. I was drowning in the music and she was the siren pulling me to sea.

When we performed the final shimmies, my hips moved faster than I'd ever experienced before. The audience of guests and dignitaries were on their feet clapping.

At last, I sank to the floor with Aliyah to bow before the royal family.

When I rose to my feet I tried to catch Leila's attention again. Her eyes glazed over me without recognition, as though the eerie fog from outside had slithered into the hall and blinded her.

"Leila!" I whispered, but my sister never looked back as she followed the other dancers out the banquet hall doors. A strange heaviness weighed me down so that I could barely lift my arms. Like I was moving in a fog, too. A prisoner of Aliyah as she held my hands in hers.

Kadesh hadn't moved, staring at me with consternation. What right did he have to be angry—after all the secrets he'd kept? Secrets of past betrothals and missing parents he wouldn't talk about. It hadn't taken me long to notice Kadesh's parents were not in attendance on the royal family dais. I felt betrayed in a way I couldn't understand, even though he'd never out-right lied to me.

When Aliyah led me back to my father's table, my legs were wooden, like a doll from the marketplace. An inanimate object dressed up in fake finery.

The princess kissed my hand and tingles of heat shot up my arm. When she lifted her eyes to mine I wanted to recoil. "You dance exquisitely, Princess Jayden," she said.

"You know who I am?"

"I know everything about you, daughter of the Nephish. Welcome to the kingdom of Sariba."

She bowed to my father, and then to Chemish and Asher. Moving with elegance, Aliyah glided back to the dais. My body sagged as though she'd pulled out my soul in tiny pieces.

Once the applause died down, it was obvious the crowd was expecting the royal patriarch to speak. King Ephrem waved a feeble hand at his nephew to do the honors.

Kadesh's fingertips touched the top of the table in front of him, skin darkened by months of sun. "Dear friends, thank you for your generous welcome home. It's been a long year, not without strife and death and loss. I'm grateful to feast my eyes upon you, my fellow citizens in this glorious land of Sariba. I'm honored to welcome guests and fellow travelers from the kingdom of the Edomites and the tribe of Nephish."

All eyes turned to us, murmurs of welcome rippling throughout the hall.

"It's a privilege to have Lady Aliyah in our presence. We're grateful for the alliance we have with the kingdom of Sheba and its princess."

Kingdom of Sheba?

I groaned within myself, feeling stupid not to have made the connection earlier. Aliyah was a princess of Sheba. Sister to the queen. That's why she sat at the royal table. I'd been a fool to worry about Kadesh marrying the Queen of Sheba. What better way to forge an alliance than by uniting Kadesh and Aliyah, a princess his own age—and the two families who ruled the world's frankincense trade?

Now I could see the resemblance between the two women. The same lavender eyes rimmed in gold. The same ebony hair, golden skin, and flawless figure.

My maid's words returned to haunt me. *Princess Aliyah* must be the girl Kadesh was betrothed to. The girl he had once imagined sharing his bed in the marriage tent.

Even the Queen of Sheba had given me a subtle warning. Although why she would caution me about her own blood sister was mystifying. Her secret messages to Kadesh in the anteroom of the palace back at Sa'ba now became even more baffling—and even more sinister.

I stared daggers at Aliyah sitting next to Kadesh side by side on the kingship dais. Her perfect red lips, that stunning face inclined toward Kadesh. She smiled prettily at his speech, reaching out a finger to touch his cloak possessively.

I didn't belong here. I was a fool to believe Kadesh's family and kingdom and obligations wouldn't have a hold on him. A hold much stronger than mine.

I'd come to Sariba only to have my heart shattered.

So I did the only thing a desert girl could do.

I ran.

26

I was gone before my father could grab me. I heard him calling my name, but I wove through the crowded room and then shot out the door.

No servant tried to stop me. No guards barred the doors. Everyone gazed at me with dreamy expressions on their faces—as though Aliyah had put a spell on everybody. How did she do it? Her otherworldly beauty? An herbal potion?

Seraiah had tried to warn me of the magic in these lands. Powerful sorcerers who worshipped gods of the underworld. But even magic had its tricks and illusions.

Aliyah had seen me rise from my seat. Watched my face drain white, the ghost of a smile on her ruby red lips. She knew I was running. For all her smiles and grace and kisses, she'd intended this outcome all along. She'd come here to intimidate me. To show off my kidnapped sister right in front of me and my father.

I didn't understand how she was connected to the Temple of Ashtoreth and the magicians and kidnappers from Egypt, but I knew deep in my belly she was. Why else would Leila be in the same room and unable to recognize her family?

The hallways and corridors were a maze. I was the rat, cornered, with nowhere to hide, and I couldn't remember how to return to my own rooms.

Finally a set of steps appeared. I raced down the staircase to an outside door. Surprisingly there were no guards standing sentry. Was that part of Aliyah's plan? If she was only a priestess-in-training and this powerfully potent, the Sariba Goddess must be formidable indeed. The realization terrified me. I wasn't safe in these lands, and neither was Leila.

Outside the doors, I found myself in the misty fog. The stuff swirled around me, thick as soup, clinging to me in the same way Aliyah had. Gray wisps ran along the paving stones.

There were no stars or moon. Which path led to the mountains and which to the sea? If there were palace guards keeping watch, they were well hidden. A fact that didn't make me feel very safe.

I ran up and down several paths with raised flower beds, nearly crashing headlong into a garden of thorny rosebushes. A perfumed rainbow of reds, yellows, pinks, and purples. I caught myself just before I fell into a fountain. Even this late at night a fine mist of water sprayed into the air.

Then I heard the sound of camels and memories crashed. A

giant tidal wave of grief. As if I'd conjured it out of the mists, my family surrounded me like specters: my mother baking over the fire, Leila fashioning a new hairstyle in the copper mirror, my father driving down the tent stakes while baby camels toddled about the campsite.

How drastically my life had changed. How complicated it had become. "Mother!" I whispered to the heavens above me. "Why did you leave me alone?"

The muttering of camels grew louder. I followed the brick path, and wooden doors appeared out of the fog. Pushing through, I entered a series of enormous barns filled with the king's camels in individual stalls. One of the camels began to bray and I almost burst out laughing. Shay stood before me, placidly eating her dinner, blinking her long, dark lashes.

"Oh, Shay." I flung my arms around her neck and she bumped her nose into me in return. I held on to her as if I was trying to hold on to the past. "I hardly recognize you with the beads and tassels of Sariba. Why do they have you locked up in here?"

Upon closer inspection, I discovered that the back of each stall opened onto a wide, spacious corral. "Aren't you spoiled? No standing in the rain. Food whenever you want it."

My milky white camel nibbled at my hair, eating some of the gold shine, and then wrinkling her nose at the strange taste. "Don't make yourself sick."

Tendrils of fog slithered through the open barn door. I'd forgotten to close it. But from out of the dark night Asher suddenly rushed through, halting when he saw me.

"What are you doing here?" I demanded. "Has Kadesh entrusted you to be my bodyguard again? Well, I don't need a bodyguard any longer. I don't need anybody."

Asher glanced down at his clenched hands, not answering at first. Then he said, "I chased you all over the gardens. Why did you run away?"

I stared at him, surprised Asher would run to my aid after what had happened to him and Laban on the desert that awful night. "Can't you tell I want to be alone?"

"You're crying," he said.

I turned away, feeling stupid for weeping, but his presence just reminded me of the mortification I'd endured in the royal dining hall.

His voice softened. "You're tired, Jayden. You've undergone a brutal journey of more than three full moons. I'm sure you're missing home, your mother."

"Don't placate me. I don't belong here at the palace, or anywhere in the southern lands."

"You belong here as much as anybody else. More so. You're the girl Kadesh loves."

"Don't speak to me of that. After Aliyah made me dance his eyes were so disappointed." I began to ramble incoherently. "I could see—it all became clear—that he—"

Asher came closer. "You know nothing."

I jerked away. "It wasn't difficult to figure out Aliyah is a princess of Sheba. And that *she* is Kadesh's betrothed. The nations of Sa'ba and Sariba—already connected by family blood and the frankincense trail—should marry."

"Who told you Kadesh was betrothed?"

"Does it matter? Once I realized Aliyah is the Queen of Sheba's sister, it all fell into place. Just please—please leave me alone," I said with a sigh. "I'll take my camel and be gone before dawn."

"You'll die before you get to the first well."

"Who will even notice or care?" I knew I was being unreasonable, but I was sick of the deceit, the running, the constant fear. My heart was so numb I wasn't sure it could still beat properly. "Maybe I should run to the Qara mountains and live there. If I wasn't here in the city of Sariba perhaps Horeb would give up. I wouldn't be putting anyone else in danger."

Asher flung his hand at my suggestion. "Kadesh would care. And so would I."

I looked down, uncomfortable, not wanting his feelings to be so plainly written on his face. I couldn't worry about him so much. We were surrounded by too many dangers and I had to keep Leila, as well as the people of Sariba, safe.

He took a step forward. "I want you to listen to me. Just listen because I'm going to tell you something very important."

My chin jerked up, surprised at his sober tone.

"Tonight, you were a vision of the land of Sariba, Jayden. Your gown reminded us of the green mountains of Qara that bring us life and every good thing. You danced with heart among those girls who just went through a piece of rote choreography. Everybody saw it. The entire room watched, hardly daring to breathe. We all felt your pure love and innocence." Asher paused, and his eyes met mine. "You are the princess they've all been waiting for."

I was speechless. Tears of remorse and shame filled Asher's eyes. Embarrassed, he brushed at them and turned away to leave.

I held out my hand to stop him. "Thank you, Asher. That's one of the loveliest things anybody has ever said to me."

He lowered himself to his knees before me while a wave of disconsolation washed across his face. "One day I will prove myself to you and Kadesh again. I will make up for all my sins." His voice strained to speak without breaking down. "I know I'm lucky to be alive."

There was a noise behind Asher, and when I looked up, Kadesh stood there, his chest heaving. His face held so much hurt it was as though he'd been physically wounded. It was obvious he'd heard our words.

"What is going on here?" he demanded. "Asher, what is this between you two? After all that happened in the Empty Sands—after Laban's execution—" Kadesh put a fist to his mouth, his own voice breaking.

Asher sagged against one of the beams of the stall. He buried his face in his hands, and then looked up with pleading eyes. "I only ran after Jayden when she disappeared . . . I was worried for her safety."

I stared at the prince I loved with all my soul, and had nearly died to find. He gazed back at me, waiting for an answer. The silence was horrible, accusatory.

"How can *you* explain?" Hurt laced my own voice. "No, don't answer. I can't do this, not here, not now."

I brushed past Kadesh, running out the barn doors again to the courtyard gardens, past the fountain still shooting water into the midnight air.

The fog had lifted a bit and I could see the path more clearly now. Lights from the palace illuminated the blossoming fruit trees and hanging willows. Picking up my skirts, I raced toward the palace door I'd sprinted out of earlier.

"Jayden!" The unhappiness in Kadesh's voice was palpable. If he wanted to explain his life, the betrothal he was obligated to fulfill, he could come to me.

I wouldn't say good-bye in a barn.

I flung open the side door and ran inside the lush hallway. My hair had come loose from its jeweled clasps, waves of curls crashing over my eyes. A servant woman walked toward me, a tray in her hands. "My bedroom," I gasped. "Please tell me which hall."

She pointed and gave me quick directions.

The outside door to the gardens opened and closed with a bang behind me. I picked up my skirts and rushed forward.

"Good evening, Prince Kadesh," I heard the woman say. "May I get something for you and Sir Asher?"

I groaned. They were *both* chasing after me.

When I found the correct hall, Tijah rose from the chair where she'd been waiting for me. "My lady, what has happened to you? There's straw in your hair!"

Without answering, I collided into the bedroom door and flung myself inside. Sobs wracked my chest. My head ached, my throat was scratchy, even my skin felt strange, as if I were coming down with a fever. The life I'd dreamed about with Kadesh had vanished this evening. Melting into the peculiar fog of this strange land.

Where would I go? What would become of me or my father? I had no idea what the rules were here. And now Kadesh had turned back into the stranger I'd met a year ago. Did I know enough about him to commit the rest of my life to him? To give him my heart and soul and never regret it?

I staggered to the sofa when Kadesh and Asher burst through the door of the suite.

Tijah gasped at their tall, looming figures filling the room. She and Jasmine scurried out of sight.

Kadesh's face was aflame. "Jayden, we *have* to talk tonight." He turned to Asher. "Leave us. This doesn't concern you."

"Stop, both of you!" I held up my hands. "This does concern Asher. You've both kept secrets from me. Whether intentionally or not. But clearly, after what happened tonight, you both *knew*. You *knew* Aliyah was—is—Kadesh's betrothed. You knew that she's sister to the Queen of Sheba. And you both said nothing."

Kadesh strode toward me, but I stepped out of his reach.

"Tonight it became obvious there is no life for me here."

The color drained from his face. "No life for you? But I want to give you all my life, all that I have . . ."

Asher circled the room. "I was trying to tell Jayden how untrue her fears are. Just now when you found us. I began to tell her what *you* should have already confided to her."

Guilt filled Kadesh's dark eyes. "I planned to tell you,

Jayden. All along. When I was in the northern deserts with your family, my life here felt so far away. I wasn't prince; I wasn't beholden to any of my obligations. And, at one point I was a dead man and none of it seemed to matter any longer."

"What didn't matter?" I asked.

Kadesh knelt before the couch where I perched, touching the hem of my green gown between his fingers. The silver ankle bracelet bumped against his palm and he held it out where it sparked under the lamp light. "I discovered a new life with you, Jayden. I didn't want to spoil the little time we had with politics, tribal alliances, and all the worries of my kingdom. Most of this last year we've spent torn apart by Horeb, separated. I planned to take you aside tonight. I planned to find a quiet place where there weren't a hundred listening Edomite ears." He shot a backward glance at Asher.

"Just *tell her*, Kadesh," Asher said. "She deserves to know . . . everything."

I shook my head. "You both talk in such cryptic terms. Kadesh, why didn't you come to me earlier, before that horrible dinner party?"

"But I did," he said. "I came to your rooms this morning but they said you were still sleeping. I didn't want to wake you after the difficult journey."

My voice quieted. "Is that the truth?"

"I swear to you, Jayden."

"I died a thousand times tonight. My servant girl told me you were betrothed to someone else. Aliyah is the sister to the Queen of Sheba. It wasn't difficult to figure out."

Kadesh sank into a chair, holding his head in his hands. "I should have forced them to wake you. Jayden, please forgive me. Even if you leave with the next spice caravan and run far away, please tell me I haven't lost you forever."

A well of sorrow rose up. "Why did you bring me to your homeland when you were betrothed to a princess of Sa'ba? I feel like a fool."

"I brought you here because I plan to make you my wife."

My throat was thick with horror at what he was insinuating. "I won't be your second wife, Kadesh. No matter how much I love you."

Kadesh grabbed my hands in his. I tried to pull away, but he wouldn't let me go. "Aliyah is *not* my wife. And she will never be my wife."

"But you're betrothed to her."

"It was arranged, just like you and Horeb. Yes, I grew up thinking we would marry, but Aliyah made a horrifying choice and I broke the betrothal."

I tried to take in what he was saying, but I still felt numb. "When did this happen?"

"Almost two years ago. Long before you found me wounded by raiders."

Impulsively, I touched the spot on his chest where the scar from the sword wound lay, the spot I'd tended to with frankincense to save his life a year ago. My eyes flickered upward. "What was Aliyah's horrible decision?"

"She joined the temple of the Sariba Goddess to train as a priestess. A woman who performs the Sacred Marriage Rite with priests of Ba'al can't be the next queen."

I was engulfed by fatigue. Horeb had no qualms about that with the High Priestess Armana. But he was only using her to gain access to the wealth of the temple.

"I'm ashamed to think Aliyah was my betrothed. Because—" He took off his crown and slammed it to the table. There *was* more, but Kadesh couldn't seem to force the words out.

Asher stood in the doorway of the suite. "Tell her why. Or I will." He paused. "I know my reckless, stupid decisions in the desert almost caused our deaths, but this—Kadesh, she needs to know to be able to live here."

"How can there be more? What else is there?"

Kadesh's face was stricken, as though all of his secrets were trapped inside a nightmare. He fell into one of the cushioned armchairs. He appeared exhausted and haunted.

I closed the hallway door and then kneeled at Kadesh's feet. I felt broken inside, as if I'd swallowed a plate of thorns. "Please, just tell me. Or your secrets will eat me alive."

"I was watching you tonight. The most beautiful girl in the room. And I watched you as you recognized Leila—the heartache when you saw that peculiar vacant look in her eyes."

"She's here at the Temple of Sariba, but I don't know why. Not after watching that Egyptian caravan steal her and the other two girls away."

"I've seen a few other Egyptians around the city today. They weren't here when I left home a year ago. I have meetings set up with my city managers later tonight. I want to know who they are and what their business is."

"You need sleep, too, Kadesh. Horeb is getting closer."

"I'll sleep after the war is over," he said drily.

"I have a new plan. I could escape to the Qara mountains. Lure Horeb away, and then, when he can't find me he would leave the city of Sariba alone."

"You are not running away," Kadesh said firmly. "We're going to get rid of the threat of Horeb once and for all."

I bit at my lip. There would be time to talk strategy for defeating Horeb tomorrow. "You spoke of Leila just now. What are you referring to?"

He glanced down at me where I kneeled on the luxurious rugs. "I've seen that hollow expression before."

"What do you mean?"

"I saw it in my mother's eyes."

I reared back, my thoughts flying in every direction. "What does your mother have to do with Aliyah?"

"My mother was ensnared into the temple religion. The rites, the ceremonies, the worship at the feet of the idol Goddess. My father and I watched her disintegrate as the Goddess's brainwashing methods worked their power on her. She became despondent, prone to nightmares and dizziness. The dizziness turned into seizures, which left her ill for days later. My father and I began to suspect she was being drugged." Kadesh's knuckles turned white on the arms of the chair and each word he spoke was slow and tortured.

Coldness spread through me. "What happened, Kadesh?" I asked, placing my hands on his knees. "Why do they drug the girls, the women?"

"The spells and potions, the incantations—it's the only way to convince a girl she'll do anything to please her Goddess. Their minds become foggy and childlike. And it numbs them to pain. After the spring Sacred Marriage Rites, there is a sacrificial offering in the summer. An offering of gratitude to the Goddess of Sariba and the God of Ba'al for the bounty of the land. For crops and new children birthed."

"Someone has to volunteer," Asher said, turning to me. "A free offering of soul and body."

I shook my head. "No," I whispered.

"My mother—the queen of Sariba—took her own life at the altar of the Sariba Goddess. She sacrificed herself. The most powerful offering ever. More powerful when it's voluntary. More powerful when you thrust the knife into your own heart. And nothing else can surpass the sacrifice when you're queen of the land."

The shock of his words sent me reeling. "Oh, Kadesh."

He put his hands on my face, holding on to me as though he was about to drown in grief. "Yes, I should have told you long ago, but I was ashamed. And guilty."

"There's nothing to be ashamed of. You did nothing wrong. The temples trap the girls."

"Before my mother's death, I'd agreed to fulfill the betrothal contract and marry Aliyah. Our marriage would bring her to the palace to live permanently—which was her intent—even though she spent more time at the temple and less time planning the wedding."

"I don't understand."

"The Queen of Sheba discovered Aliyah had forged letters to my uncle impersonating her to request the marriage ceremony be performed soon. At the time I was only seventeen, younger than most men who marry. The letters encouraged us not to wait for political reasons, despite the fact we were not at war with anyone, and were enjoying a time of peace. Trade was good, the frankincense trees thriving, and our forts along the Red Sea were under construction. The letters said there was no reason to wait, that aligning the two of us in marriage would only strengthen our forts and wealth."

"Aliyah is a liar and counterfeiter," I said. "Conniving and completely unashamed."

"In truth, Aliyah wanted permanent and constant access to the palace, not just the temple."

"If she wasn't raised here in Sariba, why was she so interested in becoming a priestess?"

"At first, she wanted to study medicine and become a physician, as some of the women in Egypt have done. The queen sent her to Babylon to live with distant relatives. Aliyah fell in love with the goddess religion, but Aliyah is incapable of true love. She only wants to control others."

"And," I said slowly, "marrying you was an easy method to gain legal access to the throne."

"She lusts for power most of all," Asher added from the corner.

Leaning close, Kadesh traced his fingers along my jaw, stopping when he reached my lips. He was uncertain of me now, and he dropped his hands, his body turning rigid. "After what the temple did to my mother I would tear it down myself, brick by brick if I could. But the temple has seduced my people. It wields political and economic power over our merchants and farmers. They fear the Goddess's wrath if they don't worship her. They live under the threat that without the power of the rites and sacrifices, the Goddess will collapse the city economically and politically. If that happened any ruler could take over easily. Death to our citizens would naturally follow."

The glow from the table lamp cast shadows on Asher's face. "But she has already brought death. The Sariba Goddess has an insatiable appetite. First Kadesh's mother, and there have been others since."

I shuddered at his defeated tone. "I suppose when Aliyah came here as your betrothed, your mother followed her to worship at the temple."

"It was a gesture of friendship and loyalty as the wedding plans began. My mother is—was kindness itself, but she had a weak constitution. She was no match for Aliyah's passionate personality and her zealous ambition."

"She has a magnetic personality," I said. "I can see people following her."

"It's even worse than that," Asher added.

The room was darkening. In the twilight Kadesh looked like a lost boy. I wanted to comfort him, but I remained still. "How could there be more?" I asked.

Kadesh rubbed at his face, quiet for a moment. "My mother was drugged a little at a time by the High Priestess. She dabbles in herbs and medicine, like the magicians of Egypt. She had spell books shipped to her. Concoctions to bring the initiate girls into alignment with her will. She has a way of weakening others' minds. Drugs that bring about confusion, memory loss, and physical weakness."

"That's why Leila and the other dancers moved as if in a dream. It explains why my sister didn't recognize me or my father."

"My mother thought she was helping me. That by offering her life to the Goddess my union with Aliyah would be stronger. Our kingdom indomitable. She'd been brainwashed. In actuality, she was slowly going insane."

The spilling of long-held secrets was taking its toll on Kadesh. He didn't look well at all. Slowly, I reached out to touch the hair along his forehead, smoothed his brow with my fingertips. "What did your father do after your mother's death?"

"I watched him turn into a madman next. His grief was horror itself. My mother was everything to him. One morning, I found him in his study, dead by his own sword."

"Oh, Kadesh, I'm so sorry." Tears threatened to spill from my eyes, but I could only reach out to wipe the tears rolling down his scarred cheek. I moved closer, our faces within a breath's distance of each other. Holding his face in my palms, I said, "I'm so sorry to make you relive these memories."

His bottomless eyes were filled with pain. "I've wanted to tell you, but I never had the courage. I didn't want to disgust you with my family's story. To bring you to a broken kingdom. I was selfish, but I wanted you so badly. I knew if anyone could help me heal this land you could with your strength and genuine unconditional love. Uncle Ephrem may not be alive a year from now, and I am his heir now that my father is gone. I needed a weapon against Aliyah. And I—"

I gave a small laugh. "You greatly overestimate me. How can I be a weapon for you? Do you want a girl to infiltrate the temple of the Sariba Goddess? To learn its secret plans and strategies? To destroy its poison and propaganda?"

"I would *never* send you to the temple. And I'm going to help you get Leila back before her mind is destroyed. I'm marrying you because my kingdom will be stronger with a king and queen on the throne who can fight to save Sariba. If you still want me for your husband."

"I'm not being fair questioning your intentions. After all, I asked you to save my family from Horeb. An enormous thing to ask of you and you've done it willingly." I turned to Asher. "So have the Edomites. You've harbored me and my family, and now you're willing to fight for our survival at the risk of your own lives and kingdom."

We'd had the threat of Horeb's armies following us for months. Now a corrupt temple with a devious and scheming priestess was laid at my feet. The Land of Sariba was treacherous. Not a safe haven at all.

Kadesh clasped my hands. He seemed to gain strength from our touch. "My uncle tells me Aliyah's influence has infiltrated the palace. We don't know who yet. Servants, guards, or cooks who do her bidding to taint the food or water supply. Once we have evidence, they'll be executed for endangering the royal family."

"The problem is the citizens don't believe Aliyah is danger-ous," I said, thinking out loud. "They only want to maintain their prosperity. How have you escaped her brainwashing?"

"I was the one who found my parents dead. First my mother at the altar, and then my father in his private rooms. Aliyah planned it that way to bring me under her influence. She thought it would show me how powerful the Goddess was and that we needed to be completely obedient to make sure the frankincense caravans kept flowing to the north. Instead, the opposite happened. I hated her and everything about the temple. My ancestors worshipped the God of Abraham, not the cults of gods and goddesses who demand your body and soul as their own. To torture or kill in the name of love is a vicious doctrine of the most devious kind. When I departed Sariba a year ago on that fateful caravan, I left knowing I had to figure out a way to defeat her. But it took so many months to return."

"Because of me and Horeb." I remembered the hazy con-fusion in my mind when I followed Aliyah onto the dance floor. "The only reason I danced tonight was because of what I ate. My food was targeted to lure me into going to her."

"I fear that's true. But many people in the dining hall tonight are loyal to the temple. Their livelihood comes from the goddess."

"That's why you looked so furious."

"Politely furious." He feigned a smile. "But you were love-lier than I've ever seen you. You dance with all of your soul, Jayden. A heart of genuine purity and trust."

"But why did you allow me to go down to the dance floor—"

"I dared not make a scene during the first royal dinner after a year. My aunts love Aliyah. They don't see the wily, crafty priestess I know. They can't bring themselves to believe it was the temple Goddess who sent my parents to their deaths. Going insane and killing yourself is not the way a queen and king should die. Their suicides brought shame to our city and caused my people to turn away from the royal family and embrace the ways of the temple even more."

Chills prickled along my neck. "How can a relatively new priestess wield such power?"

"She's been in training since she was sixteen years old and arrived from Sa'ba. The farmers say there are spirits in the mountain of the Goddess temple. That the spirits of past goddesses whisper in her ears and commune with her under the moon."

"That's where the stories come from," I said, thinking aloud. "The stories of magical spirits guarding the frankincense trees. The priestesses use those groves for their rituals. Kadesh, there is so much I have to learn about your people, but I cannot do it unless you confide everything to me. You must promise to trust me for the rest of our lives."

"I was afraid you would reject my proposal if I told you everything."

"Aliyah and the High Priestess are the ones to be rejected," I said with severity.

"Unfortunately, Aliyah and the High Priestess are now one and the same. She was recently promoted, which means her power is that much stronger."

"But she's so young." Sweat trickled down the inside of my gown. The situation just got worse and worse.

"Last night I learned that the old High Priestess was found dead in her bed two months ago."

"Dead? How?"

"The physicians couldn't determine whether it was natural causes or foul play. Despite her youth Aliyah elevated herself to the highest position at the temple by calling in favors from the other women. Using blackmail, making promises. She's charismatic and gets what she wants—and all the other priestesses admire her. To their detriment."

Asher spoke up. "The only thing left that Aliyah covets is the position of High Priestess *and* queen of Sariba."

"How will she make that happen?" The dread growing in my stomach turned poisonous.

"At the summer solstice there will be another human sacrifice."

I staggered against the desk behind me. Ceramic figurines crashed to the floor, shards flying. "I know why Aliyah brought Leila and the other girls from the Temple of Ashtoreth. She plans to make my sister the sacrifice."

27

aking Leila the sacrifice perfectly suits Aliyah's evil designs. A sacrifice to the Sariba Goddess, who will then be considered more powerful than the Goddess of Ashtoreth. That's why my sister was taken." I held my hands to my stomach, feeling ill. "Leila was probably glad to volunteer. Thinking she'd become even more divine, more special, and important."

"And the High Priestess Armana was probably paid handsomely," Kadesh added.

"Killing my sister would cause such hatred in my heart Pharez and I would leave this land—which would mean relinquishing you to Aliyah, Kadesh. All part of her plan."

Kadesh's fingers tightened around my wrists as though I'd become his lifeline to reality. "If we marry quickly, our union will slow her down."

"This is the reason the Queen of Sheba advised us to marry quickly and create a lavish wedding. But Aliyah will kill me if she has to." This couldn't be happening; it was all so insane, but I knew it was true. "My father will die. Leila's sacrifice will literally break his heart."

"Aliyah will think twice before destroying a second king and queen within two years. She doesn't want an uprising. She needs the people's docile obedience to carry out a coup."

I paced the floor. "Maybe. Maybe not." A shudder ran through me as though I were getting a premonition of my own death.

"Remember what the Queen of Sheba told us in the anteroom?"

"I can't seem to forget." I recalled the intense lavender eyes of the queen. There was something she had said that I couldn't stop wondering about and what she had meant.

Asher stepped between us. "There are many reasons to marry quickly, not just to thwart Aliyah. When you are queen of Sariba one day, Horeb will have no hold on you. He cannot claim betrothals or contracts. You can order his execution if you want."

"His execution?" I repeated. "If I did we'd have a full-blown war."

"War is already coming," Asher said soberly. He turned away to stare out the window, clearly remembering his traitorous messages that gave Horeb such a great advantage.

"And Chemish and I have been meeting with Uncle Ephrem and the generals to concoct a plan."

"That's where you've been the past two days." I'd been troubled by his secrets and the fragile trust between us. Jealous of a girl who no longer had a soul.

"Have you heard from our scouts, Asher?" Kadesh asked.

"No, and it worries my father."

"In the morning," Kadesh said to me, "we're scheduled to meet with my uncle and Pharez. We'll get the marriage contract signed. Then I'll spend the rest of the day with Chemish and the Sariba army."

"Doesn't meeting with you and the king go against protocol? The bride is never allowed to attend a marriage contract meeting."

"These are special circumstances." Kadesh gave me a tired smile. "I want you to trust me completely. I'm assigning guards directly to your suite, too."

"Am I not already protected while in the palace?"

"Aliyah, as sister to the Queen of Sheba, has access to the palace. I'm going to have to figure out a way to ban her without bringing down her wrath and causing chaos. Too many of my own servants and staff have been seduced by her cunning."

"Go carefully," Asher said. "The walls may very well have ears—and lips to impart treachery. I'll be here to protect you both. I pledge my life to you and I hope you can entrust your well-being in my hands once more."

Kadesh looked deeply at Asher, and after a moment, he nodded. "The Sariba Goddess can't steal our hearts or free will unless we give them to her."

I understood what he was saying, but everything changed

when sedition came into play. Potions, drugs, coercion, blackmail, blind obedience to a powerful being—and a citizenship too afraid *not* to worship the Goddess.

After Kadesh and Asher departed, I wanted to strip off the fancy green gown and flop into bed, but Jasmine insisted on cleaning the dress while Tijah washed the rouge and kohl from my face and applied lotion to my skin.

When I finally crawled under the cool sheets I was as tired as when I'd arrived from the desert. But now I had the weight of a thousand new worries.

Tijah lowered her voice. "Did you know there's a personal guard outside your door and one on the courtyard outside the windows?"

I was grateful for Kadesh's swift action. The peace of mind knowing guards were so close. But when the lamps were extinguished, I drifted in and out, too exhausted to sleep deeply. Shudders crawled all over my skin as though I had a fever.

I woke sometime before dawn. I'd been dreaming, but the details were elusive. I was left only with a sense of dread.

Once light appeared through the draperies, I rose and I dressed, seeking fresh air, seeking something I wasn't even sure I could define. When I ran a brush through my hair, flecks of gold dust fell into the washing bowl. The reality of the previous night returned with startling force.

Pulling on a simple dress of burgundy I stuck my toes into a pair of slippers and tiptoed past the beds of my maids. The candles in the wall sconces were melting when I cracked open the door. I almost stumbled over someone lying on the carpets.

At first I presumed it was a male servant, but then the man rolled over and grinned at me. "Kadesh! What are you doing on the floor?"

"I was hoping you'd wake early. I was about to go in and get you myself, but I didn't want to alarm your maids."

"Why aren't you in your own rooms? I'm perfectly fine."

There was a moment of silence while we gazed at each other.

"*We* are not perfectly fine, Jayden," he whispered.

I nodded, biting at my lips.

"We have an audience with Ephrem and your father in a few hours, but right now we're getting out of the palace. It may be our only chance. I want to show you my country. *Our* kingdom," he added, reaching up to stroke my face.

I gave him a wobbly smile.

Holding hands, we raced through the winding hallways and out the rear doors. A stable boy had two black Arabians saddled and ready. Kadesh helped me onto the smaller gelding and I grasped the reins.

A moment later, we flew through the rear gates and headed toward the mountains.

28

At first, I was surprised the palace guards would let Kadesh out of their sight. But it wasn't long before I noticed royal soldiers with sabers hovering in the background.

The horses skirted the city streets, taking side roads until we reached the city limits at the limestone cliffs. A series of switchbacks took us higher into the northern flat-topped peaks.

Far away in the distance, the blue-green sea sparkled with sunbeams on frothy, silent waves. Above us in the foothills of the Qara Mountains, the Temple of Sariba's towering walls rose throne-like, embedded with glittering stones of sapphire and amethyst. The towers were capped gold like the sun, so bright my eyes hurt.

Kadesh dismissed the temple with an expression I couldn't read. "Let's keep climbing. I have so much to show you."

When we nudged our horses forward again, the cry of a bird razed the air. A magnificent falcon with black feathers and a white downy breast wheeled over our heads.

"Look!" I pointed. The creature soared and then circled to fly lower and lower. The movement of his wings fluttered as a breeze against my face.

We walked deeper into the forest and the air cooled. My mood lifted as birds chattered and mourning doves called. A squirrel raced up a tree to hide behind the leafy fronds. Wild-flowers blossomed along the paths.

When we bumped legs on a narrow passage, Kadesh reached out to press my hand. My love for him created an ache in my throat.

I leaned forward in the saddle when we climbed the last steep incline. At the crest my horse's silky mane whipped in the warm breeze.

In a hollow of hills lay a picturesque lake. Ripples danced along its surface. Pine trees, tamarisk, and willows formed thick groves around the water.

I ducked under branches, the path winding its way about the shoreline. The sound of rushing water grew louder. A moment later the path turned to face a waterfall gushing down a second set of cliffs above us.

Kadesh dismounted and tied up his horse, then helped me down.

"I think you've worked a magic of your own, Prince of the Sariba Lands. You've transported us to the Garden of Eden."

"Come on, we can duck behind the water using this path."

Within moments we were standing on the edge of a limestone opening, gazing through a curtain of water pounding its way from high above to the lake below.

"Is there a river where the waterfall originates?"

"This is the last of the spring runoff. We irrigate the frankincense groves using canals and ditches."

We stood quietly, listening to the rushing water, without speaking. After several moments, Kadesh put an arm around my waist, pulling me in tight. I leaned my head into his chest. We gazed out through the dazzling waterfall to the peaceful lake beyond.

"Kadesh," I said, lifting my face. "I'm sorry for doubting you."

"It's my fault. I should have trusted you months ago with my family's tragedy."

"I remember how angry I was the day my mother died. You stumbled into our camp and then collapsed, bleeding to death. I had to take care of you. If we died on the journey, separated from the tribe, I was ready to blame you. Of course, it was only in my head I hated you." I laughed at the memory. "Until I knew that I loved you."

Kadesh brushed back my hair with his fingers, his own face in shadow from the rock overhang. From this angle I couldn't see his eye patch or the scar running jaggedly down the left side of his face. For one brief moment it was as though nothing had ever happened, as if he were whole and unblemished.

"You've endured terrible tragedies," I said softly. "To watch your parents die under such excruciating circumstances."

Kadesh surrounded me with his cloak in the damp air. I put my arms around his waist and held him tight. "I've had to work hard not to hate. Not to call on the army of Sariba to destroy the temple . . ."

His voice trailed away and I became aware of the juggling act Kadesh had to control. To keep the city safe while appeasing the Goddess and her power over the people.

"Even a land of beauty comes with a price."

I glanced up at him, his words echoing between us. "What did the Queen of Sheba mean when she asked you to take care of something? She was quite cryptic, but I had a feeling you knew what she meant."

I felt rather than saw Kadesh's reaction of surprise. "And don't try to hide it from me," I added with a small laugh.

"The queen has come to the conclusion that I might need to have Aliyah assassinated."

I gave a sharp intake of breath. "She would kill her own sister?"

"Aliyah has a peculiar hold on the people. We're not sure how to stop it. But we must to preserve our people and this country. Isn't it better for one person to die than an entire nation vanish into history?"

"But to kill her . . . murder." The idea made me sick. "The duties of a king are more ruthless than I imagined."

"I don't want to resort to that. I fear it could backfire against us, but Aliyah has gained in strength this last year. Uncle Ephrem wanted to wait and see what happened. I think he hoped the people would turn against her when my parents died. But just the opposite occurred. I fear it was a decision my uncle should have made. I keep hoping I can weaken Aliyah without killing her."

"The situation keeps getting more complicated."

"Unfortunately, my love."

I twisted a strand of his dark hair with my fingers. "And now, you must kiss me so I know you still love me."

"Oh, Jayden, I never stopped."

My arms went around his neck and I pressed my lips against his. Exhilaration rushed from my toes all the way up through my belly and into my heart. I savored the strength of his arms, breathed in the taste of him. Our kisses turned deeper and I swore I was falling into him, our spirits and bodies entwining.

He murmured against my mouth, "We'd better leave before we lose our senses in this cave."

"What better place to kiss me than a cave where nobody is watching?"

Kadesh ran his fingers through the length of my hair. "Too late for that. Behind those rustling bushes are my bodyguards."

My eyes widened.

"Our secret is safe with them. Besides, we are as good as betrothed."

My lips quivered. "Are we really betrothed?"

"In my mind we have been since the night of Hakak's wedding. When I promised my love and gave you the bracelet of my homeland. My mother's bracelet."

"Which I wear without ceasing. To wear it is to honor her, and the love you will always carry for her."

At my words, Kadesh's face twisted with emotion. "I plan to make the announcement before the court tonight."

We kissed each other one last time and then mounted our horses again. The path led into fields of grain and orchards of fruit trees. Beyond the apricots and mangoes were the frankincense groves, numberless trees as far as I could see.

I stared into the horizon. "Where do they end?"

"There are days I'm not sure they do," Kadesh answered. "All I know for certain is that the frankincense trees *do* end at the border of the Empty Sands."

We crossed an incline and rode up to a group of workers wearing white linen shifts. Getting off my horse, I approached one of the musky-scented trees. Its twisted limbs had the appearance of an old man with gnarled knuckles. The tops of the trees were a flat shape, the leaves a rich, dark green. "The branches are completely twisted, as though writhing from their limbs. Taller than I expected, too."

"The older trees are." Kadesh directed my line of sight. "See over there? A layer of mist lies on those brooding mountains. We often find frankincense trees growing naturally from outcroppings of rocks. The monsoons and cooler summers make them flourish."

Taking out a knife, he cut a piece of golden honey-colored resin dripping down the trunk. "The sap runs down in rivulets and then hardens." He pulled my palm toward him and placed the nugget of frankincense in my hand. "See? The trees weep. Creating frankincense tears for my love."

The golden piece shimmered in the cup of my hand. I

lifted my eyes to his, tears blurring my vision. Nearly a year ago Kadesh had spoken those same words to me. The day he'd given me a handful of frankincense nuggets I'd used to purchase my dagger and camel before the treacherous journey to find him.

I tucked the freshly cut frankincense into the pocket of my dress while Kadesh spoke with some of the workers about the current grafting. I was sure he had a thousand tasks to attend to after being out of his country for so long.

The orchard employees, I noticed, were careful not to stare at Kadesh's eye patch and scars, but I could see sorrow in their faces.

I kept to the shade of a wide, flourishing tree while the sun beat down. My stomach rumbled. We'd left the palace before the morning meal, and I was hungry.

Kadesh strode back, his long cloak flapping in the breeze. "I should have brought a lunch with us. We could have spent the rest of the day in our hidden waterfall lair, eating and napping."

I wagged my finger, trying not to smile at his boyish eyes.

"A man in love can always dream, can't he?" he said with a grin. "On our way home, I'm going to take you to one of my favorite places."

We took off at a gallop, following the mountain trails a different way home, skirting the switchbacks we'd taken to climb onto the plateaus of frankincense groves.

After descending a stony path, we came onto one of the cliff fingers overlooking the ocean. The expansive pristine white beach was protected by a half-moon of red cliffs edging the swirling sea. The city of Sariba was secluded, isolated by mountains and ocean.

We tied our horses to a scrub brush and stood at the edge of the cliff. I hung on to Kadesh's arm and gazed down at the pounding surf, waves crashing against jagged boulders below.

"Have you ever sailed this ocean?" I asked, trying to imagine what lay beyond the deep waters.

"It's one of my greatest dreams. Someday we'll explore the coastline in our very own ship. But nobody has gone south to the horizon and returned to tell about it."

A gust of hot wind blasted us. The sky turned black as churning clouds blotted out the sun. Something strange came over me, and I wavered on my feet. My head began to spin, as though someone were whirling me about in a circle.

"Aah!" I moaned. Pain slammed behind my eyes, so excruciating I wanted to tear my own hair out. Rip out my burning eyes and stab myself with my dagger.

An inexplicable urge came over me. To throw myself off the cliff and sail through the air like an eagle. I watched my body break against the rocks below. Bloody limbs, my head cracked wide. And then the ocean waves lifting me up and washing me out to sea.

Falling to the edge of the cliff, my shoulders trembled violently and my stomach lurched.

As if from a great distance, I heard Kadesh shouting my name. "Jayden? Jayden, are you all right?"

And then everything went black.

29

When I opened my eyes I was lying on my back. My fingers clawed at the rough red rock, hanging on while the world tilted. But the sun was shining, the sky overhead an azure blue.

Down below, the peaceful sounds of the surf wafted upward.

"What happened?" I asked weakly.

"Lie still. You're white as a corpse." Kadesh untied his water bag and gave me a small sip, cradling my head in his lap. "We were standing here enjoying the view. You became ill and fainted. Don't move until we're sure you haven't injured yourself."

My eyes bounced from his face to the sky and then back to the cliffs. "I think I just remembered my nightmare from last night."

"You didn't tell me you had a nightmare." Kadesh's voice was subdued, cautious.

"I saw terrible things. I was right here on this cliff in my dream. And I sent myself over the edge—to my death." A sharp wind brought tears to my eyes. "Why would I do such a horror?"

Kadesh wrapped his cloak around me. "You're shivering."

"I feel as though I'm burning up! My head is on fire!"

Kadesh held me close, but I pushed him away, agitated. "Tell me what this means. You *know*. I can see it in your eyes."

His face filled with such despair, a tear trickled down his face. "My mother had the same nightmares. They began a year before her death."

"What? Oh, dear God, Kadesh, *no*! Aliyah is in my mind. How can she do that?"

"I should never have let you dance with her last night. I'm a coward."

I pressed my fingers against his lips. "Please don't say that."

He clutched me against him and I buried my face in his chest, limp as a rag doll. "The Sariba Goddess is after everyone I love. She wants to torture me until I die."

"Or until you marry her," I said soberly. "She'll drug me or hypnotize to keep me away from you." I searched his face and saw truth there. "Or somehow I'll be the instrument to kill you when she's done with you and owns the Sariba Kingdom throne while her own hands will remain pure."

"Let's get home," he said softly. "You need to rest."

"I'm not sure I'll ever be able to sleep again. I don't want these loathsome visions in my mind."

"You still need to rest. I'll fetch you from your room after I meet with Uncle Ephrem and your father."

I clutched his hands, fearing this terror would drag me to the bottom of an abyss. "I'm coming with you. I won't give Aliyah a chance to stop us."

Kadesh lifted me onto his own horse, tying mine to a rope to follow behind. We descended the cliffs back to the city, silent, each of us engulfed in our own dark thoughts. When he delivered me to my room, Tijah and Jasmine were there to bathe and dress me.

"Make sure she eats a little something," Kadesh instructed. "Then please bring her to my uncle's receiving rooms in two hours. Don't let her out of your sight until then."

Tijah's eyes were wide. "Yes, Your Highness."

"Nobody comes into this room except for me or her father," Kadesh admonished.

When the door closed, I sank onto the bed, utterly exhausted.

"Lunch has just arrived, my lady." Tijah tried to coax me to try the vegetable soup and warm bread.

"I can't. My head feels as though it will lift straight off my neck."

"All the more reason you need to eat."

Jasmine piled pillows on the bed and brought me a tray so I could sit up. I finally took a few mouthfuls and bit into a soft piece of bread smeared with sweet butter. There was yogurt and fresh fruit, too.

I dozed for a bit, although I was afraid to actually sleep.

Soon a bath had been drawn, and I reclined in the warm water of the tub. I closed my eyes, thinking of the images of my death from earlier. How was Aliyah doing this? Were the spells and magic from Egypt that powerful?

When I soaked in the bathwater hot prickles began to run along my skin. The same tingling sensation I'd had when I danced the previous evening.

Slowly, as though someone else were controlling my body, I felt myself sinking under the soft white bubbles. Water instantly filled my mouth and nose, burning my lungs within seconds.

A muffled scream sounded above me.

Tijah jerked me up out of the water. "Lady Jayden!" she screamed.

I gagged, coughing and spluttering up soapy water. I lurched out of the tub and then proceeded to throw up my entire lunch into the wastebasket.

"You are ill," Tijah said. She helped me out of the bath to the lounge chair while Jasmine covered me with two thick towels.

"I'm not sick," I insisted. I didn't say what I was actually thinking. That a demon had attached itself to me—a demon by the name of the High Priestess of the Sariba Goddess.

After dropping the towel, I staggered to the dressing table. "Get me dressed as fast as possible. And"—I turned to the girls—"I want to know who is preparing my food *and* delivering it to my suite."

"Yes, my lady." Tijah and her sister worked quickly to

fasten me into a fresh gown. They dried and brushed my hair, then applied a light coating of face powder, kohl, and color to my gray lips.

A light tap sounded at the door. My father stood outside, looking uncomfortable in a white tunic and gray robe. "Are you feeling up to this meeting? You don't have to do this. The woman is not usually in attendance." He smiled forlornly. "Boring paperwork and bride-price discussions."

I took his arm, trying to smile despite my shaky legs. "I can't stay in my room any longer."

"You look tired."

"Nothing a good night's sleep won't cure," I lied.

We didn't speak as we passed housemaids carrying fresh linens. When we turned a corner, we found ourselves alone for the next stretch.

My father clenched my hand in his. "I need to talk to you, Jayden," he said softly.

We found a sofa in a small alcove. Scrolls fastened with leather straps sat on a shelf filled with trinkets and a vase of jasmine blooms. A window overlooked the gardens, the noon sun sparking yellow against a bank of rosebushes.

"We've traveled a long way to be here," my father began. "And yet, I want to be sure *you* are sure you want this marriage."

"Of course—"

He raised a hand. "Let me finish. This land is strange to us. I have grave misgivings for your future. I had the strangest dreams last night."

My stomach seemed to plunge into the floor. "What dreams?"

"We are far from our own people and our own desert ways. My dreams were a sign we should leave."

"How can we leave when we've just arrived after a long and difficult journey?" My father's face was so gray, so haggard. He would never survive a journey back to our homeland so far north of the Sea of Akabah. "I'm betraying my own king. It is treason for me to give you to a man of another tribe. We don't belong here."

"But *I* belong with Kadesh. I've risked my life and reputation to find him. How can *you* support a man who tried to murder him?"

"Misunderstandings, dear girl."

"No, Father!" I wouldn't let him take this conversation back over the same arguments. "I know what it's like to be attacked. To be left dying. To watch an innocent man maimed and blinded forever. I saw proof that Horeb killed Abimelech. I heard Horeb's own admission when he held me against my will, then chased me to the pond. He's on his way here to kill Kadesh and kidnap me. He has no mercy in his heart, only pride and vengeance."

My father held himself erect, distant. I knew my words hurt him. He didn't want to believe my accusations.

"Father, please don't stop my marriage. Horeb has aligned himself with the Maachathites and the Assyrians. Assyrians, Father! The largest army in the world. I'm sure he's promised them the chance to pillage Sariba. To steal its wealth and leave everyone in the city dead."

"But that would be all-out war. You make Horeb sound so bloodthirsty."

"I know you love Horeb. He's the son of your dearest friend. But he is not who you think he is. At least not anymore."

"When Abimelech died, he became my son. How can I go to war against my own son?"

I had no answer to such a question. "What about Leila, daughter of your blood?"

My father buried his face in his hands. "I'm losing my children, one by one."

"You haven't lost us yet. We need to get Leila back, and I know Kadesh will help us find Sahmril again. There must be a way to convince her adoptive parents to give her back—"

"I don't want Kadesh's help any longer. He has stripped me of my position as father, as a member of my own tribe, with his constant gifts." He paused, giving me a long, hard look. "I will *always* be a guest here."

Empathy flooded over me. "After everything you and Mother gave to me, I'm sorry you feel ashamed. Please come and talk to King Ephrem. War *is* coming. We must stand united."

He rose, obviously agitated. "I can't fight my own kin, my own tribesmen. I'll die willingly."

"What if they storm the palace? The Maachathites won't know who you are. They won't let you live."

"Then so be it," he said, defeat in his eyes. "I'll go find

your mother and grandmother in the afterlife."

"I wish you wouldn't say that. As though you have a death wish. Leila and I need you."

His smile was weary. "I'm not sure you actually do. The worship of the Goddess is strong here. I can feel the fear of her. A shadow lurks in these mountains. The obedience she commands isn't love." My father pressed my hand between his large ones, signs of age turning his fingers thick and crooked. "I do want your happiness. I'll stay because I love you. But I will not fight if war comes to Sariba."

We rose from the couch, but I could sense my father's unsettled heart. He was resigned, not pleased. A pensive mood lingered between us.

When we reached the royal receiving rooms, Kadesh came forward to meet us. "My uncle isn't well. We'll meet with him in his private rooms."

We followed Kadesh beyond the public rooms through another hallway.

The king's rooms were decorated in the greens and blues of the ocean. Gold leafing swirled across the high ceilings. Gilded ebony furniture sat in tasteful groupings with sumptuous pillows and vases of flowers on inlaid tables. The carpets were thicker and softer than anything I'd stepped on before. Brocade draperies adorned expansive windows, letting in light from a private courtyard.

King Ephrem sat on a lounge, dressed in robes of black and gold. His face was etched with deep gnarled wrinkles just like his frankincense trees, but I didn't think he was much older than my own father. I wondered what had caused his prolonged illness.

Earlier, Kadesh had told me his uncle was on a mix of pain potions and sleeping powders almost constantly now. There seemed to be little the palace physicians could do for him. Every time Kadesh spoke of it his face turned grim. He loved his uncle like a father.

King Ephrem beckoned us. "Come closer and sit with me." A spasm of coughing ensued. He wiped at his mouth and face and folded up the handkerchief, but not before I spied the spotted blood on the linen cloth.

"We'll make this meeting brief, Uncle," Kadesh said.

"Daughter of Pharez, let me look at you."

I curtsied in my gown, and then knelt on the lush carpets at his feet.

The king of Sariba studied my face. "My nephew has confided many things about your relationship, daughter of Nephish. He speaks of you and your father, Pharez, very highly. You took care of him after his caravan was attacked. For that I will always be grateful."

I stole a glance at my father and I could tell the king's words caused him chagrin. He didn't take praise well. His generosity was due to his own good heart and integrity.

"It was our honor to help your son," Pharez said with a slight bow. "It was the will of God we were there to help him. In normal circumstances, we would have already departed that valley."

Ephrem's gaze was piercing. "Because of the death of your wife," he said quietly.

Pharez's eyes swept up to the king's face. "That is correct."

"My queen has been gone many years," the king said. "After bearing two stillborn sons and no daughters." He gave my father a penetrating look, choosing his words purposefully. I realized the king was putting the two of them on a level station and position.

My father bowed his head, acknowledging the honor.

"Indeed, since your daughter held the position of becoming queen of your tribe, we are royal brothers, Pharez. Please. Sit down."

A male servant immediately brought a chair for my father. I admired the king's thoughtfulness toward my father, even if his words were quite direct.

King Ephrem continued. "I'm indebted to your desert generosity, man of Nephish. It *was* the will of God that Kadesh live and eventually return home. Although . . ." He paused, glancing between his nephew and me. "It took him a year before I received any messages of comfort—when I feared he was lost to a pit of quicksand or an enemy's sword."

My father cleared his throat. "I wouldn't let a man go hungry or thirsty, whether he's a follower of Abraham's God or not. It is the custom of the desert."

"Then you have no bias or prejudice."

"If God loves all his children then who am I to begrudge a morsel of food or safe passage?"

"But there was an attack against my nephew. An enemy's sword nearly killed him. Your daughter Jayden braved the desert to find him and bring him back home."

"Your nephew has filled your ear with tales," my father conceded. "But I won't speak badly of my heritage, lineage, or tribe. Especially not in times of strife and battle."

"I'm not asking you to—but here we are. And an army is on its way to make war with the kingdom of Sariba. A war we never invoked, nor sought, nor deserve."

A pained expression crossed my father's features. "Unfortunately, that's true. If you want me to ride out into the desert to stop them I will do so, King Ephrem."

"The danger is unthinkable," I said, speaking out of turn.

"I wouldn't send you to your death, Pharez," Ephrem added, agreeing with me.

"I don't believe my own nephew would kill me."

Ephrem pursed his lips. "No, but the Assyrians would kill first and identify you later."

My father's chin jerked up. I'm not sure that fact had crossed his mind. He was so eager to have Horeb found innocent of any wrongdoing his heart wouldn't allow him to see the pride Horeb cultivated and his determination to see the Sariba heir dead.

"Your daughter's soul is as generous as her father's," King Ephrem went on. "I'm sure she has her mother's beauty and gentle heart. I can see why Kadesh fell in love with her. I can also see why your would-be Nephish king wants her back."

"She belongs to him."

"Does she?"

The air filled with a cloud of tension. I clenched my fists together, wondering if my father would openly challenge the king of Sariba.

"I'd hoped to sign a marriage contract with you today, Pharez," the king went on. "I approve their marriage and Kadesh needs to marry quickly so he can be crowned upon my death."

"But surely that's many years from now," Pharez said with diplomacy.

"You needn't humor me. My death is only a few months away, if not weeks. There are problems in Sariba. Forces who wish to change our land into something else. I don't possess the energy or skills to fix this. Kadesh is the only one who can and he needs a strong queen at his side." King Ephrem glanced up at Kadesh. "And I believe he has found her."

"I have," Kadesh said, his eyes on my face.

"Please go to my desk and retrieve the packet, Son," Uncle Ephrem directed.

Instead of marriage contract papers, Kadesh spread several stone tablets on a low table next to the king.

"Pharez, come closer," the king invited. "I have something very important to show you. You need to see with your own eyes a letter I received from your cousin-brother—the previous Nephish King Abimelech. Many months ago."

The color drained from my father's face. "Why would Abimelech correspond with you?"

"Abimelech had a story to tell me. And a proposition to

make. It seems Horeb was not the first-born son. Zenos was his eldest, an heir whose nature and will was to make peace with the surrounding tribes. Indeed, he and his father were already working toward treaties with the local warring tribes to bring about a lasting truce. Using the means of trade."

"I had no idea," my father said hoarsely.

"But this eldest son, Zenos, was killed in one of those very raids he was hoping to stop."

My father put a hand to his head. "His death was a terrible loss. He had been betrothed to my oldest daughter, Leila."

King Ephrem motioned to Kadesh, who picked up one of the polished tablets and handed it to Pharez. "After Abimelech met Kadesh at the oasis in Tadmur, they had several confidential talks together, unbeknownst to you or Horeb. Please, read."

My father studied the correspondence then glanced up in astonishment. "This is Abimelech's handwriting. The symbols of his name. I recognize it."

"You have no scribe in your tribe?"

"Our tribal leaders read and write a bit, although we don't have a need very often."

King Ephrem softened his deep voice. "Abimelech knew Horeb's secret—or at least guessed it. He'd killed his brother Zenos so he could one day take the throne instead. I was deeply troubled to learn of Abimelech's death so soon after he sent me this letter. I also know the Nephish tribal council blackmailed and then stoned Jayden for the murder."

My father groaned and crossed the room to stare out the

windows. The king of Sariba was very direct. He'd spoken facts about Horeb my father hadn't wanted to admit. And proof was now, literally, in his hands.

I stood up and placed my hand on top of his. He shouldn't have been forced in this way. "I hope you'll forgive me, Jayden," my father said quietly.

"There's nothing to forgive, Father. You didn't know. Nobody did."

"The most important thing now, for us, is also stated in Abimelech's letter," Ephrem told us. "He wanted to create an alliance with the Sariba tribe. He feared King Hammurabi's eagerness to spread his kingdom across the western deserts. He feared cruel taxation was coming, and with it, oppression. His son's ambitions could lead to annihilation. Meeting Kadesh was a most propitious answer to his problems."

"Did you ever write back to him?"

"I was still pondering the proposition when word of his death arrived. Before I made such a crucial decision I wanted to speak with Kadesh and learn firsthand about the Nephish. I wanted to know why this solicitation was put forth from your king. But even if I had agreed to form the alliance, the letter wouldn't have returned in time. In fact, now I'm grateful I didn't respond. It would have fallen into Horeb's hands and he would have destroyed it—or used it as blackmail."

"What do we do now?" My father seemed overwhelmed.

"Today I want to officially make an alliance with you and your daughter. Kadesh and Jayden will arrange for their wedding to take place soon. The contract will also state Jayden will be crowned queen when Kadesh is crowned as king."

King Ephrem rose on unsteady legs. His servant walked quickly to his side, allowing the king to lean on him. He stood regally before me and my father. "Never can I align with Horeb. He is coming with the biggest armies of the world to destroy me. Now my kingdom faces annihilation. My people. And my family. The audacity of Horeb is breathtaking."

The ominous silence coming after his words was tangible.

"My dear, Jayden," he said solemnly. "You won't like hearing what I'm about to say next."

"What is it, my king?"

"There is only one way to stop this madness descending upon the lands of Sariba. And you are the only one who can do it. *You* must kill Horeb. It's the only way."

30

Alarm shot through my belly. "I don't understand. Won't Horeb be defeated by the Sariba and Edomite armies? The professional soldiers can kill him. I never want to see Horeb again. He'll try to kidnap me."

Putting his fingers together, King Ephrem listened to my concerns. "Even if Horeb were to die during the battle, his generals will never admit he's dead. They'll continue to fight. I'm certain he'll be kept away from the front lines in a safe place. There are many places to hide in Sariba. There is also his widowed mother. She will never concede his passing."

"How do you know that?" I asked, astonished.

He raised his gray eyebrows. "I've lived a long time. And King Abimelech alluded to many obstacles."

"But—why me? Kadesh can . . . Chemish . . ."

"The only way this war can end is through Horeb's demise.

And only *you* can know for certain when he is dead. Someone might disguise themselves as Horeb just to trick our army. The Maachathites are hungry for our wealth. Killing him yourself is the only way they cannot hide his death. There must be absolute proof to our warriors, and to his fighters. I'm sorry."

"I see your wisdom," I said, terror coursing through my veins. Never had I expected to hear this. How could I possibly kill Horeb myself? He'd be surrounded by well-armed soldiers.

"Come here, my son," the king said. "You as well, Jayden."

King Ephrem brought his withered palms to Kadesh's face. Slowly, he ran a finger down the jagged scar. Tears filled his eyes when he touched the black eye patch and studied Kadesh's scarred eye socket. Then, reaching for my hand, he placed it in Kadesh's, as though we were kneeling at the marriage dais.

"A true warrior king is not afraid to fight for the people he loves or to save his kingdom. You've both shown that love for each other. Willingly ready to sacrifice your own lives. That is loyalty. That is strength with a deep abiding love. Nurture it and never let it go. It will sustain you through the coming months and beyond."

A royal scribe brought a tray of writing tools to the king's desk. An official betrothal contract had already been drafted and lay on the polished wood waiting for us.

"Pharez of Nephish," the king said. "This is the agreement of betrothal between my nephew, Kadesh, and your daughter Jayden. The dowry and gifts will be exchanged. On the day of the wedding we will sign the marriage contract, making this legal and binding for the rest of their lives."

King Ephrem sat heavily in his chair and picked up the pen stylus. He signed the agreement first, and then my father added his signature. With shaking hands, I stamped my name below Kadesh's at the bottom of the covenant. To have my signature on the betrothal contract was highly unusual, but these were extraordinary circumstances. A royal union with large and weighty consequences.

My father and Ephrem shook hands and then they embraced, kissing each other briefly on both cheeks as tribal brothers did. The sight made my heart happy, but my mind continued to be troubled. My father couldn't possibly return to the Nephish people and live among them now. I was hated and despised, and now he would be as well.

He would have to live out the remainder of his life right here in Sariba. If Kadesh and I could defeat Horeb's armies and destroy Aliyah's power, we could bring a more lasting peace to this beautiful land on the borders of the ocean.

I bowed to kiss Uncle Ephrem's hand, pressing my lips against his royal ring. It was a stunning band of gold and bronze with a stamp of the frankincense tree, the sea, and halo of sun. The elderly king pulled me close, his beard tickling my chin. "Let the wedding preparations begin," he said into my ear. "And quickly! I don't want to miss it."

Kadesh caught my eye and laughed. I blushed and turned away. Then Kadesh kissed me, right in front of everyone. Uncle Ephrem clapped his hands, smiling broadly. Bubbles of joy rose into my throat. It was done. It was real. Happiness spilled out of me. Now I truly would be Kadesh's bride.

A servant brought trays of food. Steamed fish and warm bread, tea, honeyed pastries, and fruit. When we finished eating, King Ephrem's tremors grew worse, and he began to cough more frequently.

"I must put His Majesty to bed now," the servant said with a bow.

The king protested, but he looked exhausted. Wrinkles deepened around his mouth, clustering at his eyes and sinking into dark hollows.

He bade us good night and then used a cane to walk to his private room while his personal manservant followed. The doors shut behind them, and Kadesh and I accompanied my father back to his room.

"Tonight will be a quiet family dinner," Kadesh told us. "No entertainment. No dignitaries or diplomats. I want you to meet my aunts and uncles on a more informal basis. My mother's sister and her husband have a dining room in their suite. Aunt Naomi likes to entertain. I'll come to your rooms in a few hours to retrieve you. Until then, I have a battle to plan."

He smiled, trying to lighten the mood, but dread filled my heart. When Horeb appeared on the desert, people would die. Soldiers, captains, Edomites. Perhaps even ordinary citizens. There was no doubt in my mind.

After Kadesh departed, I couldn't bring myself to go back to my own solitary quiet. The fussing of Tijah and the silence of Jasmine. I needed to go somewhere private so I could ponder what King Ephrem had just told me. I also needed to figure out how I was going to bring Leila here to us.

"Do you want to join me in the gardens for a walk, Father?"

"I'd like to rest before dinner so I can attempt to be less grumpy."

"You are never grumpy."

He smiled. "That's debatable."

I kissed his bristly cheek and then moved down the hall.

I was beginning to learn my way. The palace was laid out in a series of hallways formed into two bisecting rectangles. Private suites weren't marked, but I easily figured that out by the closed, quiet doors. The public rooms had enormous arched openings. I knew there were at least two dining halls, a ballroom, government meeting rooms, and an entrance foyer with vast ceilings and splendid furnishings and columns.

I didn't know where the kitchens, storage rooms, and servants' quarters were. Probably located down another invisible hallway I couldn't begin to find on my own.

I slipped out a side door that took me to a patio with a breathtaking view of the Qara Mountains. The garden overflowed with palm trees, weeping willows, and stone pathways. On a side path, I spied a canopy and headed for it.

A domed four-sided tent had been erected in one of the far corners. On three sides the tent panels were staked, but the fourth wall—the entrance—was loose, created out of a flowing, almost sheer material, flapping charmingly in a slight breeze.

Stealing inside, I discovered the gazebo boasted its own cozy furniture. A small fountain was in the center, surrounded by irises.

Deep, comfortable sofas were positioned around the

perimeter of the fountain and plump pillows layered the couches. I pictured myself lounging here for an afternoon with scrolls of Sariba's history to read. Perhaps a harpist for entertainment. Except desert girls like me didn't know how to read. I could only recognize the cuneiform symbols for names and places. A deficiency I would need to remedy. I'd have to speak with Kadesh about getting a tutor. As his wife I'd need to be able to read orders, menus, and send my own personal correspondence.

I lifted my eyes to see a beautiful lamp hanging from the ceiling, its orb of patterned light reflecting against the walls.

"What a gorgeous room," I said aloud. "I wonder why Kadesh hasn't brought me here."

"I wonder why he hasn't either," a female voice said behind me.

I whirled around and my heart instantly began to pound.

Aliyah, the High Priestess of the Sariba Temple, stood before me. An amused smile flickered across her face. "It's such a romantic location. The perfect spot to woo the girl you love."

"What are you doing here?"

"Oh, Jayden," she said through deep red lips. "Come, darling girl. Let's sit over here and have a little chat. I think we should get to know each other better."

I glanced at the silken drapery doors, racking my mind for an excuse to escape. I didn't want to purposely antagonize her though. Her magnetism was powerful, already putting some sort of enchantment on me. I felt woozy, my head cloudy, and

I found myself drawn to her, wanting her approval.

Aliyah slipped her long, cool fingers into mine, locking us together as she pulled me toward the arrangement of sofas and pillows. I sank into the downy softness while Aliyah tucked her bare feet underneath her. Even her toenails were painted a bloodred color.

She sat sideways on the couch, smiling charmingly, reaching out to wind a lock of my hair around her finger. "How do you like Sariba?"

I swallowed, trying to remain composed. "It's absolutely beautiful, of course."

"You fit in very well here. Prince Kadesh has always liked beautiful girls."

I bit my tongue, swallowing any comment. Reason told me to flee, but I found myself unable to move. I was bound to the couch while the fountain drizzled and the scent of jasmine filled the air.

Aliyah lowered her dark lashes, her voice sultry. "Men are all the same. They want beautiful faces and beautiful bodies. That's why they come to the temple. To watch us dance before the Goddess, and then make love to the Goddess so their families are blessed."

"I thought it was to make a connection to the Divine," I managed to say. "Isn't that what the Sacred Marriage Rite is all about?"

She clapped her hands together. "I *knew* you were familiar with temple worship. I could see it in the way your body moves. In the look of your entrancing eyes."

"If you're trying to lure me into dancing at the temple, you're wasting your time."

"I'm not trying to lure you at all. I have your sister Leila for that. She's simply captivating. Always the first to be chosen by our priests or Sariba's citizens."

Now she was purposely trying to irritate me. "Let me see my sister. My father and I have a right to see her."

"All in good time, my darling girl. When the Sariba Goddess deems it. Your sister is still adjusting. She's quite busy choosing her favorite harem of men to create the divine worship experience. It's spring, you know."

"I'm quite aware of that." I was also aware she was probably lying. "You won't let us see her because you're afraid Leila will remember us. And if she remembers her family you're afraid she'll want to live with us here at the palace. You can't allow that, can you?"

Two spots of pink flared on Aliyah's smooth cheeks. I watched her take a calming breath, and then lean forward to inhale the scent of jasmine into her nostrils.

My heart raced at her closeness. Her flawless skin was mesmerizing. I found myself coveting everything about her. I wanted to flee, but her eyes never left mine. The sofa seemed to have me in its grip, the downy cushions closing in on me.

"I'm here to confide in you, Jayden, not argue about Leila. We're both women now. We can talk and learn from each other. I thought you should be aware of Kadesh's past. You should know who you're marrying. After all, he's still a stranger to you in many ways."

I balked at her insinuations, wanting to deny her words. Kadesh used to be a stranger, but we had come so far in our relationship. He had confided in me. We'd learned to trust each other.

The air was saturated in the scent of the flowers. Aliyah's perfume smelled hypnotic as it wafted into my lungs. A hint of frankincense everywhere. I stared at the winding river of water circling the couches and flowers, feeling overcome. I was stuck in an endless circle, too, with no way to escape the High Priestess. "How did you know we're marrying soon?" I finally managed to say. "Not even my maids know of it yet."

She waved a hand as though I'd asked a silly question. "I'm the High Priestess of Sariba. I know everything that goes on, my dear. Do not fear on that score."

"It sounds like something very much to be feared if you're spying on the royal family."

"Who else would I spy on?" she said with a laugh. "I'm a member of the royal family."

There was something about her voice that was making me sleepy and disoriented. I had to get off this sofa and get some fresh air.

"Poor darling Jayden. You've learned so much over the past few days, haven't you? Devastating information. That Kadesh was supposed to marry me. Promised since our royal births. We were brought up with the same royal language, the same tutoring to become leaders of our countries. We were raised to unite the entire coastline and the interior deserts—the kingdoms of

Sheba and Sariba—into one powerful country."

"That's not . . . what King Ephrem . . . said—"

Her slender wrist moved through the air. Bracelets of silver embedded with green jade stones tinkled around her hands, sweeping away my protest like a cobweb. "King Ephrem is a sick old man. Delusional. Don't pay attention to anything he says."

I was shocked at her belittling words—and the words of her sister, the Queen of Sheba, kept rising in my mind. "I can assure you I'm paying attention to a great many things since leaving my homeland."

Aliyah gave a sigh and batted her eyelashes. "Unlike *your* betrothal to Horeb, prince of the Nephish, Kadesh and I were in love," she continued, as if I hadn't spoken. "We wanted to marry. But you, Jayden. You have *nothing* to offer him or the Kingdom of Sariba. No dowry, no jewels, no powerful tribe to unite. Your life is quite . . . *un*exceptional."

"That's not true! Ephrem received a letter from my King Abimelech who wanted to join our tribes together." I knew I was grasping, wanting to prove myself to her, but why did I care so much?

She laughed derisively. "A letter from a dead king—to another king who is about to expire!"

My insecurities flared stronger than ever. This girl's beauty and wit were unmatched, but all I could do was worry about what her relationship with Kadesh had been like. Had Kadesh been in love with her? Did she still have a hold on him? Perhaps I was merely a passing fancy. An exotic toy from a foreign tribe.

I *was* uneducated, without wealth. She was right. I didn't have anything to offer Kadesh or the lands of Sariba.

Aliyah leaned in closer and I felt her skin against mine. "You're wondering if Kadesh played you for a fool?" she whispered. "You worry he'll only wed you after he marries me first—and you'll be second choice. *I* still have my marriage contract. Jayden, daughter of an obscure tribe, will be second wife to the most powerful woman of the land. Second to the High Priestess. Second in name and wealth and popularity."

I couldn't breathe. I was suffocating.

"There is *one* thing of value you bring to our marriage. Three tribes from the north are on their way here and getting closer every day. Once we conquer them, Kadesh and I will truly rule the world. It's all lovely and brilliant. Wouldn't you agree?"

"Stop!" I cried, but my voice sounded weak.

"I don't think you want me to stop. You're much too curious to know the truth about our past. You want to know if Kadesh and I did wicked things during our betrothal. I'd be glad to give you the details."

"I won't listen. Get away from me!" I moved to get up, my anger finally breaking the spell I was under, but her hand clamped down on my arm. I flung her off and pushed myself up from the couch. I tried to breathe normally, but it was almost impossible.

As I staggered to the door of the tent, Aliyah followed me, her voice like a hissing serpent in my ear. "Oh yes, you'll listen, princess of Nephish. When Leila makes her sacrifice to the

Goddess. It's spring, the time of the Sacred Marriage Rite to show the goddess how much we love her so she'll pour out her bounty upon us."

Everything I'd suspected was correct. Aliyah was using Leila to break me. To torture me into fleeing and leaving Kadesh forever.

"Don't worry," the High Priestess said, ignoring the horror on my face. "You'll get an invitation to Leila's sacrificial ceremony. But I've been thinking . . ." she tapped a finger to her chin. "Two sisters would make a *very* powerful sacrifice."

"You're insane."

"The Sariba Goddess will be more powerful than all others, even the gods of Moloch and Elkenah and Ba'al. She will rule the universe and all eternity."

"Your sister, the Queen of Sheba, is nothing like you."

"She's only my half-sister. Soon she'll be of no consequence." Aliyah's fingers encircled my arm again. "I always get what I want. In fact, I'm already making preparations to purchase another Nephish daughter."

"What are you talking about?"

"The Goddess loves girls who are young and innocent. A girl who has never kissed a man. Or fallen in love. Because she's a mere child. Barely past babyhood."

She can't be talking about Sahmril. The once lovely garden room now whirled in shades of darkness. As I wavered on my feet, my eyes searched for the opening, but all four walls looked exactly the same now.

"Oh, Jayden, don't faint yet. Leila told me all about your little sister, Sahmril. And I've found her adoptive parents . . . who, unfortunately, may not live much longer. Can you imagine?"

"I'll kill you before you ever touch—"

The High Priestess cut off my voice, as though her cool fingers were squeezing my neck. I saw a vision of myself strangled right there in the tent gazebo. My body lying on the floor. Nobody knew where I was. No servants were within earshot.

I summoned the little bit of strength I had left and shoved Aliyah away with both hands. I knew it was a weak gesture, but the woman laughed, drifting languidly back to the couch.

Her perfect white teeth glittered like a demon's smile. "Pleasant dreams, Jayden."

I fled before she permanently poisoned my thoughts and heart.

31

I ran with shaking legs to my room, then held back my anger while Jasmine and Tijah dressed me for dinner. The entire encounter with Aliyah had taken no more than an hour, but I was exhausted and frightened to the core. It didn't take long to realize that had been her purpose. She wanted to intimidate me and keep me away from Leila, including casting doubts on my relationship with Kadesh.

The hallway of the palace seemed to close in on me when Kadesh and I made our way to the palace apartment of Uncle Josiah and Aunt Naomi.

"Are you feeling all right?" Kadesh asked, tightening his hand around mine.

The unexpected pressure of his fingers caused me to jump. I sagged weakly against the wall and he gathered me up in his arms. My feet left the floor as I buried my face into his neck. A sob whimpered in my throat, but I swallowed it down.

"Who's hurt you?" he asked.

I didn't want to tell him the awful things Aliyah had said to me. "Nobody's hurt me. I'm just nervous about meeting your family."

"No, it's more than that." He lowered me to the carpet and cupped his hand around my chin. "Did Uncle Ephrem frighten you? Do you regret signing the marriage contract?"

"Oh, no, the king is kind and wise. I can see why you're so devoted to him. Why can't the physicians help him?" I asked, changing the subject.

"It's an illness that can't be treated, but I had no idea he'd made such a turn for the worse while I was gone. The healers say the stress and worry over the impending war brings on stronger attacks. He needs quiet, peace, and that is gone until we deal with Horeb and his army."

"I've asked a horrible thing of your homeland."

"The blame is completely Horeb's. His lust for you and my murder. Greed for land and wealth and power." Kadesh twisted a lock of my hair around his finger as we stood close together in the hallway. Despite his gentleness, the gesture reminded me of Aliyah. He frowned. "Something has made you nervous. Has . . . Aliyah been here?"

"Here?" I repeated.

"In the palace."

I didn't speak at first, but I couldn't continue to evade the question. "Yes, she was here. In the tent gazebo on the western side of the palace courtyards. I don't know how she knew I was there."

"She has her ways. I'm going to assign you an escort. Perhaps Asher could help. I don't want you going anywhere alone from now on. What happened? What did Aliyah say to you?"

"We talked—if you can call it that—more than enough. I doubt she'll be back."

"Your voice is shaking. She rattled you badly. She said things about you and me. No." He stopped. "She said things about me and her."

I dropped my face, unable to look at him.

"Please don't believe *anything* she tells you." He shook his head, drawing my eyes upward to meet his. "She poisoned you with lies. Yes, we were betrothed, but we didn't have any sort of real friendship. When I began my nineteenth year, she tried to get me to come to the temple. On the night of the Sacred Marriage Rite."

I took an involuntary step backward. "Did you go to her?"

"No. No! Oh, Jayden, I promise you, no. Aliyah first went there to live under the guise of tutoring the other girls. She talked about educating them, teaching them to read and write. I was ashamed to tell my parents about her invitation to the marriage rites. I pressed her, but she would never tell me the truth about her life at the temple. We all discovered too late what the temple rites actually meant."

A sick taste was in my mouth. "They appear to be well-kept public secrets."

"After my father's death, Uncle Ephrem made arrangements to send me on that caravan journey. He wanted to get me away before Aliyah seduced me with promises and lies that might confuse my loyalties. Before I left, the king contacted the Queen of Sheba and denounced the betrothal."

"I'm sure Aliyah was furious. If she's conspiring to put herself on Sariba's royal throne, can't you do anything about it?"

"I can't bring her before the courts until we have proof of treasonous action. She has an army of devoted worshippers who would fight for her. Her charisma and methods of persuasion are very polished. Since my return I've learned she's got most of the city seduced into believing whatever she says. She's generous with temple funds and the priests of Ba'al help her. They would like to be as powerful as the Egyptian priests are, influential in politics and government and making decisions on taxation and revenue. And the royal family. The Pharaoh of Egypt does nothing without his temple priest advisors. Unfortunately, most of my judges and army captains have gone to the temple."

"Aliyah has backed you into a corner. No matter what you do she will stay one step ahead of you."

"A black widow in her web." Kadesh shook his head. "Just like the Queen of Sheba warned us. At the moment I have to focus on war. Scouts say Horeb is within a week of us. I was hoping for more time. But time can be cruel in many ways."

"So . . ." I began. "You never went to the temple to see Aliyah dance, then?" Jealousy had me in a cruel grip.

"Yes, I went and watched her dance," Kadesh said quietly.

"But we never shared a bed. I promise you that, Jayden. Please believe me."

So far, everything Kadesh had ever told me had been the truth. Every promise he'd ever made he had kept. I had to stop letting my stupid fears interfere with my trust.

"If she tries to hurt you or your family, I will tear down every brick and stone of that temple with my bare hands."

I gave him a small smile. "I will tear it down with you."

"Jayden, you are my future wife and queen. Believe that until the day you die. Now let's go eat dinner. I'm ravenous."

He took my arm, and I laughed as we entered the suite. Stately furniture graced the rooms, but there were the comforts of a family here, too. Scrolls of reading materials and a sewing basket. Soft music coming from an atrium garden where a harpist played.

A glowing lamp hung over the dining table, which had been set with linen napkins, gold-rimmed plates, and brass goblets. The table literally sparkled under the chandelier of candles.

"Uncle Josiah and Aunt Naomi," Kadesh said, bowing before a middle-aged couple. "May I present my betrothed, Jayden, daughter of Pharez."

Uncle Josiah was a stout man with a salt-and-pepper beard and a hearty voice. "Is it official, then?" he asked, raising his eyebrows. "Or just a young and hopeful couple?"

Kadesh embraced his uncle. "The contract was signed a few hours ago between Ephrem and Jayden's father."

Aunt Naomi stepped forward, kissing Kadesh on both cheeks and then me as well. "Congratulations, my dears. You must bring him joy, Jayden. I've never seen my nephew looking so happy."

Naomi was an elegant woman. Her hair was pinned into exquisite loops about her head and studded with jewels. Her smile was sincere and youthful. I liked her immediately.

Servants placed dishes of seasoned meat and mounds of rice on the table along with trays of melons and berries, jugs of red wine, baskets of hot bread and garlic butter, and bowls of sweetened yogurt.

"A heavenly banquet," I said.

"I hope you'll indulge us," Naomi said with a lift of her eyebrows. "These are all my husband's favorite foods. Now sit! I can tell Kadesh is ready to eat an entire camel."

Kadesh helped me to one of the wide, soft cushions. He poured wine into my goblet and I sipped at the sweetness.

Uncle Josiah raised his glass. "To Kadesh and Jayden and the good news of a royal wedding."

One by one we clinked our glasses together, and the sound of Naomi's warm laughter filled the room.

"I was glad to have our meeting with the king," I said to Naomi. "I can hardly believe we're betrothed now."

"Your time has finally come," the older woman said. "Don't be bashful around us, Kadesh, even if we haven't seen you in a year. The food will get cold if you wait much longer. You have a lifetime to gaze at your bride."

No sooner had I scooped salad greens and yogurt onto my plate than the doors to the suite burst open. Kadesh was on his feet at once.

Chemish stood there, breathing hard as if he'd been running. "One of our scouts just arrived at the palace gates. He rode so hard to bring us news his horse is nearly dead. The other scout, Japheth, *is* dead. Struck through by one of Horeb's scouts."

Kadesh's dark eyes flamed and his palm slammed down on the table. "Where is Japheth now? Do they have his body?"

Chemish glanced at the family sitting at the dinner table and inclined his head. "I'm sorry to bring this bad news here. My apologies, my lord."

"Speak, my friend," Kadesh encouraged. "We all need to know what has happened."

"The enemy cut our scout into ribbons and burned the pieces. The smoke followed the others all the way to our borders."

"How much time do we have?"

"The armies are more than halfway between the Kingdom of Sheba and us. We haven't much more than a week."

Uncle Josiah's expression turned grave as he rose from the table. Aunt Naomi closed her eyes, her lips going white. Their young daughter, Naria, had suddenly appeared and Naomi held the girl in her lap, shushing at her nursemaid to take her back to bed.

Kadesh paced the carpeted floor, then he turned to me. "Jayden," he said. "I think we need to heed my uncle's advice.

We'll marry in three days. Can you prepare that quickly? I don't want to go into battle without being married to you."

"Of course," I said. "But is it wise to take time away from the army's preparations?"

"The Sariba Kingdom is well armed. The battle won't last long. Because of our secret groves of valuable frankincense, we're on alert at all times."

My mind whirled. My wedding. *Everything* to prepare in just days. Just as the Queen of Sheba had warned. We needed to marry before Horeb arrived, and we needed a huge royal wedding so there could be no misconstrued messages.

"Kadesh," I said. "I want to visit Leila and deliver a wedding invitation, but I fear Aliyah will never allow me to see my sister without making me grovel for the privilege."

"Surely an engraved wedding invitation from the palace cannot be refused?" Naomi said, lifting her eyebrows.

"Stranger things have happened at the temple," was all Kadesh replied. Uncle Josiah cleared his throat and I got the impression he knew the unspoken sentiments in the cryptic conversation.

My eyes met Kadesh's. He knew what I was thinking. Our wedding invitation would make Aliyah furious. Would she take it out on Leila?

I glanced into Naomi's sympathetic face. She placed a hand across the table of glittering crystal and lavish food. "Jayden, you will have the most spectacular wedding a girl of Sariba—a princess of Sariba—ever had. I promise you that. I've already begun a list. While the men assemble their weapons and soldiers, I will enlist every servant to create a magnificent wedding in three days instead of the usual three months."

Kadesh knelt at my feet and clasped my hands in his. "Jayden, will you marry me in three days hence?"

Happiness coursed through me. "Every day and forever."

Kadesh glanced over to his uncle Josiah. "Will you please prepare the marriage tent for us?" he asked. It was tradition for the marriage tent to be arranged by the groom's family.

A blush crept up my neck.

"Jayden," Kadesh added. "If we are married, Horeb cannot claim you. It's the only way to ensure our success. And our future peace and happiness."

32

The nightmares came again that night, wrestling with me, just like the prophet Jacob had wrestled with an angel. Except my angel was actually a demon named Aliyah.

I woke, sweating, my pillow clamped over my face, as if someone had been trying to suffocate me.

I had assumed the royal family's food was prepared and tasted by trusted servants. But perhaps I really was being poisoned? The idea was unimaginable, but too many strange things were happening to me.

I flung off the heavy pillow, like a chain holding me to the bed, and darted glances into every corner. Nobody lay in wait. Perhaps *I* had been trying to smother myself. Had I experienced a seizure—the same as Kadesh's mother had suffered?

My stomach lurched. I ran to the chamber pot in the dark,

stumbling my way past the tables and chairs. Silent as a shadow, Jasmine was there, holding my hair back.

After lighting the polished brass lamp on the bedside table, the maid prepared a cold cloth for my brow. I lay down while she administered it and Tijah slept on.

"Thank you," I whispered.

Jasmine nodded, running a soothing hand along my fevered arm. She held up a finger to signal for me to remain lying on the bed and then returned with a cup of cold water.

I sipped it slowly, a hundred worries battling inside my head. "What am I going to do?"

My maid gave a shake of her head. Then she made a sign for me to go to sleep, biting her lips, concern in her face.

I gripped her hand like I used to with Leila when I'd had a bad dream. "How can I sleep when my dreams turn into nightmares?"

Moonlight fell across the bedroom floor, washing the room in silvery waves. Moments later, a sheen of fog crept across the windows, sinister and lurking.

Jasmine's eyes fixed on mine, her face glowing in the night light.

"I saw fire," I whispered into the stillness. "I imagined the palace toppling, burning. I saw my sister being thrown into a deep well. I could feel her screams in my bones. How can I fight Aliyah and Horeb both?"

Jasmine's eyes welled up with tears.

I pressed her hand into mine. "I'm sorry; I don't mean to frighten you."

She pointed to her sleeping sister and then to herself, jamming her finger into her chest.

"I know you want to help, but nobody has power over the Sariba Goddess. This land is filled with a beauty that surpasses all dreams. But a specter of doom reigns, keeping us in compliance."

Jasmine pointed to my ring finger. She mouthed the name of Kadesh.

"You think I should marry Kadesh despite the coming war?"

Vigorously, she nodded, and then lifted her hands over her heart to convey the symbol of the marriage vow.

I was comforted by her assurances. "When I marry Kadesh we'll be bound through eternity. That gives me strength not to give up."

She gave a sigh then laid her head against my arm and curled onto the floor beside the bed. It was a strange gesture for a handmaid to make to her mistress, but I was touched. I wondered if the girls' mother was still alive.

I stroked her hair, feeling a maternal instinct toward her. "You're tired, Jasmine. Please go to bed. I'll leave the lamp on."

But the girl had already fallen asleep.

I watched her chest rise and fall in slow breaths. After a moment, I scooted across the comforter and lifted her featherweight body onto the mattress with me. I imagined myself and Leila as children, snuggled in our beds in our father's tent, my mother sleeping close by. My own tears now fell into Jasmine's sweet-smelling hair.

When I opened my eyes again morning sun streamed into the bedroom. Jasmine was gone. Rolling onto my back, I tried to organize my thoughts. Sleep wrapped around my tongue and I blinked, trying to fully wake up.

On my dressing table was a bowl of clean water and rose-scented soap. Fresh bread, butter, and yogurt lay nestled inside a basket. I tried to nibble at the food while I washed.

I wondered where Tijah and Jasmine had gone.

My hands shook when I applied my kohl. Then I attempted to untangle the clumped knots in my hair. The wild hours of nightmares had left me a mess. A moment later, the two maids rushed through the door.

"You're awake, my lady!" Tijah exclaimed. "We left you sleeping for just a moment while we attended to your laundry—and wedding plans!"

Jasmine's eyes sparkled. She put her hands to her lips and mouthed, "Wedding."

"We've never helped with a wedding," Tijah went on. "And a royal wedding is—is—wondrous!"

I smiled at her enthusiasm. "Not in three days, I'm afraid. I'm trying to make a list in my mind, but there are too many details."

"Lady Naomi already has a list! And a scribe to keep track of everything."

I laughed, the somber mood of the night lifting in the eager smiles of the girls.

"We're ordered to bring you to her rooms immediately. She has an entire wardrobe of wedding gowns for you to try on."

"It sounds lovely, but I need a scribe right now myself. Can you fetch one, Tijah?"

While Jasmine cleaned the room and Tijah ran out the door, I stood by the window, warming myself after days of somber fog. Soon the maid returned with a young boy named Nathan. He produced thin tablets of stone and writing tools, laying them out on the desk by the window.

"I can write well, my lady," he said, bending over the stone, ready for my dictation.

I took a breath. "To the Priestess Leila of the Sariba Temple."

His eyebrows shot up, but he didn't ask any questions, just engraved my words, inviting Leila to my wedding on the evening of the second day hence.

There was so much more I wanted to say, but it couldn't be written in a letter. I had to see Leila for myself. An invitation for her to live here at the palace with me had to be made in person. And I had to find a physician or healer to undo the confused state she was in.

When Nathan finished, he let me inspect the letter. I couldn't read most of it but I did recognize the name of Leila and my own closing the letter. "I will deliver it now, my lady. My father has a good horse I can use to climb the mountain to the temple."

"Good. Thank you very much. And Nathan," I added.

"Yes, my lady?"

"Please be careful. Deliver the letter at the servant's receiving doors, but do not enter the temple yourself."

Despite my precautions, I worried my letter would be intercepted by Aliyah.

Moments later I was delivered to Lady Naomi's personal

office and dressing rooms. The rooms were spacious, with floors of imported marble and fluttering draperies hanging at the expansive windows. I wished my mother and grandmother could be here to help me choose a dress. To be a part of this momentous time of my life. Their absence was sorely felt.

Naomi kissed me, and then ushered me to a cushioned chair in front of the wardrobe. My maidservants stepped back out of the way, but Lady Naomi said, "Girls, please be our models. Try on the various dresses so Princess Jayden can see them."

Jasmine let out a giggle when she realized she'd be wearing some of the beautiful dresses. I gave a start, having never heard her make a single noise before.

The morning passed in a blur of soft cottons and sheer silks, reds, greens, deep purples, and blues. I finally settled on a cream-colored gown with a flowing skirt made up of so much satiny material it shimmered like water at my feet. The dress boasted intricately designed beadwork and jewels along the bodice and sleeves, and a stiff open collar showed off my pale neck.

"The perfect spot to display a few royal jewels," Naomi said. "You shall have an emerald and ruby necklace with clusters of diamonds, matching bangles on your wrists, and these earrings."

She opened an ebony box that held earrings with rubies and oval-cut diamonds. "These jewels are fashioned here in Sariba by our own craftsmen. See here on the back."

The jeweler's brand was engraved in the metal. A

frankincense tree with twisted branches. "I must be living a dream," I said. "I've never seen such jewels in all my life."

"Kadesh will be giving you an entire box on your wedding day. Your father will receive one hundred camels and twenty-five Arabian horses from Uncle Ephrem."

Speechless, I stared at myself in the lace-trimmed gown in the mirror. "What shall I give Kadesh as a wedding gift?"

Naomi's mouth lifted in a smile. "Your heart. Your body. Your true self, my dear."

Emotion bit at the back of my throat. I wished my mother could see me now. It was finally happening. I was marrying the boy I loved.

The next two days I rushed back and forth between gardens and rooms, occasionally stopping Nathan, my scribe, to ask if there had been any reply from Leila at the temple. The boy always shook his head, no, and I tried not to fret, but focus on the wedding preparations. That was my task right now, other than continuing to practice with the superb sword Kadesh had given me in the land of Sheba.

We'd been in Sariba about a week now, and, after the confrontation between me and Asher and Kadesh, as well as the meeting with King Ephrem, we'd all agreed Asher needed to maintain our practice sessions.

Three times a day for an hour. Learning the proper stances and thrusts, turns and parries, helped keep me distracted and extremely busy. The day I brought my sword straight down on Asher's weapon, and then whipped around to lay my sword against his neck, he grinned—and I laughed.

"I did it," I whispered.

"I think you're ready," he said.

"Now I just need several inches of muscle on my arms and shoulders."

"Your strength is your ability to move with grace and precision. Dancing all your life has given you that. Speed and fast turns will help to keep you alive with any fighter."

I sucked in a breath and released it. A towering Assyrian warrior wearing leather armor dripping with bronze scales filled me with a terror that made my legs weak.

"Confidence will take you far," Asher added, his expression turning serious. "Believe in yourself. Believe in Kadesh. And believe in the Land of Sariba, your new home."

"We will win," I said. "We will win."

I repeated the words to give myself conviction but did I really believe it? Maybe Kadesh and I should spend our few married days sparring with each other so I would be truly ready. The thought made me smile and I shook my head, trying to banish bad thoughts.

After putting my sword away, I made a final inspection of the wedding preparations.

Palace gardeners had constructed a wedding pavilion on the garden patios that overlooked the sea. The rocky cliffs enclosed us on both sides like an embrace.

Tables were placed in position, along with chairs, pillows, and carpets. A corner was set aside for the musicians: drummers, three harpists, as well as five flutists. Another corner for an outdoor kitchen and serving area. Backdrops of flowers and fountains. Hundreds of lamps had been erected on poles, which would light up the wedding arena in imitation of a galaxy of stars dropping to the earth.

I hadn't seen Kadesh during the past two days. The tribal council, generals, and captains were having constant strategy meetings that lasted well into the night, too. I received a note from him on the second day, which Nathan read for me, his cheeks turning a bright red. "I will see you next on the evening of our wedding—under the canopy—where we will declare our love and vows and I will dress you in jewels."

Taking the note, I ran my finger over Kadesh's beautiful words, and then pressed the paper to my heart.

On the last day, I went over the wedding menu with Naomi and the palace kitchen staff. "The only thing I want for certain is sugared dumplings," I told her.

She leaned in close with a knowing smile. "The sweets of the tribal desert nuptials, yes?"

I nodded, remembering my betrothal night. The women of my tribe dancing with me and welcoming me into their world.

Aunt Naomi wiped at my eyes, which I didn't even realize had leaked tears. "Sweet dreams tonight. By this time tomorrow you will be Kadesh's wife."

I wandered back out to the gardens and watched a magnificent fountain erected. A river of water would wind its way through the patios where the guests could watch the dances. I'd been practicing my seven wedding dances, and Naomi had helped me choose the various silks and chiffons.

Tonight I planned to practice the dances until I was so tired I'd be able to fall asleep and *stay* asleep without terrible dreams waking me. After tomorrow's ceremony, I'd never sleep alone again. Kadesh would take away all my nightmares.

Leaving the wedding pavilion, I strolled down the pathway, lost in the trees and flowers. A servant bowed to me. "My lady, would you like to approve the plans for the marriage tent?"

"You mean it's close by?"

"This way, Princess."

I followed him into a three-room tent. Luxury greeted me in ridiculous amounts. Carpets so thick my toes melted into them, and a sitting room with brocade sofas and burnished lamps set into wall niches. The second room had a bed of perfumed linens sprinkled with fresh rose petals. Lilies and orchids lit up the tent with a profusion of color, in jars and urns and potted tubs.

The third partition was a bathing room, boasting our own deep-set tub for bathing. There were soaps and luxurious towels. Wine bottles in tubs ready to be chilled. Thick robes to don after bathing, and cushioned chairs for napping—or kissing.

I was overwhelmed by the romantic opulence. "Who ordered all this? Who designed it?"

The servant bowed. "Prince Kadesh made all the arrangements. He wanted it to be perfect for you, my lady."

I felt a smile curve along my lips. "Then I probably shouldn't be here to spoil the surprise."

The man didn't answer, merely bowed as I passed through.

Kadesh had thought of everything. For a year I had dreamed of lying in his arms, and now that it was here it hardly seemed real. We would have three nights of solitude . . . before Horeb showed up with his army. How many soldiers? Hundreds or thousands? I rubbed my arms against a sudden chill, feeling hunted like a lion.

King Ephrem had told me in the clearest language that I should kill Horeb. But I'd be captured or killed by his body-guards before I could even get close. And why would I need to kill Horeb if Kadesh and I were legally married? He could have no claim on me any longer. I'd be free at last, wouldn't I?

When I crossed back through the wedding pavilions and arrived at the palace doors again, twilight was descending. A liquid moon rose in the eastern sky. Tomorrow was the night of the seventh moon, the night of my wedding.

The silver orb shifted, washing streams of light against the Sariba Goddess Temple in the mountains that eclipsed the city.

The temple glowed like some kind of beacon, its tentacles stretching out to lure my soul to its heart and capture me for-ever. I pushed my way through the palace door. "You will not invade my dreams tonight."

33

In the morning I woke, miraculously still sane. No unnerving dreams or elusive demons trying to kill me. My skin was warm—not chilled by icy fear, nor hot as if burning coals pressed against my neck.

Dazed by the quiet morning, I gazed out on the peaceful courtyards.

My wedding day. And it was gorgeous.

But Leila was missing from the most important day of my life. I hadn't heard a word after sending the wedding invitation to the palace. I had no idea if she'd even received it. A great sadness filled my chest, but I would try not to mourn Leila or Sahmril, or worry about Horeb today. We had the army of Sariba to destroy them. The nightmares of my life were almost over.

A knock came at the door with a message from Aunt

Naomi. She and her personal servants would dress me for the wedding. Nervous, I could only eat a light breakfast, and then was escorted to Naomi's suite afterward.

Lady Naomi's bathing area was enormous. A large sunken bath decorated with hand-painted tiles depicting the mountains of Qara brimmed with hot water and creamy soaps. Soft white towels bordered in deep purple lay in folded piles on the vanity. Vases of flowers bloomed on tables and in alcoves. Scents from burning candles floated dreamily through the air.

"Here in our land, frankincense brings good luck to a marriage, Jayden," Naomi told me with a quick embrace. "And the children that follow."

At the mention of future babies, I smiled self-consciously. Then I quickly undressed and stepped down the tiles into the bath. The water was deep and hot, relaxing my tight muscles as I reclined.

Lady Naomi's servants used exfoliating sponges on my skin, and a shampoo that made my hair feel like fine silk.

The women's voices echoed off the bathing chamber ceiling. I gazed up at the domed ceiling and windows set high into the walls. A mural created from tiles decorated the walls. Ponds and fountains and trees, as if I were bathing in a garden.

The girls chatted about men and babies and the secrets of the marriage tent, reminding me of my betrothal night. Shy smiles tugged at my lips. Nerves whispered along my skin, settling deep into my belly as the hours ticked by. Getting closer to when I would dance for Kadesh, just like my cousin Hakak had danced for Laham.

Naomi gazed at me affectionately. "It's going to be a marvelous wedding day, Jayden. One to remember for the rest of your life."

After the bath, I pulled on a silk robe and Naomi instructed me to lie down on a soft mattress. "We have the henna ready. My women are experts at painting beautiful symbols of the Sariba lands."

The feathery paintbrushes were like butterfly wings on my skin. Lady Naomi had one of her musicians play the harp to soothe me. Other servants brought lunch and delicacies as well as fresh fruit and ice-cold water, which soothed my feverish nerves.

By late afternoon my makeup was done. My lashes were brought to life using the exotic thick kohl, my eyebrows plucked, and the juice of red pomegranate stained my lips. I sat in the chair for the curling of my hair. Jewels were added and a light sprinkling of gold flakes as the final adornment.

At dusk, I slipped into the cream-and-gold bridal gown. My hair fell in thick curls down my back. Shimmering tiny jewels had been woven throughout the ringlets.

Naomi had me stand before the mirror while the lamps were lit. Golden light glowed around me. As if I had become the sun and all light radiated from me. "Kadesh couldn't have chosen a more beautiful girl to be his queen."

"Thank you so much for all you've done for me," I told her, kissing her cheeks.

"Don't spoil your makeup, dear girl. Are you ready to meet your husband?"

Her personal servants flung open the doors of the suite while an array of palace servants flanked the wide hallways to watch me walk through to the wedding pavilion.

Just outside the door Uncle Josiah stood next to my father, who took my arm. "You look like a vision, Jayden," he said. "Just like your mother on our wedding day."

"I do? Then I am completely and utterly happy."

"There's great joy in your eyes. Kadesh is a fine man, a fine prince, and has great intelligence to outwit his enemies. I've spent the past several days watching him prepare and I'm impressed. But for now, forget the rest of the world exists. This is your time."

When we stepped into the gardens, the real world seemed to drop away when I entered a fairyland of lights. Frankincense wafted through the air, and tables were loaded with exquisite delicacies. The laughter and chatter of guests, friends, and family, including Sariba dignitaries and council members, filled the night with a warm happiness.

My father escorted me through the crowd. The guests bowed to me in their party finery, murmuring congratulations. I heard whispers of approval and comments on my beauty. I lowered my head to hide my nervous smile.

The pavilion was enchanting, bursting with flowers and delicately crafted columns. Tinkling fountains and carpeted paths. I turned my head this way and that as if I was eight years old again and I'd been granted permission to stay up all night at the grandest party of my life.

Naomi was on my other side, in position as my surrogate

mother. "Try not to look *so* deliciously happy, my dear girl. Decorum must still be in attendance. We are the royal family, after all."

She squeezed my hand playfully and I smothered down a laugh. Naria, Naomi's daughter, stood close with a basket of rose petals. She bounced on her toes, eager to spread the flowers over me and Kadesh by practicing on a few guests.

I pasted a solemn, royal expression on my face and then—suddenly—there was the wedding party standing at the dais. Chemish and Asher and King Ephrem on his throne. Chemish grinned broadly with a fatherly look while Asher's eyes drank me up. I purposely let my gaze sweep past him, a twinge of guilt at ignoring the boy, but searching for Leila in the crowd of guests. I hadn't received any response from the invitation I'd sent. If that was her doing or if Aliyah had intercepted my letter I'd probably never know, but the thought of my sister not being here to see me married left an empty spot inside. We'd been torn apart by so many circumstances this past year, and the gulf between us was wide.

Of course, there were Edomite soldiers bordering the wedding procession. Men who had come such a long way for me and Kadesh. Men who had forsaken their families to fight alongside the Sariba army. Gratitude filled me. An abundance of blessings had surely followed our trials and hardships.

Finally, my gaze settled on Kadesh. His stare was piercing, sober, and filled with love. My soul wanted to take flight and soar into the heavens with him. I imagined us later tonight, locked in each other's arms while the world dropped away.

Royal guards already surrounded the marriage tent so we wouldn't be disturbed.

A rush of longing ran up my legs and into my belly, filling me with devotion and passion for this beautiful man who finally belonged to me.

A heartbeat later I was at his side. He grasped my hands, pulling me close. "Hello, my darling Jayden."

Whispering into his ear, I teased, "Is that all you can say to your bride?"

A small sound of emotion escaped his mouth. "There are no words to describe your exquisite loveliness. I love you."

Impulsively, I wrapped my arms around him. "Oh, Kadesh, I love you with all my heart."

The crowd laughed at our unexpected exuberance, indulging us.

My father walked up the steps of the dais to join King Ephrem, who also held the title of High Priest of Sariba of the order of Abraham. Commissioned to pronounce Kadesh king of Sariba when the time came. Soon we would all sign the final covenant, signaling our marriage was sealed forever.

Two stewards were in position as court witnesses. The king motioned to us and then Kadesh and I stepped to the table where the contract papers were laid. Chemish and Asher stood beside us as personal witnesses. Celebratory wine had already been poured into gold-rimmed goblets.

The wedding party raised our glasses to one another and then took a single sip of the pungent juice. When the contract was signed, we would face the wedding guests, lift the goblets high, and then drain them in a final gesture before the crowd exploded into shouts and cheers. A bevy of trumpeters stood ready to blast a chorus of rejoicing and triumph for the future king and queen of Sariba.

Speaking in a low voice, Uncle Ephrem said, "Now is the time to express any doubts or any concerns." Up close, the king's demeanor was pale and his hands trembled. He was not well. He'd risen from his sickbed only to see us married.

I bent across the table and kissed his wrinkled cheek. "Thank you, King Ephrem, for welcoming me into your home and into your family. I will honor you for all my life and with all my heart."

His hooded eyes were sly as he winked at me. My breath caught. In that moment, I saw the image of my grandmother in his countenance. I glanced up at the heavens, knowledge washing over me that my grandmother and dear mother were there beside me on this happiest of days.

Ephrem's face broke into a hearty grin. "I take it neither of you has any concerns nor wish to withdraw, then?"

Kadesh gripped my hand in his, his eyes fastened to mine. "I don't think anybody has anything to say, my king."

With tremulous fingers, King Ephrem picked up the stencil and dipped it into the pot of ink to sign the official marriage scroll, but the safe cocoon of my wedding suddenly turned surreal, as though I'd been thrust into a dream.

The world around me shattered.

Shouting broke out behind us and high-pitched screams

rang through the crowd. Swells of commotion filled the air, rising in my ears, turning reality into a nightmare.

Not a second later, Chemish gave a gasp, lurched forward, and then crumpled to the earth.

"Chemish!" Kadesh cried, dropping to his knees beside the Edomite leader.

I reared back, my chest exploding with shock. An arrow was lodged in Chemish's back. His eyes were closed and he was lying very, very still.

"Father!" Asher screamed.

Kadesh glanced up at me, his expression one of horror. The next moment he yelled, "Get down, Jayden!" He pushed me under cover of the dais just as a second arrow whistled over our heads and punctured the backdrop of the platform.

Screams filled my head while wedding guests and servants scattered. I watched our friends and family dart under awnings and race down the terrace steps of the tiered gardens. Scrambling for their lives. I tried to find my father but he'd disappeared.

"Assyrians!" a soldier yelled above the fray. "Maacha-thites!"

"What's happening?" I choked out. Under the dais table, I crouched on my knees, my wedding dress draped about me while I stared at Chemish. The end of a foreign arrow protruded from his back. It couldn't be real. This wasn't happening.

Asher broke off the arrow and rolled his father over, heaving as he panicked and felt for a pulse.

Kadesh's face was wild. "Are you all right, Jayden?"

I nodded without speaking while we crouched together, watching in a daze while the people of Sariba were running about the palace grounds and shouting.

My face was numb, my limbs heavy with a crushing weight. I wished I had my dagger, my sword, anything. The royal guards were somewhere in the commotion, but who was the enemy? Which direction were they coming from? It was too hard to tell in the twilight.

When Kadesh rose to his feet I pulled at his fingers, but they slipped from mine. "Kadesh, no, they're going to kill you!"

No sooner had the words left my mouth than a horde of men on horseback surged through the wedding pavilion. I sat frozen while they hacked down the canopy tent poles with long sabers. Tables were upended, throwing plates and goblets and cutlery all over the grass. The food tents fell in heaps. Screams and shouts spun a web of haze over the last images of my wedding day.

In the midst of the commotion, I heard Naomi's voice screaming, "Naria! Naria!"

Across the stone pathway, the young girl stood in terror among the fleeing people who were knocking over chairs to get to the safety of the palace. Scrambling to my feet, I raced for her, scooting behind an overturned table just as one of the attackers galloped past on his horse. I stared at him: a man with long, black hair and a foreign head cloth dangling over his face. Even when the lamplight grazed his profile, I didn't recognize him. I didn't know any of them.

Crawling across the pathway seemed to take an eternity. Finally, I reached Naria and pulled her down to the grass, covering her with my body, just as Asher had covered mine during the stoning at Tadmur.

Over my shoulder, I watched Asher trying desperately to waken Chemish. Tears streamed down his face as he flung the arrow's broken end across the brick pathway. The horsemen were closing in from the perimeter. Would they shoot Asher next? Was Chemish dead? None of us were safe out here in the open.

I'd lost sight of both my father and the king. All was a chaotic crush.

"Naomi!" I shouted. I could see the woman stumbling about under the shadowy pavilion, frantic to find her daughter. "I'm over here!"

No more than a minute had passed since the first arrow struck Chemish, but the Edomites were already fighting. They slashed at the invaders with their swords, trying to bring them down off their horses. One horseman fell off with a thud to the stones, and his horse screamed. A second horseman was pulled off his steed while another table laden with wedding dinner crashed to the ground. My ears were ringing.

The world had erupted into madness.

Staggering to my feet, I stepped on the hem of my wedding gown. "Naomi! Here!" I scooped up Naria's wriggling body and thrust her into her mother's arms. "Go! Back to the palace!"

Thankfully, she didn't question my order, just disappeared

into the confusion, and I ducked again, hiding under the same table when a third foreign rider galloped by. Thoughts tumbled about while I watched the scene. The intruders didn't seem to be trying to kill any of the guests. Just creating havoc and destruction. Only Chemish had been shot. Why had he been singled out?

Instantly, the answer came. Chemish had been standing next to Kadesh. They weren't aiming for Chemish. They had been aiming at Kadesh. The attackers didn't appear to be Nephish or Maachathite, or Assyrian, either. Was this chaos the work of King Hammurabi, the ruler of Babylon? He was a master at toppling kingdoms and regimes by taking out their kings in a single decisive move.

I tried to gauge my luck at getting back to the dais to help escort King Ephrem to safety. Surely he was cowering as I was, unable to escape.

But before I could get up and run, the backdrop behind the table parted. A girl in wedding finery with a mane of man-icured black hair rose to her feet behind Ephrem's throne. A moment later, she slipped through the rear panels. I sucked in a breath when I recognized Aliyah.

The Sariba priestess glanced about to make sure the path was clear. Then, with quick, sure steps she ran down a set of garden stairs into the shadows of the night.

I slumped back on my heels. Had Aliyah ordered this reign of terror? To destroy our wedding? To kill Kadesh so she could take the throne? But that made no sense. It served her interests better if she could get rid of me and then seduce Kadesh with her hallucinating potions, so she could reign with him. Her powerful tools of potions and persuasion would eventually create a puppet king to do her bidding.

With Aliyah on the throne, the legitimate King of Sariba would fall under her spell and ultimately be rendered useless.

The scheme unfolded before my eyes: Aliyah getting rid of Uncle Ephrem and then Kadesh, too. But this attack couldn't be attributed to the High Priestess. The traitorous plot worked best with Kadesh alive, not dead. At least until they were married and an heir safely planted in her womb. She had secretly attended my wedding tonight for some other reason.

Scratches stung my hands from crawling across the stone paving. My wedding dress was grass-stained. Jeweled combs tumbled from my hair. But I was dry-eyed as I watched the wild scene unfold in front of me.

Ten Edomites attacked each horseman, hacking them down, their hands and swords dripping with blood. The horses ran like crazed beasts, shredding flower beds and knocking over urns, the whites of their eyes wild.

In the hazy distance I caught sight of a few stable boys trying to trap the horses, calming the creatures with their expertise, the animals adorned in foreign bangles and saddles.

Finally, after what seemed an eternity, the wedding guests had all retreated to the palace, the fighting stopped, and an eerie silence reigned. The Edomite horsemen regrouped across the pavilion from me.

I rose to my feet, staggering in my gold sandals. I stared across the lawns, the broken pavilion canopies, the overturned tables and smashed flowers and food. I couldn't seem to take a full breath. My wedding was in utter ruins.

The dead bodies of the invaders littered the beautiful rugs and carpets. Without speaking, riding slowly, their swords still held aloft, the Edomites spread through the gardens and along the walls, securing the perimeter. A few remained standing in the center of the wedding pavilion, their chests heaving after the brief battle.

From the darkness, Kadesh's face came into focus. With both hands, he wrenched me toward him, lifting me up against him and burying his face into my chest. He held me tight, not speaking, his breath warming my skin.

I held his head in my hands, kissing his hair. "Kadesh! You're alive!"

His arms crushed me. "*You* are alive. I thought I'd lost you. I couldn't find you."

Slowly, he released me and I slid down along the length of his body, my feet touching the ground again. "I've spent most of the time hiding under various tables. How is Chemish?" I had to ask, but I feared the worst.

"He's badly hurt. The physicians are working on him now."

"Oh no! Look!" Under the dim light of one of the hanging lamps, I spotted Asher. He was no longer at the dais kneeling over his father, but straddling the body of one of the intruders. His arm reared back, ready to thrust the man's sword into his chest. I shuddered with a terrible memory. I'd once swayed over Horeb, ready to plunge my dagger into his heart.

We raced across the paving stones, the circle of my wedding gown dragging through the dirt. I clenched the folds in my fists so I wouldn't trip.

When we reached Asher, the invader's eyes were open and he was gasping for air, not dead, not yet.

"I found him, Kadesh," Asher said, his voice rough with rage. "You're speaking with the prince of Sariba now. Talk, man, before I cut out your heart."

Kadesh held up a hand to stop the boy's impulsiveness. Killing the invader too hastily wasn't to our advantage. "We'll spare your life," he told the man, "if you tell us who ordered this invasion."

The man gave a hollow grin, his teeth red with blood, words coming out in spurts. "Horeb, king of the Nephish."

"What is your position in his army?"

"Scout. Surprise chaos." He choked on his own blood and spit up a mouthful.

I turned away, my stomach dry heaving.

"Are you Maachathite or Assyrian?" Kadesh demanded.

"Neither. I'm Basim, leader of the marauders from the mountains of Sa'ba. Horeb let us out of prison. We helped him with horses and supplies to cross the final desert. Our families will be well paid."

"Mercenary soldiers!" Asher spat out. "Shall I kill him now, Kadesh?"

"No. Get one of your Edomite brothers to take him to the palace jail on the other side of the compound."

"Stop," I said, surprising myself. "Not yet." The filthy man of Sa'ba glanced up. He laughed when he saw my ruined wedding dress, red dribbling from the corner of his mouth. It was all I could do not to spit at him myself. "Before you get to reside in the fine prison of Sariba, answer my questions. Where is Horeb now? How many days from here?"

The wounded man sneered at me, his eyes raking over my figure as he realized I was the bride. "Are you his betrothed?"

I stared at him coldly.

"Horeb wanted me to tell you that he'll see you at the full moon."

His words were chilling. Tonight was the full moon.

"Take him away!" shouted Asher to two of the Edomite soldiers.

They carried him off, but his moans were already haunting me. "Kadesh," I whispered, staggering when I turned to him. "The full moon is tonight."

Kadesh glanced up at the sky, his face grim. "That raider is lying just to frighten us. Oh, Jayden," he began. The anguish in his face was almost more than I could bear. But I had to bear it for him. It was time to truly become his wife in all things, despite the fact that the marriage contract hadn't been signed yet. What timing of the mercenary soldiers. They'd stopped the wedding at just the right moment.

I kissed Kadesh's cheek. Smoothed my hands down the royal robes he'd worn for our wedding ceremony. "Where's my father? And Uncle Ephrem? Did they escape with their servants back to the palace?"

"I don't know. I haven't seen them since Chemish was shot."

We stared at each other, and then raced back to the dais.

"Go to your father," Kadesh told Asher. "He needs you now. Send one of the physician's servants to us when you have word of his condition."

The young man shook his head. "He's unconscious. For now, I'll stay with you, my prince. I want to protect you and Jayden if there are more enemies lurking about."

Kadesh put a hand on the boy's shoulder. A thousand unspoken sentiments passed between them.

The dais was dark, the candles snuffed out. Hope flared that both Pharez and Ephrem were safely in the palace.

But then a muffled cry came from behind the black dais curtains.

Quickly, we skirted to the rear and found my father kneeling on the ground over the form of a body. The body of the king. King Ephrem's bodyguards stood at attention, their faces bleak as though trying not to weep.

Kadesh fell to the earth beside him, lifting the king into his arms. "Uncle!" he cried.

I knelt on the other side of him and stole a glance at my father who slowly shook his head.

It was easy to see that the King of Sariba was dead. His face was gray, his jaw slack, his body eerily still.

Kadesh's face wrenched in grief, and then tightened grimly. "If that marauding horseman did this to my uncle, I will personally have him hung and quartered."

My father pressed Kadesh's shoulder. "No, Son, there's no arrow or sword wound. It appears King Ephrem collapsed during the assault. I think his heart failed. The attack was too much of a shock."

34

At midnight on the evening of my wedding day, we said good-bye to King Ephrem.

His bodyguards and personal servants gathered long, gnarled pieces of frankincense wood to create a funeral pyre on the soft, white sands of the beach. Gentle waves lapped the shore in a voiceless melody.

The King of Sariba was now voiceless, too. A long era of peace and prosperity gone with him. News of the king's death spread like wildfire. The country had been plunged into mourning. I watched the preparations, numb from the last few hours. I was supposed to be married right now. Lying in the arms of Kadesh within the marriage tent. I wondered where the marriage contract papers were. Lost in the chaos somewhere. I hadn't even thought to search for them. Were they drifting in a fountain, or torn into pieces and trampled underfoot?

Or had Aliyah taken them? The sudden thought turned me cold. Was that what she was doing at the dais? I should have chased the girl down and ripped her hair out in the process.

Who would sign the marriage covenant now? I was adrift, lost. Defeat stared me in the face. Our fate had turned, our future uncertain once again.

King Ephrem's body was already stiff on a gilded deathbed, crafted from his beloved frankincense trees. I kissed his cheek and whispered my good-bye. Kadesh held the man in his arms. The man he'd called father over the past two years. The sound of his grief burned a hole in my heart.

Uncle Josiah stood stoic and silent, the old general suppressing his grief. Naomi wept bitter tears, rivulets of drying salt on her face.

A crowd of Sariba's citizens was gathering on the shoreline along with the palace servants, heralds, maids, and gardeners. King Ephrem's longtime body servant, assistants, and scribes stood in small groupings with somber faces, trying to hide their tears, but not succeeding.

The Edomites formed a solemn contingent behind the palace soldiers and captains. Ironically, everyone still wore their party finery.

A light breeze whipped the hem of my wedding dress against my legs while trumpets played a mournful version of the Sariba anthem and the king's soldiers marched in solitary lines, halting at the funeral pyre.

Four men at each corner of the deathbed lifted the king's

body and placed it on the bed of logs. A hundred pounds of the finest golden frankincense tears was wedged among the logs and sticks. A sweet, musky scent filled the salt air.

An hour earlier, Kadesh had dressed his uncle's body in the royal regalia and purple robes he'd been given when crowned King of Sariba. The king of Sariba was grand even in death, his face peaceful. Aged with love for his people and his country. At the signal of the king's vizier, the captains of the two guard details lit the pyre of wood with torches. Flames snapped at the dry frankincense wood, and then shot into the sky. Soon an inferno roared, backlighting the ocean's waves washing along the foaming sand.

King Ephrem's profile was outlined in the blaze, and I flinched in sorrow. Despair washed over me while the tide brushed the beach like a painter's canvas.

I couldn't seem to absorb all that had happened tonight. My mind flashed with images. The exquisitely decorated wedding pavilion. The beautiful rooms of the marriage tent waiting for Kadesh to carry me through the doorway. Chemish falling forward with a horrible thud at the dais. Confusion and horror and flashing swords. Asher's boyish tears making my throat ache. My own paralyzing terror when I'd scooped up Naria.

Aliyah slipping away into the night.

Uncle Ephrem pronounced dead by my father.

I gulped down the emotions that threatened to swallow me while I watched fire eat up the body of the beloved King of Sariba.

After long moments of tears and wails coming from the

mourners, Kadesh trudged through the sand to where I stood in silence next to Uncle Josiah and Aunt Naomi.

Josiah turned to him. "We have to talk, Kadesh. Immediately. About your kingship."

The light of the pyre flickered across Kadesh's face, the dark patch held against his eye appearing as a black, empty hole. "Please, uncle. I'm watching the man I loved rise to the sky in ashes. I can't think of the next step, not yet."

"You must," Josiah said in a low voice. "Asher told me what that invader said. You need to be crowned before the king of the Nephish arrives."

"We have a few days to discuss all these details," Kadesh said, his voice as somber as the sky.

"You don't know that," Josiah said. "What if they're closer than we think?"

"And what about their wedding?" Naomi spoke up. "Jayden as queen?"

The muscles in Kadesh's jaw clenched. The demands on him were already beginning. He turned to me and placed my palms to his lips. "Your wedding was destroyed by mercenary soldiers hired by Horeb. You deserve so much better. You deserve everything but I need to gather my generals immediately. My people are now fully aware war is coming. The entire land is filled with terror. This has become so much bigger than we ever imagined. I need to rally my people. Assure them they'll be safe."

I couldn't seem to breathe. Even if we married in the

morning there would be no time for each other. Grief was eating our emotions, and the coming war consuming our minds.

"Jayden, I need to be crowned before I can sign the marriage covenant for myself. At least we have the papers crafted before Uncle Ephrem died. But to marry you in one of the anterooms of the palace, sword and daggers stuck in my belt on my way to battle. Unable to take you to the marriage tent. In good conscience, I can't make you a widow on your wedding day."

"Kadesh," I whispered. "The marriage covenant papers . . . I don't know what happened to them. They're missing." I was sure I was dying. My heart ripped piece by piece from my ribs. Once more Horeb had come between us. Death to destroy our happiness.

Naomi was now weeping. "This is no way to begin your life together. Marred by tragedy and war. It will forever be a blight on your union and the country. Many citizens are already murmuring that the High Priest of Ba'al and the High Priestess of the temple should be king and queen of Sariba."

Inwardly, I groaned. Every piece of me was as cold as the bottom of the ocean. Aliyah had been preparing the people a long time for just this occasion. She'd seen ahead into the future when Kadesh didn't return home for a year. She'd laid her own plans to thwart us.

"We can't let that happen, Kadesh. You've fought too hard just to watch your country taken over by traitors. I'll do whatever you ask of me. Fight by your side. Or disappear into the desert to save your kingdom."

"Oh, Jayden." Fiercely, Kadesh dropped to his knees and kissed my palms, gazing up at me. "You are too good. Too brave."

I tried not to laugh in my despair. "No, I'm terrified. But instead of cowering in the palace waiting to hear of your death, I will fight by your side with the rest of your army. Together, we will defeat Horeb."

Our eyes locked, remembering King Ephrem's charge to me to kill Horeb.

Josiah stepped forward, his eyes golden from the flames devouring the funeral pyre. "By dawn's light I'll have the kingdom's council assembled and we'll crown you King Kadesh of Sariba," he said.

Asher moved into our circle of grief, placing a hand on Kadesh's shoulder. His own eyes were red from tears and smoke.

"How is your father?" I asked him.

"Feverish, in a coma. But the physicians have cleaned and stitched up the wound. We have hope he will live. If," he added solemnly, "the frankincense works and God is willing to spare his life so I can take him back home to my mother."

I thought of Isra in the red canyon lands, so many miles away, not knowing her husband was gravely wounded by an arrow meant for Kadesh.

Sudden shouts sounded from the cliffs above the beach. We stared up at a band of Sariba soldiers gathered there. One of them signaled down to us. A signal of urgency, of distress.

"Our horses, Asher!" Kadesh shouted. "Quickly!"

Raw nerves gripped my belly. "What's happening?"

Two Arabian steeds as well as Asher's horse reached us in seconds, ridden by palace stable boys who spoke so excitedly it was almost gibberish. "We saw them! People on the desert, my lord!"

The boys handed up the reins and Kadesh and I leaped onto the horses' backs, galloping across the soft sand. Asher was swift on our heels as we urged the horses up the trail to the cliff overlook.

Behind us, Naomi cried out, but her words were lost to the wind.

I tucked my wedding gown up under my legs and my hair was battered by our speed, wind and salt air ruining the carefully crafted curls. Sending gold dust streaming into the ocean's breakers.

From the top of the half-moon cliffs, the black endless ocean spread below us, and the city twinkled with lights before us. Deceptively harmless, as though no tragedy had happened that night. As though Sariba had not lost its beloved, old king.

On the hills to the north, the Sariba Temple glistened under the moonlight, a thousand lamps bringing its courtyards closer than they appeared. The temple seemed to mock me, to laugh at my tragedies.

We rode a mile west to the edge of the desert. I clenched the horse's reins in my fist, my thighs tight against its flanks, dread creeping cold fingers along my neck.

Dismounting at the edge of the city, we stared into the distant desert. Pinpricks of light out on the empty sands betrayed our eyes like the fragment of a dream.

"Are those lights from the Kingdom of the Queen of Sheba?" I asked, praying my eyes were playing tricks on me.

Kadesh shook his head. "Sa'ba is more than three weeks' journey from here. Those lights are only one day's journey from where we're standing."

A hot summer breeze rose up from the desert floor, whispering a lament through the hollows of the Qara Mountains.

Asher's tone was bitter. "Those lights up ahead are the army of Horeb."

Fear tasted vile in my mouth, as if the smoke from Ephrem's death pyre had scoured my throat.

A soft cry strangled me, and Kadesh reached out to enclose me in his cloak. His touch was warm and reassuring, but I knew the worst of our nightmares had finally arrived.

We stood still, breathing each other in. I was aware of Asher's eyes on us. Aware of his resignation over the strength of the bond Kadesh and I had. But I was also deeply aware of the young man's profound devotion and love for us.

Damp sand puckered my wedding dress, the odor of ashes and death rising from the silk. Hot blood pumped through my veins, giving me a headache, but I shivered.

An eerie resolve laced Kadesh's voice. "Within a fortnight we'll stake every one of their heads on the city pylons. Horeb will sorely lament the day he left his homeland and came to the Lands of Sariba."

We turned to face the shimmering lights coming toward us on the desert.

Horeb had found us.

Author's Note

THE STORY BEHIND THE STORY...

The Forbidden trilogy takes place during the Bronze Age. Bronze is a soft metal, but can be crafted into swords and weapons, although they often needed to be re-tempered after hard use because there was the risk of bending or breaking. Damascus (located in Syria) has long been famous for its sword-making, and the type of metal and forging process created beautiful wavy patterns in the weapon.

During the Bronze Age cuneiform writing was invented and grand cities dotted the shores of the Euphrates and Tigris Rivers, the country of Egypt, as well as along the coast of the Mediterranean Sea. Many of these ancient cities boasted sophisticated indoor plumbing, dams, and reservoirs, although running water was usually only enjoyed by royalty and nobility.

The city of Mari on the banks of the Euphrates River had a high standard of living. The city was so coveted and strategic that King Hammurabi, who was king of Babylon, laid siege to the city in 1759 BCE, which quickly fell. King Hammurabi created a code of laws for his kingdom and enforced them by creating judges and courts. Stone stele engraved with King Hammurabi's code of laws have been found during archeological excavations and one of the original stones can be seen in the Louvre Museum in Paris with copies of Hammurabi's Code in the Metropolitan Museum of Art in New York City.

Despite the grand cities of Egypt, Jerusalem, Damascus, Babylon, Nineveh, and others, hundreds of thousands of people, perhaps even millions, lived a nomadic lifestyle herding camels, sheep, and goats. They lived in goat-hair tents that were rolled up and moved by camel to follow the rains to places where flowers and shrubs sprang up overnight for their animals to eat. Every few days or weeks they'd pick up their stakes and move on, relying on travelers and scouts to give them information about the weather—or how to avoid their enemies. Dozens of tribes lived in these vast deserts, but the nomadic, or Bedu tribes, also enjoyed oases during the hot summers, and marketplaces in the various cities to purchase food and other supplies.

Jayden's family belongs to the tribe of Nephish (or Naphish), who was a prince of Ishmael, the son of the prophet Abraham in the Old Testament. Abraham's grandson Jacob had twelve sons, who came to be known as the leaders of the Twelve Tribes of Israel, but many people don't realize that Ishmael also had twelve sons, who were called the Twelve Princes of Ishmael. These sons spread throughout the Middle Eastern lands and became the Arab and nomadic tribes we know today.

Because Jayden's family are close descendants of Abraham, they were most likely followers of the true and living God of Abraham, whose monotheistic beliefs were followed for centuries after the prophet's life. In this same part of the world, other religions sprang up including worship of the gods of Ba'al, Moloch, Ashtoreth, the gods and goddesses of ancient Egypt, and others where people of the cities built temples for them. So there were polytheistic people living side by side with the descendants of Abraham.

Over the last hundred years, the countries of Jordan, Syria, Saudi Arabia, and others have encouraged their nomadic tribes to live in the cities, where they can take advantage of education and have access to medical care, which means the number of bedouin people have been dwindling for the last several decades. But still today, there are tens of thousands who live a nomadic lifestyle in the Middle East with their tents and herds.

Two years ago I traveled throughout Jordan and visited Petra and Wadi Rumm, home to many nomadic people. My husband and I had the great experience of meeting several families who live in tents and caves in these stunning and breathtaking landscapes. They were welcoming, generous, and even extended an invitation to an upcoming wedding.

We also drove a 150-mile portion of the King's Highway, which used to be the ancient Frankincense Trail—the same trail Jayden would have traveled with Kadesh's caravan while escaping the army of Horeb. From Damascus to the lands of Sariba, or the frankincense lands, is about 2,400 miles. The details in *Banished* about nomadic wells, the terrain, the Red

Sea, and the land of the Queen of Sheba are based on my personal research as well as the writings of archaeologists and explorers whose work I've read over the past fifteen years. (Please read the Author's Note in *Forbidden* for more details about the trilogy and the land of Sa'ba.)

Frankincense trees only grow naturally in one place—on the coast of the Arabian Sea—near where the modern port of Salalah, Oman is today. A few miles from the coastline, groves of frankincense trees grow in the foothills of the Qara Mountains. Because the Empty Quarter lies between this lush and bountiful land and the nearest cities, Sariba was extremely isolated and kept secret. It was a dangerous journey. Even during the Roman Empire armies lost their way and tens of thousands of Roman soldiers died in the desolate land between Sa'ba and Sariba.

The difficulty in moving the ancient spice—used lavishly in temples, and for embalming and medicine—more than 2,000 miles to the cities of Egypt and the lands of Canaan, Syria, and Babylon caused frankincense to be worth more than gold. Later, the magnificent city of Petra (ancient Edomite lands) in the first and second centuries BCE became the crossroad for caravans of spices, gold, and silk on the Frankincense Trail. Look up images of Petra online and prepare to be amazed. I also have a Pinterest board with pictures from my trip. Please browse!

Regarding funeral customs, Abraham and his wife, Sarah, were buried in stone sepulchers according to the Bible, and, of course, in Egypt people were mummified and buried in a variety of pyramids or tombs underground. But many ancient cultures such as the Greeks, Romans, Norse, as well as ancient tribes of Africa, used funeral pyres. Since we don't know the history of the people of Sariba, or any details about their city or kingdom, I drew on the possible custom of a funeral pyre for King Ephrem for a people who didn't have caves close at hand, and there is no archeological evidence of pyramids, or burial grounds.

In the case of King Ephrem in *Banished,* Kadesh and Jayden didn't have the luxury of time either. Since frankincense was their livelihood and so valuable at this time period, it made sense to me that it would be an honor to use the special wood in the funeral platform and pyre to send their king to the after-life.

The names I used for the Qara Mountains and the Hijaz Mountains are modern. We don't know what people in the eighteenth century BCE called these mountain ranges.

As a side note, after Roman times, the world of Sariba and the lands of frankincense disappeared from history. Nobody in the Western world knew they existed until European explorers in the Empty Quarter stumbled upon the bountiful and abundant land on the Arabian Coast in the late nineteenth century.

To see a map of the Forbidden trilogy, please go to my website: www.kimberleygriffithslittle.com or here for a pdf: www.kimberleygriffithslittle.com/forbidden-map.pdf.

ACKNOWLEDGMENTS

I'm very lucky to have fantastic people in my life, including people who are patient when dinner isn't on the table and soup & sandwiches—or pizza—is de rigueur. Again. Although I personally consider pizza a food group. I'm blessed to have talented and creative family and friends who help me with teacher's guides, book club guides, bookmarks, gorgeous graphics, swag, mailings, and book-launch parties: my sister Kirsten, who is a teacher of extraordinary talent, my daughter Milyssa, and Jan Lewis at authorsidekick.com.

Each book I write is a wild adventure, and a never-ending learning curve. At least I have brilliant people who don't roll their eyes when they read messy first drafts and give my work insightful feedback with a few brainstorming sessions thrown in. Endless gratitude to my superreader son, Jared, my daughter Milly, and my dear friend and author, Jacqueline Garlick, for reading *Banished* and being there when the angst and fears become overwhelming. I love you guys!

I'm grateful for the wonderful friends I've made over the last fifteen years at the Society of Children's Book Writers and Illustrators New Mexico chapter, especially long-time friends Carolee Dean, Caroline Starr Rose, Kersten Hamilton, and Lauren Bjorkman. Thank goodness for weekend retreats in Taos where we can talk all day and night—and throw in a little bit of writing, too.

The launch year of *Forbidden* has been a thrilling ride of meeting new friends and readers at conferences and bookstores, through Twitter and Facebook, and receiving many wonderful and touching emails. Thank you for all the kind, gushing messages about *Forbidden*. You make the journey so much brighter. It was a dream come true to travel to Book Expo America and meet my lovely and amazing editor, Karen Chaplin, as well as so many of the people who helped my book along the path of publication. I'm grateful to my editorial director, Rosemary Brosnan; my copy editor, Maya Packard; and all the publicists, marketing folks, and art department geniuses for brilliant and gorgeous covers. Consider yourselves showered with virtual chocolate.

Overflowing thanks go to Adams Literary, for all the wonderful things they've brought into my life. Their inspiring optimism, hard work, and friendship makes the writing life a thousand times better. Hugs and kisses, Tracey and Josh!

Thank you, Justin Cook, for the gorgeous book trailers you helped me create. Stunning actress Sela Vave made the perfect Jayden. It was a thrill to film "on location" in the pseudo deserts of Jordan, aka southern Utah. Justin, I'm honored to have known you since your kindergarten days.

Finally, I was blessed to go on a book tour with my dear friend Martina Boone, and a whole bunch of other YA authors I love and admire, as well as my Young Adult Series Insiders cohorts. We traveled from Baltimore to D.C., through Virginia, North and South Carolina, ending at YALLFest in Charleston. It was an incredible road trip filled with great conversations, good food, and lots of map reading and hotel hopping. It was a thrill to meet hundreds of young adult readers and fans. I'm grateful to the many booksellers who generously helped me launch my YA debut, especially Park Road Books in Charlotte, North Carolina, for the fabulous party on *Forbidden*'s official birthday. Thank you!

I have Pinterest boards about belly dancers and my Middle Eastern trip right here: www.pinterest.com/kimberleylittle.

Please visit my website, www.kimberleygriffithslittle.com, to watch the book trailers and download free teacher's guides and book club guides—or drop me a note!

TURN THE PAGE FOR A SNEAK PEEK AT
THE EPIC CONCLUSION TO JAYDEN'S STORY

1

Last night should have been one of bliss. After all Kadesh and I had been through—the loss of my family, the trek through the harsh desert . . . this should have been our night, the first as husband and wife in the marriage tent.

During the months of hardship and terror, I'd imagined us sipping wine and bathing in a marbled bath of bubbles. Lying in perfect luxury on a golden bed, together at last.

Instead, Kadesh and I were like lost children, orphaned by the sudden death of his uncle, King Ephrem, at our wedding ceremony, which had been irrevocably shattered mere hours ago.

"Come," Kadesh said, tugging at my elbow. His other arm went around my waist as he helped me mount my horse. We rode down the winding cliff path back to the beach where we had just sent off King Ephrem in a royal funeral pyre.

Those ominous lights we'd just spotted in the distance from the top of the cliffs had imprinted fresh horror on my mind. Strangers on the desert were never a good sign, but hundreds of lights on the desert spelled doom. Horeb's army was so close, so inevitable. There was no avoiding the war that was about to descend on us in all its wrath and fury.

Beside me, Asher, the Edomite prince, muttered, "No time left for planning or training. Horeb's armies will be here before nightfall tomorrow."

My horse brayed, as though the animal understood the gloomy words.

Kadesh frowned at the young man with disapproval. "Don't worry, Jayden," he said, trying to comfort me. "We're ready for them."

Despite his trying to calm my fears, I was beyond being worried. Within the next fortnight, Sariba would either survive or fall to its doom—and take the lives of everyone with it.

The crowd of mourning citizens and palace servants, guards and king's soldiers began to disperse when we reached the funeral pyre. Shadowy figures drifting up the sandy beach back to the paths that led to the city above. Silent specters. Muffled tears.

While King Ephrem's pyre burned out, the last of the red flames snapped at the salty sea air, devouring the body of the King of Sariba.

A hot wind whipped at my bridal gown. I wanted to scrape

the horror of the night from my sight until my eyelids were raw.

The acrid smell of smoke and ashes chafed at my nose and throat. I was sure that no amount of water could ever quench my thirst again.

Gripping my hand, Kadesh lowered himself before the funeral pyre, pulling me with him. On my knees in the soft sand, while waves rushed along the shore, I bowed my head. Tears slipped down my nose, conveying my devotion and love to the kindly old king.

King Ephrem had welcomed me as his nephew and heir's betrothed, including my father into his household. We were part of his family now and he was ready to lay aside the safety of his kingdom and people in order to provide us shelter and a new home.

I was grateful for his love, but apprehensive about Kadesh's inevitable crowning. The sooner it happened the better when three threatening armies were now at the kingdom's doorsteps. His crowning would calm the citizens and show leadership and strength. The man I loved was vulnerable, just as much as I was.

Kadesh's heart was tender, and too magnanimous. And, blinded in one eye as he was, he was not the perfect specimen of a fearless soldier and commander in chief. His physical obstacles might not endear confidence unto his army.

Reaching out to me from the blackness of midnight, Kadesh lifted my fist to his lips and kissed my fingers. We knelt in the sand, trembling and clinging to each other. "I give you all that I am, Jayden, daughter of Pharez. All my heart and all my protection, for as long as I take breath."

"We will fight together," I said, my voice catching. "Horeb now, and any future adversaries. We must trust each other implicitly. You must let me do my part."

"I'm not sure I'm ready for the latter." His mouth crooked into a small smile as he brought me close. "Dear God in heaven," Kadesh whispered into my hair, his hands cupping my head. "Help this kingdom. Help my people. Help us as their servants and leaders."

Swirls of fine sand rose and I closed my eyes. "Let's go home," I said softly into his ear.

Kadesh motioned for Asher to take our horses back up to the city, and then he and I walked together, our hands in a death grip, not wanting to let go. Our shattered wedding, King Ephrem's death, and the impending war overwhelmed us into silence.

When Kadesh and I staggered into the palace, my eyelashes were crusted with the salt of the ocean.

Servants rushed to attend us, bedraggled and dirty as we were. Wall sconces flickered with lowered late-night flames. We gulped down a goblet of water each, but the cool drink hurt my burning throat. All I could smell was ashes and death on me, my wedding dress, even my skin.

Waving away any more food or drink, Kadesh kept me moving past the columns and carpets of the entrance foyer, as though fearing I would collapse onto the floor. A fainting bride would never do in the public rooms with the eyes of the servants on us, despite the lateness of the hour and the few discreet guards on duty.

With Kadesh's arms around my waist, our fingers tightly laced, we maneuvered the hallways, the train of my wedding gown trailing dirt along the deep-cut carpets.

Kadesh pushed open the door to my suite, light from the hall falling across the carpets.

All at once, my legs gave out, and I faltered on the threshold, reaching for the doorjamb to stay upright. Kadesh swung his cloak around me and lifted me into his arms, carrying me into the suite.

To my right came the sound of whispers and the soft close of the door to the bathing and dressing area; my maids prudently disappearing at our unexpected appearance.

I pictured them waiting up for me, worried after the destruction of the wedding, the sudden death and funeral pyre of our king. Rumors were already spreading like wildfire over the sight of the enemy armies bearing down on us.

At the moment we all needed rest, but my mind whirled with a thousand thoughts.

Kadesh strode across the room to my bed, tossing the extra pillows aside. Gently, he laid me down on the coverlet, the folds of his cloak still caught around my body. I was distantly aware of the shushing sound my ivory wedding gown made against my legs.

Kadesh knelt beside me and slipped off the gold sandals from my feet, allowing them to clatter to the floor.

I caught at his tunic with my fingers. The fabric was smudged with ashes as well as dirt from the fight with the marauders who had attacked our wedding—and had shot an arrow into Chemish's back. We didn't know whether the King of the Edomites still lived or not.

"Any word from Asher about his father's condition?" I asked, my voice hoarse in the eerie stillness of the suite.

Kadesh shook his head, and my eyes burned with a fresh wave of grief. I choked it back, not wanting to break down. I had to be strong. Guilt might wrack my conscience at bringing Horeb to the doors of Sariba, but I could not give in to panic.

"Shh," Kadesh whispered. He rose from where he knelt on the floor and lay down next to me, curling me into his chest.

My fingers clutched at his back, pulling his warmth tight against me to stop the shivering. I didn't realize how cold I'd been until now. "Tonight was our *wedding*—" I began.

"Don't think of that, Jayden," he said softly. "It will tear you into pieces. The future is still there, waiting for us. I promise. Now you need to sleep."

I took a deep breath, keenly aware of his musky smell mixed with dirt and ash and blood. My limbs were limp and I was exhausted, but my mind continued to race with a hundred images. "There will be no more peaceful sleep until Horeb is defeated," I said in a broken voice. "Or we are dead from his invasion."

"Tomorrow will be a long day," Kadesh said, his eyes on mine. "I'll have your maids bring you a sleeping draught to help you relax." I shook my head, but he placed his hands on both sides of my face, staring deep into my eyes. "Tomorrow Sariba will crown me as its new king. I must legally hold the throne before Horeb attacks."

"How soon will the armies descend on the city?"

"It won't be tomorrow, that is for certain. They're still half a day's journey away, and they'll need to set up camp, find water in the hills. Plan their first battle strategy. Remember, this land is foreign to them. They'll be sending out their scouts if they haven't already. The city will remain closed, our own army at the gates, our own scouts in the hills to bring news of their movements."

"Kadesh?" I whispered, his hair falling against my neck in the darkness. "I can't stay in my suite pacing the floor for the next many weeks, hoping you'll come home. I have to be at your side as your queen—even though we weren't married tonight."

His eyes flicked away and then back to mine. A deep sigh rose from his chest while he brought me closer. "I don't like you being part of this. I can't stand the thought of Horeb seeing you. Of hurting you again."

"Yet King Ephrem said *I* was to kill Horeb." My stomach churned when the words caught in my throat.

Kadesh pressed his lips against my forehead, his face hovering above mine. "Stay in bed tomorrow. Rest up for what lies ahead. Get your strength back."

"I am strong—"

He rose to a sitting position and let out a small chuckle. "A girl who crosses the desert and takes on the Edomites will never be underestimated by me."

I gave him a small smile, wishing we were still lying together on the bed. I was cold, chilled, and terrified.

"I must go before the palace is filled with gossip about my presence in your room at such a late hour."

"What are your plans tomorrow?" I asked.

He lifted an eyebrow. "What are *your* plans tomorrow?"

"Actually, I intend to get my sister from the temple. She wasn't at our wedding tonight, even after I sent her an invitation. The High Priestess Aliyah stopped her from attending, I just know it. I must talk to her and convince her to move to the palace. It will be safer here. I—I don't even know if she's still alive . . ."

"She is," Kadesh assured me. "You shouldn't leave the city, even to go to the temple. I'll accompany you."

"You have a war to prepare for. I won't waste your time."

"The forest between here and the temple might not be safe."

"If Horeb's army actually makes it that close to the city then we are all doomed."

"True. We'll face him in battle on the desert, between the frankincense groves and the foothills of the Qara Mountains. Far from the city gates. I plan to go out tomorrow with my scouts to see what we can learn."

"Wait until my return from the temple. I want to go with you."

"You are determined. We won't be riding out until night-fall. I want Horeb to think he's got a temporary reprieve. There won't be a sign of any of Sariba's scouts or soldiers. Silence from us—despite my secret convoy of soldiers already hiding in the foothills."

"Then we have quite a day ahead of us. Which means you must kiss me," I added softly.

"With all my heart."

He leaned in and gently kissed me, his lips warm and comforting. "Soon I can say that I am your queen," I murmured.

"To me, you already are."

"Being married to you almost seems like a dream now." I brushed away the tears leaking out of my eyes. "A dream that will remain elusive forever."

Kadesh gazed into my face, pensive. "After all this is over, I'm not sure the marriage tent is good enough for us. I want to take you to the place my parents would often visit when they needed a reprieve from royal life and duties."

"Where is that?"

"An ancient stone castle, or fort, almost two hour's ride from here in the mountains. It was abandoned and in disrepair, but my father fixed it up for my mother when I was young. They had many happy times and memories there."

I gave him a shaky smile. "It sounds perfect."

We finally broke apart. Kadesh's mouth was tight with grief, but his features were filled with an angry passion. "I vow to you, Jayden, that we will overcome the terrible deeds of this night. We will win."

"I believe you," I whispered to assure him. But did I actually believe that we could abolish three armies of Assyrian,

Maachathite, and Nephish soldiers? To defend the city without the slaughter of innocent families?

Kadesh had not been crowned King of Sariba yet either. He'd also been away for a long year, recovering from the caravan raid and helping me search the city of Mari for my sister, Sahmril, while under siege.

Unfortunately, Aliyah—in her role as the temple High Priestess—had used that year to her advantage, gaining the trust of the city, showing off the fruits of the temple. With Kadesh's absence and King Ephrem's ill health, she'd had free reign to influence the army's leaders and Sariba's mayors and city council. Further, she had aligned herself with the Egyptians who were now living here and weaving their magical spells and charms. How dangerous that would prove had yet to be seen, but the knowledge made me incredibly uneasy.

"There's wisdom in your being crowned as soon as possible," I said. "To thwart any coup from your army—or Aliyah's influence. You must act quickly."

"I've been watching a myriad of thoughts moving through your head," he said with amusement. "You're weighing everything out."

"How can you tell?"

"Your eyes go distant. Then you take a breath and hold it while you're thinking. I always know when I'm about to get a barrage of ideas." He tightened his grip on my waist. "Please return from the temple as soon as you can tomorrow. You can't miss the king's crowning."

"*Your* crowning," I emphasized, running a finger along his

cheek, my heart tugging at the thick white scar along his face from Horeb's sword that had gouged out his eye. "Who will do the honor of crowning you king?"

"Uncle Josiah, my closest relative to the throne. He's in line as my successor. When Uncle Ephrem was a young man, the High Priest Melchizedek from Salem crowned him king, but there's no time to get him here when the journey takes months."

"This will all be over long before then" I said soberly. "Horeb's men will likely be under orders to capture me and take me to him."

"I won't let that happen, Jayden, but if you stayed safely at the palace that risk lowers," Kadesh added pointedly.

"Many people will die over the next few weeks, all because of me. I can't sit idly by while everyone else takes all the risks. The High Priestess also wants to get rid of me and take you and your kingdom for herself. Death might be the easiest way, but who will try to kill me first, Aliyah or Horeb?"

READ
THEM ALL!

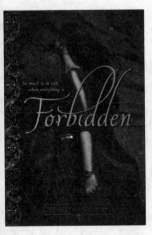

JOIN THE

Epic Reads

COMMUNITY

THE ULTIMATE YA DESTINATION

◀ **DISCOVER** ▶

your next favorite read

◀ **MEET** ▶

new authors to love

◀ **WIN** ▶

free books

◀ **SHARE** ▶

infographics, playlists, quizzes, and more

◀ **WATCH** ▶

the latest videos